MW01048429

The Druid's Son

OTHER TITLES BY G R GROVE:

The Storyteller Series:

Storyteller

Flight of the Hawk

The Ash Spear

Guernen Sang It: medieval-themed poetry

Guernen Sang It: King Arthur's Raid On Hell And Other Poems

Guernen Sang Again: Pryderi's Pigs And Other Poems

The Druid's Son

G. R. Grove

i Dari - pob hwyl!

Lulu.com

GG

First Edition: October 2012

Published by Lulu.com
Lulu Press, Inc.
Morrisville, NC, USA

for Aldertree Books

ISBN: 978-0-557-11990-5

Set in 12 pt Garamond by Aldertree Books,
Denver, CO, USA.

—CONTENTS—

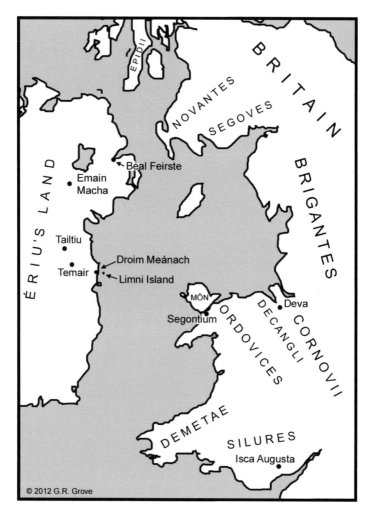

Figure 1. Parts of Britain and Ireland in 60-80 AD.

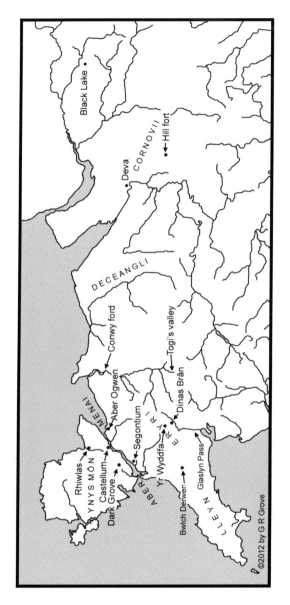

Figure 2. Part of Western Britain in 60-80 AD.

The Thing Unexpected

Harvest was over. The corn from the poor stony fields had been gathered safely into the barns, and the sheep and cattle brought down from their high summer pastures to graze on the stubble and manure the fields with their droppings. Only the pigs were still in the oak-woods below, fattening on acorns. Soon it would be Samhain, the time of the blood-feast, the time of slaughter.

The woman standing in the house-place doorway and looking up at the misty hills was thinking of another slaughter, a spring blood-letting which had changed her world forever. Not long after Beltane of the previous year, it had been, when the word they had all dreaded came from Môn: the Red Crests had crossed the Aber Menai, and destroyed the Sanctuaries of the Druids. Those who had been supreme in Britain for longer than any living man could remember were now a broken rabble, hunted fugitives in need of shelter themselves.

It had seemed impossible to her, as if the black earth had gaped beneath her feet, or the sky of stars fallen upon her, and yet it had happened. Before many days the first wounded survivors had reached her mountain valley, followed in a little while by half a dozen of the Druid Priests themselves: lean grave-faced men in fire- and blood-stained robes, with the high shaven foreheads of their kind, and their eyes still dark with grief and loss. The people of the valleys had taken them in and made them welcome, and shared their spring-scanty food and ale. The woman in the doorway remembered that first night—the crowd of weary strangers in her father the Chieftain's fire-lit hall, the low murmur of talk, and the silence where there should have been bard-song. She remembered the man who had been seated in the place of honor beside her father: a dark-bearded man neither young nor old, whose solemn face yet bore the marks of past laughter, and whose deep-set eyes were gentle, and wise beyond his years. Lovernos, they had called him, Lovernos the Fox—the last Archdruid of Ynys Môn. The woman smiled a little sadly, thinking of him, and her hand went unconsciously to her swollen belly, where she carried his child. Spring-born, the boy would be: for

Lovernos had told her, speaking with *awen*, that it was a son she carried.

Motion caught her eye in the twilight distance, and she left off remembering. Five riders were coming up the valley track from the south. As they came closer, she knew them, for four of them were her brothers and cousins, gone these three moons and more as part of an escort for Lovernos and his band. The fifth was an older man in worn dark clothes, gray-bearded, and with short-cropped gray hair above his forehead where his tonsure was still growing out—for it was no longer safe in Britain to look like a Druid. By the time he dismounted stiffly before the hall door, she had fetched the guest-cup, and offered it to him now.

"A blessing on the house," he said formally, as he took the carved ash-wood cup and drank.

"Be welcome, Honored One," said the woman. She remembered him now as one of Lovernos' men, Cunomoros by name. "Come in to the fire."

"Gladly," said the man, following her into the hall through the curious crowd which had gathered there. "The nights are cold here now."

"And will be colder still before long," said the woman. They stopped beside the hearth-place, and the man held out chilled hands to the flames.

"It is accomplished," he said quietly.

"I thank you for the news," said the woman. "Did he… did he suffer much?"

"No," said the man, "it was clean. I struck the first blow myself; after that he felt nothing."

"I am glad," said the woman, and paused, biting her lip, her eyes bright with unshed tears.

"He sent you this," said the man; and reaching into his belt-pouch, he pulled out a battered silver ring which she knew well. "Keep it for the boy until he can wear it."

The woman took it and looked at it, then closed her hand tightly upon it. Cold though it was from the autumn chill outside, yet she felt the power in it still, as if some spark of its former owner lingered. "You are so sure," she said wonderingly, "so sure I will bear him a son." And at the words, she felt the child stir for the first time in her womb.

"Yes," the gray-haired man said simply, and stretched out his hands again to the fire. Then he met her eyes, and something passed between them. "I was sent back," he said softly, "to be the boy's teacher…and his foster-father as well, if that would please you."

The woman looked at him, and saw for the first time the strength in his face, and the wisdom. "Yes," she said after a moment. "It does. He will need a father, and I am going to need a new man. Come with me now, and I will show you…your home."

He was born in mid-spring, in the month of Edrini, at the time when the days and nights are equal—a fine healthy boy, with a tuft of his father's dark hair, and his mother's blue-gray eyes. He was a quiet baby, eating and sleeping readily, causing no trouble, and born in a fortunate year: a year of good crops and good weather, when all things throve. He grew fast; it seemed to his parents no time at all before he was crawling, then walking. That was when the trouble began; for although the boy would play peacefully with other children, and loved his foster-father's company, he liked best to be alone among the hills.

"Have you seen Togi?" asked his mother one evening. Cunomoros, washing the garden soil from his hands at the water butt, looked up.

"I have not," he said. "Not since midday. I thought that he was with you."

"And I thought the same." She sighed. "Perhaps he will come home soon for his supper." Cunomoros looked up at the surrounding hills, where the slow summer twilight was deepening into dusk.

"Perhaps," he said. "But I think that I will go and look for him all the same."

The boy lay listening to the bats, watching them as they flew swiftly on their dark irregular hunting courses through the clear evening air, and hearing their high thin voices. The human voice calling his name he had ignored now for some time. The night was too fine for going indoors, and he was not yet sleepy. His empty belly he ignored also, as a thing of no importance: at this he had already had much practice. The bats were more important. He had never seen so many at one time before, and he thought there were several kinds among them, some large and some smaller. In a little while he might understand their words.

His father's voice was closer now; soon he would be found. He should have picked a more hidden spot in the rocks, but this smooth patch of open, sheep-cropped turf on which he lay gave him a better view of the bats, and of the pale summer stars behind them. It was too late now to move. Instead he watched the jerky flight of the bats as they twisted and turned in the air in their pursuit of their prey. He had found a dead one the summer before; the short brown fur had been soft, and the body amazingly light. He had kept it in a cleft in the rocks until something—perhaps a fox—had found and stolen it.

A dark shadow blotted out part of his sky. "So there you are, Togi," said his father's voice. "Why did you not answer me? You must have heard me calling."

"I was not ready yet." The boy's eyes still followed the bats. What must it be like, he wondered, to fly so swiftly and so well, skimming through the darkness like a ghost, free of all restraint?

"Well, it is time we went back." Cunomoros stretched down a hand; reluctantly the boy took it and was hauled to his feet. "You mother will be worried."

"Let go, I can walk by myself. Why would she be worried? She knows I know these hills."

"Women are like that. Besides, there are wolves."

"In the summer?" The boy leapt up onto a gray boulder and picked his way from rock to rock, his bare brown feet gripping surely, his arms lightly extended to keep his balance.

"Sometimes. Other things as well. What were you doing up here?"

"Watching the bats. Does nothing hunt them?"

"Nothing that I know of. They move too quickly, and never in a straight line. That is their protection; no one knows where they will be next. Remember that, if you are ever pursued, and do the thing unexpected." Unseen in the darkness, Cunomoros frowned, his own thoughts going back seven years to a pursuit and an escape. The Red Crests had hunted them then, sure enough, but Lovernos had been too clever… He put the thought away with practiced ease, and held out a hand to his son. "That is a good lesson for you: do not forget it."

"I will remember." The boy jumped down and paused. "Father…?"

"What?" The man stopped, waiting.

"Is it true they are spirits? That they speak with the voices of the dead?"

"The bats?" said the man, frowning. "It might be so. Where did you hear this?"

"I do not know," said the boy, moving on through the heather. "Only, I remembered it… Is it true?"

"Perhaps it is," said the man, following him. "But only those as young as you are now can hear them; I cannot. As you grow older, you will cease to hear them, too."

"That will be a pity," said the boy. And softly, half to himself, "Then I must listen as much as I can now, while I am still young." And they went on down the mountain.

He was seven years old, and it was Samon, the beginning-of-summer month: time to start his warrior training. This was the first thing he had thought of when his eyes opened that morning. Quietly, so as not to awaken the small brother who shared the bed-place with him, he rolled out from under his blanket and stood up on the packed earth floor of the hut. His mother and the new baby were still asleep, for the dancing had gone late, but his father was up already as always, standing in the doorway to view the pale sky, and combing his long gray hair and beard with his fine-toothed bone comb. The boy ran quick fingers through his own rough-cropped dark hair, and straightened the sleeveless woolen tunic, belted at the waist with a strap, which was all that he wore in summer—his father was particular about these things. Then he picked up his small belt-knife from the place where he had left it the night before, and tucking it under his belt, followed the man outside. "May I carry the basket, Father?"

"You may." Cunomoros handed him the covered willow basket, but kept the glazed pottery jug he carried in the crook of his left arm for himself. "Is it too heavy?"

"No," said the boy stoutly. In truth, it *was* heavy; there must be more than a few oatcakes in it this morning.

"Good," said Cunomoros, and they set off up the hill. The sun had not yet risen, and all the world was fresh and new—a good omen for the first day of summer. Later it might be warm, unless the clouds came. In the pens some of the shepherds were gathering their bleating flocks, ready to drive them up the mountain to the summer pastures, where they could feed on the rough grazing well away from the village crops; tomorrow the cows would follow with their calves. Some of the young men and women would be up there with them all summer, milking the cows and the ewes to make butter and cheese, and storing the resulting winter-food in cold stone-lined rooms dug into the hillside. The boy almost wished he was going; he loved the solitude of the high places; but he had work to do here below, learning his manhood skills from the arms master, and his priest-craft from his father.

At first the path wound back and forth on the steep slope, then it straightened out. The hilltop was empty except for the low ring of ancient gray stones with the burnt-out remains of last night's bonfire in its center. There was only the song of the wind through the gorse and heather, and the far-off cry of a hunting hawk, dancing suspended on the bright air. They stopped beside the big stone on the far side of the circle, and the boy put down his heavy basket in the grass. He watched while his father stirred the gray embers of the bonfire into life and fed them, first with small twigs and the dry stalks of last year's willow herb, then with bigger pieces of split alder wood from a pile which had been left behind for this purpose the night before. Tendrils of white smoke arose, and small flames licked greedily at the wood. When the fire was burning strongly, Cunomoros stood erect and lifted his hands in the dawn prayer. The first light of the rising sun touched his brown face as he did so, and turned his gray hair and beard to silver. He began to chant, and the boy added his high voice to the song. This part of the ritual he knew well and loved.

When the prayer was finished, Cunomoros turned to the offering, after first adding more wood to his fire. From the willow basket he took out a stack of flat oatcakes and a joint of raw meat from the previous evening's sacrifice. At the scent of the cakes, the boy's stomach rumbled; but the Gods must be fed first. Cunomoros broke the oatcakes one by one into the greedy flames, then laid the meat across them. A black smoke went up, and an odor compounded of burnt and roasted flesh. He added a few more pieces of wood and stood back. "Are you ready?" he asked.

"I am." The boy pulled the knife from his belt and unsheathed it; the sharp edge, bright with much honing, shone in the sunlight. Reaching around to the nape of his neck, he seized a tuft of hair and hacked it off; then, still holding it in his left hand, he jabbed the point of his knife with practiced care into his left thumb, so that a fat bead of blood burst out and ran down into his palm. Closing his hand, he mixed the blood into the hair. "I give myself today to the Gods who bred me, to the Gods who fed me, to the Gods who led me. May I always walk in their path." Opening his hand, he dropped his offering into the fire, where it vanished in a puff of flame. Then he stepped back, smiling.

"Well done," said Cunomoros. "Let me see your hand." The boy held it out; the cut was small, and had almost stopped bleeding. "Good. Keep it clean as I have taught you."

"I will." They stood side by side and watched the fire for a while. When the meat was charred to black ashes, Cunomoros poured ale from the jug to extinguish the flames. A hiss and a cloud of pungent steam arose. When the jug was empty, he lifted his voice again in a chant, and again the boy joined him. Then silently they picked up their burdens and started back down the path, leaving the hilltop to the kestrel and the morning wind, and to the Gods.

That afternoon Togi went to begin his warrior training, along with half a dozen other boys born in his year. He knew most of them well; they had played together since they could walk, rolling and wrestling like puppies in the rushes of the hall during feasts, swimming naked in the icy waters of the stream which made its way by leaps and bounds down the valley, and gathering birds' eggs on the moors in the spring and nuts and bramble-fruit in the autumn. The use of the three-pronged fish-spear and the birding bow they knew already; now was the time for them to learn the way of those weapons used against men, and to hone their woodcraft until they could pass silent as shadows through the oak-woods of the lower valleys, or lie in ambush on the bare hillside hidden only by a patch of rough grass and their utter stillness.

Old Crotos, an elderly warrior who had passed his youth in the war-band of the local king and had the scars to prove it, looked them over as if he had never seen them before. "None of you," he told them, "are a patch on what your fathers were, and *they* were a poor lot—always supposing you *had* fathers, and were not merely found under a bramble bush." The boys grinned sheepishly, knowing this for old custom. After a while Crotos set them to work casting spears at a straw target. Togi was neither worse nor better than any of his fellows, but he set himself doggedly to improve. As his father said, one could never have too many skills. Presently Crotos dismissed them, telling them to be there earlier tomorrow.

Togi went home, to find his father hoeing the bean patch behind their hut, which stood a little apart from its fellows. Without being asked, he went to fetch the big wicker basket, and began filling it with the hoed-up weeds. For a while they worked in companionable silence; then Cunomoros paused to rest. Leaning on his hoe, he asked, "How did it go?"

"Oh—well enough," said Togi. "Mostly we threw spears."

"Mmm," said Cunomoros, and began to hoe again. After a little more silence, Togi said, "Father?"

"Yes?"

"Does a Druid also need to be a warrior?"

"Mmm," said Cunomoros. "Well—no, and yes. In days past, it was not necessary. We were respected for our learning, and for our magic; no one would have dared to lift a weapon to us. But nowadays…" He paused, thinking how to phrase this.

"Since the Red Crests came?" said Togi.

"Since the Red Crests came," agreed Cunomoros. "They do not honor us or our Gods. We cannot cease to be Druids; but in the future, it may be well if we are able to defend ourselves with steel, if need be, as well as words, and with war-craft as well as magic. Remember, Lugh of the Light is a warrior as well as a Druid, and a Bard, and many other things; and what the Gods do not disdain to do, men should never cease to try and accomplish."

"Mmm," said Togi, and carried the basket full of weeds away to dump them on the midden. When he came back, he said, "You will still teach me every day?"

"Of course. Every morning, and whenever else there is time."

"Is there time now?" asked Togi. His father looked at the still un-hoed bean rows and smiled.

"We can recite as we work," he said. "Let me hear yesterday's lesson." And in time to the hoe strokes, they began to chant.

Half of his days now were spent under the supervision of Crotos. Here the boy learned the use of spear and shield, and practiced with a scaled-down wooden sword—against the possibility that he might someday own a real one—the swinging strokes which could take off an enemy's arm or head in battle. He learned, too, the rules of the boy-pack; and this, for one who had always preferred his own company and that of the mountains, was a harder task.

The younger boys were often set to compete with or learn from their elders, and sometimes Crotos nodded off in the warm afternoons, when he should have been watching them. At first the boy had no trouble; they were all of them feeling their way like new hound puppies in the pack, and Togi—his full name was Togidubnos, but no one ever used it unless he was in serious trouble—had early weighed up his fellows with his usual calm good sense, and taken care to be on friendly terms with most of them. But in any group there is always an exception, and the exception in this case was a hulking ten-year-old called

Ivomagnos, two hands taller than any of his fellows, and large and strong in proportion.

It was Togi's bad luck to be matched often against Ivo at weapons practice, not because he was the other boy's match in size or strength—none of them were—but because he had a certain quickness which made him better at this game than the rest. It was just as if he knew where Ivo's wooden spear-blade would be before it arrived, and could always move aside in time, or block it with his own light wooden shield. It was true that he scored few hits in return—Ivo's greater strength could always beat down his blows—but this was no consolation to the bigger boy, who was used to having things his own way. At last, when Togi had danced aside from one of his lunges for the ninth or tenth time that afternoon, to the laughing jeers of some of the older boys, Ivo lost his temper and charged. Hitting the other's shield with his own, and with all of his considerable weight, he knocked the smaller boy to the ground and landed astride him. "You little rat," he cried, "twist away from this, if you can!" And grabbing Togi's throat with both hands, he began to choke him.

Clawing unavailingly at the bigger boy's hands, Togi knew that he was in trouble. The sweating red face above him was beyond his shorter reach, and the weight on his small chest had already driven all the air from his lungs. As his world swung and darkened around him, he did the one thing that he could, the unexpected thing: he made himself go limp. Then, as Ivo, thinking the fight over, relaxed his grip and leaned back, Togi grabbed the bigger boy's wrists and pulled himself up off the ground. His rising head met Ivo's nose with a satisfying crunch, and Ivo screamed. Togi twisted out from under him, and came to his knees. Then he yelped in his turn as Crotos' dog-whip, impartially used, lashed them both. They fell apart, panting.

"What is this?" said Crotos. "Cannot I take my eyes off of any of you young fools for a moment without one of you trying to kill another? To do it by accident is bad enough; I expect nothing better from such untrained cubs. But to do it by intent... Well, stand up, both of you, and let me see the damage."

They stood, well apart, Ivo trying to stanch the blood which was still pouring from his nose. Crotos looked them over in silence for a while, running the lash of his dog whip through his fingers. There were nervous giggles from some of the other boys, but he fixed them with a rheumy eye and they became silent and serious. "Huh!" he said at last. "Ivo, go down to the stream and wash the blood off of your face, and whatever it was you did, do not do it again. Togi, pick up your weapons and try a bout with Lugo. Maybe he is fast enough to hit you. The rest of you, go on with what you were doing. This show is over!"

They scrambled to do his bidding. Ivo, his hands still on his streaming nose, gave Togi a glare which promised future vengeance, then went off as bidden to wash his face. Togi, ignoring his grazes and bruises, picked up his wooden spear and shield and faced Lugotorix, a thin red-haired youngster who was one of the unofficial leaders of the boy-pack. Lugo grinned at him. "That was a good move," he said. "I saw it. Did you do it by intent, or were you lucky?"

"Some of both, I think," said Togi, grinning back.

"Ha!" said Lugo, and laughed. "Well, show me now what you can do now with your spear... No, feint first. No, like this... quicker... quicker... good! Now I will try... watch my eyes... How did you do that?"

"I do not know," said Togi, panting, as they paused; he had dodged the thrust at the last moment.

"Huh!" said Lugo, and laughed again. Then he sobered. "Keep an eye on Ivo. He holds a grudge."

"I know," said Togi.

"Do you?" Lugo grinned again. "You know a lot for such a little fellow. Well, one more bout, and then we will rest."

They sparred again. This time Lugo was faster, and feinting low, managed to graze the younger boy's left shoulder over his shield. "Enough for now. Crotos will be letting us go for the day soon. Are you all right?"

"Yes," said Togi. "Thank you. It was a good lesson."

Lugo laughed. "I wish," he said, "that I knew how you manage to be so quick. Well, you may have need of it before long. Go on, now. You can go."

Togi was stiff the next day, but Ivo's face was a mess, and not being popular, he came in for a good bit of teasing. The looks he gave Togi were frankly murderous, but Crotos kept them apart, and presently Ivo's nose healed, and the other boys lost interest. So the summer slipped by. Lughnasa came, and everyone was busy with the harvest. The sheep were brought down from the high pastures, and the ewes separated from their lambs, and the rams put with them to tup. The cattle came down in their turn, and the girls and youths who had spent their summer with them brought down the stored butter and cheese. In the oak woods the pigs fattened upon acorns.

The mornings were frosty now on the hilltop when the boy and his father made their dawn prayers and offerings. Sunrise was later and farther south; Togi learned to track it against two aligned stones of the little circle. He knew the cries and the flights of the commoner birds now, and their meanings. One morning as they chanted, a flock of geese passed over calling, so low that the beat of their wings was loud in the still air, every perfect feather shining in the early golden light. The boy's eyes followed them with awe and longing, the words of the chant momentarily forgotten; then he remembered himself and took up the song again with his father. "Where are they going?" he asked when it was finished.

"Far to the south," said Cunomoros, "to a land where summer lingers most of the year. They go and come with the tides of the light, along their broad pathways in the sky. Every year they have made that journey, since the time when the world began to be, and all things living first crept from the cold and darkness, to see and adore the rising Sun. Each year at midwinter, when the light turns back from darkness, we remember that first morning, and recreate the world with our songs and tales. So it has been and will be, until at last fire and water reclaim the world, and cause a new beginning."

The boy nodded absently; he had heard this tale before, but always loved it. "Tell me again about the tides."

Cunomoros smiled. "The tides of the light wax and wane with the turning of the year, following the sun, as the tides of the ocean rise and fall following the moon. The ocean is the great water which laps the coasts of Britain, and cuts us off from Ériu's Land to the west, and from Gaul to the east. One day you will see it yourself."

"Have you journeyed over the ocean?" asked the boy, his eyes still following the flight of the geese, now distant black specks in the clear air.

"I have. In my youth I myself traveled to Ériu's Land, and there I learned many mysteries. There were many of us on Môn who went there to study in those days, and many from that country who came to learn from us. Your blood-father got his birthing in the north of that great island."

The boy nodded again; he had been told this before, too, but it was only a story to him; Cunomoros was the only father he had ever known. "And did you go to Gaul?"

"No," said Cunomoros sadly. "The Red Crests destroyed the Sanctuaries there before I was born. Everywhere they come they bring destruction. May the strong Gods keep them from Ériu's Land, for that is our last retreat. When the oak groves of Ériu are cut down, there will be no more Druids."

"Until the world is reborn?" said the boy.

Cunomoros nodded slowly. "Yes. Until our world is reborn."

The Red Crests

The days grew shorter; winter came. They celebrated Samhain, remembering the dead. The pigs were brought up from the oak woods, and the young boars slaughtered. For a while there was fat pork and blood sausage in plenty for everyone.

The days grew shorter still, and the nightly cold increased. Around midwinter there was snow, and at night the howling of wolves in the high hills. Togi's small sister took a fever and died; his mother wept for a while, then things went on as they had before. And the year turned, and turned again; and twice spring came, and summer, and harvest. And that second year after the harvest, when Togi was nine years old, the Red Crests also came.

They were only a small party, escorting the tax carts: for the local King had been defeated that summer in battle, and had been forced to pay tribute. Some of the King's men were there, shame-faced, to uphold the levy. It was not much more than they would have paid to the King; but it *was* more, after a poor harvest; and there would still be the need to feast the King as well when he came on circuit. The people watched, grim-faced, as their grain was carried out from the barns in its heavy wicker baskets. There would be hunger this winter, more hunger than usual: for the poor mountain fields never yielded quite enough, even in good years.

Togi watched with the rest, and heard the murmurs among the people. This was his first sight of the fearsome Red Crests, whose advent had changed his world before ever he was born. Lean, dark-haired men, they were, the most of them, not much different in appearance from the tribesmen they had conquered; but their weapons were better made, and their steel shirts well-polished, and their discipline a new thing entirely. Their officer was young, but old in his work; he looked at the gathering crowd as a shepherd looks at sheep, but less fondly. With tramping and stamping the soldiers loaded the baskets of grain into the carts, and the small shaggy native ponies hauled them away under the urgings of their foreign drivers. When all of them were gone at last, creaking their way down the rough valley road, Crotos drove the boys back to their weapon practice. Togi was not the only one that afternoon to see, in the straw target at which he launched his spear, the shape of a Red Crest soldier.

That evening, hoeing the beans with his father, he asked, "Why did we not fight them? They were not so many; there were many more of us."

"Mmm," said Cunomoros. "Only so many today. How if we killed these, and they came in their hundreds, or tens of hundreds, to demand the blood-price? What then?" Togi was silent. "I have seen their armies," said Cunomoros. "I saw them cross the Aber Menai, when they came to Môn. A river of men, all shining with fish-scale armor; a flood of men, like storm-waves upon the shore. We could not turn them back then. Boudicca could not defeat them, though she outnumbered them a hundred to one. Only if all the tribes of Britain were to rise as one people, could they be defeated; and that will never happen now."

"Why not?" asked the boy.

"Because the only force which could have united all the tribes at once," said Cunomoros bitterly, "was the Druids. And the Red Crests knew it, and for that reason they destroyed us."

"Not all of us," said Togi seriously. "You and I are still here."

"Yes." Cunomoros smiled. "Yes, so we are. And since we are, let me hear yesterday's lesson again, with no errors this time." And as he listened, he continued to hoe the beans.

"Father," said Togi later that evening, as they sat beside the fire in their hut, "tell me again about Môn."

Cunomoros smiled, setting aside his empty supper bowl. "I have told you all of that tale many times. Well, what would you like to hear?"

"About the Black Grove," said the boy, "and the going under the ground."

"The manhood ritual? Hmm," said Cunomoros. "You are young to be thinking of that." Togi had grown a good bit in the past year, but manhood among the tribes was fourteen.

"And you know that I cannot tell you all of it: it is *geas* on the initiates not to tell."

"Tell me what you can."

Cunomoros sat staring into the fire for a little while. It was dying down, and he reached absentmindedly for a few more sticks from the pile beside him to feed it. Togi's mother was cleaning the wooden bowls and the stew pot; the small brother was doing his drowsy best to stay awake for a little longer in order to listen. The night outside was still and cold; in another moon it would be Samhain. He remembered autumn nights on Môn; remembered the feasts and the rituals; remembered the sacrifices; remembered, also, his youth…

"I was born on Môn," he said after a while, "and there I grew to manhood. My father and mother were Priests and servants of the Gods, and I got my teaching in the Sacred Groves. I thought to spend my whole life there in service to the Shining Ones, but the Gods had other ideas… No man can outrun his destiny.

"When I was thirteen, I went with a handful of other boys my age to the Black Grove, near the eastern shore of Môn, where the Aber Menai flows between her and Eryri. There were old men there whose job it was to prepare us for what was to come; generations of boys had passed through their hands, and they knew their craft well. They taught us the songs to sing as we walked the Dark Path; the omens and portents to read; the Friends and Foes who live within the earth, beyond the stars, beneath the sea, and help or hinder the Seeker. We learned how to fast, and how to control our minds and our bodies; we learned the use of the drugs which assist in the crossing of the Veil. We learned the questions to ask, and the answers to avoid, on that journey. And one by one, as Samhain drew near, they took us into the darkness, and sent us on our quests."

Cunomoros sat dreaming for a while, watching the fire and remembering. His woman had finished her tasks and bundled the small brother, limply asleep, into the bed he still shared with Togi. She sat down then beside the fire to get its last warmth, and watched her elder son as he listened to the oft-told tale. His eyes were bright and eager, his lips a little parted as he drank in the words. More and more she saw in his face the likeness to his dead father: the same straight nose and wide cheekbones, the same dark hair and thick brows, the same gray eyes, changeable as the light upon clear water…

"Tell me about the hill," said the boy softly, "the hollow hill which took you into the earth." Cunomoros looked up smiling, putting aside his dream.

"It is more of a mound than a hill," he said, "like the cairn on top of Penwyn. It was built very long ago, so long that even we cannot count it, by the First Men who came to these islands in the days when the Gods still walked among them, and taught them their crafts. The first people built many such places to honor their dead, and in many of them their spirits still live. At Samhain they awake… I have seen them."

"What are they like?" asked the boy eagerly.

"That," said Cunomoros, "I cannot tell you: it is forbidden. But when you see them, you will know for yourself." He stretched, straightening his back with an effort, and yawned. "Time now for bed." Standing up, he reached down a hand to his wife, and she took it with a smile.

Togi rolled himself under the blanket along with the small brother. The last flickering flames of the fire set shadows quivering in the thatch, and painted moving light on his closed eyelids. That night he dreamed of ghosts who spoke with bats' voices, and of flying through the air, light as a leaf, beneath the silent stars.

Samhain came, and the autumn slaughter. The feasting was somewhat less generous than usual after the depredations of the Red Crests, but the blood offering was poured as always on the hilltop, and the fires lit; and places were set afterwards in the hall for that year's dead. The other boys dared each other to run though the ghost-haunted woods, but Togi walked by himself on the hills, and watched the stars. His work with his father and with Crotos now kept him busy throughout the day; only at night could he steal out sometimes and be alone, to hear the voices of the Gods or spirits. If his parents noticed these absences, they held their peace: Cunomoros because he knew what sort of man he was raising, and what went into the making of a Druid; and his mother, more simply, because she trusted and loved him.

Midwinter came, and with it the King of the Ordovices, as he did most years. It was customary at this season for him to travel around the land with his *teulu*—his household warriors—receiving entertainment from each village as he came to it: an indirect form of taxation, paid without the need to move the food. The King was a youngish man, tall and loose-limbed, ruddy-faced and red-bearded, with a merry eye. He sat in court for most of one day, hearing claims and counterclaims, and rendering judgments. His men hunted in the hills on horseback, and brought back two bucks and a doe to supplement the feast.

These warriors were all young, the best of their tribes; one or two bore livid scars from the summer's fighting; and on all of them was a sort of grimness, a lingering anger at their defeat. The older boys hung around them, asking for battle-stories, and came in for much rough teasing; but Togi spent as much time as he could manage with their Bard, a lean red-haired young man called Cingetos, who sang the King's praises in hall in the evenings, and entertained them all afterwards with tales of magic and wonder. He and Cunomoros were well acquainted, and the Bard had much to tell the old Druid about what went on in the land.

On the third afternoon of the King's visit, the two of them were seated on a wooden bench in front of the feast hall, enjoying the thin December sunshine and the cups of ale which Togi had just fetched for them. The King and his war-band were off hunting, together with the Chieftain and most of the warriors of the tribe, and the place was left to the women and children, and the two men on the bench.

"So the tribes are quiet for the moment," said Cunomoros, ending a thoughtful silence.

"Quiet enough," said the Bard, "but it is the quietness of exhaustion. The Red Crests have beaten us on all fronts, and we lie up to lick our wounds, and plot new strategies."

"Until summer? Or will it be longer?" asked Cunomoros.

"Na, I am not knowing," said the Bard. "But I think it will be two years, at least—perhaps three or four—before the war-summons goes round again. We lost too many men last summer; so did the Silures. It takes time to raise and train new warriors." He cast a glance at Togi, crouching at their feet. "Will this be one?"

"Na," said Cunomoros, smiling a little in his beard, "or at least, not one for the sword only. He follows his father's path."

"Which now cannot be named," said the Bard, and his answering smile was grim. "The Red Crests have burned the Groves wherever they have found them; they have proscribed the Three Orders. All must offer submission, first to the Emperor, and then to the Emperor's Gods. Beyond that, we bards may sing as we will, as long as we speak no treason. It is not so with your order."

"So it was in Gaul," said Cunomoros, nodding, "or so the old men told me. Well, at least the Red Crests do not yet hold the North, or Ériu's Land. We may rise again."

"As surely as the sun rises tomorrow," agreed the Bard. "But after how long a night?"

"Longer, I think, than any of us know," said Cunomoros, and sighed. "Maybe this boy will see the dawn."

"Maybe," said the Bard slowly, and looked down at Togi consideringly. "He is growing fast. How many years has he now?"

"Nine," said Cunomoros.

"Ten in the spring," said Togi, who had been silent until then.

"Ho!" said the Bard, and laughed. "And eager for manhood. So were we all, eh, Cunomoros?" And to Togi, "Do you sing?"

"All the chants," said the boy proudly, "and many of the reckoning songs. I shall know them all soon."

"He has learned many," agreed Cunomoros, "and has a good voice. But why the questions?"

"A thought occurred to me," said the Bard slowly, "or half a thought, at least... I travel much with the King, especially in the summers. When the boy is a little older, I might take him with me sometime, to see more of the world. A singer's boy would attract no attention from the Red Crests, and there would be nothing to mark him out as different."

"It is a good thought," Cunomoros agreed. "In two years, perhaps, or three, he might be ready. I will teach him as much of your art as I can."

"What do you think, then?" said the Bard to Togi, who was listening wide-eyed. "Would you like to travel with me—let us say—three summers from now?"

"I would!" said the boy eagerly. "I would, most gladly!"

"Work hard, then, at your lessons," said the Bard, "and in three years—we will see!"

"I will be ready," said Togi, and the two men laughed.

"Well," said Cunomoros musingly, "why not? He must go forth someday, and this would be a good beginning. For the place of his fate is not here. I have read the omens, in the smoke and in the fire, in the water and in the wind. Over land and over sea he will travel, and through darkness to light… That is the shape of the pattern, but the end I have not seen…" He shook himself then, putting off the *awen*, and saw the boy and the Bard staring at him; and he smiled. "That is enough prophecy for today. Run, now, boy, and bring us more ale." And Togi took the empty cups and ran, but his heart was singing within him at the thought of the adventures which lay ahead. What price he would pay for them, he did not yet know.

It was a lean, hard winter, and the grain which the Red Crests had taken was sorely missed before spring. The King had remitted some part of the customary food renders, but could not remit it all, for he had his own people to feed. There was heavy snow around Imbolc, and some of the lambs were born dead, which meant a smaller flock next year; and the milk of the ewes was less than usual because of the lack of new grass, so that there was little to spare for the fresh cheeses which the people of the valley so needed at this time.

Crotos sent his older boys out on the hunting trail, shooting and trapping where they could. Togi found himself better with his birding bow than the others his age; it was if his hands knew just where his target would be before it arrived; but the snow had driven many of the birds down to lower country, and his bag was poor. Cunomoros put his herbal lore to work and joined the women, foraging on the hills and along the wood-shore; the roots he brought back were strange and bitter in the pot, but they helped to fill the empty belly, and did the eater no harm. Even so, he himself went without some days, to give the small oatcake which was his share as an offering to the Gods. Togi would have given his as well, but his father would not let him: he was growing again, and needed all the food that he could get.

It was on Beltane Eve that the next thing happened. Togi had helped his father light the bonfire on the hill, and carried the flame to the valley to light the cleansing-fires—the fires between which the sheep and cattle were driven to insure their health and fertility for the next year. The older men were drinking or drumming, the younger ones drinking and courting—for couples often paired off at this time of year. The boys who were too young for either were gathered at one side, eating their fill of roast meat for a change and boasting. The older ones, including Ivomagnos and Lugotorix, who had recently turned thirteen and would have their manhood rituals next year, were bragging about what they would do on the war-trail against the hated Red Crests when they were warriors themselves. Ivo had never forgotten the broken nose Togi had once given him—it had healed crookedly to remind him—and he never missed a chance to make fun of the younger boy. "And what will you do, little priestling," he said now, "when you come to manhood? Hide still behind your father's skirts? It will be a threadbare defense against the Red Crests' spears!"

Togi laughed. "My spear is as sharp as yours, Ivo, and my aim is better. I do not think it is I who will be shamed before the tribes."

Like all of the thirteen-year-olds, Ivo had been at the heather ale when the men's backs were turned, and the flush of anger now added color to his already red face. It did not help that Togi's aim with either spear or bow was truly better than his. He cast around in his ale-fuddled mind for something biting to say, and found it. "Will you bring your Druid magic, then, to help us fight? The magic which failed your father at the Aber Menai? It could not stop the Red Crests then, or why are you here, little afterthought in the mountains? Why are you not a Priest's son on Môn?"

Some men grow red-faced with anger, but Togi was not one of them. Instead he grew pale, and his grey eyes darkened in the twilight. "My father's magic did not fail," he said carefully and distinctly, each word dropped like a stone into a deep well. "But even magic cannot turn back an army by itself. I will strike my blow against the Red Crests before I die, and it will be a bitter one. But you…" He paused, staring with narrowed eyes at and through Ivo, to something only he could see. "You will fall in your first fight, Ivo, and be food for ravens, and only your kin will mourn you."

"That is enough," said Lugo strongly, thrusting himself between them as Ivo started forward with his fists clenched in anger. "No more, either of you: this is a night for feasting, not for fighting. Togi, keep your mouth shut until you are grown; Ivo, you should not have baited him. Come on, all of you, and let us see if we can get another pitcher of ale while no one is looking! I for one am dry with talking!"

They followed him, most of them eagerly, Togi more slowly. He was still trying to master his anger, and to understand the moment of vision which had spoken through him, as if some other being was using his mouth. He had heard his foster-father speak like this before, but had not understood how it felt: like a horn being blown through by the wind, with no control over the music it made; like the words which one spoke in a dream, not knowing beforehand what one would say. To be powerful and yet powerless, blown light as a leaf on the gale, riding helplessly the strength of some force beyond oneself: this was the Seer's gift, the gift of *awen*. It was both a gift and a burden: a weapon not lightly to be used. This much he knew, by training and by instinct. What more it was, he would later learn. He only knew now that it was like a sword in his hand, which before had been empty, and that Ivo had been afraid.

That summer the Gods answered their people's prayers, and sent a good harvest. It was all gathered safely into the barns, and the boys were picking the little half-wild russet apples which grew on the south slope of the hill, when the Red Crests came again. They were not unexpected, for the King had been forced to promise five years of tribute to get his peace, but they came as welcome as a black frost in springtime, and as deadly.

Once more the men and women had to stand and see their winter food being taken away by the black-browed foreign soldiers, under the watchful eye of their centurion. There was more muttering than the year before; last winter's hunger was still sharp in everyone's memory. Togi felt a red hatred rising in him as he watched, and he saw the centurion's face through a bloody mist. He focused that hatred; felt it bright and sharp and solid as a spear; was about to launch it with his mind toward his target—then Cunomoros's hands came down hard on his shoulders, and Cunomoros's voice hissed "No!" in his ears. Startled, Togi looked up into his foster-father's face, seeing it set and angry as his own had been, but cold, cold. "No," said Cunomoros again quietly. "This is not the time."

"He is our enemy," said Togi as softly. "He should die for what he is doing to us!"

"Perhaps he should, and perhaps he will," said Cunomoros, his fingers still gripping the boy's thin shoulders tightly. "But this is not the time or the way. Be silent for now, and watch. We will talk later."

All of this had passed in moments, unnoticed by anyone else. The Red Crests finished loading the grain, the drivers cracked their whips, and the patient ponies drew the high-wheeled carts away down the long rough track which ran the length of the valley, the soldiers marching after them. Crotos drove the other boys back to their apple picking, and Cunomoros released his son to go with them. Togi went with his mind shaken and confused. What had he been about to do, and why had his father stopped him? He thought about it in snatches in the orchard, but came to no conclusion. Only the next morning, on the quiet hilltop after they had chanted the dawn prayer, did Cunomoros explain.

"You know the Triads of Right and Wrong Action, do you not?" he said. Togi frowned.

"Of course I do."

"Good," said Cunomoros. " 'Tell me, then, O Seeker, the nature of Anger.' "

" 'Anger,' " said Togi readily, quoting the well-learned lesson, " 'is of three kinds: the just anger which moves a brave man to avenge injustice; the vain anger, which flares up in a fool or a drunkard at a trifle, and causes needless quarrels; and the coward's anger, which serves as a cloak for his fear.' "

"A true word," said Cunomoros. " 'Tell me, then, of what element is it composed?' "

" 'It is composed of fire,' " said Togi. " 'The just man's anger burns bright and clear like the hearth-fire, which gives warmth and light. The drunkard's anger burns roaring and dangerous as the wild-fire, which brings forest and field to ruin for no cause. And the coward's anger burns bitter and sullen as covered coals, which can maim or harm with no warning.' "

"Well spoken," said Cunomoros. "And what do these three angers have in common?" This was not a usual question, and Togi frowned.

"Fire," he said at last. "Fire, which can help or harm."

"And of what sort," asked Cunomoros, "was your anger yesterday?"

"A just anger," said the boy, "against those who do harm to my people.

"You say truly. But what was it that were you doing with your anger, there in the crowd?"

"I—was making a weapon of it," said Togi slowly. "A spear, to strike the chief Red Crest. To kill him."

"A spear, made with your mind?"

"Yes. And I was—about to throw it—when you stopped me."

"And what do you think would have happened, when you threw this spear?" asked Cunomoros.

"I—I do not know. But I wanted to kill him, to see him fall dead."

"And if he had?" said Cunomoros. "What would have happened then?" Again Togi frowned; his thoughts had gone no further than the picture of his hated enemy dead at his feet.

"The soldiers might have killed me," he ventured at last.

"You only? When they saw no weapon, when they saw only magic—Druid magic?"

"Mmm," said Togi. "They would have looked for the Druids, and killed us both?"

"They might not have troubled to search," said Cunomoros. "I have seen a village that the Red Crests had sacked. Pray to the Gods that you never see one."

"They might have killed us all," said Togi, his eyes wide and dark at the horrors he was imagining. "But…but…"

"It did not happen," said Cunomoros, and put his hand on the boy's shoulder. "But what?"

"Could I—what I was doing—could it have worked?"

"Yes," said Cunomoros simply. "You have the seed of that power in you: I have seen it. I will teach you what I can about its uses, but I cannot teach you much. Someday you will control that magic; but until that day comes, you must control yourself. Otherwise it will be like the drunkard's anger, which can flare up and destroy many good things in a moment. So when you feel anger or hatred, pause and remember my words."

"I will," said the boy. He was shivering. Cunomoros put an arm around him and hugged him.

"Come on," he said, "let us go and see if your mother's barley bannocks are ready. I am hungry, even if you are not."

In the autumn woods the pigs foraged for acorns, and the boys and girls for nuts. Togi brought home sacks full of the little brown hazels, and his mother ground them on the stone into meal to mix with her barley-meal. Toasted on the bake-stone before the fire, they made fine nutty bannocks. Sometimes there was a little meat—he was becoming good now at shooting squirrels, his feisty little red competitors for the nuts—or a bite of hard summer cheese to go with the bannocks; sometimes beans—the crop had been good that year—or a handful of green-stuff from the wood-shore or from the frost-touched remains of the garden. There had been apples, too, for a while, the bruised ones which needed to be eaten early, and bramble-fruit; but those were gone now.

His mother was with child again; the baby, she said, should be born around Imbolc. He would have to work harder at his hunting, though they would get their share of the meat from the herds and the flocks—their share of the pig-slaughter, too. Cunomoros had been suffering lately with the joint-ail; it was worse in the winter cold, and made it hard for him to climb the hill some mornings. Their lessons, though, went on as before; in addition to the endless lists and memory-songs, he had begun to teach Togi the language of Ériu's Land. The importance of this was shared between them without words, but Togi knew what it meant: one day he too would cross the sea to a land where the Druids still held power.

"A great green land it is," said Cunomoros, "green and mild all year round. A land of many long-horned white cattle, of fierce chariot-fighting warriors and beautiful long-haired women. A land of much magic, where at the right seasons the Old Ones still walk among us; where the Gods still linger in the hollow hills, and hear our prayers. The great Sanctuaries have many Priests and teachers, Druids and Seers and Bards; wonderful is the chanting at Beltane on the Hill of Uisneach, and great the sacrifices at Temair on Samhain Eve. Even Môn in her heyday could not surpass them... Your blood-father came from that land, from the mountains of the northwest. As a youth he came to Môn to study, and with us he found his fate..." He fell silent then, staring into the fire, and Togi did not disturb him. He had thoughts of his own to follow: he had been dreaming again.

It always began on a high hill: sometimes by the cairn on Penwyn, sometimes at a place he did not know. Yet to say he did not know it was false, for he had been there many times now; he knew the shape of the land, the color of the rocks, the strange gray light of the world-between-the-worlds, like a misty dawn but colder. He knew the moment when the sound would come, the sound of far-off horns, brazen and deep, bronze-mouthed and braying, echoing in the high hills. He saw the change of the light; saw the winding dust-white road appear which led to his high place; saw the man climbing toward him, far-off but clear. Sometimes he stood and waited; sometimes he started down to meet the stranger; but always the light faded, and the dream slipped away. Maybe it was one of those things which Cunomoros said he would be better able to control when he was a man. Maybe...

Cunomoros sighed, and came back to the present. "Let me hear that last verse again," he said, "and this time take care with your accent." And so the lessons went on.

Samhain Night

He was eleven years old now, tall for his age but slender. They had celebrated his name-day, as always, on the fifteenth day of Edrini, the Bright Month, halfway through the spring. He stood, said Cunomoros, between seasons—possibly between worlds, although Beltane and Samhain were the true boundary days. He himself thought sometimes that this was true, for he also stood halfway between priest and warrior. Although he would not reach manhood for three years, he came closer every day.

The new baby had been born at Imbolc, a strong healthy girl. The labor had been long and hard; his mother had bled much, and suffered a fever afterwards; and even now, with Beltane approaching, she was not really well. Cunomoros and Togi had cared for her and the child, with some help from the other women of the village, and Tritos, the small brother—no longer so small, for he would start his own weapon training soon. Togi had learned much herb-craft and house-craft in the process, and had become a good maker of oatcakes—when there was meal enough to make them. Between the Red Crests and the King, there had been little enough of that year's harvest left for the people who grew it.

The young Bard—Cingetos was his name—had come again with the King's war-band at Midwinter. He had listened to Togi's singing, and grinned. "That is well enough for a beginning," he had said, "but you have much to learn yet, lad; also you need to be older before you can travel with me. We will talk again next winter." Togi had been disappointed, but perhaps it was just as well: his family would need his help this summer, with his mother still so far from well. But soon, very soon, he would—escape was not the word; he was not imprisoned here, or unhappy. But there was a wider world out there, and he yearned to see it. He told no one of his dreams.

The manhood rituals were held during the three days just before Beltane. One by one the boys were taken into a stone hut on the mountainside, set aside for this purpose, a hut whose walls had been built by the Old Ones themselves. It should, said Cunomoros, who led the rituals, have been a cave or a hollow hill, but this was close enough: sunken into the hillside, half below ground, the hut's gray stone walls were almost hidden by brambles and gorse bushes, and its roof was of thick green turf rather than golden thatch. The boys stayed for a night and a day in the dark, and came out as men at sunset. That was all Togi knew, all he was allowed to know—until his turn came. The young men came out quiet but triumphant, and were given new spears that evening by their fathers or foster-fathers. Then the next night there was the Beltane feast, with dancing and drumming, and cauldrons brimming with the carefully kept heather ale and mead.

Late on that Beltane Eve, Togi passed Ivo and Lugo, who had just completed their own manhood rituals, and had the new tribal markings raw on their arms to prove it. They were drinking and laughing with a girl—a girl not much younger than they were, with merry eyes and long black curls and swelling breasts beneath her sleeveless linen kirtle. "What was it like in the darkness, all that time?" she was asking. "Were you not afraid?"

"Afraid? Of what? Mice, or shadows?" laughed Ivo. "Na, not I."

"Afraid of ghosts—of spirits," said the girl, and giggled.

"I saw no ghosts," said Ivo. "Did you, Lugo?"

"None," said Lugo. "Although… you talk of what is forbidden, Ivo."

"Was there no Druid magic, then?" asked the girl.

"Bah!" said Ivo. "What are Druids nowadays? Old men, dressed up to scare children. Or boys like that one." And he pointed at Togi, who had stopped to listen. "Would *you* be afraid in the dark, little priestling?"

"Let be, Ivo," said Lugo, but Togi came toward them.

"Not I," he said. "I know the ways of darkness, and of magic. I can go places where you would not dare, new-made warrior!"

"Name one!" said Ivo promptly. And when Togi paused to think, "Name one, little boy, or eat your words."

"Would you go, then," said Togi slowly, "to the cairn on the top of Penwyn on Samhain night—go before sunset, and spend the whole night there alone, without fire, without steel, without company?"

There was a silence, for the cairn on Penwyn was known to be haunted ground. Long ago a hunter, lost in fog and darkness, had spent the night sheltering beneath its stones, and been found in the morning stark mad. The tale, passed down through generations, had lost nothing in the telling.

"Not I," said Lugo.

"Nor I," said Ivo. "Would you go, then, little boy?"

"I would," said Togi boldly, "and I will."

"We will hold you to that," said Ivo with malice. "Remember, you two others, what you have heard him say. And when he fails to go—as fail he will!—let us all call him braggart, and coward!"

"Na," said Lugo, frowning. "Let the boy alone. Togi, you should not boast so, but I will not hold you to it."

"What I have said," said Togi deliberately, "I will perform. Let you all remember!" And he walked away. Behind him he heard nervous laughter, but he did not look back.

"So what," said Cunomoros the next morning on the hill, "is this tale I am hearing about you?"

"Mmm," said Togi. He was not surprised; Cunomoros always knew everything that happened, sometimes before it did so. "It is nothing much."

"That is how you think of it, then?" said Cunomoros, "To walk among the dead is nothing much? Excuse me, I thought it was my student that you are, and not my master!"

Togi bit his lip. "Well, but Father, I could not help it."

"Could not, or would not? I have spoken to you before about anger. Is this how you show your self-control?"

Togi sighed. "Na, you are right. But he insulted you—he insulted all the Druids… and me. I could not—I *would* not let it go by. Should I have done?"

"That is fairer speaking," said Cunomoros evenly. "And insult is hard to bear. At least you are truthful, with me and with yourself. Do you feel ready for this challenge you have undertaken, which frightens grown men?"

"No," said Togi. "But I will have to do it. Will you help me to prepare?"

"So far as I can," said Cunomoros, and smiled. "Beyond that, it is in the hands of the Gods."

"Then I must make offerings," said Togi seriously.

"That will be a good start," said his father.

Summer passed all too quickly. At sunrise on the hill, hoeing the beans in the morning, tending the afternoon stewpot, or walking in the long evening twilight, Togi learned all that Cunomoros could teach him of ghosts and spirits and phantoms. There were spells to memorize, tricks and incantations, promises and questions, pitfalls to avoid. In the hut at evening around the dying hearth-fire, Cunomoros told them stories which left little Tritos, listening wide-eyed, afraid to go outside for a necessary journey. Even Togi's mother, nursing the new daughter, protested sometimes, laughing a little, that he frightened her—she would not sleep herself tonight, no, not a wink, unless he set strong spells to protect them all! Only Togi showed no fear, and drank it all in; and if he dreamed afterwards of horrors, he did not wake to tell of them.

Autumn brought the Red Crests back again. There were less escorting soldiers with the carts this time; perhaps they thought that the tribesmen were cowed, or perhaps they had need of men elsewhere. There were rumors of unrest in the North; the Brigantes had not yet made submission. Togi watched in bitter silence the stealing of their sorely needed grain; he was learning to control his anger, and to be patient. The time for revenge would come later.

The King's visit came early that year. He was trying to whip up support among the tribal chieftains, said Cingetos the Bard, for a possible move against the Red Crests next spring. Not war, Cingetos thought, not yet; but some sort of threat which would help him in an appeal against the taxes. Certainly the people could not support this level of extortion for long; either the Red Crests or the King would have to reduce their demands. If not, then there might be a new King soon; such things had happened before.

"What is this I hear," said Cunomoros, "about rebellion in the east?"

"Some young men of the Corieltauvi did it," said Cingetos. "Some of that tribe joined with Boudicca in her revolt, and all of them were punished. Resentment is still strong. These lads attacked a small body of the Red Crests, and killed a few. Their villages were burned as a result. It was also said…" He paused.

"Yes?" said Cunomoros. "What was said?"

"That the Druids were involved," said Cingetos. "It may even be true, though I doubt it. The Red Crests, however, believed the rumor. They are offering good silver to anyone who denounces a Druid."

"Ah," said Cunomoros. "And have any claimed the reward?"

"Not yet," said Cingetos. "Not yet."

Togi had been listening as usual, sitting on his heels beside the bench where the two shared cups of ale in the pale autumn sunlight. A tremor of fear went through him, and, as if his thought had called them up, Ivo and Lugo came strolling out of the feast-hall door beside him. Had they heard Cingetos' words? He did not know; they were laughing at some joke one of them had made. Ivo's eyes slid sideways for a moment as he passed the group by the door, but there was nothing in that—nothing but a prickling of the short hairs on Togi's neck. Then they were gone, and he turned his attention back to his father and the Bard.

"I do not know," Cingetos was saying. "The Druids are, if not honored, at least still feared by most. But where there is enmity, where there are old grievances, festering still in the dark—who knows? I would not say it was impossible, but surely not here."

"I wonder?" said Cunomoros. "I wonder? I think none of us is safe any more." His eyes went to Togi, and he smiled. "Are you still of a mind to take the boy with you next summer for a few moons?"

"Yes, I think so," said Cingetos, also smiling. "If all goes well, and he still wants to go. He does not know how heavy my hand can be."

"What do you say?" said Cunomoros to Togi. "Will you risk it?"

"Gladly," said Togi, smiling. "If the Gods allow."

"We are all in the hands of the Gods," said Cunomoros.

Three days to Samhain, then two. Togi was sleeping badly; all that Cunomoros had taught him rose up in his dreams and laughed at him. He had been mad, mad, to issue this challenge, but he must go through with it. Ivo had not forgotten, and had been baiting him about it the last few days; but even if he *had* forgotten—even if everyone had—Togi himself could not forget, could not back down. *The only way forward is through.* He could not remember where or when he had heard that phrase, but it echoed in his mind. Be it so, then. He would go forward, or die in the attempt; there was no other way open to him now.

At last the afternoon of Samhain Eve arrived; time for him to start climbing the mountain, if he was to reach the cairn before sunset. Cunomoros was going with him partway. He kissed his mother, and stepped out of the hut, to see Ivo and Lugo also waiting for him. "What is this?" he asked.

"We are going up with you, to make sure you *do* go," said Ivo, grinning wickedly. "And I am bringing this"—he patted the coil of rope he carried over one shoulder—"to make sure you stay. Otherwise, how are we to know where you spend the night?"

"You might trust his word," said Cunomoros. Lugo looked shamefaced, but Ivo only grinned wider.

"I would rather trust this rope," he said. "Words come too easily to him."

"I am ready," said Togi, ignoring him. "Let us go; sunset will not wait."

"Yes," said Lugo, "it is time."

Penwyn was not high as mountains go, but the slopes were steep and rugged. They followed sheep tracks upward through the heather and the red frost-burned bracken, changing direction from time to time, but always climbing. From the valley below they could hear the distant lowing of cows and the bleating of sheep, but up here there was only the occasional cry of a hunting hawk, hovering on the wind, or the croak of a raven beating black-winged across the pale sky. Togi's thoughts were mostly concentrated on keeping up with his older companions, and on looking back from time to time at Cunomoros, who was lagging behind. He would not think about what lay ahead.

The sun sank lower, and evening shadows began to creep across the valley, but up here they were still wrapped in warm amber light. The bracken and heather fell away, and there was only thin sheep-cropped turf between pale golden stones. Ahead of them on the summit the shape of the cairn appeared, a long, low mound surrounded by a ring of boulders. At one end of it, two taller stones stood up, leaning against each other, to frame what must once have been an entrance, and now was only a small brushy hollow, like the mouth of a shallow cave. That must be where the long-ago hunter had sheltered, on a night of mist and fog. Togi shivered.

By the time they reached the cairn, the sun was two hand's-breadths above the horizon, and the first-quarter moon which marked the beginning of Giamon hung high and silver above. There would be light for those going down; moonlight for half of the night, unless clouds came up...or fog. A cold little wind was blowing from the west, stirring the small leaves on the bushes at the foot of the two tall uprights. The three of them stopped—Cunomoros was some way behind by now, but still coming—and stared at the stones.

"How do you plan to use that rope of yours?" Lugo asked. He was smiling a little maliciously; it was obvious that there was no easy way to tie Togi to the stones—or in fact to anything else. Ivo frowned, looking back and forth from the stones to the younger boy. Togi stood silent, keeping his face still, and watched as his father breasted the last slope. "You cannot simply bind his arms and legs," said Lugo reasonably. "It will be cold tonight; he may need to move about in order to keep warm. I think you will have to trust to his word after all, Ivo."

"Ah, have it your own way!" said Ivo in frustration. A crafty look came into his face. "I would not trust his bare word, but an oath—a strong oath—might do. Will you swear one, little priestling? You should be good at this."

"I will, gladly," said Togi. "What oath would you have?"

"The strongest oath," said Ivo. "The triple oath. That should bind you, if anything will."

"I swear," said Togi carefully, "to spend the night here in this place, without fire, without steel, without living company, and not to stir between sunset and sunrise. I swear it by my blood, and by my name, and by my *awen*. If I break this oath, may the green earth open and swallow me; may the seas rush in and drown me; may the sky of stars fall upon me and crush me out of life forever."

"And I swear," said Cunomoros somewhat breathlessly, coming to a halt beside his son, "to stand as his guarantor, by the same oath. Are you content?" The wind blew back his hair from his lined brown face, and rippled his gray beard; above it his eyes were very bright, and fixed on Ivo, who moved uneasily in their glare.

"Yes," he said reluctantly. "I am satisfied."

"Then let us settle my son to his watch," said Cunomoros, "and start back down as soon as may be. It will be dark long before we reach home, and there are rituals I must perform tonight, lest the spirits of our ancestors be displeased, and bring misfortune upon us."

They were gone, and he stood alone on the mountain. The sun was setting slowly behind a bar of golden cloud, a cloud which glowed bright as iron in the smith's forge; bright even as the forge-fire itself. Overhead the first-quarter moon rode high and silver, and in the mingled light the stone uprights at the closed entrance to the cairn looked warm and friendly, like the door-pillars of a great hall. If only he knew the way of it, he could walk through that door, and join the Old Ones at their feasting.

Samhain night…the Feast of the Dead. In the Chieftain's hall below, the places would be set for those who had died in the last year. Soon they would rise from their cold beds, and leave their grave-mounds, and swim upon the currents of the air, calling in their high thin voices to those who could hear...

He was no longer afraid. He had set his course; what would follow was his fate. He bent to rearrange his wooly nest in the stunted heather, close beside one of the uprights, where the mound gave him a little shelter from the wind. He was wearing the new brown wool tunic which his mother had woven that summer, and the thick hooded cloak she had made for him the year before. Cunomoros had left him his own cloak as bedding, and even Lugo had offered his as well at the last moment. Only Ivo had remained stubbornly hostile, but after four years Togi was used to that. He sat down on Lugo's cloak and huddled his father's around him, leaning back against the sun-warmed stone, and gave himself to contemplation of the view before him. Peak after peak, the mountains stretched away to the south, hazy blue summits dark now with evening shadows. His village in the valley below him was hidden by the swell of the slope. He was alone with the mountains and the sky.

Wrapped in its own cloak of glowing cloud, the sun slipped below the horizon. All at once the light was dimmer, and the moon brighter. Like a sword-blade pulled from the smith's fire, the bar of cloud cooled slowly—gold to red, red to gray, gray to black. In the darkening sky, the first pale stars appeared, and the boy greeted them by name. The wind whispered through the short grass, and behind the stone on which he leaned, a lonely cricket sang. Everything else was silent as a held breath. Within the mound, he could feel the dead awakening.

Slowly at first they awoke from their year-long slumber. Ghostly white bones moved and stretched in the dark. Most of their kind, the boy knew, had gone on to the Summerlands, to live a second life there, or to be reborn into a new one here. These were the stubborn ones, bound by will or duty to the land where they had once lived: the guardians, the gate-keepers, the watchers at the ford. Beyond even the counting of the Druids were the years through which they had dwelt here. They were part of the flesh of the land now, like the mountains. Like the standing stones they had raised, they endured. And on this one night above all others, they emerged to survey their vanished kingdom, and to feed on the life of any who barred their way.

Slowly they rose from their cold couches, leaving behind the dry bones they no longer needed, the green bronze blades, the twisted torques and arm rings—for these had been Kings and warriors of their people, and Priest-Kings before ever there were Druids. As pure spirits they stood in the solid darkness, stretching out their senses to the world outside their mound. The boy outside felt their ghostly touch, and shivered despite himself. He knew that they were hungry for warmth and blood, after so many years of dry earth and cold stone. And he had nothing with which to ward them off, no fire nor steel—his belt knife had gone with Cunomoros—nor living company, unless one counted the cricket behind the stone…

Even as the thought passed through his mind, he heard a rustling in the grass beside him, and with the quickness of a fox he twisted to his knees and pounced. He felt the small soft body writhing under his hand, and tightened his grip, then cautiously sat back to examine his prey. In the white moonlight the mouse peered at him from between his fingers with beady black eyes, whiskers aquiver. He grasped the long tail which hung loose with his other hand, but it never moved, frozen in panic stillness. A warm-blooded morsel of life, it might yet buy him his life. Without looking he knew that the ghostly door behind him was opening, as the first of the dead emerged.

Bodiless as fog, in the remembered shape of his body, the dead King came from the mound. The golden circlet he had worn in life encircled his pale brow, but his lunate breastplate of gold was that of a Priest. The moonlight picked out the lines engraved on its phantom surface, and gleamed in dark eyes where no living eyes could be. Behind him came others—warband, comrades, retainers—solid shadows with ghostly spears and ghostly swords. Seeing the boy they had sensed, they paused to look at him. And Togi rose up from his blankets, still holding the mouse, and spoke.

"The Gods' blessings on you, Old Ones, and my welcome. How may I serve you tonight?" His voice was high and clear, like his dawn invocations; wonder had forced out fear. The Priest-King gazed at him in surprise. Since those who put him into the ground had departed, seldom had he met a living human in this place, and never one so calm. Togi felt himself weighed and measured, blood and body and spirit, and stood the test.

"Why are you here, man-child, all unafraid?" asked the ghost at last. His words were strange beyond telling, and yet the boy understood them.

"In fulfillment of a vow," he said. "And in defense of my father's honor, and my own."

"Those are good reasons," said the ghost, his hollow voice echoing on the wind, but his meaning piercing his hearer's mind. "And while I lived, I might have done the same. Yet still it is a foolish thing that you have done. For speaking with the Dead, there is always a price. Do you know that price, young warrior?"

"I am twice the son of a Priest," said Togi. "I know that the price is high, but also that it depends on the asker. What price will you take tonight, Old One? Blood or spirit or life? And will you grant me knowledge in return?"

"Speak first your name," said the ghost, moving a little closer. His silent followers crowded close on his heels, their dark eyes gleaming, and a cold hunger came out of them all in a wave. Togi wanted to step back, but he knew that he must not. If once he moved, they would be on him like wolves on a lamb. And he knew that he must not speak his own name.

"My blood-father was a fox," he said slowly, thinking it out as he went, "and I am his cub. He gave his life for his land, for his people, against the red ravagers. Over land and water they came hunting him with steel and fire, but they could not catch him. Me he hid in the darkness, to work his revenge. The gray wolf raised me here, and taught me magic, to dance on the mountains and know the names of the stars."

"That is a good answer," said the Priest-King, and again he moved a little closer. "And for that I will give you a choice: you may pay the price with either blood, or spirit, or life. If I take blood from you, you will live, but be maimed in your body. If I take spirit, you will live, but be maimed in your mind. If I take your life, you may join my company forever, and journey each Samhain with us on the winter's winds, or depart, if you wish, to the West, to the Isles of the Blessed. The choice, Fox's Cub, is yours to make, and yours alone."

Despite himself, Togi was shivering now, as the cold hunger of the ghosts reached out and enveloped him. He did not want any of these choices; he wanted to live, and grow up, and travel, and do great deeds. He wanted—he pulled himself up on the brink of panic, and felt the mouse wriggle against the tightening grip of his right hand. And a bubble of laughter rose up in him, and he remembered his plan.

"Blood, or spirit, or life, you named, Old One," he said, trying to keep his voice steady. "But you did not say that it has to be *my* blood, or *my* life. Here is blood and life for you, both together." And he held up the mouse by its tail.

The ghost stared at the mouse, which swung head-down from the boy's fingers, paws scrabbling jerkily at the night air. It was a very small life, but it *was* alive—and warm. And the night was passing, and in the valleys below there would be offerings, and perhaps other lives on which to feed. And the boy was clever, with a cleverness the ghost dimly remembered in himself, long ages ago, when he had been a man...

"A bargain," he said. The mouse jerked once below Togi's hand, and hung still. He opened his fingers and let it fall, and thought that it vanished before it hit the ground. Then the ghostly troop flowed around him like cold fog on a rising wind, silver in the silver moonlight, and were gone. For a moment he thought he heard them calling to each other, crying out in high thin voices which rose and fell eerily in words he could almost understand. Then these too dwindled in distance, and he was alone on the mountain with the moon.

He stood for a long time listening to the silence and thinking. Then he curled up in his three cloaks at the foot of the tall stones and slept. He did not see the ghosts stream back to their barrow at dawn; the next thing he knew was sunlight on his face, and his father's voice calling his name. He sat up yawning, to see Cunomoros and Ivo and Lugo all looking down at him.

"Well," said Cunomoros smiling, "did you have a quiet night?"

"Oh, mostly," said Togi, and yawned again. "I did have some company for a little while."

"What kind of company?" asked Ivo suspiciously. "You swore you would stay here alone."

"Well, there was a mouse here for a while," said Togi. "But it is gone now."

"No other company?" asked Lugo, looking around at the bare mountaintop.

"No other *living* company," said Togi, and yawning again, stood up. "Did you bring me anything to eat, Father? I am starving!"

"I did," said Cunomoros, and reaching into the breast of his tunic, he pulled out a cloth-wrapped bundle. "Your mother was up before dawn at her baking, and I know there will be plenty more waiting for us at home."

"That will be good," said Togi, and grinning, opened the package and stuffed half an oatcake into his mouth. They had not gone far when a thought struck him. "Go on, Father," he said. "I will catch up with you." And running back, he knelt and placed half an oatcake at the foot of the tall stone. "I thank you," he said to the spirit of the mouse, "for my life." For sacrifices, as he knew, should always be acknowledged; and sooner or later, all debts must be repaid.

Dinas Brân

Cingetos returned two days after Beltane, and this time he came alone. Moreover, he brought with him a spare pony, a young gray gelding with a black mane, on a leading rein with his packhorse behind his own stolid bay. "After all," he said to Togi with a grin as they led the horses to the paddock, "I can hardly expect my singer's boy to walk behind me while I ride. Besides, it will be good practice for you." Certainly it would be that, thought Togi, for the mountain people were spearmen, not cavalry, and he had only received the basic lessons in horse-manage which were part of his warrior training. He would have to learn as he went.

Cingetos sang in hall that night for the tribe's entertainment, but afterwards, instead of sleeping there, he came back with Cunomoros and his family to their hut. Seated on a low stool beside the hearth-fire, and with a cup of good ale in his hand, he sighed. "I am here," he said to Cunomoros, "to make good on my offer, if it pleases you and the boy—and if you think that he is ready. Twelve years old now, is he not?"

"Since the middle of Edrini," said Cunomoros. "As to being ready—yes, I think that he is, although it grieves my heart to lose him, even for a little while. For how long will you take him? He is not yet done with his schooling."

"Until Lughnasa, at the least," said Cingetos, and yawned. "Until Samhain, at the most. It will depend upon the King's circuit. I must rejoin him soon."

"Does he call a hosting this year?" asked Cunomoros. "I mind what you said two years ago at midwinter."

"Not yet," said Cingetos. "And if war comes, I will send the boy back."

"If you have a chance," said Cunomoros.

"Yes," said Cingetos honestly, "if I have a chance."

Togi's mother had listened silently to all of this, but the next morning she called the boy aside. "Is it sure that you are, little cub, that you are ready?" she asked.

"I am," said Togi. He had been growing again over the winter, and was now almost as tall as she was, though his face still had its boyish roundness. His dark, rough-cropped hair—almost black, but for a hint of red in strong sunlight—hung loose on his shoulders, and his brows were thick and dark above his clear gray eyes. Smiling a little, his mother fished something out of the neck of her tunic: a battered silver ring, which had hung on a thong around her neck for as long as the boy remembered. She pulled the thong over her head now, and held it out to him.

"I think it is time that you had this," she said. "It was Lovernos'—your blood-father's. He sent it back to you by Cunomoros before he died, while I still carried you in my belly. You teethed on it, though you would not remember that. Now it is yours."

Togi took the ring by its thong and held it up, gazing at it in wonder. He had never questioned the source of this thing which she had always worn, often though he had seen it. It had been a familiar part of her, like her blue eyes, or the dark hair which was beginning now to be streaked with gray. Slipping the worn thong from the ring, he held it on his palm, tasting it with his mind as Cunomoros had taught him to do. There was a small design deep-carved on the face of it, blurred at the edges with much wear but clear in the center, of a figure holding a many-spoked wheel, which might have been Lugh, and might have been some other God. He sensed something in it which was not of his mother, something—someone—strange and yet familiar. He tried it on, but found that it was too large even for his index finger, and put it back on its thong. "Are you sure you would not rather keep it safe for me, Mother," he asked, "until I am a man?"

"So Cunomoros thought," his mother said, still smiling. "But I think differently. Yet better it is that you wear it around your neck for now, little cub, safely out of men's sight. When the day comes to put it on, you will know; for you are Lovernos' true son, and this ring was made, as he told me, for a Druid Priest."

Togi slipped the worn thong over his head and tucked it under his hair, inside his brown linen tunic. The ring felt odd against his skin for a moment, and then right. "Thank you, Mother," he said, and hugged her. "I will keep it safe."

"Keep yourself safe, too, little cub," she said, and kissed him. "And come back to me in the autumn, for I shall miss you." And with that she turned away and went into the hut. It was time to start the supper stewpot, and the little daughter was crying.

Three days later Togi rode away from the home he had known all his life, with little else but the clothes that he wore, and the worn silver ring hanging on its thong inside his linen tunic. His good hooded cloak and new wool tunic were strapped on Cingetos' packhorse along with the Bard's own gear; his only weapon was the horn-handled belt-knife—larger than his old one—that Cunomoros had given him on his last name-day. He felt very proud to be riding thus, following his new master, on a bright summer morning when all the world was in bloom. He had no notion of the adventures that lay ahead. Cunomoros did, but he kept the foretelling to himself, and only offered extra sacrifices to the Gods.

They were two nights on their way to the King's *rath* at Dinas Brân, set on a round-topped hill in the heart of the mountains, and Togi enjoyed it all. Cingetos set a slow pace out of consideration for the boy's lack of horsemanship, but in truth he himself found it no hardship to dawdle, enjoying the gentle weather and stopping from time to time to get down and stretch his legs. The country was green and lush with early summer; the sunshine was warm; and there were no Red Crests anywhere to be seen. The first night they lodged in a chieftain's hall, where Cingetos sang for their supper, and the second afternoon saw them climbing the long slope to Dinas Brân. Below them, a wide lake reflected the pure blue of the heavens; on either side, gray-headed mountains towered above pale green forests; and above them, white-headed eagles and red kites soared across the sky. It was a land built for Gods, or giants; the heartland of a people, and the proper home for a King.

Regenos—for so the King was called—had recently rebuilt his chief court here, in a place which had been strong and holy time out of mind. His fortress had no walls, nor needed any, for the cliffs below protected it; the one winding approach from the north was easy to watch and defend. Here he had his long thatch-roofed wooden hall, his storehouses and stables, his brew-house and bake-house, and quarters for his serving-folk. Cattle and horses were herded for him on the lower slopes of the hill, and grain came up on pack-ponies, the path being too steep for carts. It was a Raven's Fortress indeed—for that was the meaning of its name—in the heart of Eryri, the Eagles' Country, and—so far—secure.

Cingetos exchanged jests with the watchmen on the way up, and slipped off of his horse at the top with a sigh, scrubbing a lean hand over his bony face and pushing back his tangled red hair. "The stables are over there," he said to Togi, pointing. "Take our ponies there when you have unloaded them; I will show you later where to stow our gear. We will sleep tonight in the hall, with the King's *teulu*, which is my proper place when I am here, and yours too, now that you are with me." And he turned away, leaving the boy to his tasks.

Togi did as he was told, taking time to look about him. Seeing new places, meeting new people, were meat and drink to him, and he took it all in. The men and women going purposefully about their business here were not many, but to him a host of strangers. He wondered what the King's Druid would be like, and where they would celebrate the morning sacrifices. There had been none which he had seen in the place where they had stayed the night before.

Presently he asked this question of Cingetos. "Hush!" said the Bard softly. "Yes, there is a man here who makes offerings to the Gods in due season, but do not call him a Druid. I thought you had listened enough to your father and me to know that the use of that name is forbidden now."

"I am sorry," said Togi, frowning. "Yes, I do remember now. But it seems so strange! There is not a morning since I could walk that I have not greeted the Sun with my father."

Cingetos laughed. "Well," he said, "if you rise to make dawn-offerings here, do not wake me! The King's household sits late at their mead and wine when they can, as you will see. Put our gear under that bench in the corner; it will be time for feasting soon." And indeed young men in sweat-stained tunics were already drifting into the hall, laughing and joking among themselves, to throw themselves down on the benches which lined the long room and call for ale. Women came with cups and pitchers; serving-men came to set up the trestle tables between the benches and the hearth-fires, which burned in a long stone-lined pit down the center of the earth-floored hall. Before Togi knew it, the place was full of people, and the King himself came in to take his seat at the end away from the door.

Regenos was a big man, tall and very muscular, with reddish hair and beard and bright blue eyes. The few times when Togi had seen him on circuit, he had always been richly dressed, in a many-colored woolen robe festooned with strings of amber and red and blue glass beads; but here in his own hall he made less display. The only things fine about him tonight were the heavy gold bracelet, like a twisting serpent, which he wore on his left arm above the elbow, and the gleaming blue steel of the razor-edged blade with which he cut his meat. Otherwise many of his war-band outshone him in color and splendor; but no one, however ignorant, would have taken him for anything other than a King.

Three men had followed their King into the hall, and now went to sit beside him. In answer to Togi's questions, Cingetos told him that the first, a tall black-bearded man called Orgetos, was the leader of the war-band, and the second, a fair youth called Cloutios, was the King's half-brother and shield-bearer. The third was an older man, plainly dressed in dark clothing, with a lined face and gray-streaked hair. "Who is he?" asked Togi.

"Sennos," said the Bard. "And he is—"

"I know *what* he is," said Togi softly. Cingetos looked at him in surprise.

"Is it so obvious?" he asked.

"No," said Togi slowly. "But—"

"Like knows like, I suppose," said Cingetos, and laughed. A serving-man put a platter of meat on the table, and he reached out to take some. "Eat now," he said. "Soon I must sing. Stay here, and"—he laughed again—"keep quiet if you can. It may be a long night."

For a boy bred up in a poor mountain valley, the King's feast was a revelation. Togi ate more good roast cow-meat that night than he sometimes got in a month at home, and drank more heather ale than he had ever had before in his life. Only the barley bannocks, he thought, were not so good as those which his mother made, although this did not stop him from eating three. Tucked into a corner of the hall, unnoticed by the others, he listened as Cingetos sang his first songs, praising the King and his war-band, and accompanying himself on a small square wooden-framed lyre. Afterwards the Bard sang other songs, comic ones which had the young men pounding the time on the tables and roaring along with him. By the time it was all over—the platters cleared away, the tables stacked, and the King long since retired to his private room—Togi was half-asleep on his bench. But when Cingetos shook him awake, he did his share to spread their straw pallets on the floor, and tumbled down upon his own just as he was. His last thought before he slid into a deep pool of sleep was a regret that he might miss the dawn sacrifice.

Despite his weariness, he awoke the next morning, as always, before sunrise. It took him a little while at first to remember where he was. The shadowy hall, lit only by a last few flickering flames in the long hearth, was full of the sounds of slumber: many men's deep regular breathing, and the occasional grunt or snore. Cingetos beside him lay curled on his right side, his long bony face, relaxed in sleep, looking younger than his years. Cautiously Togi pushed back the cloak he had used for a blanket and got to his feet. Taking care not to step on any of the sleepers, he made his way to the doorway and slipped out past the leather curtain that closed it. His time-sense had not betrayed him; it was the hour before dawn. A blue trail of smoke was rising from behind the kitchens, where the bakers were firing their ovens, but otherwise the place was quiet. Where would the offering be made? Following his *awen*, he walked south, through a huddle of thatched bothies and storehouses, and in a short time came out on the edge of the little plateau which crowned the fortress hill.

Awe-struck, he paused to gaze around him. To his left and right and behind him, the great bald-headed peaks reared up, but before him the ground dropped steeply away into a forested valley, where oak and ash mingled their early summer leaves, bronze-green and palest green-gold. Before him in the distance he could see other mountains, still blue-shadowed in twilight, but no match for the giant on his right. *Yr Wyddfa,* Cingetos had called it yesterday: the Place of the Grave. Even as he watched, the first sunlight touched its peak, painting with rosy light the gray crags still seamed with traces of last winter's snows. Back home at this time, Cunomoros must be making his familiar offering, but Togi had nothing here to give. Instead, he lifted his empty hands to the mountain, and began to sing.

His song praised the mountain and the sun, and the Shining Gods who had set them both in their places when the world was new. It was rough beginner's work, and not very long, but he sang it with all his heart. When he had finished, he stood for a few more moments with lifted hands, then dropped his arms and turned through a half circle toward the east.

"That was a fine offering," said a man's deep voice behind him. Startled, Togi turned his head and saw the gray-haired man he had noticed the night before. Sennos, Cingetos had called him: Sennos, the King's Druid.

"The altar is there," said Sennos, and looking where he pointed, Togi saw that what he had taken for a cliff edge was not quite sheer. Instead, rough-carved stone steps led down for twice a tall man's height to a broad ledge, invisible unless one stood just above it. "Take this," said Sennos, extending a covered basket, "and follow me."

"You do not know me," said Togi wonderingly. "You do not know who I am."

"I know *what* you are," said Sennos quietly. "That is enough for now."

The basket was heavy, and the steps steep, so Togi went carefully. The ledge, however, was more than wide enough for two. Against the cliff face stood a small square altar, a fore-arm's length each way, carved out of the living stone. Small rock plants grew in crevices around it, and early violets bloomed at its base, but its top was darkened with fire and with the stains of past offerings, not yet washed away by the rain. Sennos set the jug he had carried on the stone beside the altar, and took the basket from Togi. Within it was a small warm bannock, fresh from the day's first baking, and a young cockerel, bound but still indignantly alive. Sennos took wood and kindling from a pile beside the altar and arranged it carefully on the top; then, taking flint and steel from his belt-pouch, he struck a spark onto his prepared tinder, and blew it into a flame. Chanting the morning prayers, he drew his belt knife and cut the cockerel's throat, holding the jerking body while it spilled its blood into the flames. He cut off the head and added that as well, then set the rest aside and took up the bannock, which he crumbled into the fire. When all was consumed, he handed the jug to Togi, saying, "Extinguish it now." Togi poured ale onto the dying flames with a practiced hand, chanting the proper prayers as he did so. "Yes," said Sennos when it was finished. "You have done this before."

"Many times," said Togi. "My father was—is—a Priest."

"So I thought," said Sennos, and smiled in his gray beard. "And I remember you now: you are the boy who came with Cingetos yesterday. Where did he find you?"

"In my mother's house," said Togi. Sennos gave a bark of laughter.

"Yes," he said again. "You do right not to tell nowadays. But the prayers which you chanted I know, and I know where I myself learned them. Were you born on the holy isle?"

"No," said Togi. "But my—my teacher was."

"Ah," said Sennos. "Then I think I could give him a name."

"Mmm," said Togi. "It might be so." Sennos laughed again.

"Na," he said, "I will not try your silence now. For how long are you with the Bard?"

"For the summer," said Togi, "to learn and travel and see the land."

"Then we will have time to talk," said Sennos, "for I also travel with the King this summer." He put the body of the cockerel back in the basket and covered it, then picked up the empty jug. "Let us go up now," he said. "There will be food in the hall soon, and I am sure that at your age you are hungry."

"I am," said Togi grinning, and followed the King's Druid up the rock-cut stairs.

At the top, Sennos went off to put away his jug and basket and to wash the cockerel's blood from his hands, leaving Togi to find his own way back to the hall. When he came into it, although not much time had passed, it seemed a different place. The door-curtain had been pulled aside to let in the morning light, and the fires built up. Some of the young men who had slept there were still rolling up their straw pallets to put them away under the benches, but most had finished and gone elsewhere—probably to visit the latrines. Cingetos, however, was still there, sitting on a bench and combing his fingers through his rumpled hair. "I do not suppose," he said when he saw Togi, "that I need to ask where you were. Did you find Sennos?"

"He found me," said Togi. "This is a most wonderful place, master. What shall we do today?"

Cingetos laughed. "You," he said, "can spend the morning grooming our ponies and taking them down to the paddock near the foot of the hill. We will be here for some days, and there is no point in leaving them in the stables, where they will have to be fed. When you get back, I will find the time to examine you on your bardic knowledge. You are not with me merely to look at the world."

"That will be good," said Togi. The serving-men were coming in to set up the tables, and he hastened to put away his bedding. Breakfast would be very welcome, and he thought that he could smell fresh wheaten bread.

So began the pattern of Togi's days at Dinas Brân. Each morning he was waiting for Sennos above the altar ledge before dawn, to exchange a word of greeting, and help by carrying the basket down the steps. One day it was raining too hard to light a fire; instead, Sennos scattered a bread-offering to the winds, and Togi poured the ale upon the bare stone. Another morning there was fog, and they both groped their way cautiously toward the cliff-edge, wrapped in a chill gray blanket which muffled sound. Those days were not uncommon, but the fine days were best.

Sennos asked the boy no more questions, but answered readily when Togi asked about some details of ritual which differed from those that he knew. "The rites are not fixed entirely in form," the old Druid said. "In outline, yes, and in many set phrases; in the Gods to be praised, and their attributes. But there is room for variation, and new things, such as the praise-song I heard you offer. Knowledge and wisdom; inspiration and memory; foresight and understanding: these are the qualities of the Three Orders, but any one man may share in the gifts of all. Name the Three for me."

"Druids, Bards, and Seers," said Togi readily. "But the greatest of these are the Druids."

"In many ways," Sennos agreed. "Yet I think sometimes it is the Bards who will last the longest of us three: for without our Sanctuaries, how shall we Druids properly teach those who come after us; how shall we replenish the numbers of our kind?"

"There are Sanctuaries still in Ériu's Land," said Togi hesitantly. "Or so I have been told."

"There are," said Sennos a little sadly. "Once men traveled from that island to Môn, to learn the final mysteries. Now I think it is the time of the return flow, the ebb tide. And if, even there, our line should finally fail, we may truly be forgotten."

"Until the world is reborn," said Togi.

"Yes," agreed Sennos, "until our world is reborn."

Most afternoons Togi spent with Cingetos, learning and reviewing the basics of song-craft. Cunomoros, said the Bard, had given Togi a good grounding; but as the old man was not a Bard himself, there was a limit to what he could teach his son. Therefore he, Cingetos, would take up the work; and he did so with a will. Togi's memory was already well trained; learning by heart was easy for him, and he eagerly drank in the Bard's lessons, and began, in his free moments, to put them to his own use.

All too soon these patterns were broken, for Regenos was ready to set out on his summer circuit. They would go first, said Cingetos, to his northern territory, following the Afon Conwy to the sea, with side-trips, of course, here and there to visit his subordinate chieftains. After that they would make their way west along the shore, if the Red Crests did not interfere.

Unstated but implicit in this plan, said Cingetos, was the King's intention to gather support against the Red Crests, in hopes of diminishing their tax levies. The Bard was not confident that he would succeed.

"The Red Crests have the whip hand over us still," he said to Togi as they sat in the sunshine on a quiet bench outside the hall. "The tribes have not forgotten the losses that we suffered three years ago. There are still too many young men missing from our ranks, too many who went to feed the ravens. A glorious death is good, but its memory does not strengthen the shield-wall, though I say it who sang their praises. In five years, perhaps, we might fight them again and win—but I doubt our people will wait that long. The thought of more hungry winters will goad them to action—and they need little goading… Well, we shall see. Perhaps the threat of revolt will do more for us than the action itself. Now, let me hear that last song again, and this time, with the correct ending."

The morning when they rode out from Dinas Brân was bright and warm and sunny, a beautiful summer day halfway between Beltane and Midsummer. They did not leave very early, for there was much to be done in the selection and packing of gear; the collecting and loading of ponies; the final decisions, even, of who in the King's household was to go and who to stay. It was well toward midday before they were all gathered, and the company began to make its way down the hill. First came half a score of young men of the *teulu* with their captain before them, all of them mounted on fine horses with silver-studded bridles, brightly-painted round leather shields on their shoulders, and long bronze-studded scabbards slapping their thighs as they rode. Their cloaks were thick-woven wool of the true warrior scarlet, clasped on the right shoulder with red-enameled brooches of bronze. Next came Regenos himself on a tall red stallion, his cloak many-colored above his checkered woolen tunic, and his gleaming jewel-set sword-hilt of purest gold. With him rode his shield-bearer and his Bard and his Druid, all of them richly dressed and well-mounted, though none so much so as to outshine the King. After these came a gaggle of serving-men leading pack-ponies, Togi among them, and finally more of the *teulu* as a rear-guard. They left behind them, in a cloud of dust and a relative silence, the King's wives—he had at least two—and assorted children; the last dozen or so of the *teulu* who were to guard them in the King's absence; and a number of serving-folk who heaved a collective sigh of relief at seeing the rest of them gone. Soon enough they would all be back; but for now Dinas Brân could relax and be for a while at peace.

Togi was sorry not to be riding with the Bard, but his place in the pack train was also of interest. He had begun to have acquaintances among the packmen and other servants; for solitary though he was by nature in so many ways, he was also endlessly curious. One of the grooms, Castos by name, a dark curly-haired boy only three or four years Togi's senior, ranged up beside him now as the path widened. "A good day for travel," said Castos, "if it does not rain."

Togi gazed at the sky and sniffed the air as he had seen his father do. "Na," he said, "I think that it will not—not for a day or two, at least."

The other boy laughed. "Is it a weather prophet that you are, as well as the Bard's apprentice? Not that yours is a bad guess for this time of year. Well, I hope you are right—I hate riding in the rain!"

"Will we be seeing your home this summer?" asked Togi. He knew that Castos, like most of the boys and young men at Dinas Brân, had been fostered with the King for training, to earn, if they were good enough, their warrior's place in his retinue.

"We will," said Castos, smiling. "As I think I told you before, I come from Aber Ogwen, on the west coast. Have you seen the sea before?"

"I have not," said Togi, "and I want to. But is not the coast near Ynys Môn?"

Castos laughed. "Well, Môn is near the coast, but not near *all* of the coast—you will see. What have you heard of Môn?"

"I heard what the Red Crests did there," said Togi briefly. "How soon will we reach your village?"

"Oh, not for five or ten days," said Castos. "I will be glad to see them all again, my parents and brothers—it is a year now since I came to serve the King. I am hoping that he will take me into his *teulu* in a year or two, when I am older, but serving him like this is a good way to begin. Some of his young men let me join in their weapons practice already. Maybe I can help you to join us, when you are of warrior age."

"Mmm," said Togi thoughtfully. "That might be good. But I have a lot to learn first."

"I want to be a captain," said Castos, "and lead my men against the Red Crests in war. My father says we gave up too easily last time—I shall not make that mistake!" A shadow passed across his face for a moment; then he laughed. "Let me hear that song again you were making, about Orgetos—it was not bad."

"Na, in a while and a while," said Togi, and grinned. "It is not finished yet. Tell me instead where we will be staying tonight."

"At the head of this valley, at Pennant, just below the watershed," said Castos. "They are generous with their feasting there; you will like it."

"I am sure that I will," said Togi. And they rode on in companionable silence in the summer sun.

The village of Pennant was set in a rich green valley with high peaks looming on every side, and the hospitality was all that Castos had promised. The next day saw them climbing a narrow trail up a steep slope to cross over into the drainage of the Conwy. Togi was glad that Cingetos' ponies were mountain-bred and sure-footed; for himself, he would rather have walked that trail on his own two feet, but was ashamed to show it. Instead he watched the people in his party, and the eagles and red kites soaring above him, and silently recited his morning prayers. Just over the watershed they came to the next village, a stone-built huddle of bothies thatched with bracken and heather which made him think of the manhood hut in his own valley. The people here were more shepherds than cowmen, and the feast that night was of sheep-meat, and little flat griddle-baked oat-cakes tasting of leeks and wild honey.

Slowly they worked their way down the Nant-y-Gwryd valley, staying each night at a new village. The weather was fine for the most part; the King slept in the chieftains' huts, the *teulu* in the feast-halls, and Togi and the other serving-men under whatever shelter they could find, or sometimes none at all. Togi cared for the Bard's ponies and gear; Cingetos sang to entertain their hosts; and Regenos talked a great deal with the local chieftains, although to what effect it was not always clear. Sennos talked with no one, so far as Togi could see; but each morning the Druid made the dawn offering, asking the favor of the Gods on them and their undertaking, and each morning Togi joined him. Sometimes one or more of the village people came as well, bringing their own small offerings to be blessed; sometimes afterwards they asked Sennos for a charm, or a curse, or a healing spell, and generally he gave it to them. Now and then he talked for a while with some old man or woman who was the Priest or Priestess of that valley or village. "They have no training as we do," he said once to Togi afterwards. "They only do as their fore-fathers or fore-mothers did before them. And yet they also honor the Gods—the little local Gods of their kindred—as truly as we ever did, when we gave offerings to the Shining Ones in our great festivals. Remember, boy, the importance of the hearth-Gods, and the spirits of the land. They are the very root of our religion, and powerful in their own spheres. Never neglect them."

"How do I find their names," asked Togi, "when I come to a strange place, if there is no one there to ask?"

"By making offerings," said Sennos, "and listening. When they speak, you will hear."

"I will remember," said Togi thoughtfully, looking at the land around him, just touched with early sunlight.

"Yes," said Sennos, "you will."

That night Togi dreamed, as he had not for a long time, of ghosts: hungry ghosts with high thin voices, riding the winter winds. When he awoke, the summer stars were paling above him, although it was yet a long time until sunrise. He had slept that night alone, wrapped in his cloak, in the dry grass beside the horse pasture, preferring the pure air and the silence to the smoky, crowded hall. Now he lay and listened to the quiet ripping sounds of the grazing ponies tearing up their mouthfuls of sweet green grass, and the distant songs of the early-rising birds. There had been something else in his dream, he thought, something beside the ghosts: something familiar. Turning onto his side to sleep again, his hand brushed the leather thong around his neck, and he felt inside his tunic the hard shape of the silver ring his mother had given him. Since leaving home he had showed it to no one, and seldom thought of it. Now he pulled it out and looked at it closely in the pale light, seeing the small figure of the God with his many-spoked wheel. It was a ring, his mother had said, made for a Druid—for a Druid Priest. He was a long way as yet from that goal, but one day, if the Gods were willing, he would reach it, perhaps in the Sanctuaries of Ériu's Land. Thinking about that prospect, he smiled; and pushing the ring back into its hiding place, fell asleep again, still smiling.

He would always remember his first sight of the sea. For some days they had been following the broadening stream of the Conwy, and the night before had slept in a village at the top of its tidal range. Baked salmon had been a part of the meal, a delicacy Togi had never before encountered: so pink and rich and succulent it had been, and so different from the flesh of any land animal. He understood immediately why this creature was accounted one of the foods of the Gods. As to whether it was also the food of wisdom, as the legends had it, he was unsure; he did not feel any wiser after eating it, but only pleasantly full. Perhaps some salmon contained more wisdom than others, and the wisest ones were harder to catch; he would certainly have to sample any others which came his way, in order to make a fair judgment.

He was awakened before dawn the next morning by the crying of gulls. All that day he watched them circling overhead, their long white wings cutting slices out of the sky, and their raucous voices echoing above the big blue-green river. Castos told him that they lived mostly on fish, especially dead ones which they found along the tide line. Togi remembered Cunomoros' explanation of tides; it would be good to see them for himself.

Their path was climbing a hill now, away from the marshy banks of the Conwy. Suddenly, as they reached the top, he saw the river again on his right hand, wider even than before; and on his left, a great gray-green, silver-shining mass of water, larger than any lake he had ever seen or imagined. He caught his breath for a moment in astonishment at its size. As the path led downward again he lost sight of most of it, hidden by a last outlier of the mountains, but he knew it was still there. Its scent was strong on the freshening wind, a mixture of salt and fish and other things he could not yet name. A strong sense of anticipation rose up in him; he knew that this great restless being held a part of his destiny. As they splashed through a stream and wound their way across the rough grazing toward the village beyond, he thought that he could faintly hear that great beast's movements, beating eternally against the land.

When his chores were done, and the evening feast was over—more fish, but not salmon this time—he climbed some way up the hill behind the village to get a better view. Wide and wider the water stretched out as he went up, colored with a many-faceted reflection of the slow summer sunset. He sat for a long time on the shoulder of the ridge watching its movements. Soon he would see it closer at hand.

"Where shall we celebrate Midsummer?" he asked Sennos two mornings later, as they were preparing for the dawn sacrifice. Beltane had fallen late that year, and the moon which had been almost full when he came to Dinas Brân had passed her first quarter again.

"A good question," said Sennos thoughtfully as he arranged his wood on the turf-built altar they had just made. "Somewhere, I think, between here and the Red Crest's fort at Aber Seint—the place they call Segontium. Unless we were to cross to Môn—but I do not think Regenos would dare that."

"Why not?" asked Togi, scraping wood shavings from a stick with his knife, and piling them under the firewood.

"Because the Red Crests have forbidden it," said Sennos harshly. "They want no crossing back and forth between the holy island and the rest of Britain, for they know why some of us would wish to go there. They have beaten us into the earth, and mean to keep us there."

"Mmm," said Togi. "Could one or two men cross? How *do* you cross to Môn?"

"By boat," said Sennos, taking flint and steel in hand. "There are treacherous currents in the Aber Menai—the strait between the island and the land—and even if there were not, it would be a very long way to swim."

"Mmm," said Togi again. "I can swim a little, but—but perhaps not that far." He had learned the art in the valley stream at home, but doubted his proficiency against the ocean. "I would like to see Môn, at least a little of it."

"And I," said Sennos slowly, "would like to walk her fields once again, and feel her roots beneath me. Well, we shall have to see." He struck sparks to Togi's tinder, and blew them into a flame. "It is," he said, "in the hands of the Gods—as always."

"As always," agreed Togi. "May they be kind."

"Master," said Togi to Cingetos later that day, "a question."

"Only one?" laughed Cingetos. "When were you without them? Well, we have a little time before supper. Ask it."

It was late afternoon, and they had finished the day's travel; their gear was stowed away under cover, and the ponies released to their grazing. They were walking in a thin gray sea-mist among the few wind- and salt-stunted apple trees of the orchard, while Cingetos gave Togi an overdue lesson in song-craft. The Bard stopped now and turned to face his student. He realized with a shock that the boy had been growing again. The tunic which had fitted him at Beltane was now a finger's-breadth shorter in the sleeves, and the top of his dark head was even with Cingetos' eyes. Unaware of these thoughts, Togi smiled up at him. "Would it be allowed," he asked, "for me to leave you, just for a few days?"

"Why, what is this?" asked Cingetos, diverted. "What had you in mind?"

"Sennos says," said Togi carefully, "that we will be near Ynys Môn soon. He would like to visit it, and I would like to go with him." It was always better, he knew, to keep to the exact truth in such things; or so Cunomoros had taught him.

"Umm," said Cingetos. "I am not sure that would be wise. The Red Crests keep watch over Môn, because they know that it is important to—to those I will not name. It could be dangerous."

"I am not afraid," said Togi. "It would only be for a day or two: what harm could come to us?"

"More," said Cingetos grimly, "than you can imagine… Well, I will speak with Sennos. Now let me hear that last lesson again, with the correct rhymes."

The next day Togi began to get glimpses of Môn. At first it was only a low misty line on the far side of the wide green waters of the bay, but day by day as they rode westward along the coast it became clearer. Togi found himself disappointed: somehow he had expected something grander than this low range of green and brown hills. He told himself that when he came closer, when he actually walked upon that hallowed island, and saw its ancient stones and holy places, it would be different; but he was not entirely convinced. Neither Sennos nor Cingetos had spoken again about his desire to go there, but he did not think they had forgotten. He did his work for both of them, and tried to be patient.

"Tonight," said Castos one morning as they sat their ponies waiting for departure, "we will be in Aber Ogwen, my home. Wait until you see the richness of our pastures, and the size of our cattle! Yes, and taste the mead and ale my uncle brews—there is nothing like it!"

"Mmm," said Togi. "Are your people fishermen as well as farmers?"

"Of course!" said Castos scornfully. "All the coastal villages take harvests from Manannan's fields as well as from their own—we could not live so well without it. We fish the Aber Menai every day."

"Mmm," said Togi again. "You fish from boats, then, do you?" He had seen boats—another new thing to him—drawn up on the beach by all the coastal villages they had visited, but it was as well to make sure.

"Of course," said Castos. "How else? You would not catch much with a fish trap in the shallows, not the way the tides run through that strait."

"Well," said Togi, "do you ever cross the water—the Aber Menai—to Môn?"

"We used to," said Castos, "before the Red Crests came—or so my father told me once; I do not remember it myself. We still go there now and then, to take traders who want to cross, but not often. Why?"

"If someone wanted to go—or maybe two people—would one of your folk take them?" asked Togi.

"They might." Castos frowned a little. "It would depend. Who wants to go? You? And—who else?"

"Me, certainly. About the other, I am not yet sure," said Togi honestly.

"Well," said Castos, "I cannot promise, but I will ask my father. You and the Bard? Or you and the—the Priest?"

"I am not sure," said Togi. "I will tell you tonight."

That evening he went in search of Sennos as soon as he had dealt with Cingetos' gear and ponies. This he had never done before; it had seemed natural to join the old Druid only for the morning sacrifice, as had been their pattern since the beginning. Now he could not wait until morning; he must take this chance while it offered. Otherwise it might not come again.

He found Sennos walking along the shore, his hands clasped behind him and his gaze fixed, as it seemed, on the sand before his feet; but at the sound of Togi's footsteps, light though they were, he looked up. It was a long, considering look he gave the boy, a glance which weighed and measured him through and through. "Yes," he said then, before Togi could speak. "I have spoken with Cingetos, and he releases you to me for a few days. Will they take us over tonight?"

"I do not know," said Togi. "Maybe. Is that what you wish?"

"It would be better, if we mean to go at all," said Sennos. "The weather may change tomorrow."

Togi looked at the high, thin clouds gathering in the west, and nodded. "I will see what my friend has arranged."

"That will be good," said Sennos; then more softly, as if he spoke to himself alone: "I should like to walk Môn's fields once more, before I die."

Castos was not in the feast-hall; after some casting about, Togi found him at last in his family's hut. This was a good-sized round dwelling on the seaward edge of the village, stone-built and sod-thatched, its roof held down against the winter gales by ropes of twisted heather. He found the family at their meal, a more elaborate one than usual in celebration of their younger son's visit. They greeted him warmly when Castos told them who he was, and invited him to join them. "Na," said Togi, "I would do so gladly, but I must attend my master soon in the hall. I came only to find out if Castos has spoken to you yet about my question." All eyes turned to Castos at this, which was, Togi thought, answer enough.

"What question is that, my son?" said Castos' father.

"He was asking," said Castos, "about a passage to Môn, for one man, or possibly two. Is it two, Togi?"

"Yes," said Togi. "Tonight, if it may be."

"Tonight!" cried Castos, but his father only nodded.

"Better before the storm," he said. "How soon?"

"After the feast, I think," said Togi.

"That will be good enough," said the man. "The light lasts long on the water. Meet me at the shore when you are both ready."

So it came about that later that evening, in the slow summer twilight which painted the glowing clouds with red and gold, Togi found himself cautiously boarding a low, narrow wooden-framed leather boat. Neither he nor Sennos owned much in the way of baggage, and Togi had left most of the little he did have behind with the Bard. His good hooded cloak, however, came with him, and his horn-handled knife. What Sennos had, or had left behind, he did not know. As they pushed out from shore he felt himself launched into adventure, into another chapter of his life. At last he would walk upon the holy land of which he had heard so much.

There was not much wind, and at first the water was almost calm. The fisherman rowed easily but steadily, and steadily the gap between them and the shore behind them widened. No one spoke; it seemed as if to do so would break the spell by which they passed across this strange country. The tide was high, and they rode easily above the golden sands beneath them. Farther out, the surface was rippled by a current which set toward the south, but the fisherman seemed unperturbed, steering his craft easily toward the far shore. And at last, as the western clouds were cooling from red to gray, they grounded on the sand of the holy island—the sand of Môn.

Thanking the boatman, who nodded curtly and pushed his craft out to return, the two waded up the beach through the last dying waves. "Where are we?" asked Togi, looking around wide-eyed. "Are we near the Black Grove?"

Wringing seawater out of the skirts of his long dark robe, Sennos chuckled. "Not very," he said. "That is some way south of us along the shore. We will walk that way, and look for a place to spend the night. I doubt that all the people who lived here once are gone. Come along, then, and do not talk: I want to listen to the land."

They walked slowly southward through what seemed a deserted country. At first they followed the coast, but presently they came to an overgrown track leading westward, and Sennos turned into it. It brought them to the top of a low ridge with a wide view to the west and south. Empty fields stretched out before them, once cultivated but now thick with weeds, their dry-stone walls crumbling from neglect; but they saw no hearth-smoke, no buildings, no herded sheep or cattle. In the distance a raven called, and another answered it. Other than that, there was only the sound of the wind in the grass.

"Fourteen years," said Sennos bitterly. "Fourteen years, and still a desert. This was a rich land once, and well farmed. Now there is nothing." He began to walk again, following the ridge crest southward. Togi followed him silently; there was nothing to say. He hoped that it would not rain, as the clouds in the west were growing thicker, and it seemed likely that they would have to spend the night in the open. In the pale summer twilight they trudged slowly on.

Abruptly the ridge came to an end, where a steep-sided valley cut its way inland. Patches of small, scrubby trees grew along its bottom, with here or there a gap where the twisted remains of a larger oak showed through the young growth. Turning inland, Sennos began to descend the slope, wending his way through the knee-high bracken and thorny clumps of yellow-flowering gorse. He walked like a man who knows his way, and yet is unsure of what he will find at its end. Togi followed him wearily, beset with a growing sense of ill-omen. This was not how he had imagined his visit to Môn.

In the valley's bottom they came at last upon a well-worn path, which even in the fading light showed the tracks of many ponies. Now at last Sennos paused, looking up and down the valley. "Listen!" said Togi suddenly. His younger ears had caught the sound of hoof-beats in the distance.

"Get down!" hissed Sennos, waving him back into the brush. No sooner had they taken shelter than there was a flicker of movement higher up the valley, which resolved itself after a moment into a body of horsemen, coming quickly closer. "Down!" whispered Sennos again, enforcing his command with a hand on Togi's shoulder as he joined the boy on the ground, face-down in the tall bracken.

The horsemen passed by in a jingling of bridle fittings and a rhythmic smother of unshod hooves. After they had passed, Togi raised his head slowly to look after them. Even in the faint gray light from the rapidly clouding sky, he could make out the glint of metal on heads and shoulders, and the shape of the tall spears they carried. It did not need Sennos' hoarse whisper beside his ear to tell him that this was a patrol of the hated Red Crests, and that the down-valley path which led back to the sea was closed to them. They would have to take their chances in the low rolling hills of Môn.

Togi squatted in the doorway and watched the rain pour down. He was cold, wet, and hungry, but none of these were new things to him. He was also worried. After avoiding the Red Crests they had walked on for some time, until around midnight they had stumbled on a ruined homestead, and taken shelter in the one building which still had some part of its roof. Curling up in the driest corner, they had slept on and off during the rest of the short night, until their empty bellies had wakened them. Now they waited for dawn. If there had been anything here to burn, Togi thought, he would have dared the chance of the Red Crests seeing them, and built a fire for warmth; but he could see very little: only a few piles of dead leaves in the far corner where they had slept. The blackened stone walls and the charred thatch of the roof testified to the long-ago fire which had destroyed this place. How long ago? Fourteen years, thought Togi, looking at the ash saplings which had taken root amidst the fallen stones, would be about right.

Sennos sat hunched in a corner, drawn in upon himself. He had spoken very little since they saw the patrol; nothing at all since they took shelter here. Looking at him in the gray light of approaching dawn, Togi thought that the old man had aged ten years overnight. Well, they could not stay here; once the rain let up, they would have to move, Red Crests or no Red Crests. Castos had said that his folk ferried traders across, so somewhere on Môn there must be other people. The problem would be finding them without being found themselves.

"Sennos," he said impulsively, "where is the Black Grove? The place where the manhood rites used to be held?" Sennos raised his head slowly and blinked.

"South and east of here, I think," he said. "Why do you ask?"

"I want to go there," said Togi. Sennos looked at him for a moment, then shrugged.

"Why not?" he said listlessly. "It is as good a place as any. We will go as soon as the rain lets up." And half to himself, "Maybe there I will find what I seek."

On such a morning it was hard to judge the moment of sunrise, but suddenly Togi felt that it was near. Time to make the offering... "Sennos," he said, rising from his haunches, "let me have your flint and steel."

The old man blinked again, then wordlessly extracted them from his belt pouch and held them out. Togi took them; then, rummaging in the far corner, found a handful of dry twigs and leaves. On the driest spot he could find near the doorway he laid them all down, then went back for more. Fragments of rotten wood, dead weed-stalks, and a few seed pods from last year's willow-herb joined the pile. Kneeling beside them, he struck sparks onto the driest tinder again and again, until at last one caught. Carefully he blew it into flame and fed it with his unlikely fuel. It would not last long, but perhaps long enough... With his knife he hacked off a little of his dark hair; then jabbed the knife point into the ball of his left thumb. A bead of blood sprang out, and he mixed it quickly into the hair, then dropped blood and hair together into his tiny fire, speaking the dawn prayers as he did so. "O Shining Ones, brighten my path; give me your strength and protection..."

A sinewy hand reached over his shoulder and dropped something else into the flame, and Sennos' voice joined his in the chant. And from the east, as the early sun rose, a single ray of daylight pierced the clouds to shine upon their crude altar. It lasted only for a moment, but that was long enough: Togi knew that their Gods were with them after all. As the fire flickered out, he stood up. "Let us go," he said. "It is time."

"It is indeed," said Sennos. And rising, they went out into the wet gray morning, heading south.

Duck's eggs from a late clutch which Togi found by the edge of a pond made their breakfast, that and a few handfuls of green-stuff. Out of long practice he foraged as they walked. The rain diminished to a drizzle, and then to a pearly mist through which the strengthening sunlight broke in golden beams. The mist sometimes obscured the low hills through which they passed, but also it helped to hide them from any watching Red Crests. Sennos seemed now to know where he was going, and Togi was content to follow, listening to the distant bird-calls and enjoying the freshness and growing warmth of the morning. Twice more they passed ruined homesteads, and once the charred remains of an oak grove, half-hidden under tangles of white bindweed and rosebay willow-herb, where great trees had been hacked down and burned. Toward midday they crossed a low saddle between two ridges, and Sennos stopped and pointed. "There it is," he said. "The Hill in the Black Grove—or what is left of it."

Amidst a scattering of burnt and fallen trees, Togi saw a low, round, grass-grown mound. It reminded him of the cairn on Penwyn at home, but it was bigger—wider than the King's great hall on Dinas Brân was long, and easily twice as high. Despite the bright summer sunshine and the destruction of its surrounding oak grove, the place felt cold to him and dark—winter-dark. "Let us go closer," he said abruptly. "I want to see—what is there."

"As you wish," said Sennos dully. Slowly they went down the slope, passing a single tall gray standing stone. Circling sunwise around the mound, they came to the entrance, which stood open behind its cloaking weeds, a gaping black mouth into the earth. "The rising sun shines into it at Midsummer," said Sennos. "It would have done so this morning, for we are almost at that day."

Togi walked slowly toward the opening. No one, he thought, had gone in there this summer; perhaps not for several seasons, for the old stalks of the willow-herb, the white remnants of last year's seeds still clinging to them, stood undisturbed amidst the new growth. He could feel the darkness inside the mound, and the sense of something waiting. It was more than an entrance, it was a Gate—a Gate between the worlds. If he could pass through it, he might find himself in another world—in the Otherworld—in the feast-hall, perhaps, of the Shining Gods themselves…

"Do not go in," said Sennos' voice behind him, and at the same moment Togi stopped, as if he had struck a wall. It *was* a wall—a rampart—a barrier; it was a door which he had no way to open. His eyes saw nothing but blossoming plants, and sunlight, and a gap into a green hill, but his mind felt a barrier as cold and solid as stone. He touched it, worried at it, feeling for an entrance…

"No," said Sennos again, and the old Druid put a restraining hand on Togi's shoulder. "It is forbidden. You have not been prepared. Come away."

"But what is it?" asked Togi, taking a few reluctant steps back. "What do I feel?"

"Come away for now," said Sennos. "I will tell you later. This is not a safe place to be just now."

Togi stopped. Looking around him at the green mound, and the black fallen trees, and the pale sky overhead, he took a deep breath, then another. "Yes," he said after a moment, as much to the spirit of the place as to Sennos. "I will go now, for I am not ready. But I will come back." And turning, he walked away to the south without a backward glance, and Sennos followed him.

As the day cleared, the mountains of Eryri took shape out of the haze to the east. "We need to turn more toward them," said Sennos, looking at the distant peaks. "The farther south we go, the closer we come to the Red Crest fort at Aber Seint, and the harder it will be to find someone to take us across. There are marshes and quicksands on the south coast of Môn as well. In the west of the island I think we would find more people, but that is a long walk, and the King is expecting me to meet him again before he faces the Red Crests."

"Is there anyone left in this part of Môn, other than the Red Crests?" asked Togi. "We have seen no signs."

"We had better hope there is," said Sennos.

"Why," asked Togi as they walked, "could I not go into the mound? I know I have not had the training my father told me of, but it was more than that. It was like a wall, a—a barrier I could feel but not see. I have felt nothing like it before."

"How many holy places have you visited?" replied Sennos. "But no, I know what you mean. Many would not feel it, and they might go in. But they would see little besides a dark passage, and other things of this world. When the time is right—when you have had the right training—you will know how to pass that barrier, and you will see things that those who enter easily would never see. You have a long road ahead of you—do not be impatient."

"But where can I get that training?" asked Togi. He was not feeling particularly patient. "Who will teach me, now that the Sanctuaries are gone?"

"I do not know the answer," said Sennos sadly. "I will teach you what little I may. But I think in time you will find the rest for yourself."

The sun was low in the west, and they had been following the coast for some time, when at last they saw ahead of them a welcome thread of wood-smoke which marked a fishing village. "Now," said Sennos, "we will see." They approached cautiously, but the people, although astonished to see strangers, were friendly. They were welcomed into the headman's house, and given seats by the fire, and wooden bowls full of savory fish stew. Hungry though he was, Togi was almost too tired to eat. Once he lay down, he did not stir until someone shook him awake in the pale dawn, to eat again and then go down to the beach where one of the fishermen waited to take them across to the mainland. All the way across Togi gazed back at the island. Nothing much had happened to him there, but he knew that he would be back. He would not soon forget the fallen trees and burned-out homesteads, or the emptiness of what had once been a fertile land.

They found the King encamped at Aber Seint, not far from the Red Crests' fort. Regenos was in a foul mood, said Cingetos, for few of his promised levies had come to join him, and the Red Crest commander was unimpressed by his pleas for remission of the tribute. "He knows as well as we do that we cannot afford to fight him yet. We are still too weak. In two or three years, it may be a different story; or we might make common cause with the Silures or the Deceangli. But for now, we waste our time here… What did you think of Môn?"

"Mmm," said Togi. "I did not see much of it. There are not many people there. Did the Red Crests kill them all?" For some reason he had not wanted to ask Sennos.

"Many of them, I think," said Cingetos. "Mind you, I was only a boy when it happened, younger than you are now, so I only know what I have been told. It was always said to be a rich land."

"It is not rich now," said Togi thoughtfully, "but I think it might be again."

"Only," said Cingetos wryly, "if we could get rid of the Red Crests."

"Yes," said Togi. "That would have to come first."

Cingetos laughed. "And you know how to do it?"

"Not yet," said Togi seriously.

"Be sure," said Cingetos, still laughing, "to tell me, when you find out. Now, in the meantime, let me hear that song you were making, if you have finished it. I think that is more in your scope just now."

They left Aber Seint the next day, heading back into the mountains, and there they celebrated Midsummer with feasting and fires. Togi fell back into his old routine with Sennos, and they did not speak again of Môn. Only sometimes Togi caught the old Druid watching him with a puzzled frown. For himself, he continued to enjoy his summer's travels, and was sorry to see Lughnasa approaching. Still, it would be good to be home again. He had much to tell Cunomoros, and much to ask.

Sennos Again

Harvest came, and the Red Crests followed; winter came, and brought the King. Cingetos came with him, but without Sennos. "Na," said the Bard, in answer to Togi's question, "he does not travel in winter. Too old, he says, to leave his fireside at this time of year."

"Ah," said Cunomoros, draining his last cup of ale, "I would say the same. Old bones do not take kindly to winter journeys."

They were seated by the fire in his hut after the evening's feast, sharing a little quiet conversation before bed. Togi had mentioned Sennos to his foster-father after his return, but he thought now of a question he had not asked at the time. "Father," he said to Cunomoros, "you told me once that you know Sennos. Was he on Môn with you when the Red Crests came?"

"He was," said Cunomoros. "He fought in the defense, and likely has the scars to prove it. But we went different ways afterwards. How he came to be with Regenos I do not know."

"Nor I," said Cingetos. "He was already at Dinas Brân when I came there, five years ago. But that brings me to another question, Togi. Would you like to travel again with me next summer?"

"Mmm," said Togi, frowning a little. "Yes, I would, but...it will be my manhood year—my training year, I mean. I think I should stay here and study. I have a lot yet to learn."

"Ha!" said Cingetos and laughed. "You have a lot of bard-craft still to learn, too, lad. Is that less important?"

"I—think it may be," said Togi, flushing. "I am sorry."

"I believe I am insulted," said Cingetos, but he was grinning. "Na, never worry, lad. But do practice what—little!—I have taught you. Maybe we will travel together again, some summer when you have more time."

"Mmm," said Togi again. "Maybe we will." But he did not sound convinced, and Cingetos forbore to press him further. What Cunomoros thought of this he did not say.

"I wonder," said Togi the next morning as he and Cunomoros were walking down the hill after making the dawn offering, "if I did right in my answer to Cingetos last night. It seemed at the time the right choice, and yet…"

"Why did it seem so?" asked Cunomoros.

"Na, I do not know," said Togi. "A—a darkness over that journey, it may be. Something I did not want to face…"

"Mmm," said Cunomoros. "And yet there are good reasons for you to go. You may not have another chance to study with the Bard, and he can teach you things that I cannot."

"I know," said Togi. They walked on for a while in silence.

"Is it a danger to yourself that you see," asked Cunomoros quietly, "or to others?"

"I—both, I think," said Togi.

"To us here?" asked Cunomoros.

"No," said Togi, frowning. "To—those I will travel with, and—and others. But…"

"Will your going cause the danger?"

"No," said Togi again. "But—but it will make me part of it…"

"Will you learn things of value on this journey?" asked Cunomoros.

"Yes," said Togi, and after a moment, "I am answered."

"I think so," said Cunomoros. "Not all learning is pleasant, but sometimes you must pay the price." Togi sighed.

"I will speak to the Bard again before he leaves," he said. "Maybe he will still take me."

"I think he will," said Cunomoros with a smile. And they walked on down the hill.

Winter was long and hard; spring came late and welcome, and with it Cingetos came again. He came on a sunny afternoon two days before Beltane Eve, bringing with him the gray pony which Togi had ridden the year before, and he came in some haste. "Can you be ready tomorrow?" he asked Togi as he slid down from his bay horse beside the boy. "Regenos is starting his circuit early this year, and he wants me back as soon as may be."

"I can," said Togi, stroking the bay horse's nose. "But why the haste?"

"There is talk of rebellion against the Red Crests," said Cingetos as Cunomoros joined them. "Are you content, Cunomoros, for me to take your son on such a journey? For I tell you truly, we may see bloodshed before summer's end."

"If he is willing," said Cunomoros slowly, "then he may go. Togi? You are thirteen now, almost a man; it is for you to choose."

"I will go, Father," said Togi. "You were right." Cunomoros smiled.

"Then take the horses to the paddock, and make your gear ready," he said. "Cingetos, come with me to the hall for the guest cup. We will need to talk for a while, and I must start the Manhood Ritual soon."

"I am sorry to come upon you so suddenly," said the Bard a little later, as they sat in the sunlight on the bench outside the feast-hall. "But Regenos has had news which disquiets him. The harvests were bad in the north last year; a Red Crest patrol was ambushed by some of the young hotheads among the Brigantes, and a village burned in retaliation. If we have a good corn crop this year, all may yet be well, but…"

"But the spring snows delayed the planting," said Cunomoros wryly, "and the outlook is not good."

"As you say." The Bard grimaced. "Pray to the Gods, Priest, for a warm summer and a good harvest. There are two more years of the tribute renders to run; and after that, who knows?"

"Who indeed?" said Cunomoros sighing. "I will make offerings."

"So, I think, will we all," said Cingetos, and tilted his cup to pour the last drops of his ale onto the ground. "So will we all."

Togi had begun to notice girls. It had come upon him gradually during the last winter. They had always been there, of course, but aside from his mother and his small sister, he had had little to do with them, so much had his mind been concentrated on things of the spirit. Now his body was reminding him, often at the least convenient times, that it also had a word to say in their partnership. It was a new dimension of his world, and he looked forward to exploring it. But he wished that it was a little more under the control of his mind.

Not that he had done much other than think about the subject so far. True, there was one little dark-haired girl of about his own age—Huctia was her name—who had caught his eye lately. They had exchanged a few words now and then in the feast-hall, and she had seemed friendly. He had thought of approaching her on Beltane Eve after his duties were over, and trying for a kiss, at least—providing she had not already gone off with someone else. No chance of that now... Well, maybe in the autumn. In the meantime, the world was wide, and half of it women. Perhaps on his travels he would have more luck.

So he was thinking as they rode up the winding trail to Dinas Brân. Unlike the previous year, they had made the trip in one long day. The sun was already low, and the blue shadow of Yr Wyddfa was stretching out to cloak the fortress hill when they reached it, but the mountaintops to the east were still basking in spring sunshine. In the courtyard Cingetos slid down from his mount with a sigh. "Take the ponies to the stable for now, and put our gear in the usual place," he said to Togi. "I will go and look for Orgetos, to see when the King intends to ride. When I left he was planning to celebrate Beltane here first, but one never knows with kings." And he set off across the compound, greeting friends on his way. Togi unloaded their gear, and led the ponies toward the stable, noticing familiar faces as he went, and the small changes any place undergoes in a year. Already he felt at home in this high aerie, and was sorry they would not be staying long.

He was rounding a corner on his way back from the stable when he almost collided with Sennos. Both of them took a step backwards in surprise. Togi thought that the old man had aged visibly over the winter: the frown lines in his thin face were deeper graven, and his hair and beard were whiter; he seemed shorter also, but that might have been because Togi himself had grown. "A good day to you, Honored One," he said respectfully. "Have you been well?"

Sennos stood frowning at him in silence for a while, as if trying to remember who he was. "The Gods' blessing on you," he said at last. "Do you travel with the Bard again this summer?"

"I do," said Togi. "Do you come with us?"

"I do," said Sennos briefly, and made as if to go.

"And may I join you for the dawn offerings as before?" asked Togi. It seemed somehow necessary to ask. Sennos hesitated.

"You may," he said at last. And half to himself, "But I wish I knew..." He shook his head, and abruptly walked away in the direction of his quarters. Togi went on to the hall, turning over the old Druid's last words in his mind, but he came to no conclusions. Time, he thought, and the Gods, would reveal all. For now, he was more interested in his dinner, and in what Cingetos would sing that night.

He was up before dawn the next morning, waiting for Sennos at the cliff edge. As he watched the stars slowly dim and wink out against the growing light, he was struck again by the majesty of the mountains around him. Surely the Gods were walking on those summits, in the high places beyond the reach of men. Down here in the courtyard and on the hill below, they would be lighting the Beltane fires tonight, but the great peaks above would be dark. It should not be so, he thought; the very mountains should reflect the strength of the Sun God... As he thought it, the first sunlight touched the tip of Yr Wyddfa, and for a moment the last of the winter's lingering snow seemed to burst into flame, red-gold against the mountain's gray head. It came like a gift and an answer; he felt the strength of the God fill him; and as he had done a year before, he lifted up his hands and his voice in a song of praise.

"That was well sung," said Sennos' harsh voice when he had finished, and as before the old Druid was there with his basket and jug. "Now come below with me to make the offering."

"Thank you, Honored One," said Togi, turning to face him. "May I carry your burdens?"

"As you wish." Sennos handed them over, and silently they descended the rock-cut stairs. Only when the offerings had been made and the fire extinguished did he speak to Togi again. "You may help me tonight, if the Bard can spare you."

"Thank you, Honored One," said Togi again. "I think that he will. Is there anything else that I can do to help you?"

"Not before tonight," said Sennos. "I will see you then."

Togi spent part of that afternoon with Cingetos, being tested on his memory of what the Bard had taught him the summer before. "Not bad," said Cingetos briefly at the end. "We ride in two days—even the King will not interrupt the festival with travel. Have a new song ready for me to hear as we ride, on some topic related to the feast."

"I will," said Togi, grinning. "May I have time tonight to help Sennos?"

"You may," said Cingetos, grinning back. "I may have a little business of my own to tend to tonight as well. But mind," he added, "how you go with that old man. Do not tell him more than you need—about anything."

"I will not," said Togi more seriously. "He is—changed—from a year ago. I do not entirely trust him, but I can still learn from him."

"That is wise," said Cingetos, and grinned again.

They stood upon the threshold of Beltane, for all days begin in darkness. Although the sky above them was still bright, they were already in the shadow of Yr Wyddfa. Now they waited as evening climbed up from the valleys to engulf the peaks to the east. Slowly the light withdrew as the tide of darkness drowned it, and the half-moon which starts all months brightened above them. At last day was gone, and under the first pale stars Sennos knelt and struck the sparks to kindle the new flame from which all the fires in Dinas Brân and on the hill below would be relit. Togi stood beside him with a resin-soaked torch, ready to catch that flame and carry it to the dark pile of wood waiting on the highest point of the fortress hill. Carefully the old man blew on his tinder, and suddenly a little bud of fire blossomed. He fed it with straws and dry twigs until it grew and strengthened, then, "Now!" he rasped, and Togi held down his torch.

The fire caught at it eagerly and blazed up, and Togi carried it quickly to the bonfire; then, when that was ablaze, he ran on, through the upper gateway and down the hill, the torch he carried streaming ragged flame behind him. Men waiting by the path yelled and clashed their spears against their shields, women shouted greetings, children shrieked with laughter and followed him as he ran. He reached the bottom out of breath but exhilarated, and threw the torch which was scorching his fingers into the waiting pile of wood and tinder. As soon as it caught, he snatched a blazing branch to light the second fire. All around him people were laughing and yelling; there was a bawling of cattle and a bleating of sheep as the men prepared to drive their herds and flocks between the fires. Back on the hilltop Sennos would be making solemn offerings, but here there was a party atmosphere, and for once Togi was glad to be a part of it.

Someone shoved a wooden cup slopping with ale into his hand; someone began to pound out a rhythm on a skin drum. Togi drained his cup in one gulp and threw it away, then joined a group of young men and women beside one of the fires. He was tall for his age, and a stranger; they let him in gladly, knowing him only as the fire-bringer. Someone began a dance; soon they were all dancing and yelling. Later there was more ale, and a laughing dark-haired girl, her smiling face gilded with firelight, who grabbed his hand and drew him to run between the flames. In the sweet darkness of the summer night afterwards, Togi got more than one kiss. He did not go back to the fortress hill until almost dawn.

If Sennos noticed that he was out of breath when he arrived, just in time for the offering, the old Druid made no comment, but Cingetos in the feast-hall afterwards looked at his pupil and laughed. "I also," he said, yawning, "had a fine time last night. I think we will have no lessons this afternoon; it is a good day for sleep." Togi did not disagree.

Slowly the King's party moved from one village to the next through the greens and golds of early summer. Looking about him with a knowledgeable eye as he rode, Togi saw that the crops were not as advanced as they should be; the late spring snows and frosts had left their mark. The farmers knew it, of course; there was an unspoken tension in the people. They brought generous offerings to Sennos when he made prayers to their Gods for good weather and good harvests. Even a normal corn crop could mean hunger now, with the Red Crests taking their share; a poor one would be ruin and starvation. Togi saw it in the women's anxious eyes, and in the men's weather-beaten faces; only the children seemed innocent and at ease. For himself, it weighed on him sometimes, though he was only Sennos' assistant: to speak to the Gods for men was no light task. In good times the Priest maintained the balance, the right relationships between all parts of the world. In bad times the success of his offerings could mean life or death for the members of his tribe.

Bard-craft, he was learning, had also its own demands and rewards. It was not only the interplay of words, the elaborate songs or tales which entertained or taught. The Bard was the memory of the people, the keeper of knowledge and lore. He held up a mirror to the King, showing him for which qualities he was praised, and for which he would be remembered. He sang the feats of brave warriors, granting them the undying fame for which they bled and died. The laws were not his field, though he must know them: that was still the part of the Druids, such of them as were left; but like the Druids and the Seers, he was sustained by *awen*, the fire from heaven by which they were all inspired. Togi drew this new knowledge in, and made it a part of him. Cunomoros had been right, and he himself had been right to come: there was much that he could learn this summer.

There was also the possibility of war. The *teulu* was aware of it, as were the little war-bands of the local chieftains with which they mingled at night in the feast-halls. The rumor of what had happened in the lands of the Brigantes had passed among them, and grown in the telling. The young warriors were restless, eager to show their war-like skills to the King's men; there were spear-throwing competitions in the afternoons, wrestling and running, and boasting in the mead-halls at night. These things Togi avoided, so far as he might. His eye was as straight as that of any boy his age, and his arm as strong, but it was not for the warrior's arts that he had been born.

So the early summer passed, as they wended their way among the mountains and through the coastal villages. The King and his Judge spent afternoons hearing disputes, and the local elders testified before them as to the history and custom of the land. At Cingetos' direction, Togi listened to many of these discussions: dull though they were, they were grist to the Bard's mill, and the basis of the Druid's law. They were part of the King's work as well, for his wisdom was not only displayed in battle. That might come later, but for now his arts were those of peace.

As in the previous year, they celebrated Midsummer again not far from Caer Seint, but this time there was no mention between him and Sennos of another visit to Môn. All the better, thought Togi; and yet something in him longed to walk those fields again, and to dare the magic of the Dark Grove. Patience, patience, he said to himself: perhaps, once he was a man—perhaps even next summer… But always a cloud came between him and that goal. Then he would be restless, and his sleep troubled by dreams which he could not remember on waking, and the silver ring of his blood-father weighed heavy against his breast. Sennos spoke little to him on any subject that summer, and made no effort to teach him: the old man seemed to be withdrawing into some dream of his own. That it was not a good dream, Togi could see. He spoke of it once to Cingetos. "Yes," said the Bard, as their ponies ambled side by side in the afternoon sunshine, "I have seen it myself: he is changing, and not for the better."

"I think," said Togi slowly, "there is an anger in him. He has less care in the sacrifices these days: he only wants blood. There was one morning…" He shut his mouth firmly on the words. The death of animals was a daily thing to him, but it should be seemly. To do otherwise was a pollution, and an ill omen.

"Hmm," said Cingetos, frowning. "Well, there is nothing I can do. Better not to challenge him: it is he who is the Priest. Only…"

"Yes," said Togi, answering the thought rather than the words, "I will be careful."

It was not all ill: there were good times. Togi was growing more confident in himself, and he found that some of the young women in the villages responded to this. He remembered his experiences of Beltane Eve, and built on them, exchanging smiles and glances with pretty young maids. Midsummer's Eve was particularly sweet, and he got more than kisses, but he found the appetite grew as it was fed. Winter at home might be barren in contrast, but that dark season would bring new challenges of its own.

Lughnasa was near, and they were circling through the mountains, when the news came of the raid. The Deceangli to the east had broken the borders, and driven off the cattle from three villages on the Conwy's eastern bank. At once the warriors were excited, and young men came streaming in from the lands around to join the King's hosting. Overnight the whole complexion of his progress changed. He rallied his troops the next morning, and they set off eastward in haste.

"I should send you home," said Cingetos to Togi as they rode together in the baggage train. "You are too young for this hosting."

"Not much younger than many," said Togi. "Next spring I will be a man."

"Then is then, now is now," said Cingetos. "Would you go if I sent you?"

Togi sighed. "I—yes, I would," he said. "But is this not part of my education as well? A Bard must know war."

"That is true," said Cingetos grimly. "Very well, come along; but whatever happens, stay close to me. At least we do not ride against the Red Crests."

"Not this year," said Togi.

They caught the Deceangli halfway to their borders; the engagement was brief but bloody. Togi hung back with the baggage train, as he had promised, but he heard the weapon-clash, and the screams. Outnumbered and surprised, the raiders put up little resistance; before the afternoon was far advanced, they were streaming away, leaving their stolen cattle behind them along with some of their dead. Regenos and his men pursued them, but not far; long before sunset they came trickling back, to gather up their own dead and wounded and drive the regained cattle back to the pastures around the nearest village, where their owners could reclaim them.

"What did you think?" asked Cingetos of Togi that evening, as they stood outside the smoky hall to get a breath of fresh air before seeking their blankets. Overhead the summer-pale stars shone silently down, but the sounds of drunken boasting and singing were still loud behind them. Togi was silent too for a while, frowning. He had seen his friend of last summer, Castos, die of a spear through his guts, his great plans to be a battle-leader gone with the blood which poured out between his desperately gripping fingers. Young men and old, they died all alike, paying the price for their loyalty to their King. He had listened as Cingetos praised those fallen heroes in song, and knew that their names—for a while—would be remembered. It was a noble death, and fitting to a warrior. All these things he knew in theory, but to see them for the first time was hard. He sighed.

"Will it be like this," he asked, "when we fight the Red Crests?"

"No," said Cingetos. "That will be much worse. This was a merry afternoon's gentle play in comparison. When the Red Crests come in war, they will not come to steal our cattle, but to destroy us. Ask your father or Sennos what it was like on Môn."

"Maybe I will do that," said Togi softly. Cingetos gripped his shoulder.

"Come on, let us put our blankets in the stable tonight," he said roughly. "I am tired, if you are not, and it will be quieter there than in the hall."

"Sennos," said Togi two mornings later, "were you born on Môn?" They had just completed the dawn offering, and were starting back toward the hall. The old Druid stopped still and stared unblinkingly at Togi.

"No," he said after a moment. "I was born in Kernow, and went there as a man. Why do you ask?"

"Oh," said Togi, "I wondered how long you had lived there before the Red Crests came."

"How long?" said Sennos musingly. "Two and twenty years—almost half my life, and the better half at that."

"What was it like?" asked Togi.

"Before?" said Sennos. "It was good. A peaceful, settled land and a fruitful life. I studied in the Groves, and served the Gods. I was a law-speaker, and a teacher, and a diviner. I stood high in the Council. I should have been Archdruid myself before I died, not a powerless wanderer on the roads in the train of a petty king."

"What happened?" asked Togi.

"Happened? The Red Crests came, in their hundreds—in their thousands," said Sennos. "They crossed the Menai and landed, despite the tides and all our offerings and prayers. We fought them then, with spears and with swords, and whatever other weapons we could find, but they were too many. They cut us down like grain, as they cut down the oaks. You have seen…"

"Did you fight?" asked Togi softly. Sennos hardly seemed to see him now; he was looking into some unimaginable horror of his own; but he answered all the same.

"Yes, I fought—I, who had never carried a sword, or struck a blow in anger. I did all that I could, but they beat me down with their shields. I lay unconscious until nightfall amidst the piles of the slain. When I came to myself and saw…" He paused, his face working. "I walked all night. There was fog…and fire…and screams. The Red Crests killed everyone in the villages, everyone they could find. Sometimes I had to hide…" He drew a deep breath. "At last I found the survivors on the western isle, but by then it was too late. The Archdruid was dead, and they had set the Irish fox in his place."

"Who?" said Togi, startled. This part of the story he had not heard before. Sennos looked at him, and seemed to see him again.

"Lovernos," he said harshly. "They set him in the place which should have been mine—a young man, hardly more than

a student, but with a glib tongue. Well, he got no good by it."
He gave a bitter laugh. "His so-called friends did for him in the
end, and I, whom he had supplanted, have outlived him by
twice seven years. That is revenge of a sort..." He looked
harder at Togi's face, and his eyes widened. "So that is who you
are. I should have known, there was something about you...
But he never raised you or trained you; he is dead and in the
ground... Who was your teacher, Fox Cub? Who was it taught
you your craft?" He took a step forward, pale eyes blazing, and
grabbed the neck of Togi's tunic as if to choke the answer out
of him.

"Let go!" The boy threw up his hands to break Sennos'
grip, and felt the worn leather thong around his neck part. The
ring spun out, shining in the morning sunlight, and Togi caught
it neatly one-handed. Sennos stood staring again.

"Let me see it," he said hoarsely after a moment. Slowly
Togi opened his fingers, ready to close them again on his
treasure if Sennos tried to snatch it, but the old man did not
move. "So he did not keep it," he said musingly. "How did it
come to you?"

"From my mother," said Togi quietly. Sennos gave a
twisted smile.

"Did he leave it with her, after he planted his seed? I
would not have thought so."

"No," said Togi. "My foster-father brought it back to
her after he died."

"And who is your foster-father?" asked Sennos. He
seemed almost normal again, and Togi found himself answering
before he thought.

"Cunomoros," he said. Sennos gave a crack of laughter.
"Why do you laugh?"

"Ask your foster-father when you get home, Fox Cub,"
said Sennos. "And greet him for me. The Gods have a sense of
humor after all, it would seem... But for the rest of this trip, I
think I will make the dawn offerings alone." And he strode off
toward the hall, leaving Togi staring blankly after him.

He thought about it all that day while he rode and did
his customary tasks for the Bard. They were traveling
southward again, toward Dinas Brân, and it was almost time for

him to go home. It was not far now; if he borrowed the gray pony from Cingetos he could be there by tomorrow night, and that would be good. And yet, and yet... It felt like running away, and he had never run from anything in his short life—until now.

That evening while Cingetos was singing, he slipped out of the hall and made his way to the nearest clump of oak trees. Under their dark branches he made offering, pouring out his supper ale onto the twisted roots, and placing his bread and meat on a flat stone. Then he lifted up his hands and prayed: "Lugh of the Light, Many-skilled, Druid and Bard and Warrior, show me the right path, that I may gain honor and wisdom, and face down my fear." He stood for a long time listening to the silence of the forest and the beating of his own heart. At last there came into his mind the memory of the Beltane fire, blazing, warming like the sun... *Do what you were born for,* said the flames in his mind. *Make the offering. Serve your people by serving the Gods.* He felt again the rough wood of the torch in his hand as he ran, smelled the smoke and burning resin, saw the crowd of fire-lit faces cheering him on. Running—running *to* the place of sacrifice, not away. He smiled, and thanked the God silently; and the next morning he joined Sennos as usual for the dawn offering.

The old man was kneeling, arranging his sticks and tinder on the turf-cut altar he had just built, but when he saw Togi coming he got stiffly to his feet. "Why," he said without preamble, "are you here? I told you to keep away."

"I come to serve the Gods," said Togi, standing still. Sennos looked at him for a long time, his eyes traveling over the boy and coming to rest at last on his face. His own face gave nothing away.

"Very well," he said at last. "Light the fire." And his hand went to his belt, where he carried the sacrificer's knife. He unsheathed the blade, a shining foot-long piece of razor-sharp steel, and stood holding it lightly in his right hand. A little smile played about his mouth within the frame of his gray beard, but it did not reach his eyes, which were dark and cold.

Slowly Togi knelt beside the altar and picked up the flint and steel from where Sennos had dropped them. He struck his sparks carefully and bent to blow on them, all too aware of his vulnerable position. The short hairs on the back of his neck stood erect, and the skin between his shoulder blades prickled and felt cold. He could imagine all too clearly the blow, the pain, the blood, the falling into darkness, but he kept his eyes on his task. A little tongue of flame sprang up beneath his fingers, and caught the twigs which he offered it, and grew. He fed it carefully, then stood up and turned to face the old Druid. He was almost surprised to find himself still alive.

Sennos' eyes were wide and dark, and the knuckles of the hand which held the knife were white with tension, but he had not moved while Togi lit the fire. After a moment he sighed, and turned to take the offerings from his basket in the usual way. The red cockerel's blood hissed into the flames, and he lifted his voice with Togi's in the dawn chant. When the rites were over, he only said, "You may help me build the Lughnasa fire tomorrow, when we reach Dinas Brân." With that he turned and walked away as if nothing had happened. Maybe, thought Togi, nothing had. But he never spoke of Môn, or of Lovernos, to Sennos again.

The High Powers

He turned fourteen on a day of mixed rain and sunshine, with the bare black branches of the forest thrashing against a tattered gray sky in the gusts of a cold north wind. There were presents from his family—a thick hooded cloak of crotal-dyed wool from his mother, which had been on her loom all winter; a lathe-turned wooden cup of storm-felled oak, highly polished, from his brother Tritos, who was apprenticed now to the village wood-carver; even a pierced stone on a hand-braided cord from his little sister Vera; but Cunomoros had given him no present that morning. "That," the old man had said with a smile, "will come later. For now, son, welcome to your new estate." For of course, by the custom of the tribes, he was now a man—or would be, after the manhood ritual at Beltane.

It had been a hard winter, and a hungry one, between the late harvest and the Red Crests and the King, but his mother had saved enough barley-meal aside to make him his favorite bannocks, laced with wild honey and cooked on the flat bake-stone beside the fire. He protested that he could not eat them all, and shared them with his brother and sister, although his stomach was still grumbling emptily when they were gone. The stew which came later would deal with that, for he had been lucky at his hunting the day before, and had killed a fat badger, out for its early-morning stroll; the meat was already bubbling in the pot, and filling the hut with good odors. He and Cunomoros, of course, had been up before dawn as usual to make the morning offering, though it was Togi nowadays who carried the jug and basket, and fetched up the firewood beforehand to build the sacred fire. On some mornings it was all that Cunomoros could do to climb the hill, especially when the track was slick with rain or melting snow. The snow was gone now, or should be, until autumn. Maybe next winter he would make the offerings himself on such days, leaving his father to sit below by the fire. The old man had earned it.

On some mornings now they had company, for Cunomoros had taken a second student, a young man called Valos who had come to him after Samhain, asking to be taught the rudiments of the priestly craft. A year older than Togi, he was a sturdy brown lad who mostly worked with the shepherds, although he was not of their blood. His mother had been an incomer, one who had sought refuge in the mountains a few years back after escaping from the Red Crests; now she was dead, and Valos was left alone. A silent youth, a little lame in one leg from some childhood injury, he had a retentive memory, and seemed grateful for such time as Cunomoros could spend with him. Whether he would ever make a Priest, thought Togi, was another question; only time would tell that—time, and the Gods.

In the meantime, Togi's work must go on. For him this meant more hours of study and memorization, in addition to the time he spent hunting or at weapons practice. The latter was becoming more urgent for all the young men; Cingetos had told them at Midwinter, when he paid his customary visit with the King, that there were still rumors of war. "Empty bellies fill soon with grievances," the Bard had said wryly. "Like snow-laden branches, the people's patience eventually will break. Already we hear it creaking in the night." When he thought of the Red Crest solders taking his people's hard-won grain, Togi was as eager as any to fight; but he also remembered the death of his friend Castos the summer before. Castos would never now become the great war-leader he had had it in him to be, and that was a loss both to him and to his people. Togi had his own goals, and wanted to live long enough to reach them. They did not include an heroic death at the age of fourteen.

He had not told his family much about his previous summer's adventures, and nothing at all about Sennos' bitter words. He had wanted to ask Cunomoros about them, but the time never seemed right. He was not sure, anyway, what to say. *Why did Sennos laugh when I told him that you were my foster-father?* No, it made no sense...or perhaps too much sense, of a kind he did not want to think about. At last he set it aside, to concentrate on the things Cunomoros was teaching him. Because of who and what he was, his manhood ritual was to be different from that of the other young men of the tribe.

"I cannot make it the same as mine was in the Black Grove," Cunomoros had said. "This place is different, with different paths and energies, different spirits in the land. Moreover, some of what you will undergo must be the same as that of the others. But for you, there will be additional tests and dangers first, and for these I have prepared you, so far as it is in me to do—and so far as it is allowed. Some things you must learn for yourself."

"How will I know what those things are?" Togi had asked. They had been digging manure into the garden, ready to feed the beans which would be planted later that month, and Cunomoros had paused to catch his breath. The exercise had warmed them both, but the north wind was sharp. Above them the mountaintops were hidden by skeins of ragged, fast-moving cloud. Togi could just see the manhood hut high on the side of Penwyn, appearing and disappearing as the clouds swept by. It looked very far off and lonely.

"You will not know, until the time comes," said Cunomoros, picking up his shovel again. "That is why you will be spending some nights alone on the mountain, starting at the new moon. It is time you began to practice walking the Dark Path, the spirit path, and that is best done in silence, away from the places of men."

"Mmm," said Togi, driving his shovel into the black garden soil to loosen it. "Will this be different from the meditations you have taught me already?"

"Yes, and no," said Cunomoros. "It begins with meditation and with trance, but it goes farther—much farther. I will tell you more when the time comes. For now, chant for me the names of the Guardians and Guides which I have taught you." And in time to his digging, Togi began to chant.

As they climbed the mountain, the new moon was a pale sliver in the golden western sky. They were not going far this time, only far enough to be well away from all people. Togi was wearing his new woolen cloak and his old tunic, now rather short in the sleeves—he had shot up again over the winter, and was now as tall as Cunomoros. The night would be cold, for they were only just past the sun's half-year point, but this first time, at least, he would have a fire; journeying in darkness would come later. He carried the old willow basket, which contained a horn lantern and a black pottery flask sealed with a wooden stopper. Cunomoros followed, leaning heavily on his oaken staff.

After a while they found a good spot in the lee of a stony ridge, sheltered from the wind but with a clear view of the dark eastern sky. In the fading twilight Togi gathered wood and started a fire. "You should go down now, Father, while there is still a little light," he said as he knelt to blow on his tinder. "I can manage now on my own."

"There will be starlight enough to guide me later," said Cunomoros, smiling, "and I have the lantern. Build up your fire a little more, and sit down." Togi did as he was bidden, and Cunomoros sat beside him. They watched the flames for a while in silence, enjoying the warmth and their shared companionship. "Are you ready?" asked Cunomoros softly at last.

"Yes." Togi felt calm, but also excited. This was a new challenge, a new milestone on his path.

"Good." Cunomoros took the black pottery flask from their basket and pulled out the wooden stopper. A faint minty aroma escaped; he sniffed it, and nodded. "This is not too strong, but it will help you to begin. Are you comfortable? Are you ready to walk the path?"

"Yes," said Togi again. He was sitting cross-legged by the fire, in a position he could maintain for hours. "I am ready." Cunomoros handed him the flask.

"Then drink this draught, Seeker," he said formally, "and with it begin your travels. In the fire is your first Gateway. Open it and pass through."

Togi took the flask, and drank. Under the mint there were other flavors, darker and more bitter. His memory identified each of them as he replaced the stopper and set the flask down. On an empty stomach—he had been fasting since morning—he felt the effects of the drugs almost at once: a lightness, a buoyancy, as if he were a bird about to test its wings. Smiling, he stared into the fire, his eyes wide and dark, his breathing shifting already toward trance. Cunomoros watched him for a while, then picked up the discarded flask and lit his horn lantern with a twig from the fire. Togi never stirred, and after a little longer his foster-father stood up stiffly, stretched, and backed away from the fire. He paused there for a long time, ignoring the increasing chill which gnawed at his old flesh and settled into his bones. It was hard to let this child-man of his fly free, but it must be done. He wanted to put more wood on the dying fire to keep his boy warm, but he stayed where he was. At last, long after moonset, he lifted his basket and lantern, and softly limped away.

Togi never heard him go. He was deep in trance now, riding the currents of the fire. He had gone through the Gate to meet the first of his Protectors—providing that he could answer the questions which he knew would be asked. He rose and fell like a spark on the wind, tumbling in the turbulence of flames and laughing as he flew. Searing heat was all about him, but he was untouched by the fire, because he was a part of it. Its hissing and roaring were all around and through him; it spoke not in words, but in pulses of light, red and gold and blue. *Who are you?* it asked him suddenly. *Why are you here?*

Silently he replied, *I am the Son of the Fox, and I seek my inheritance.* The flames hissed and crackled, laughing around him.

By what right do you claim it? Speak carefully, or we will burn you...

By my art, and by my tongue; by my words, and by my mind, by the fire which burns in me and in every living thing, I call upon Gofannon, the Master of Fire.

The light around him dimmed to purple, and the heat withdrew. He was suspended in a great space. A dark voice spoke now in his mind, a voice of iron. *You have called upon me, and I have come,* it said harshly. *Ask now what you will.*

Togi smiled within himself. *I ask to learn, Lord: to control the power of Fire; to gain the strength of Iron; and to call upon your protection in my time of need.*

What will you give for this? asked the iron voice. *For nothing comes without price.*

When the day comes, said Togi, *I will pay the price demanded. How can I know it, before my need arises?*

There was a long silence, echoing, endless. *Good,* said the iron voice at last. *Follow me, and learn...*

A spark in the fire, a hammer on iron, an ore in the earth, a sword in the hand... He was all of these things, and more, during that night. The voice of the fire, and the Fire-Master, spoke through and around him, singing to him, teaching him, and at last returning him to his own body, his world, his life.

There was red light on his closed eyelids, but it did not flicker like fire, and he was cold, cold as burnt-out embers. He opened his eyes slowly with a great effort, and beheld the rising sun. Stiffly he stood up, every joint of him aching with cold, and smiling raised his chilled hands and hoarse voice in the morning prayer. He had paid the price of knowledge, and survived the first of his tests. In a little while, after his rites were finished, he headed back down the mountain to begin the day. Below, in the garden, it would be time to plant the beans. Behind him the ashes of the fire stirred faintly in the morning wind, and then were still.

The moon was new again, and once more the two of them were walking on the mountain. The beans Togi had planted after his first trial were a hand's-breadth tall now, lifting their first pale green leaves to the spring sky, and some of the bushes and trees along the wood-shore were wearing a faint haze of green buds. This time the trial would be different; this time there would be no fire. Instead, they followed a stream which had cut a deep cleft into the hillside. On either side of them as they walked, the sides of the cleft grew steeper; they threaded their way through tangled bushes and fallen trees, sometimes on the rocky banks of the stream, sometimes wading though its icy pools. At last they reached their goal, where the stream dropped in a shimmering silver curtain of spray from a slot three men's height or more above them, to splash and foam into a wide pool. Behind the sheet of falling water was a shallow mossy ledge, where here and there clumps of fern clung to the cliff face. To reach it, thought Togi, critically surveying the rocks on either side, would not be easy, but it could be done...
"There?"

"There," nodded Cunomoros, taking the black pottery flask from his basket. "I think you will find there is room enough. Are you ready?"

"I am." Togi twisted the folds of the cloak which he was carrying slung over his shoulder through his belt to keep it secure and to free his hands. "Let me have the flask."

"Do not drink it until you reach your seat," said Cunomoros, handing it over. "It will affect your balance." Togi took it and shoved it under his belt on the side away from his cloak. "In the water is your next Gateway, Seeker," said Cunomoros more formally. "When you are ready, open it and pass through."

"I will," said Togi, smiling. He waded slowly through the edges of the pool, looking for a place to start his climb. The rocks were glistening wet with spray from the falls, but he found a foothold, and then another. Clinging with hands and sandaled feet, he edged his way up and sideways through the icy curtain of spray, heading for the ledge. He was almost there when the rock beneath his right foot gave way and rattled down into the pool. Twisting sideways to protect the flask, Togi slipped and followed it, landing with a splash in the boulder-strewn waters below. The pool was deep enough to give him some protection, but not enough; he came to his knees coughing and gasping, rubbing his bruises and half shaken out of his wits. But before Cunomoros, who had watched in helpless horror as he fell, could plunge in to help him, he was on his feet again. "Na, na, Father," he said, holding up one dripping hand, palm-outward, "I am—all right. I do not—need help."

"Are you sure?" asked Cunomoros anxiously, hesitating on the edge of the pool. "Do you want to continue?"

"Yes," said Togi firmly, shaking the wet hair out of his eyes and pulling himself together. "This is nothing. Do not worry." And wading directly through the waterfall—he could hardly get any wetter, he thought—he began again to climb.

This time he reached his perch safely. The ledge was a little wider than it had looked from below, which was all to the good. He spent a while wringing some of the water out of his woolen cloak; then, wrapping its clammy folds around him, he settled down with his back to the stony cliff face behind him, and drew out the flask from under his belt. Pulling out the wooden stopper, he sniffed the contents; this one was different, he thought, and yet in many ways the same mixture as the first. Drinking it down with a grimace—for it was bitter—he restoppered the flask and set it on the ledge beside him; then, closing his eyes, he gave himself over to the music of the falls. Below, Cunomoros watched him for a while, and then went quietly away.

This time Togi found it harder to start his trance; he was cold, and his right knee throbbed where he had struck it on a rock in the pool. Shivering, he sucked a bruised knuckle and tried to find a more comfortable position on the wet stone. He began to feel dizzy, and to wish that he had put this challenge off until tomorrow; one day would not have made much difference. Too late now to back out... His teeth were chattering and he clenched them; the sound of the water seemed to be inside his head, a pounding, bubbling rhythm which beat with the beat of his blood. His eyes would not focus, so he closed them, and leaned his aching head back against the rock face, trying to slow his breathing. He was sliding—slipping—floating away into the dark...

This time there was no control, no easy riding of the current. He twisted and turned in the water, dragged down and pitched up again, helpless as a log in a flood. A cloudy green darkness enveloped him, blinding him, filling his mouth and nose, flowing into his belly and chest, numbing and dissolving his strength and will. A little more and he would lose himself in it, never to return; already the edges of his thought were mere tendrils of brook-weed in its flow. Slowly he sank deeper, deeper, into the cold waters which flowed within the earth, into the greater darkness. His consciousness was slipping away, but it did not matter... did not matter... And yet it *did*. He was Togi...Togidubnos...son of Lovernos the Fox...and he was *not* yet ready to die, not yet ready to drown...

The waters laughed around him and within him, a rolling, pounding laughter like the crashing of waves on the beach. *Little cub*, said the waters, *do you think your strength of will can overcome ours? All things which live come from us and return to us. Who are you, that you should choose your time?*

I am the Son of the Fox, said Togi to the waters, *and I have come to seek my inheritance.* The waters laughed again, gurgling and chuckling through his flesh, blinding his eyes, dissolving his very bones.

That is nothing to us, said the waters. *By what right do you claim it?*

By my will and by my word, by my art and by my strength, by the water which flows in every living thing, said Togi, *I call upon Manannan, the Lord of the Sea.*

There was a silence then, a deep green silence. Togi ceased to tumble in the flood, and hung instead suspended in it, unmoving. After the buffeting of the waters, this was a relief. Almost he felt he could sleep here in this quiet darkness, but he did not dare to, for he knew that from that sleep there would be no awaking. Instead, in a slow inward chant, he made himself recite the names of all the rivers of Britain, north to south, east to west. He was just finishing when he became aware that he was not alone in the darkness. *You do well,* said a huge voice, *to count the names of my children. You have called upon me, little cub, and I have come. Ask now of me what you will.*

With an effort Togi pulled his straying wits together. *I ask to learn, Lord: to control the power of Water; to gain the strength of its flow; and to call upon your protection in my hour of need.*

What will you give for this? asked the huge voice. *For nothing comes without a price.*

When the day comes, said Togi, *I will pay the price demanded. How can I know it, before my need arises?*

There was a long silence, echoing, endless. *Good,* said the huge voice at last. *Follow me, and learn...*

A drop of rain in a cloud, a breaking wave upon the shore, a deep well in the earth, a strong tide in the sea... He was all of these things and more that night. The voice of the water, and of the Sea God, spoke through and around him, singing to him, teaching him, and at last returning him to his own body, his world, his life.

He opened his eyes slowly to the cloudy light of dawn. He was so cold that at first it was hard to move, hard to even remember who and where he was; but at last he pushed himself to a sitting position on the ledge, and with numb fingers forced the black pottery flask back between his belt and his bruised ribs. Groaning, he slid stiffly down the rock face, and picked his way painfully around the edge of the pool. His right knee was bruised and swollen, and he looked around until he found a dead alder branch to use as a staff, then hobbled on. When at last he came out of the cleft into the wider valley, he saw that the sunlight was just touching the high hilltops. Smiling, he stopped and leaned his staff against him, and lifted his hands and his hoarse voice in the dawn prayer. He had passed his second test, and he was still alive. Behind him the stream flowed ever onward over its falls, and the pool gurgled quietly.

There was no moon in the sky as Togi climbed the mountain. His third test fell near the end of Quimon, the extra month which comes once in five years to keep the seasons in their proper alignment with the sun. Waiting the few days longer until the new moon appeared would have brought him too close to Beltane itself. As it was he would have only three days to prepare himself between this journeying and his manhood ritual; but it would, he thought, be enough.

He came alone this time to make contact with the High Powers, the Gods and Goddesses of the Sun and Moon and Stars. With Lugh of the Light he was already familiar, having offered to him every morning since he could remember; but the Goddess of the Moon he did not know well, or the Shepherd of the Stars. There would be others as well, other paths and powers: but the Clear Gate might also be harder to find. And this time he would be journeying without the drug.

Even without Cunomoros' company, he climbed slowly, for his right knee was still stiff from the bruising he had got in the waterfall's pool—a useful reminder of the physical as well as spiritual dangers which might lie along his path. Well-trained and gifted though he was, he was still only a man, and he too could fail.

He was making for the top of Penwyn, not far from the cairn of the Old Ones. In the long spring twilight—Beltane fell late this year—he had no need for a lantern in order to see his way. The ghosts would not be awake, although he could feel their presence as he came nearer. There was only the singing of the wind in the grass and heather, and the distant churring of a nightjar from the shadowy slopes below. The valleys below him were already pools of darkness compared to the bright heights of the northern sky.

He chose a spot just below the summit, on the east side of a jut of rock which would shelter him somewhat from the wind, and settled down on the pad of his folded cloak, putting to one side the other things he had brought with him: a small bundle of firewood, a leather bottle filled with clear spring water, and a packet of bread and cheese wrapped in a clean cloth. These could wait until he needed them; if all went well, he would be here for two nights and a day. Resting his back comfortably against the warm stone behind him, he set himself to contemplate the Path which lay before him.

As the twilight deepened, the summer stars appeared, palest in the pale north and brightest in the dark south. He watched their slow wheeling and reached out with his mind to their Shepherd. Gradually his awareness of his own body fell away; he floated among the stars in the depths of the sky and heard their slow song, faint as the voices of the bats which he had loved to watch as a child. For a moment Cunomoros' voice spoke in his memory: *if ever you are pursued, do the thing unexpected....* And his own voice answered: *I will remember...* But the voices of the stars and of their Shepherd were louder, and the remembered words floated away into the great darkness which now enclosed him. He waited, slowly reciting the names of the summer stars as he had seen them before that darkness fell, and at last the star-song fell silent. Yet Togi knew that he was not alone.

Who are you, and why are you here? asked the Shepherd's silver voice in his mind. It was a calm, mild challenge compared to those Togi had encountered before, but the will behind it was cold and hard as ice.

I am the Son of the Fox, he replied, *and I come to seek my inheritance.*

In his mind the Shepherd laughed. *What inheritance is that, Child of Earth? And by what right do you claim it?*

My inheritance is the knowledge of the Sky, and the powers of the Sky, said Togi. *And I claim it by my will and by my word, by my art and by my act, by the Light which shines in every living thing.*

I can give you only the knowledge of the Stars, and of Darkness, said the Shepherd, and behind his voice was a tinkling like the sound of frozen branches in winter. *Do you still wish it?*

Yes, said Togi.

Then take, O Child of Earth, the thing for which you have asked, said the Shepherd.

There was a long cold silence. In it, Togi felt the chill of the Shepherd's sky sink into his flesh like the cold of a midwinter's night. Needles of ice pierced him; his breath choked and froze in his throat; his eyes were blinded and sealed closed by frozen tears. Only his hearing remained, and in it, the chiming sound returned and grew louder. Then he felt himself lifted and whirled by winds such as he had never known before, thrown spinning down the length of the years to a time before life, before light, stripped and battered and torn until only the cold core of his mind remained. At last, when even that spark of spirit was flickering on the edge of extinction, he did the one thing which he could do: with all the strength remaining to him he called upon Lugh, the Lord of Light.

The winds ceased, and he hung motionless, still and blind and battered in silent blackness. And at last a great golden voice spoke in that silence. *Who calls,* it said, *upon Light in the Darkness? And who is it that seeks for the Sun in the bosom of old Night?*

I call, Lord, said Togi. *By my father's name and by his ring, by his life and by mine, I call: I who have walked your path and served you since I could stand.*

There was another long silence. Then the golden voice said, *You have called upon me, Fox Cub, and I have come. Ask now of me what you will.*

I ask to learn, Lord: to summon the power of Light; to gain the inspiration of your Awen; and to call upon your protection in my time of need.

What will you give for this? asked the golden voice. *For nothing comes without a price.*

When the day comes, said Togi, *I will pay the price demanded. How can I know it, before my need arises?*

There was a long silence, echoing, endless. *Good,* said the golden voice at last. *Follow me, and learn...*

A midsummer sunrise, a beam of light in darkness, the heat which ripens the grain, a blazing sunset... He was all of these things and more that night. The warmth of the sun, and the voice of the God, spoke through and around him, singing to him, teaching him, and at last returning him to his own body, his world, his life.

He opened his eyes slowly to the bright light of midday. He was still leaning back against the rock, the sun warm on his face and body, and all around him rose the singing of the larks. The Sun God's last words still echoed in his mind: *Look for my pale Sister at evening. She will expect you...* This time the trial was not over; there was yet more to come. But so far he had survived; he was alive.

His mouth was dry, and he drank some of the water in the leather bottle, then stood up and made a slow circuit of the mountaintop. The day was fine and fresh, with a strong breeze from the west. After a little thought he returned to pick up his possessions, and moved to a similar spot which faced that way. The new moon would be visible only briefly at sunset, if at all, and he must be ready for her. Sitting down again upon his folded cloak, he leaned his back against this new sun-warmed rock, and dozed, remembering the lessons he had learned in the previous night's visions. His belly was empty, but he paid it no heed; fasting would only aid him in his quest, and was to him no new thing.

At last the sun dropped slowly toward the western horizon, clung for a moment, great and fat and golden, to the mountaintops, and then slipped behind them. With its going the first faint sliver of the new moon appeared, a hand's breadth above the peaks. In that instant Togi called out to her with his mind. Then, as she dropped in her turn behind the mountains, his spirit followed her into the palely glowing sky.

Again he hung suspended while the summer stars appeared around him, but this time his focus was the Moon. Within her bright rim, sharp and shining as the silver blade of a sickle, he saw the rest of her pale body. He held up his hands as if to touch her, but she was beyond his reach—infinitely beyond his reach. But she was aware of him, and spoke smilingly in his mind, with a woman's soft voice. *Why are you here, little cubling?* she asked. *You have come a long way.*

I come to learn from you, Lady, said Togi. *To gain such of your secrets as you would share.* He felt strangely diffident with this Goddess—a new thing for him in his journeying. It was not like the awe he had felt with her great Brother, or the fear the Star Shepherd had put on him. This Queen of the night had a different relationship with men.

She laughed now in his mind, but tenderly. *Much of my magic you can never own, Fox Cub. Do you not know mine is not a magic for men?*

So I have heard, Lady, said Togi slowly. *Yet I ask that you teach me such of it as I may understand.*

That I will do freely, said the laughing voice. *Follow me now, and learn...*

Is there no price for your teaching, Lady? asked Togi in surprise.

Na, cubling, said the Moon's voice, *or not in the way you mean. My price you will pay each time you offer me worship, and gladly pay it. Is it not good?*

It is, said Togi, beginning to understand. *Teach me, then, Lady, tonight...*

He opened his eyes at last to the pale sky of dawn, to find himself curled in the grass at the base of his yesterday's stone. Knowing from the light that he had a little time yet until sunrise, he stretched slowly, smiling. The Lady had indeed taught him things he was glad to know.

Yawning, he sat up and drank more water from this flask, then untied his bundle of wood and began to build a fire. He was hungry, and ate a little of his bread and cheese to sustain him on the long walk down the mountain, then offered the rest on his fire as a gift to the High Powers. At sunrise he greeted the Bright Lord with joyous song, then gathered his few belongings and set out for home. He felt well prepared for his fourth and final test, which would come with that of his year-mates in three days. Behind him a thread of smoke from his fire drifted and vanished, and the larks rose rejoicing on the bright morning air.

Coming of Age

Two days before Beltane, Togi found himself standing outside the feast-hall in the late afternoon sun along with eight other boys his age. They ranged from big yellow-haired Pasutagos, who had turned fourteen a few days after the previous Beltane, to little dark Vindex, whose name-day had fallen a mere two days ago. All of them were nervous and cracking jokes to cover it, boasting of things they had done in the past and would do in the future. They were well acquainted, of course—they had mostly shared their seven years of warrior training together—but this did not mean that all of them were friends. In any group of more than two people, there are always rivalries and alliances, and Togi's year-mates were no exception.

"I," said red-headed Sagos, throwing out his narrow chest, "have slept with more girls than any of you. There are few in the valleys who have not felt my spear!"

"Pah!" said little black-haired Bogos. "They may have felt it, but I am betting that it was only to laugh at its limpness! Now I—"

"What do girls matter?" asked pale-haired Ambios. "Any true warrior can have his pick of them. Now I, I went along last summer when Lugotorix led a raid against the Deceangli—"

"You may have gone along to start with," said Vindex slyly, "but I heard that Lugo sent you back as soon as he noticed you were there."

"Not true!" cried Ambios, flushing. "We raided their pastures and brought back many cows!"

"Two bullocks and a dry heifer, more likely," said Sagos.

"When was this great cattle raid?" asked Togi. "And where? I do not remember it, but I was away."

"It was half a moon before Lughnasa," said Ambios, "in the hills east of Conwy. Why do you ask?"

"That is odd," said Togi thoughtfully. "For I was traveling with the King when he fought the Deceangli in those same hills just before Lughnasa. Strange that I did not see you or Lugo there." Vindex snickered.

"You, with the King?" said Ambios scornfully. "Why would he want you with him?"

"I went as student to his Bard," said Togi, "at the Bard's invitation."

"Oh, it is a bard that you are now, is it?" asked Ambios. "I thought you were a fledgling Priest."

"A man may be both," said Togi. "Two talents are better than none."

"Do you put insult on me, then?" cried Ambios, now very red in the face.

"Not I," said Togi, smiling. "I have no need to." Ambios clenched his fists.

"Be quiet, you fools!" said Pasutagos urgently. "They are coming for us now." All of the boys assumed an air of studied innocence as Cunomoros and Crotos came out of the feast-hall together with Bratronos the Chieftain.

"Well," said Crotos, looking them over and shaking his gray head, "I have done my best with them, Bratronos, hard work though it was with such poor material. They are yours now, Cunomoros—maybe *you* can make men of them."

"Na," said Cunomoros seriously, "I will neither make nor unmake them. I will only show them what they are."

"Do not destroy them all in the testing, Honored One," said Bratronos jestingly. "I need new spears!"

"I think there will be one or two left, at least," said Cunomoros. Slowly, without further words, he looked the boys over one by one, as if weighing them coldly in the balance, and Togi saw with startled respect the aura of priestly authority which his kindly father could assume. When Cunomoros' glance came to him, he kept his own face sober. This was not hard; it was as if a stranger looked out at him from his father's familiar eyes. For the first time Togi wondered what Cunomoros' role had been on Môn, and Sennos' words came back to him: *The Gods have a sense of humor after all, it would seem...*

"Follow me," said Cunomoros to them all impartially, and turned toward the path which led up Penwyn. Togi put his disquieting thoughts aside, and set his mind on the manhood rites to come. After that, perhaps, it would finally be time to ask questions.

With its gray stone walls half hidden by brambles and bushes, and roofed as it was with thick green turf rather than golden-brown thatch, the ancient manhood hut seemed, when they reached it, more like a cave than any dwelling of men. It had been built, legend said, like the ghost-haunted cairn above it, by the First Men, or by the Gods who had walked among them in those high and far-off days. Its doorway was blocked by a hanging curtain of dark leather, and its gray lintel-stone was so low that even little Vindex had to bend almost double to enter it when his turn came—for Cunomoros, after entering it himself, called them in one by one after him, in a deep echoing voice which seemed to come from a much larger space than this hut could possibly contain. Perhaps, thought Togi, the place was bigger than it looked—as indeed it might be, if it was not entirely of this world... At last, when he was the only one still waiting, he heard his name called, and followed the others inside.

The leather curtain swung closed behind him, cutting off the sunlight, and he stumbled blindly down two or three shallow steps, straightening cautiously from a crouch as he did so. The hut was dim and cool, with only the faint light which leaked in around the edges of the curtain to give him any sense of where he was. Cunomoros, or his assistant—for there seemed to be one or more people helping him, although Togi had not seen anyone else arrive—took him by the shoulder and blindfolded him loosely with a strip of rough woolen cloth, then led him to his place among the others, and without speaking, urged him to sit down on what seemed to be a pile of deerskins laid out on the bare earthen floor. Even that measure seemed unnecessary, for the light from outside soon faded, leaving them all sitting silently and uneasily in the dark.

After a while someone near the back of the hut—it was hard to say exactly where—began to tap on a skin drum, very softly, in a heartbeat rhythm. The sound went on and on relentlessly, now faster, now slower. The air began to thicken with a smoky scent like burning herbs, although there was no fire to be seen. Togi knew that scent, and smiled to himself in the darkness; it was harmless stuff compared to the potions he had recently drunk. His confidence had risen again, after that strange moment in the courtyard, and he felt himself very nearly master of the situation, an initiate among novices, who had already done things the others could only dream of.

Time passed slowly. Now and then he heard a rustling noise, as one of the boys shifted position restlessly; nothing was happening, and their initial fear had changed to boredom. Almost imperceptibly, the smoke was thickening, and there was another scent mingled with it now. Despite himself, Togi yawned. Suddenly the drumbeat stopped, and in the back of the room a light began to grow. He could see it through and around the edges of his blindfold: a steady light such as a candle might give. From the direction of the light Cunomoros' voice spoke again, calling one of the boys by name: "Pasutagos—arise, and come to me." A shadow crossed the light, then two shadows returned. There was a pause, and the light almost went out, as if a lantern had been shuttered. The drumbeat began again, louder than before, and under its sound Togi could faintly hear voices, Cunomoros' and Pasutagos', in a question and answer rhythm; then all three sounds stopped at once. Again the light brightened; footsteps came back, and two shadows; and Cunomoros' voice called: "Sagos—arise, and come to me."

Eight times the pattern was repeated, and at last it was Togi's turn. When his name was called, he got lightly to his feet and walked directly toward the light, hardly needing the touch of the escort's hand. He sensed rather than saw a hanging curtain which was put aside before he reached it; it swung closed behind him, brushing the backs of his legs. Cunomoros' voice spoke again, still with that strange echo: "Togidubnos son of Lovernos, you have passed the age of manhood, and have come here today to gain its full estate. Are you ready to face the tests which await you?"

"I am," said Togi.

"Hold out your hands," said Cunomoros. Togi obeyed. Something cold and hard and round was put into his hands: a large cup, he thought, but an oddly shaped one. He moved his thumbs across it, testing its surface, and they encountered depressions, two smooth rounded depressions of uncertain depth. Even before his blindfold was removed, he knew what he was holding. Dark in the ivory bone, the skull's empty eye-sockets looked up at him from between his hands. Its top had been cut cleanly across, and the bowl thus created was full of some dark liquid which looked red in the candlelight. Despite himself, Togi shivered. "Blood and death wait always in the way of the warrior," said Cunomoros quietly. "Are you ready to accept this fate?"

"I am," said Togi.

"Then drink," said Cunomoros. Togi looked for a moment longer at the thing he held, seeing the fine cracks in the ancient bone, and the polished places where many hands had touched it over the years. This too had once been a man. With a faint smile he lifted it, and drank reverently. Honey and mead were in it, and the juice of crushed berries, together with some underlying bitterness which he could not immediately identify. He lowered the empty skull; and Cunomoros, still with that stranger's face, took it from his hands. "You have set your foot on the way," the old man said. "Now you must walk the path. Fear also awaits the warrior. Go you now, and sleep: in your dreams you will meet the thing that you most fear."

The blindfold was put on Togi again, and the silent escort led him back to his place. The room was quiet except for the deep breathing of his year-mates; already he could hear a few snores. He stretched out on his back in the cool darkness and relaxed, and almost at once he slept.

It was the old dream again, the one which he remembered from his childhood. He stood once more on a hilltop bathed in the gray light of the Otherworld, and looked down on a land which he should know. Far off in the distance he heard the sound of horns, brazen, bronze-mouthed, and braying, echoing in the green valleys below him. He saw the change of the light; saw the winding road appear which led to his high place; saw the man climbing toward him, small and distant and clear. This time Togi started down to meet the stranger; this time he knew he would succeed.

His road twisted as it descended, and trees and bushes sometimes blocked his view; but whenever he could see clearly, the man was still there, walking steadily up the road toward him: a dark-haired bearded man in a knee-length white garment, with touches of gold glinting at his throat. The stranger moved easily but not quickly: a young man, perhaps, at the end of a long journey. Something about him seemed familiar, and not only from the dreams; and yet Togi was sure that this was no one he knew in the waking world. He quickened his own pace.

Somewhere in the woodland to his right, another horn sounded: not like the deep-voiced horns he had heard at first, but one with a lighter, fiercer note. The stranger on the road below him started and threw up his head, like a stag who hears the hounds, then looked about him quickly, as if seeking a hiding place. But there was none; the road there was straight and open. Seeing this, the man stopped still, and raised his hands in a formal gesture, then began to weave a pattern with them in the air before him. For no reason that he could name, Togi started to run. Even as he did so, fog rose from the ground around him like smoke from a fire, and the clear landscape dissolved in a blur of mist. Between one stride and the next, the smooth surface of the road changed to a rough hillside clothed in gorse and heather. Togi stumbled to a halt, and stood panting.

The bright horn called again, and figures appeared in the mist to his right: marching columns of men in the garb of Red Crest soldiers, with shining silver armor on their bodies and square red-painted shields in their hands. Togi could have escaped them in the mist, but instead he stood staring in fascination which slowly changed to horror. The faces inside the helmets were those of dead men, bloody and torn by the crows; even as he watched the flesh dropped away to show the white bone within. Behind them as they marched the mist began to glow, gold and red as fire; it *was* fire, fire and smoke and destruction, and somewhere in that fire, he knew, was his home and family—what was left of them. He started to run toward the fire, but the dead soldiers blocked his path. Their mindlessly marching feet trampled the ground into mud, and their eyeless faces watched his every move. When he tried to dodge around them, they struck him down with their shields and drew their swords. He could not save his people; he could not even save himself. He had not done what he was born for, and he was about to die...

Someone was holding him down; he struggled and cried out. Someone was shaking him. He must be blind, for it was dark—dark… He put up his hand to his face, and felt the blindfold, and memory came back to him. He was in the manhood hut with his year-mates, and the pale light of early morning was seeping around the curtain which covered the door. Slowly he sat up. Whoever had shaken him—had that been real?—must have gone, for there was no one beside him now. Some of his fellows seemed to be awake, for he could only hear one or two still snoring, one or two breathing in the deep rhythms of sleep. *They* must not be facing their fears, he thought wryly. He hoped that he had not cried aloud, like a child with the nightmare. He brooded on that for a moment, then set himself to remember his dream. The first part of it was already fading, but the last part was horribly clear…

"Pasutagos." It was Cunomoros' voice again. Togi heard the tall boy get to his feet and walk toward the light in the back of the hut. The heartbeat rhythm of the skin drum started up again, masking whatever was being said. After a while the drumbeat stopped, and Pasutagos came back, stumbling a little, and sat down. Eight times the pattern was repeated, and at last Togi heard his own name. This time he arose more slowly and made his way toward the curtain which was drawn back for him. He stopped just inside it and stood waiting.

"Sit down," said Cunomoros. Togi sat, hearing the weariness in the old man's voice as he did so. His blindfold was removed; in the candlelight he faced once more—not his foster-father, but the Priest. "Tell me your dream," said Cunomoros. Togi told it all slowly and exactly, or as much of it as he remembered. Cunomoros seemed to brood for a moment, frowning. "Is it the Red Crests you fear?"

"No," said Togi; and then more slowly, "No, I think not. Not them, but the destruction that they bring. I was powerless to stop them. They will grind us all into the earth, as they did on Ynys Môn. We will go down into silence, and be forgotten, unless…" He stopped, surprised by his own words.

"Unless…?" said Cunomoros.

"Unless… Na, I do not know. The *awen* has gone," said Togi, and sighed.

Cunomoros nodded. "It comes when the time is right... Warrior, you have faced death and fear. One more test awaits you: the test of pain. Go back to your place now, and think on what you have learned, and what you would suffer willingly for the good of the tribe." The blindfold was put on Togi again; he arose and returned to his place. Around him he heard the others stirring restlessly, but he had much to think about. There had been something else in his dream, someone... Na, he could not remember. At last he lay down again and slept.

When he awoke, the faint light from the doorway was shading toward evening. He heard restless stirrings: his year-mates were all awake. The ritual was almost over, except for the final test. The test of pain, Cunomoros had called it: the process by which each of them would gain the tribal mark which he would carry for the rest of his life. Once in times long past, or so Cunomoros had taught him, young men had carried elaborate patterns cut and tattooed into their skin, but nowadays the design was simpler. It was the way in which it was put on that mattered.

"Take off your blindfolds," said Cunomoros' voice, "and move your bedding back against the walls." Togi and his fellows did as they were told. As they cleared the central space, Cunomoros brought a small firepot into the middle of the room and set it down, removing the lid carefully with a wad of cloth. The coals inside the pot glowed cherry red, licked by little tongues of blue flame. "Gather in a circle and sit down," said Cunomoros. "The time of your last test is at hand."

The boys sat or squatted in a loose circle around the firepot as Cunomoros produced a long iron rod and placed one end of it in the coals. That end, as Togi knew, was the brand: a deep-carved design like the face of a mountain cat, about as wide as a man's thumbnail. The old man set a wide clay bowl and a jug on the ground beside the firepot, then drew the long sacrificer's knife from his belt and unsheathed it. The edge of the blade glittered red in the light from the glowing coals, as if it were already blooded. "Pasutagos," said Cunomoros, "are you ready now to face the test?"

"I am," said the tall boy.

"Then stand up and hold out your left arm," said Cunomoros quietly, "and do not move." Pasutagos held out his bare left arm, palm up, and Cunomoros quickly drew the knife across it, making two shallow intersecting cuts which bled freely. "Let your blood fall in the bowl," he said. Smiling, Pasutagos held his arm over the bowl, and watched the drops of blood gather and fall. Wrapping his wad of cloth around the handle of the brand, Cunomoros drew it from the fire. "Hold still," he said, and pressed the glowing iron accurately against the bleeding cuts with a hiss. Pasutagos made no sound. Cunomoros placed the brand back in the coals and said, "Well done. Sit down. Sagos, are you ready now to face the test?"

"I am," said the red-headed boy.

"Then stand up and hold out your left arm," said Cunomoros, "and do not move." One by one he marked them, and each shed his blood into the growing pool. Some flinched a little at the touch of the iron, but no one made a sound. At last Cunomoros came to Togi. "Togidubnos son of Lovernos," he said, "are you ready now to face the test?" A few eyebrows went up; not everyone had known the name of Togi's blood-father.

"I am," said Togi calmly.

"Then stand up and hold out your left arm," said Cunomoros, "and do not move." Togi held out his arm, and watched dispassionately the action of the knife. It stung a little, but no more. As his blood dripped into the bowl, he watched Cunomoros lift the brand. No one would have known from his face when it went home, although the pain was intense. Cunomoros placed the brand on the ground to cool and said, "Well done. Now comes the final test." Bending, he took the jug and poured its contents into the blood bowl, until the mixed liquids filled it. Then lifting it carefully, he straightened. "Stand up," he said, and waited while they rose. "In this bowl you have mingled your blood; you are all blood brothers now. But there is one more thing which must be done to seal that bond: each of you must drink. Pasutagos, will you begin?"

"I will," said the tall boy. Taking the bowl, he drank, then handed it on to Sagos. The red-haired boy's hands shook a little as he took it, for this was unexpected; but he drank and visibly swallowed, and handed the bowl on to Vindex. Slowly it went around the circle, some drinking more readily than others, but none refused. It was still half-full when it came to Togi, who as always was last.

To leave anything behind would be wrong, he knew; such a sacrament could not be discarded, and there was no proper fire here into which it could be poured. This thought passed in an instant; he took the bowl and drank all its contents down, as if it were fine ale. More than half, he thought, was the same flavored mead which he had drunk from the skull cup—was it only the night before? He lowered the empty bowl and handed it back to Cunomoros, who smiled faintly for the first time since the ritual had begun.

"Well done," he said again, setting the bowl on the ground. Taking a small pot from his belt-pouch, he unstoppered it and smeared the thick black ointment it contained on each boy's arm in turn, to seal the cuts and color the scar which would form. Then he stepped back, and looked them all over once more. "All of you have faced your tests," he said, "and all of you have passed them. Let the promises you have made in this place never be broken. Now say with me the Great Oath."

They said it with him, loudly, triumphantly, so that the dark room echoed and the stone walls shook with the sound: *As a man of the Ordovices, I will freely face pain, fear, and death to defend my land and my people. If I break faith with them, and with my honor, may the dark earth open and swallow me, may the seas rush in and drown me, may the sky of stars fall upon me and crush me out of life forever.*

"Remember always," said Cunomoros when they had finished, "what you have done here, and what you have sworn to do. Now go back to your families, and make ready for tomorrow night's celebration. I will follow soon."

One by one the young men made their way out, stooping under the low lintel and blinking in the late evening light, until only Togi was left.

"Father," he said then, "may I help you here? For I think there are things to be done before you can leave." Cunomoros had been covering the firepot, but at this he looked up and smiled.

"Yes," he said simply. "Thank you, my son." And his face was familiar again, and Togi smiled back.

It was three days later; they had just made the dawn offering, and were walking down the hill again under a high bright sky. "Father," said Togi, speaking suddenly out of their shared silence, "I have a question."

"Yes?" said Cunomoros, smiling. "What question is that?"

"How did my blood-father die? How and why?"

Cunomoros was silent for a moment. "Mmm," he said at last. "That is a short question, but it requires a long answer. Let us find a good spot to sit, and I will give it to you. It is right that you should know it all, now that you are a man."

"That was my thought also," said Togi.

They found a ledge of rock in the warm early sunlight and sat down. "I have been expecting this," said Cunomoros, "since you told me two summers ago that you had met Sennos. What did he say to you?"

"Mmm," said Togi in his turn. "He told me about the coming of the Red Crests, and how they destroyed Môn. I saw a little of that myself when I went there with him. And he told me how he fought in the defense, and how the Council had chosen—had chosen my blood-father to be the new Archdruid instead of him. I do not think," said Togi carefully, "that he liked my blood-father, or you. When I said that you were my foster-father, he laughed."

"Ah," said Cunomoros. "No, there was never any love lost between us. But he would never have been chosen Archdruid, much though he desired it; indeed, it was the strength of that desire which worked against him. Your blood-father took nothing from him, whatever he may think." He sat for a while in silent thought, and Togi waited. "We chose Lovernos as Archdruid," Cunomoros said at last, "because despite his youth, he seemed the most fit to lead us in those perilous days. He had a degree of vision—not only *awen*, but clear seeing—which comes seldom to men, and as often to the young as to the old. He directed us wisely—as wisely as any mortal man could. Some of our treasures and people he sent for safety to Ériu's Land, to one of our Sanctuaries there; others of us he dispersed around Britain, to keep our knowledge and practices alive for our people here. For himself, he kept nothing at all. His gold torque—for he was nobly born—and the Archdruid's jewels of office he put into the lake—the Lake of Small Stones on Môn—together with the other offerings. His very life he gave in the end, as a sacrifice to the Gods."

"Mmm," said Togi. "How, then, was I begotten?"

"By good intent," said Cunomoros seriously. "When he knew his fate, he did not think it right that his line should end with him. He hoped to beget a son who would have some part of his talent, and carry on his work. So, I think, does every man." He smiled a little. "In that, I think he succeeded."

"And his death?" asked Togi, ignoring this last. "How did he die?" Cunomoros sighed.

"This will not be easy to hear," he said, "but it is your right. He died as a sacrifice—by the triple death—at his own will, and was put into the earth at a holy place five days' journey east of here, to be the Guardian of our land. The Red Crests hold that country now, but if I can, I will take you there one day... When he was dead, I brought back for you, at his own request, the one thing from Môn that he had kept until then: his Priest's ring. It was given to him there by the Archdruid himself when he took his final vows, not long before the Red Crests came."

Togi's hand went unconsciously to the ring where he wore it still on its knotted thong inside his tunic, but his mind was dealing with Cunomoros' earlier words. "The triple death," he said slowly. "You have told me about that before, but..."

"Yes," said Cunomoros. "He died by the noose, and by the knife, and by the water. But he felt none of these; only the first blow briefly, which stunned him, before the rest was done to him. I know, for it was I who struck him; my hands held the noose and the knife, and helped to put him into the water when he was well dead." He held them up before Togi's fascinated gaze. "I was a sacrificer on Môn, Togi; I had killed men before. Not many, I grant you, but enough to know how it should be done. Lovernos did not suffer."

"So that was why Sennos laughed," said Togi after a moment, "when I told him that you were my foster-father. He said that the Gods had a sense of humor after all."

"Did he?" asked Cunomoros with a twisted smile. "Yes, that sounds like him, and it might seem that way to some... Well, that is the tale; or its bones, at least. Do you need more?"

"No," said Togi. He drew a deep breath, and let it out in a sigh. "I must think on this." He stood up abruptly. "I am going to walk on the mountain. I may be gone for some time."

"That is wise," Cunomoros said quietly. "Walk and think; take as long as you need." Togi nodded jerkily without speaking, then turned and walked away. Cunomoros watched him out of sight and sighed, then stood up and started on down the hill.

As always when he was troubled, Togi sought the high places. It was not even a conscious decision, but an instinctive turning toward the Shining One—Lugh of the Light, to whom he had made so many offerings—as a child in trouble turns to the parent he trusts. Slowly, as he climbed Penwyn, passing the manhood hut and heading up the steep track which led to the Cairn of the Old Ones, the pieces in his mind fell together to make a pattern of sorts: Sennos' face, flushed with anger; Cunomoros' face, kindly and concerned; the sacrificer's knife, equally deadly in their different hands; their dawn offerings; his own blood dripping into the bowl; the desolation of Môn; the arrogant Red Crest soldiers; and the worn silver ring, sent by a dead man to the son he would never see, to a seed planted in darkness and in hope... With his mind's eye he saw Cunomoros' lifted hands again, now stained with the blood of his blood-father, and felt the blow, and the noose, and the knife, and the dark waters of the pool, as if it were his own flesh which suffered them, his own body which died, falling into darkness... Blood shed demanded repayment or revenge, but how could he demand either from the man who had raised him, how take the blood-price for a father slain from the only father he had ever known?

On the top of Penwyn he stood still, and held up his hands to the sun. "O Shining One, Lugh of the Light," he prayed aloud, "show me the path I must go, for I think both paths—to demand or to not demand vengeance—are equally wrong." Then he gathered heather-twigs and dry bracken and built a fire, and having no other offering, cut a lock of his hair and moistened it with a few drops of his own blood, and dropped it into the flames. It burned away, leaving a silence in his mind where he had expected the words of the God. Very well, he would wait. Sitting down beside his dying fire, he composed himself for meditation.

The long summer day was drawing to an end before he had his answer. He had pulled out the ring and was playing with it, turning it between his fingers so that it caught the light. From the hand of his blood-father, by the hand of his foster-father, it had come to him: a gift, a promise, a destiny. *Father,* he thought, *I wish I could speak with you, and ask you what I should do.* And oddly, as it seemed, there came into his mind an image of the mouse which he had offered to a hungry ghost on this very mountaintop three years before. The mouse had been a helpless sacrifice; it had not consented to its fate, and therefore he, the sacrificer, had owed its spirit an offering, a sort of very small blood payment.

Lovernos, however, had died—what had Cunomoros said?—by the triple death, at his own will. That was the distinction. As well ask blood-price of the knife, or the rope, or the water, as of the man who had used them. The half-healed brand on his left arm caught his eye, and he remembered Cunomoros' hand, steady on the sacrificer's knife. No compensation was due there, either, for he had consented to that action, and by his consent had set the doer free. Consent was the answer.

He sighed and stood up stiffly. His fire was long since out. It was time to go down the mountain and face his foster-father again—as a man.

Cunomoros was in the garden, leaning on his hoe at the end of one row of beans. He had finished the hoeing, but had not yet gathered the weeds, which lay in small piles here and there between the rows. He looked tired and old, but his face as he watched Togi's approach was calm. Without speaking Togi fetched the big wicker basket and began to gather the weeds, then carried them in it to the midden. When he returned, he said, "I am sorry that I was gone so long."

"No matter," said Cunomoros. "Did you find what you sought on the mountain?"

"Yes," said Togi, and after a moment, "Thank you, Father."

"That is good, then," said Cunomoros, and smiled. And putting their tools away, they went in together for supper.

Summer in the Hills

It was customary among the tribes for the new-made warriors to spend some part of their first summer as men with the flocks and the herds in the high hills. They helped the older shepherds and cowmen, and aided the young women to milk the beasts, and to make and store the resulting butter and cheese. They also provided a first line of defense against possible cattle raiders—a not inconsiderable danger.

Togi had gone up a few days after Beltane with the last of the ewes and the late lambs. He was no shepherd, but in truth the two old men and their dogs who herded the flock had needed little help from him. He had been up to the summer pastures before, of course, but not to stay, and he was looking forward to the experience. This year he would be no one's servant boy, as he had been the last two summers when he traveled with Cingetos, but a free man among men. He took a light spear with him—a hunting spear, not his new war spear—and felt very proud.

The first person he saw when he reached the camp was Valos, Cunomoros' new student, who had come up with the first flocks. The brown lad was squatting beside the main cooking fire outside the stone-built huts, taking dark sods of peat from a coarse-woven sack and adding them to a neat pile already there. Firewood was scarce in the high pastures, but there were areas of blanket bog, and one of the young men's tasks each summer was to cut and stack slabs of peat to dry, ready for use the following year. Seeing Togi, Valos stood up, smiling and brushing his hands against the skirts of his sleeveless woolen tunic to rid them of the clinging crumbs of the dark stuff. "You are here, then," he said. "I wondered when you would come. Is all well at home?"

"Well enough." Togi gazed around the circle of low thatched buildings with interest. "Where shall I put my gear?"

"You can put it in that one," said Valos, pointing, "with mine. Come, I will show you." He led the way into one of the huts. Blinking in the dimness within, Togi followed him. "Back here," said Valos, indicating a pile of freshly cut heather and bracken beside his own bed-place. "I saved you a space, I thought it might be good if we were together."

"My thanks," said Togi, dropping his cloak and carry-sack on the pile and laying his spear across it. "Yes, it will be good to talk. Who else is here?"

"Two of your age-mates," said Valos, "Pasutagos and Vindex, and three of my foster-cousins, from my foster-father's line. The others are quartered in other huts; but some will be out with the herds at any given time." He laughed. "Otherwise we would hardly have room to move! Come out now, and I will show you the rest of the camp."

"You know it well," said Togi, following. Valos smiled.

"Like the palm of my hand. Five summers I have spent up here, since my foster-father Gennetos took my mother to wife."

"Mmm," said Togi. "I remember him. Was it this time last summer that he died?"

"Yes." Valos shrugged. "His kin amongst the shepherds still give me a place in their huts, but we are not close. I think some of them still regard me as a cuckoo in their nest."

Togi nodded. He vaguely remembered a little of the talk when old Gennetos took Valos' foreign mother and her half-Red Crest son into his house. The old man had got little good by it; she had died after two winters, leaving him to raise the boy alone, as he had promised her. "He gave you your spear at your manhood feast?"

"He did," said Valos, leading the way across the compound. "One of his own, too, though not the best. My foster-uncles and cousins have the others now." He came to a halt beside the wall of the sheep fold, empty now but for an old ewe and two small lambs, and stood leaning his hands on the lichen-covered stones. "These two," he said, "we have put to a foster-mother, since they lost their own mothers, and she her own lamb. We clothed them at first in pieces of the dead lamb's skin, to cover their foreign scent, but now they are accepted. In a few days we can let them out to pasture together, and I think all will be well." His square brown face was calm; he knew what he was saying. Togi met his friend's dark eyes with his own gray ones, and nodded.

"Yes," he said deliberately. "I think all will be well. Cunomoros asked me to continue your lessons this summer, whenever we have the time— if it pleases you."

Valos smiled. "That," he said, "would please me very much—very much indeed!"

As always, Togi woke before dawn, and lay for a moment in the stuffy darkness of the sleeping hut, wondering where he was. The snores of the other young men around him and the occasional rustle of bedding as someone turned in his sleep reminded him: he was in the summer camp. Beside him Valos' slow breathing showed that the brown lad still slept. Togi hesitated for a moment, but they had made no arrangement the night before. Besides, he wanted to be alone this first morning, to feel the spirits of the place and make his own bargains. Groping above his head, he found his belt and sandals where he had put them the night before, then quietly rose and made his way cautiously to the door.

Outside it was cool and fresh, the early stillness broken only by the distant bleating of the sheep and the occasional song of an early-waking bird. Putting on his sandals, he headed for a nearby hillock which he had picked out the day before as having a good line of sight to the east. Reaching it, he gathered a handful of dead heather twigs and a few bits of dried grass, then stood to watch the growing light. Around him the land was awake, plants and animals, birds and insects, all going about their summer business. Early bees hummed in the golden-blossomed furze, and a hunting kestrel dropped suddenly from her hovering to strike at a mouse in the grass, and rise with breakfast for her waiting chicks. Below in the camp a wisp of smoke arose as someone stirred the sleeping embers to life, and Togi, watching the glowing east, knelt to light his own small fire. A spark of light, like another fire, appeared on the shoulder of the eastern hills, and as the sun rose he lifted his voice in a song of praise, then stooped again to add his offering—a bit of last night's bannock—to the small licking flames. The day, he thought, was well begun.

"Why," asked Valos presently, as they sat together eating their breakfast porridge on the hard-packed ground outside the hut, "did you not wake me this morning?"

Togi swallowed a well-chewed mouthful before answering. "I was not sure," he said slowly, "if you would have wanted to come. Shall I wake you tomorrow?"

"Of course," said Valos. He scooped up more porridge from his bowl with his well-worn horn spoon, then paused with it halfway to his mouth. "That is, if you wish me to join you? I am not meaning to intrude."

"Mmm," said Togi, chewing again. He was still thinking. "I thought"—he swallowed—"I thought to have the first morning to myself, to be honest. But tomorrow you would be welcome. You have made the dawn offering with us—with me and my father—several times, after all."

"I have," said Valos nodding. "Thank you." He scraped the rest of the porridge from his bowl, then licked it clean. "It is strange," he said, "how right it feels to me to make that offering, for the Gods are rooted in the land, and in the people of the land—or so Cunomoros told me. And I am not of this land by blood, and only half by my raising. How then can I be acceptable to them as a Priest?"

"Mmm," said Togi again, frowning. "My blood-father was not of this land, and yet he became a Druid on Ynys Môn. I think that the Gods make their own choices." Finishing his food, he stood up. "But now I think it is time for work. What should I do today?"

"You came up with the late lambs yesterday, did you not?" said Valos. "Did you see where they are pastured?" Togi nodded. "Then go and join them, and do whatever Bro and Conn ask you to do. I will be there later, but I have tasks to finish here first. Oh, and take your spear—you should not need it, but it is always well to be prepared. Give me your bowl and I will wash it with mine." Valos grinned. "That is one of my tasks for today. Your turn will come, O Priest!" Laughing, Togi complied, and went to fetch his spear, the better to guard the sheep from non-existent dangers.

Slowly the warm days passed. The moon, which had been almost full when Togi arrived, waxed and waned, and appeared again as a slender crescent, and Midsummer came. They did not make much celebration of it in the hill camp, but Togi and Valos noted it, and held their own observances on the evening. Seeing their fire on the hillock, a few of the other youngsters drifted up to join them, until they had a small crowd. There was no heather beer with which to make merry, for the scanty grain stores in this hungry time before harvest were too precious to spend any of it in brewing, but they managed a fair amount of merriment nonetheless, singing and dancing around the fire to the beat of Valos' skin drum. It was a friendly night, a happy night, and Togi cherished the memory of it afterwards.

"Do you speak the Red Crests' tongue?" he asked Valos one morning, while the two of them were walking up together from the camp to the peat cuttings, their task for the day. "You were what, nine summers old, when you and your mother left them?"

"I was," said Valos slowly. "Yes, I spoke it in those days, but it has been so long…"

"Could you teach me such of it as you remember, then?" asked Togi.

"I could try… Why do you ask?"

"It is always good," said Togi, "to learn what one can of one's enemies."

"Ah," said Valos. "Yes, they are your enemies. Mine, too, though I carry their blood in my veins. My mother told me…" He paused, and Togi waited, walking in silence beside him, his coarse-woven peat sack slung over his left shoulder and his wooden spade swinging loosely in his right hand.

"My mother," said Valos after a while, "was of the Iceni, from the east of Britain. The Red Crests took her captive with many others after Boudicca's revolt failed—you have heard tell of it?"

"Yes," said Togi briefly. "Go on."

"They raped her," said Valos, "and afterwards sold her as a slave to a merchant, who passed her on as a favor to another man. I am not even sure which of them was my father… She did not tell me this, of course—I was only a child—but I heard her speaking of it once to a friend, and afterwards I remembered, and understood… Oh, yes, the Red Crests are my enemies, too."

"Mmm," said Togi. "In a way, then, we are brothers, for both of us got our begetting from the same cause." And he told Valos briefly what Cunomoros had told him of the destruction of Môn, but leaving out the story of Lovernos' death. That was still too personal, too close to the bone, to share. "I am luckier than you," he said at the ending. "I still have my mother and my foster-father, and blood kin all around me. But the Red Crests stole my heritage just as they stole yours. Perhaps one day we can help to win it back—brother."

"Yes," said Valos. "Perhaps we can." He stopped and held out his right hand to Togi, who grasped it strongly. "You may count on my spear beside you in that fight—brother," he said, and Togi smiled.

The moon reached her first quarter, and the month was Dumen, the Middle-of-Summer month. The weather stayed warm and dry, and the grass, which should have been abundant, withered and turned brown, so that the sheep grazed it down to the roots and had to be moved often to new pastures. Some of the cows went dry, and the butter and cheese, carefully prepared by the young women and stored in stone-lined caves dug into the hillside, was less than it should have been. Togi and his people watched the sky, but no clouds came from the west, although he and Valos increased their offerings as much as they could, sometimes going to bed hungry. The kitchen girls noticed, and gave them extra scraps, but still the Gods withheld the needed rains.

What was bad for the pastures, however, was sometimes good for the herdsmen. Valos had his eye on one of the young women, a broad-hipped lass with flaming red hair. They walked together often in the warm twilight when all of their chores were done, and on these evenings Valos came very late to bed. Togi teased him about it, and the brown lad laughed. "It is true that I fancy her," he said, and sighed. "But I doubt her father would give her to me. Still, it is sweet now and then to lie together in the summer grass, and I can dream. Are there none of the girls who appeal to you, brother?"

Togi considered the matter. "One or two, perhaps, but... Na, I am not ready for them yet. I have still too much to learn and to do, to waste my time with girls." This was not entirely true. There was one little dark-haired lass—Huctia was her name—who smiled at him sometimes when she passed, and whom he had fancied the summer before. Of late he had seen her more often with Ivomagnos, his old tormentor. It would be pleasant to take her away from Ivo, and Togi thought about it sometimes, but he could see no way to do it. Women, moreover, were unpredictable, and he was not ready to be tied down. Perhaps when he was older—seventeen, or even eighteen—but not yet.

In the meanwhile, there were other things to think about, such as hunting. Meat for the pot was always welcome, and hares were abundant on the grassy hillsides. A throw-spear was no good against them; they could twist and turn too quickly, and Togi had not thought to bring his bow. Rocks, however, were also plentiful, and he began to carry two or three good-sized pebbles in his belt pouch. At first he had no luck, but presently he got in the way of it, and hit his target more often than not. When he brought in his third kill—a big buck hare—Pasutagos, who was helping Huctia with the cooking that day, greeted him with raised eyebrows. "How," the tall youth asked, "do you do it? Are you casting a Druid's spell on them?"

Togi frowned, for that word was not to be spoken. "Na," he said, "I hit them with rocks, that is all. It is not hard."

"Not hard for you, it seems," said Pasutagos with a grin. "But for the rest of us—well! I should like to see that rock throwing!"

"Come with me tomorrow, then," said Togi, "if they can spare you here, and you will see."

The word went around that evening, and by the time Togi set out next morning he had half a dozen followers. In vain he protested that traveling in such a pack was no way to hunt hares. No one would stay behind, least of all Ivomagnos, who had happened to be visiting the camp the night before and had heard the story from Huctia. Valos was not among them, although when he had seen what was happening, he had offered to come. "Na," had said Togi. "I know that Conn is needing you with the ram lambs today, and I do not need your help in hunting hares." And when Valos was silent, he had added, "There is no danger. No ill will come to me of it." And Valos had nodded and left it at that.

Now, as he climbed the hill, scanning the grass ahead of him for any signs of movement, Togi wondered if he had been right to turn down his friend's offer. The young men following him kept well back, but he knew that some of them at least were hoping to see him fail. He was not popular with everyone; he spent too much time alone, and some of them suspected him of working magic. And in that, of course, they were not entirely wrong—only in their ideas of what that magic might entail. It was not something which could be used lightly, like an old wife's charm muttered over the cooking pots, or the string of nonsense words that kept the nightmare at bay. It was an opening of one's self to the universe, to see and feel and taste and smell everything that was around one, and by aligning one's will with that of the Gods, to work changes in the world. This much Togi knew from Cunomoros' teachings and from his own experience, although he lacked as yet the power and focus to cause great changes. One day he might own that focus, might command that power, but not yet. Unconsciously knowing which way a hare would jink next, and throwing a pebble to just that spot, was about the extent of it so far, he thought wryly. And even then, it only worked for him perhaps one time in three—but that was better than most other men could do.

A flicker of movement in the grass ahead of him distracted him from his thoughts, as a big buck hare broke cover. Togi hefted the stone he had been carrying and threw, but not quickly enough; the hare jinked and the shot missed by a hand's breadth. Behind him he heard Ivo give a crack of laughter, to be hushed by Pasutagos. "Hist!" said the tall lad. "That is only once. Go on, Togi. We will follow."

"Then follow quietly," said Togi, taking another stone from his belt pouch. He heard Ivo laugh again, but less loudly. Trying to focus his mind on his task, Togi started up the slope again. Somewhere ahead of him the hare had gone to ground. The question was, where?

This time he saw the motion at once; the hare had moved again, but in cover, and the range was too great. Even as the thought flashed through Togi's mind, his arm was already in motion. The hard-thrown rock fell short, and the hare bolted, vanishing over the brow of the hill. Behind him Ivo guffawed, and Togi whirled to face his tormentor. "If you can do better, Ivo, then come and show me the way of it. Let us advance together, and whoever hits his target first wins."

"Na, why should I do that?" asked Ivo, taken aback. "It is you who claims to be such a good shot, and not I."

"Ah," said Togi, and suddenly smiled. "You admit, then, that you cannot do better! That is good hearing!" One or two of the other youngsters laughed, but Ivo frowned.

"I did not say that!" he protested. "I am as good a shot with a stone as you any day—na, I am better!"

"Then why not take my challenge?" asked Togi, grinning. "Show me what you can do, and I will admit it! Is that not fair?" he asked the others.

"Fair indeed!" laughed Pasutagos, and little dark Vindex echoed him. "Yes, Ivo, show us what you can do!"

Ivo shook his head like a baffled bull, but he could see no way out. "Oh, very well," he grumbled. "Yes, I will show you what I can do, little priestling." Bending to a stony patch on the hillside, he grubbed up two or three pebbles at random. "I am ready," he said. "Let us start. Only do not get too close to me, and spoil my aim!"

"No danger of that," grinned Togi, and the other young men laughed. "I am not wanting your embrace!"

Ivo glared at him. "Be careful you do not provoke it, then," he said. "You would not enjoy it! Now, let us start!" And he set off up the hill. Togi followed him, a little behind and to one side, still grinning.

The next hare they flushed was too far away to hit, but Ivo threw regardless. His stone fell harmlessly a spear's length behind the creature, and the others laughed again. Ivo's ruddy face grew redder still, and his scowl darker, but Togi said nothing, and they went on up the hill.

For some time they climbed in silence. Perhaps, thought Togi, there were no more hares left in that area. Ivo was muttering to himself, and Togi heard one or two whispers in the group behind him. Maybe they would all give up and go back soon.

Even as he thought this, he knew that he was wrong. A big hare bolted suddenly out of its form close ahead of him, and Togi threw at once. His stone struck the running animal in the head, and it fell stunned, tumbling forward as the last kick of its strong hind legs made it somersault. Ivo, taken by surprise, threw even as it was falling, and missed by a hand's-breadth. Then Togi was running forward to collect his prize. The stunned hare was still breathing, and he finished it off quickly least it recover and escape. Then Ivo was there, confronting him. "That was not fair!" he cried. "You distracted me by throwing from behind me!"

Togi laughed. "Is it my fault you were unprepared? What a hunter you are, Ivo! Own now that I am the better shot—*you* cannot hit a dead hare, much less one that is running!"

The other young men laughed, and Ivo scowled. "Maybe not," he said, "but I can hit *you*!" And he lobbed his remaining stone straight at Togi's head.

Startled, Togi threw himself sideways, and the stone only grazed his left ear. There were shouts from the others, but he ignored them, standing poised on the balls of his feet, ready to dodge again or to fight, and meeting Ivo's eyes. He thought for a moment that the big young man was going to charge him; he looked like murder. Then Pasutagos, running forward, grabbed Ivo by his shoulder and spun him around. "Enough!" he cried. "You might have killed him!"

Furious, Ivo tore himself free. "Na, I could not!" he spat out. "He is too fast!" And he turned toward camp.

"Ivo!" called Togi, and Ivo looked back. Something in Togi's appearance stopped him.

"What do you want now?" he asked impatiently.

"The next stone you throw," said Togi softly, "will be your death."

Ivo laughed. "Is that a threat, priest-boy?"

"Na," said Togi. His eyes were wide and dark, looking through and beyond Ivo at something only he could see. "Na. It is a promise."

Ivo laughed again and turned away, and most of the others followed him, but Pasutagos and Vindex did not move. After a moment Togi drew a deep breath and let it out in a sigh.

"Your ear is bleeding," observed Vindex dispassionately. Togi put up a hand to feel it, then looked at the blood on his fingers in surprise. He had not felt the pain until now.

"It is nothing," he said.

"Why did you say what you said?" asked Pasutagos. "You looked—strange."

"I do not know," said Togi slowly. "But I spoke the truth… Come on, I want to take this"—he lifted the dead hare by its hind legs—"back to camp before I join the shepherds. We have already wasted too much of the morning with throwing stones."

The moon waxed, and waned, and waxed again to her first quarter, and the month was Riuros, the End-of-Summer month. Lughnasa would fall late this year, but in the meantime the work went on, in the valleys and on the hilltops. Riuros was sheep-shearing month.

Togi had no skill with the big iron shears, and this was work for experts. His task was to collect the heavy, stinking fleeces into bundles and carry them to the storage area. Presently they would be taken down the mountain by pack-ponies, where they would be washed and carded, dyed and combed and spun by the women, who would spend the winter weaving them into cloth on the big bottom-weighted vertical looms to provide next year's new clothes. Any extra could be traded for other goods, for the cloaks made from the wool of the mountain sheep were valued throughout Britain and beyond.

Valos was in the thick of the shearing. Although no match in strength or experience for some of the older men, he had a deft hand with the shears and an endurance which many others his age lacked. Togi was impressed; he had thought himself as fit as any his age, but the brown lad far outstripped him. Laughing, he commented on it one evening, but Valos only smiled. "You have spent more time exercising your mind than I have," he said, "and it shows. You can memorize a new song or chant in one or two hearings, while I stumble after five. I have had only my body's skills with which to make my way, and so I have had to make the best of them. Each of us makes what he can of what he was given."

Togi was silent for a while, thinking what to reply. The two of them were heading for the little stream which flowed past the camp, planning to wash off some of the day's sweat and dirt. The water was low from the dry summer, but still cool and clear between the gray boulders of its bed. Someone in the distant past had built a rough dam across it at a little distance from the huts, and the resulting pool was a popular spot on warm evenings.

"It is true," he said at last, "that I have spent my life so far in study whenever I could. A Druid Priest is not made in a season, or in a handful of years, and it was to be a Priest that I was born. But a good shepherd is as valuable in his way, I think, as a good Priest."

"Our laws do not say so," said Valos wryly. "When we both come to our full strength, your honor-price will be higher than mine. Is it not so?"

"It is," said Togi, "supposing we still live under our own laws by then, and not those of the Red Crests. I have heard—" He broke off, listening to the sounds of splashing and laughter from the pool ahead. "I think we will have company tonight."

"That should be good," said Valos, and then, as an afterthought, "Ivo has gone back down again."

"Good," said Togi, and smiled. "I can do without his company."

"He has lost face," said Valos, "and will want to win it back again."

"I know," said Togi quietly. "But—*hai*, Vindex, Pasutagos, is it only you? I thought from the noise that it was a herd of bullocks splashing here, at least!"

"Come in and join us, then," called Vindex, "and we shall be *two* herds!" And he threw himself belly-down again in the water with a great *smack*. Wasting no time, Togi and Valos stripped off their tunics and leapt in to join the others, rolling and splashing in the chest-deep pool.

"So," said Pasutagos presently, drifting lazily on his back, "how is the sheep-shearing going?" He and Vindex had been with the cow-herds that day.

"Almost over," said Valos. "Perhaps another five score of them, by the tally sticks. After that it will be time for the marking, before we separate the lambs."

"In good time, then," said Vindex. "Will you be going down to help with the reaping soon?"

"Na," said Valos, "I stay with the sheep."

"I will be starting down soon with the pack-ponies," said Togi. "Are you going, Pasutagos?"

"Not yet," said Pasutagos, yawning. "Someone has to stand guard, after all, against cattle raids. Now is the likely time, and I am the best warrior in our year."

"Hear him!" said Vindex, grinning. "O great warrior!" And swinging his arm, he sent a wave rippling across Pasutagos' face, so that the blond lad choked and spluttered, and came up swinging blindly. His response hit Togi, who splashed him back in turn; soon water was flying everywhere. At last they stopped, panting and laughing, and subsided again. "*Hai mai!*" said Vindex then. "What warriors we all are!"

The sound of laughter made them all turn. Three young women stood on the path watching them. "What warriors indeed!" said one, a shapely redhead. "Will you drown all your enemies as you have done yourselves?"

"Come in and see!" cried Vindex. "There is room!"

"And still a little water left as well," said Valos, smiling. "Come and join us, Casta."

The redhead laughed. "Will I be safe, with such wild men?"

"With me, you will be" said Pasutagos promptly. Vindex laughed.

"And why is that, brother?" he asked slyly. "Can we guess?"

Pasutagos reddened. "I did not mean—" he began, pushing back his wet yellow hair, but Valos interrupted.

"Huctia, Seda, come and join us. The water is fine."

Little brown-haired Seda giggled, but dark-haired Huctia took up the challenge. "Why not!" she cried. "Come, sisters, together we will be safe enough." Untying her belt, she dropped it, then unpinned one shoulder of her worn linen dress and let it fall, and the other two copied her. Then, seizing their hands, she led them into the water with much laughter. Vindex held out his hands to her, but she ignored him. Her eyes slid over Togi, who had been all this time silent; she looked at Pasutagos and smiled. "Will you keep me safe, great warrior?" she said.

Pasutagos blushed like fire, and stammered an answer. Huctia laughed and took his hand. Casta had joined Valos, and they were laughing and joking together. Vindex was doing his best to attach Seda. Togi had a sinking feeling: what could he do to keep from being left alone? Then, in his mind, he heard Cunomoros' remembered voice: *if ever you are pursued, do the thing unexpected.* Certainly he was not pursued, but… Suddenly he laughed. "Vindex!" he called, wading toward them. "Look what is coming!" And he pointed to one side.

"What?" Vindex turned his head. Under the water, Togi tripped him, and he fell backwards with a splash, his hands flailing wildly. While he was still struggling to get to his feet again, Togi reached out to take Seda's hand.

"You see this poor fellow cannot even stand up, he is so unsteady!" he said, grinning. "You had better come with me—you will be safer!" Seda laughed, then laughed again as Vindex surged up dripping, his wet black hair blinding him.

"But will *you* be safer?" she asked. "I do not think…"

"I will, if I stand behind you," said Togi quickly, as Vindex cleared his eyes and glared at him. "Perhaps *you* can protect *me* ?" Seda laughed again.

"Yes, I think I can," she said. Togi slipped quickly behind her and put his hands on her bare brown shoulders. Her skin was smooth and soft, and a loose lock of her hair brushed his fingers. A shock ran through him, but he kept his eyes on Vindex, who was looking uncertain.

"I feel safer already," said Togi, still grinning. Reluctantly Vindex laughed.

"My vengeance will come," he said lightly, "and it will be terrible."

Togi laughed. "You can see me already shaking with terror," he said. "Now go away, and—and help the cooks with supper! Seda and I have many things to discuss." Vindex grinned and went.

Togi stoked his hands slowly down Seda's arms, then turned her to face him. She smiled. "That was well done," she said.

Her eyes were deep blue; her young breasts were pale and pointed, with pink nipples. She looked up at him with unshadowed friendliness. Slowly, carefully, he bent and kissed her.

Soon there was no more splashing in the pool. Above it the birds sang in the summer silence, undisturbed except for the distant bleating of the sheep.

Revolt!

The harvest was poor that year. The dry summer was followed by unseasonable rains just before Lughnasa, which beat down the grain and left it moldering in the fields. At least the five years of tribute were over: they would only have to share their salvaged crop with the King—or so the people thought, until the Red Crests came again.

They were not entirely unexpected; the rumor had gone round the valleys some days before. King Regenos had protested unavailingly, but the Red Crest officer in Segontium would not listen: his orders came from the provincial governor Julius Frontinus in Londinium, he said, and any appeal must go there. Regenos had sent messengers, for what good it would do him; in the meantime the tribute carts creaked their way up the valleys, under rather heavier guard than had been customary of late. They came to Togi's valley on a sunny autumn day near the end of Anagan, the Harvest Month, when the young men and boys were bringing in the last of the late apples from the orchard.

Togi put down his basket of apples near the entrance to the feast hall, and stood staring with the rest. A crowd was gathering as the news went round: old men and women, boys and girls, warriors and young wives, muttering angrily to each other or silently watching. Bratronos the Chieftain pushed his way through them to confront the Red Crest officer. "Why are you here?" he asked with dignity. "We have paid our five years; it is over."

"I am here on orders," said the officer. His British was not bad, though he spoke with a heavy accent; he must have been some years in the province. "I have come to collect the usual tax. Tell your people to stand aside."

"There must be some mistake," said Bratronos. "We owe you no *tax*, we are a free people. You must talk to our King."

"Your king has no authority over me," said the officer patiently. "Only the Emperor and those he has set over me can command me, and their command is that I should collect the tax from you. Tell your people to stand aside, and no one will be hurt."

"We could not pay you your *tax* even if it were due," said Bratronos with rising anger. "The harvest was bad; we have barely enough for ourselves this year. If you take our grain, we will starve."

"That is nothing to do with me," said the officer. "I am here to collect the tax; I cannot remit it. For the last time, tell your people to stand aside."

"No!" said Bratronos. He planted his feet more firmly and glared at the officer. He was a big burly man, past middle age but still strong, and he towered over the Red Crest. "I will not stand aside. I have sworn to defend the life of my people, and I will do so to my last breath. Let you go back to your ruler and tell him we will not pay."

The officer sighed, and spoke some words loudly in his own language. His soldiers, who had been leaning casually on their big red shields, lifted them and locked them in line. At another command they drew their swords and started forward, leaving a momentary gap through which the officer stepped back, and closing it when they had passed him. As they reached Bratronos the closest one struck him on the side of the head with the flat of his sword, then hit him again with his shield as the Briton crumpled. Stepping over his body, they continued their steady advance. Women screamed, children shrieked and ran. Some of the younger men and boys, caught weaponless, tried to grapple with the soldiers bare-handed, while others, Togi among them, picked up stones and pieces of firewood. Already blood was flowing.

The officer called another command in his language, and the line of soldiers halted. "All of you," he cried then in British, "stop fighting and go to your homes. Let us collect the tax and we will leave you in peace. Otherwise we will burn the thatch over your heads."

"Not before we kill you, Red Crest," called Ivomagnos, and threw a stone at the officer. It struck him on his armored shoulder, and he staggered, then barked another order to his men. Several of them sheathed their swords, seized one of the short javelins they carried behind their shoulders, and began to throw them. Ivo took the first one through his throat, and fell with a strangled cry. Togi, sighting on the man who had thrown it, let fly his stone, then ducked as another javelin hissed past his ear.

"Stop!" It was Bratronos, who had staggered to his feet, bruised and bleeding. "Stop fighting, O my people! This is not the time! This is not the place! Stop fighting, and listen to me!"

The Red Crest officer barked another order, and the soldiers ceased to throw. Slowly the Britons gave back before them and stood silently waiting. Bratronos limped forward, ignoring the Red Crests, and passed through the line of shields. He stopped beside Ivo's body, which lay motionless in the dust, his blood pooling darkly under him.

"We will take payment for this day, O my warriors," he said then, "and it will be a rich revenge. But if we fight now, our women and children will die. We will meet these Red Crest thieves on the battlefield, and show them there what men are made of. But not here, not now. Our day will come." He turned to face the Red Crest line. "Take what you came for today, and go. But if you come back again, we will pay you in steel and in blood."

"Grain will do for today," said the officer. He spoke to his men, and they stacked their shields, then tramped their way to the granary. The people of the village, Togi among them, stood stone-faced and silent, watching as their winter's food was taken away. He knew that it was no longer a question of whether war would come, but only of when. He did not need his *awen* to know that it would be soon.

As Ivo's body was being carried away by his silent kinsmen, Togi found himself suddenly face to face with Lugotorix. "Well," said Lugo tersely, "you were right, three years ago: he fell in his first fight, and he will not be much mourned. Can you prophesy now what will come of it? I could use some good news."

"Na," said Togi, shaking his head. "It does not work like that; the *awen* comes when it will."

"A pity," said Lugo. "We will have to make do with other things, then. I did not love Ivo, but he was a man of the tribe, and I will have blood for his blood if I can."

"I think there will be plenty of that," said Togi, "plenty for all of us." And turning, he walked away, leaving Lugo staring after him.

Cunomoros was in the garden, not hoeing for a change, but inspecting the root crops. "I wish," he said absently, "that I had planted more parsnips this year... You are unhurt?"

"Yes," said Togi. "You have heard, then?"

"Enough," said Cunomoros, and sighed. "Was anyone seriously injured? Other than Ivo, I mean."

"None that I saw," said Togi. "But—Father, I predicted it—his death, I mean—three years ago...and again in the summer camp!"

"Yes," said Cunomoros, looking at him for a moment. "There is always a first time... But predicting is not causing, unless you misuse it of intent. The *awen* comes when it will; you are only the instrument through which it breathes. Strive only to be a pure one."

"I will remember," said Togi soberly.

"Yes," said Cunomoros, and smiled a little. "You will."

It was half a moon later, near the middle of Ogron, the Middle-of-Autumn month, when the next news came round: King Regenos had summoned the leaders of all the tribes to a council. It was Cingetos who brought the summons, and stayed the night to discuss it. After the tumult in the feast-hall was over—for of course every man there had to have his say, usually more than once—he came to Cunomoros' hut for a last cup of ale before turning in. "I did my best," he said sighing, "to explain what I understand very imperfectly myself... Regenos is angry and upset, of course, but it is more than that. He knows how hard this winter will be for all our people."

"Why," asked Cunomoros, "did the Red Crests demand another year's tax?"

"Do I know?" said Cingetos wearily. "Na, but I think—or at least, I have heard it suggested—that the commander at Segontium wanted the taxes for himself. A bitter irony—I am sure you will laugh with me!—is that Regenos' appeal to the Governor in Londinium, while it did us no good, spoiled his plan as well: Frontinus will take most of the profit now, such of it as does not go to Rome, leaving the commander no better off than he was before… So, at least, say the words on the wind." He drank more ale. "They are all of them a corrupt people, the Red Crests, rotten clean through with this insane lust for gold. It is more to them than honor, or praise, or fame. And yet they are so strong—so bitterly, coldly strong, like their own steel. How can men live so?"

"I do not know," said Cunomoros, shaking his head. "I have never understood them. I only know that in pursuit of their madness, they may be our destruction." He turned to Togi, who was listening silently. "Is there more ale in the pitcher? We are too gloomy tonight."

"A little," said Togi, looking, and poured the rest into Cunomoros' cup. "I can go up to the hall and get more, for our honored guest." And he gave Cingetos a half smile.

"Na, we will send your brother," said Cunomoros. "Tritos, go and get us more ale."

"Yes, Father," said the boy, and taking the pitcher, ran out.

"A good lad," said Cingetos. "And that brings me to another thought… Togi, would you like to come with me to this council? It would be good for you, I think, so see how such decisions are made—or not made, as the case may be."

"I should like to come," said Togi, "if you can spare me, Father?"

"For a few days, I think we can," said Cunomoros. "But Cingetos, what is the council to decide? You were interrupted before you could explain."

"Na, I am not sure myself," said Cingetos. "But the talk all through the mountains is that we have borne enough, and more than enough, from the Red Crests; it is time we pushed them back—if we can. I told you about the Silures, did I not?"

"How the Red Crests defeated them last summer? Yes. Is there more?"

"A little. Some of their leaders have sought refuge with the King, and are loud in urging him to make war on our common enemy."

"Mmm," said Cunomoros. "Words are cheap when you risk nothing, having nothing left to lose."

"So I think," said Cingetos, and fell silent. Tritos came back with the ale jug, and filled first the Bard's cup, and then his father's. Togi shook his head when the jug came to him; he was thinking.

"What strength do the Red Crests have in Segontium?" he asked Cingetos. "Could we defeat them?"

"That is a good question," said Cingetos, "and I do not know the answer. I think we might, if we could lure them out of their fortress, but that could be hard. There are a few of them on Môn as well, and more in their bases in the south, holding down the Silures."

"Môn," said Togi thoughtfully. "I did not see many of them there two summers ago… Could we take it back?"

"Um," said Cingetos, scratching his thin red beard. "I do not know. Perhaps, but we would have to deal with Segontium first."

"It is good land on Môn, is it not, Father?" said Togi.

"The best," said Cunomoros.

"Remember that thought, then," said Cingetos, "when you come to the council. Although I doubt you will be the only one to think of it…" He drank off his ale, and yawned. "I am for bed now," he said. "We will have a long ride tomorrow." When he had gone Togi banked the fire and joined his brother under their shared blankets, back against warm back. Tritos was soon snoring, but Togi lay awake for a while, thinking of Môn as he had seen it, as it once had been, and as it might be again.

The short autumn day was already dying behind the shoulders of Yr Wyddfa with sullen banners of red and gray cloud when the two of them reached the steep track which led to Dinas Brân. With the oaks and ashes of the valleys stripped of their leaves, and the mountains wearing tattered cloaks of new snow, Togi thought that the fortress hill looked a much grimmer place than it had in summer. The guard posts were well manned, however, and torches burned brightly in the King's crowded courtyard when they clattered to a halt there. "See what you can do for us in the stables," said Cingetos as they dismounted. "I doubt there is much room, either there or in the hall, but I will find us bed-space somewhere—with

Orgetos if nowhere else." He grinned. "It is my right as *bardd teulu* to sleep in the Captain's lodging if I wish, though I do not often wish it!"

Togi unloaded their gear as usual and took the ponies to the stables, where the chief groom, after some argument, found space for them. Then he followed Cingetos more slowly to the hall, looking about him as he went. Here and there he saw a familiar face, but not the one he was seeking. He had not asked the Bard what had come to Sennos in the past year, and he was curious as to what the old man's position might be in these changed and perilous times. If the Red Crests could be pushed back, it might be safe to publically call oneself a Druid again...

Sennos was not in the hall, but a great many other people were—mostly the young men of the war-band, but with a fair admixture of graybeards. These, Togi thought, would be the headmen from those valleys which had first received news of the council. His own people would probably arrive tomorrow; he and Cingetos had ridden ahead. He stacked their gear with a pile of others' near the back of the hall, and looked for a place to sit on the crowded benches. He had just found one when there came a lull in the hall noise, and the King came in.

Regenos looked much as he had the year before, if less genial, but his reddish hair and beard would not show gray for some years yet. Not so for dark-haired Orgetos, who followed him in. It was the third man of the party, however, who drew Togi's gaze. Sennos' hair, which had been gray-streaked two years before, was now as white as bleached bone, and there was a stoop to his thin shoulders which had not been there before, as if his years weighed heavily on him; but his pale eyes were as keen as ever, and were searching the hall for new faces even as he found his seat. They paused for a moment on Togi, and he knew himself recognized, and then dismissed. The dawn offering, he thought, would tell him more; but clearly Sennos, now taking his seat at the high table, was still a power in the King's court.

The feast that night was less rich than in former years; even the King's court was feeling some effects of the bad harvest; but meat and mead were still plentiful, and Togi took his share. Cingetos did not sing that night, but spent a while talking with the King and with some of the other men at his high table. Two of them caught Togi's eye: burly broad-shouldered men with brown weather-beaten faces and curly black hair and beards, whose richly colored clothes looked much the worse for wear. They sat close to the King, but not immediately beside him: visitors, perhaps, but not of the first rank. Working his way through a generous platter of boiled cow-meat, Togi thought that they might be the exiled leaders of the Silures whom Cingetos had mentioned. They had a look of defeated men: a sort of sullen anger mixed with shame, such as he had seen in Lugo's face after the Red Crests came. He wondered what they would have to say in the council.

"Well," said Cingetos cheerfully when the feasting was over, and the King and his councilors had gone, "I think I have found a better place for us than Orgetos' lodging, where all the talk will be of war tonight. Bring our blankets and follow me." Curious, Togi did as he was bidden, and followed the Bard as Cingetos wove his way through the compound, stopping at last before a plain wooden hut not far from the southern cliff-edge. When he tapped on the doorframe a man's voice bade them enter. Togi followed the Bard into a warm smoky herb-scented room dimly lit by the fire in a brazier. "This is my sometime student," said Cingetos to the room's inhabitants. "Togi, this is Lucotios, the King's physician, and his daughter Resta. They have offered us bed-space here while the council fills the feast-hall."

"Greetings, Togi," said the tall gray-haired man by the brazier. "I remember you from two summers ago, although you may not remember me." But Togi did not hear him; he was gazing at the girl beside Lucotios as if he had never seen a woman before. For small and slender though she was, with a tangle of pale hair turned to spun gold by the firelight, and wide dark eyes which looked back at him with friendly curiosity, it was clear that she was a woman and not a child. Togi felt a tide of heat surge up his body into his face, and was aware that he was blushing. He blinked, and turned his attention belatedly to his host.

"I think I remember seeing you, lord," he said, "but I had no speech with you." He was still aware of the girl with every fiber of his being, but dared not look at her again. "Where shall I put our blankets?"

"Over there will do," said Lucotios, pointing. "Resta, bring cups and wine for our guests. You will take a cup, Cingetos—or did you have enough in hall?"

"Na," said Cingetos, "I will drink with you gladly, old friend—I spent most of my time in hall tonight talking, and there is a thirst on me still. Togi, if you bring the rest of our gear, I think Lucotios will give it house-room for a while."

"Gladly," said Lucotios.

"I will fetch it, then," said Togi, and left them. He was glad for the chance to recover himself in private. The cold night air felt good on his flushed face, but could not still the tumult raging in his body. How could the mere sight of a girl, he wondered, have such an effect on him? He was uneasily aware that he must have behaved like a fool. And he was going to be sleeping in the same room with her tonight... He took his time about his errand, but eventually he had to go back. This time when he pushed the door curtain aside, he saw only Cingetos and Lucotios, sitting on either side of the brazier with cups of wine in their hands.

"Na," Lucotios was saying, shaking his head, "I do not know what is in his mind. I am no diviner like Sennos, to trace the future in a cock's intestines, or the fall of a handful of yarrow stalks. I do not plan wars; I only try to repair the results." Then seeing Togi, he smiled. "Come and join us, lad. There is a cup here waiting for you, and Resta has gone to get us more wine. It was a long ride you had today; you will both be tired, and ready soon for your beds, but another cup will not harm you."

"I will be glad of it," said Cingetos, and laughed. "You keep better drink than I get in the King's hall, old friend."

"Regenos is generous to me," said Lucotios. "The fruit of the grape is one of the few good things the Red Crests have brought us. I got the taste for it when I sojourned in Gaul, long years ago; it is a good medium for many draughts, and strengthening by itself."

"Were you a long time in Gaul, lord?" asked Togi, taking a stool by the brazier, and raising the cup Lucotios gave him to cautiously taste it. He had never drunk wine before. Sweet and harsh together, he thought, like bramble-mead mixed with sloes. He rather liked it.

"Yes, lad," said Lucotios, "I spent a score of years there, from when I was a youngling like you, traveling with my father, and never thought to end my days in Britain. I met my girl's mother there, wooed and wed her…" He sighed, and drank more wine.

"Was she much like her daughter?" asked Cingetos, regarding his empty cup with sorrow.

"She was," said Lucotios. "Blithe and fair as midsummer, and wise with it… She died in childbed, and our son with her; all my skill and knowledge could not save her. After that, Gaul had no savor for me; I came back to the north, where I began… Ah, Resta! Did you get it, then?"

"I did," said the girl, coming into the firelight. "Let me fill your cup, Father."

"Tend to our guests first, love," said Lucotios amiably, and she filled Cingetos' cup, then turned to fill Togi's. He held it steady with an effort; she stood so close that he could feel her warmth, and catch a trace of her scent, half woman and half sweet herbs. He felt the heat rise in his face again, and was too tongue-tied to thank her before she moved on to fill her father's cup.

"Ah!" said Cingetos, smacking his lips. "Each cup is better than the last!"

"The steward was already abed," said Resta, smiling. "Matura got this for me from the King's own store; she is still grateful to you for curing her grandson's fever." Lucotios laughed.

"What a well-trained daughter I have!" he said.

Resta smiled. "Why, I have had a cunning father to teach me," she said.

"What have you heard around the court," Cingetos asked her, "about this possible war? For I think you hear things that your father and I would not hear."

"Very little," said Resta, and her laughter was quenched. It made her look suddenly older. "Only what any woman would say."

"Which is?" asked Cingetos.

"That neither war nor peace will be good," said Resta seriously, "for in both we will lose things of value. If we do not fight, our people starve, and if we do fight, our warriors die in battle. There is death before us either way."

"That is true, and more than true," said Lucotios, and sighed. "Ah, me! Fill up our cups again, daughter, and yours as well: we need what merriment we may achieve while life is yet with us."

They drank, and drank again. By the time he sought his bed, Togi's head was spinning with the wine. He carried with him into sleep a memory of Resta's face, flushed with drink and firelight, her pale hair and dark shining eyes, and the sweet shape of her body beneath her woolen kirtle. His dreams were strange and restless, and his sleep disturbed.

When he woke at last, it was to see Resta rekindling the fire, blowing the banked coals in the brazier to life in the predawn darkness much as his mother did every morning with their hearth fire at home. He lay and watched her for a few minutes, then rolled out of his cloak and sat up. Seeing the movement, she smiled at him. "Good morning," she said softly, so not to disturb the others. "You are awake early."

"Always." Togi rubbed his face and yawned, then combed his fingers roughly though his thick dark hair. It was shoulder length now and still growing—a man's hair, not a boy's. He stood up, wrapping his cloak around him. "I go to make the dawn offering with Sennos."

"Ah. So it is a—a Priest—that you are, and not a Bard?"

"Half a Priest, at least." He smiled at her sleepily, no longer disturbed by her presence. "Do you and your father breakfast in the hall?"

"Most days," said Resta, smiling back. "But times like this, when the hall is full of visitors, I make griddle-cakes for us here."

"Will there be some for me, when I come back?" asked Togi.

"There might be," said Resta, "if we do not eat them all first." She grinned.

"Then I shall hope," said Togi, grinning back, and went out quietly, leaving her to her baking.

The sun was not yet up, but the sky was bright and clear. Togi made his way to the cliff top above the altar. There was no sign of Sennos, so he waited, looking up at the silent snows on the crest of Yr Wyddfa. As always that high place drew him; someday, he thought, he must climb there: what a place it would be to greet the dawn! Just as the first rosy light touched the mountain's top, he heard rapid footsteps, and turned to face them. "Good morning, Honored One," he said.

"So it *was* you in the hall last night," said Sennos. "I thought so, but after two years… Take the basket, we are late."

It was true; the sunlight was creeping down the high ridges. Togi took the basket and followed the old man down the steep stone steps. The ledge seemed smaller than he remembered, and the altar still held the ashes of the previous day's fire. Sennos brushed them roughly away and built a new fire with wood from the pile kept there. The offering which he took from his basket was a fresh barley loaf and a small jug of ale. He did not explain his lack of a blood sacrifice, and Togi did not ask. Something in Sennos' face made him very aware of the drop behind him.

When the dawn prayers were over and the fire had been quenched, he followed the old Druid back up the stairs. Sennos took the basket from him with a muttered, "Thank you," and walked away as rapidly as he had come. Almost, thought Togi, watching his departure thoughtfully, as if he wanted to avoid any questions… He shook his head, and turned back toward Lucotios' hut. There might still be griddle cakes, and he was hungry.

The council began the following evening. All day the last stragglers had been making their way up the hill; the feast hall was full to overflowing, and there were lords of fifty spears bedding down in the stables with their horses. Togi felt himself fortunate to sleep on Lucotios' floor, although he was still not as comfortable in Resta's presence as he would have liked. It was nothing that he could predict: a look, a touch, the fall of light along her cheek, or the scent of her shining hair: any of these things, or a dozen other, could wake the tumult in his blood. Then a tide of heat would rise into his face again, and his tongue would stumble on the simplest of words. He would have liked to be away from her, yes; and he would have liked to be away from her, no: he craved her company as meat craves salt. He was glad of the morning offerings, for then, at least, his mind was single; however much he might distrust Sennos, in that situation he could wholly trust himself. The beginning of the King's council, however chaotic, was a welcome distraction.

And chaotic it was. The benches were full, and the floor; the heat of the packed bodies in the hall exceeded even that of the central hearth-fires; and the noise, as men struggled to be heard, or shouted each into his fellow's ear, seemed to shake the very roof-beams. The King's silencer pounded in vain on the pillars for quiet; but at last Orgetos' stentorian bellows made themselves heard, and gradually the noise died away to a grating surf-sound of grumbling whispers. Over it, the King's clerk began to call a list of names, and strong male voices answered. Togi saw many men whose faces he remembered from two summers ago: minor lords of hill forts, chieftains of small farming or herding communities like his own, headmen of fishing villages: all the people whose lives were threatened by the Red Crests' latest demands. No women, of course, except for the few who peered in around the door-curtains: this was a meeting for men, although men and women alike would feel its aftermath. This decision was for the warriors of all of the tribes to make; although the King would hold the casting vote for war or peace, he would go against his people's decision at his peril.

Regenos opened the discussion. "You all know why you are here," he said. "The Red Crests have broken the treaty we agreed on five years ago; they have come stealing our harvests, and they threaten us with war and ravaging if we resist. Only last summer they attacked our neighbors to the south, the Silures, and enslaved them. Now they treat us as if we too are already their slaves, to be dealt with as they wish. If we make no resistance, they will go on, loading us with one indignity after another, until we wake one day to find ourselves slaves indeed, with their shackles on our wrists, and our freedom a forgotten dream. I say we must fight them now, while there is still time. Does anyone disagree?"

Several voices spoke at once, interrupting each other. Regenos raised his own over them. "Softly, softly! Carnos, you first, then Maiorix. After that, we will see."

"O King," said Carnos, a big burly red-haired man who was head of a fishing village on the north coast, "how can we fight them? They are too many. If they could crush the Silures in a summer, can they not do the same to us?" There were murmurs of agreement, but not many. Togi, watching from his perch on a pile of gear at the back of the hall, saw many heads shaken. "All very well for you, Carnos," cried a man nearby, "you can always catch more fish. It is not your whole summer's labor they are stealing, with no chance to replace it until next harvest!"

"Quiet, there," called Orgetos. "Wait your turn, Ambiorix."

"Na," said Regenos. "Let him speak, for he has truth in his words. What would you say to that, Carnos? Can you feed the mountain folk with your fish, as well as your own people?"

"Na, you know that I cannot," said Carnos angrily.

"Shall we starve, then, while you fish in peace?" asked Ambiorix. A chorus of voices were raised in agreement. Carnos' red face flushed darker in response. Regenos held up a hand.

"Enough for now," he said. "Let Maiorix speak."

"My thanks, O King," said Maiorix, a grizzled elder with a gray mane and beard as curly as a ram's fleece. "Carnos and Ambiorix have both made good points. True it is that we cannot sustain the Red Crests' plundering of our harvests for much longer, when even in good years we barely have enough for ourselves. True it is also that they are strong, too strong for us to defeat alone in open battle. Yet a pack of hounds, working together, can bring down a stag or a wild boar which could easily kill any one of them alone. How, then, if we look beyond our own borders for allies? All the tribes of Britain are not yet enslaved, and even our brothers the Silures might still throw off their chains and stand beside us. The Red Crests cannot fight us all at once."

"There is truth in what you say," agreed Regenos, "and I have already sent messages to some of the other tribes. But such plans take time. Who else will speak against war?"

There was a sea-surge of voices, but no one took up the challenge. After a few minutes a lean dark man near the front of the hall called out, "I would speak, O King."

"Do so, then, Camulos," said Regenos. Camulos half-turned to face the others.

"Most of you know me," he said. "I scratch out a living with my cousins in the hills above Aber Seint, which the Red Crests call Segontium. But I was not born there. My family were fishers and farmers on Môn, before the Red Crests came. The earth of that island is clay of our clay; her rocks are bone of our bones, her rivers flow in our blood. I remember the richness of her fields, the abundance of her harvests. Who holds Môn need never hunger, for she can grow grain to feed all Eryri. She is a prize worth having, a fortress worth defending. This is our chance to take her back—we may never get another!"

There were voices raised in agreement: "Môn! Take back Môn!"

"A good plan, if we could do it," said Regenos. "But can we? There is still the question of numbers, of strength."

"There may be many and many of the Red Crests in Britain," said Camulos. "I do not know. But there are only ten score of them, at most, at Caer Seint—I have seen them and numbered them, I and my cousins who work beneath their walls. And on Môn herself there are far less, only a few hands of them. Let us once take back that island, and they cannot dislodge us."

"They did so once before," cried a dissenter. "Ask Sennos—he was there."

"Yes," called another man, "ask Sennos! Ask the Druid!" At the forbidden word, a little shiver of silence went through the crowd. Togi felt it in himself; it stroked down his spine like ice. For a moment there was a darkness in his sight, a roaring in his ears; he wanted to cry out a warning, but he struggled against the words which were choking him. This was no time or place for prophecy. Man though he was now in years, in this company he was still little more than a boy in experience, and unknown to most of those here. He took a deep breath, and another; his vision cleared, and he saw Sennos standing beside the King.

"Yes," the old man was saying, his deep voice ringing through the hall, "I was there. I saw the battle, and the destruction. Ask what you will of me, and I will answer. But this I tell you truly." He paused, and there was silence, a silence so profound that his listeners might have been turned to stone. Into that silence he spoke, measuring out his words like pieces of silver dropped into a deep pool. "Môn was ours once, and can be again. If we win her back, I think that we can hold her, but our success or failure lies with all of you. As for me, I will give my last drop of blood, my last breath of life, to cleanse her of the Red Crest filth, and keep her free."

"Free for the Druids to rule there again?" called one voice. Sennos shook his head.

"Na," he said slowly, "we will never rule there again. But our people may. Is there anyone here who would not fight to take back our heritage—to take back Môn?"

Again there was a silence. Sennos turned to the King. "Lord King," he said formally, "you have your answer."

"I do," said Regenos. And to the men in the hall, "Who will speak for war?" The shouts of agreement seemed to shake the walls. Regenos let them yell for a moment, then held up one hand. "We are agreed, then, on a war—we have only to plan it. But first, set up the tables here as best you can, and let the serving men come in. Tonight we will feast. Tomorrow will be time enough for another council—a war council!"

War Council

It was early afternoon of the following day when the war council began—a cold day of low gray cloud and icy mizzle rain, and a bitter knife-edged northern wind which whined around the doors and windows, pushing the leather curtains aside, playing cat-and-mouse with the hearth-fires and torches, numbing feet and fingers and chilling the blood. There had been no visible sunrise that morning, only a lightening of the mist, and Togi and Sennos had not lingered at their devotions. Indeed they had scarcely spoken, other than in the business of the rite, for there was nothing new to say. The rest would come later, in the council.

There had been little discussion in Lucotios' house the night before; the hour had been late, and they were all tired. Cingetos had only made one comment as they lay down to sleep. "There will be heroes in this war," the Bard had said, yawning, "but I wonder... Will any of us be alive afterwards to sing their praise?" He had sighed, and stretched out on the floor, rolled in his cloak. Only Togi had heard his last muttered words. "If not, we may all go down into darkness, and be utterly forgotten..." They had stuck in his mind, and he had carried them with him into dark dreams which troubled him until morning.

The feast-hall, however, was not dark that afternoon. Heath-fires flamed high, and torches burned bright on the roof-pillars, as if to hold back the threat of winter outside. Regenos in his high seat blazed in a robe of red and gold, brilliant as a stormy sunrise, with heavy golden bracelets on his sinewy brown arms, and a twisting golden torc at his throat. All of his officers that day shone in bright colors—all of them but Sennos. The old Druid wore instead a plain robe of bleached wool, white as his bone-white hair, and girdled with a dark belt set with plaques of silver. His pale eyes shone with suppressed excitement in his worn face; he had come, thought Togi, to the brink of his desire—the recovery of Môn. Togi could feel that same excitement in himself at the thought: to walk that hallowed ground again, and remake the Sanctuaries into what they had been in his fathers' day… He pushed the vision aside, for Regenos was beginning to speak.

"I have taken first counsel this morning," the King was saying, "with my household, and with some of my advisors. Our problem is this: do we begin our war with the Red Crests at once, braving the onslaught of winter, or do we wait until spring? Both courses have their advantages and their dangers. If we fight now, we can hope to take our enemies by surprise; more, we may recover some of what they have stolen from us before they can take it away. But we will fight alone, with no time to gather allies; and the weather will not be our friend. If we wait until spring to strike, we may gather friends to stand beside us, but the grain renders the Red Crests have stolen will be beyond our reach, and we will be weakened by hunger. I would hear your counsel, O men of the Ordovices, for I am not sure in my own mind which course to prefer."

"This is a difficult question you set us, O King," said Camulos, the man who had spoken the night before for the retaking of Môn. "And I am not sure how to answer it, for you state the balance of choices very justly. Yet I would choose to strike now, so soon as may be, and that for two reasons."

"What reasons are those?" asked the King.

"My first reason," said Camulos, "is this: I have seen the walls of Caer Seint, and they are very strong. To destroy the Red Crests, we must lure them out of their fortress to a place where we may fall upon them unaware. One man, or two, might keep such a plan secret from Samhain to Beltane—perhaps! But how long can all the tongues of the tribes be silent? I think that well before spring they would hear of our plans, and be warned."

"A good point," said Regenos, overriding the growing murmur of disagreement. "And your second reason?"

"It is only this," said Camulos. "If we retake Môn, in part so that she can feed us, we must be on her ground in time to plow and plant a crop. Summer-sown corn has no chance to ripen, and warriors in the field can neither sow nor reap. If we are going to win our war, we must do so long before Beltane; otherwise the Red Crests will have no need to defeat us, for we will have defeated ourselves."

"But how can we fight a winter war," broke in Ambiorix, "with empty bellies in the snow? The thing is impossible!"

"There might be a way," began Camulos, but a surge of voices overrode him, agreeing with Ambiorix.

"Silence!" cried the King, his voice breaking through the tumult. "Let him speak." Gradually the shouting dwindled to a murmur. "What is your way, Camulos?" the King enquired. "Do you have a plan?"

"Half a plan, so far, O King," said Camulos with a grin, "but I hope that we can improve it. Our grain—or so those who work beneath the walls tell me—is still in Caer Seint, waiting for the ships which will take it away. If you were to send to the Red Crests now, and offer to buy it back—Gods know your people will need such aid this winter!—they might hold it there for a time, while you raise the price agreed…"

"What? Pay the reavers who have robbed us to return what they stole?" cried Carnos. "We would be a laughing-stock before all the tribes of Britain. I would die first!"

"Na, na," said Camulos, "I did not say we would buy it, you fool, only that we might make the offer, as a ruse—for with such enemies as these, truth is wasted! Then, when they are expecting gold, we can give them steel instead—break through the gates, maybe, when they come to bring out the grain, or take their wagons by ambush in the pass, and their escort with them…"

"Good thoughts," said Regenos, interrupting Carnos' angry reply. "Yet there are many of us here, and likely as many plans. I will hear other voices, before I make my decision. Who will speak next?"

"I will, O King," said Maiorix, shaking back his gray mane. "How if we attack Môn first? That will draw the Red Crests out of their fort, and we can fall upon their rear when they least expect it. Crush them between us, maybe, as they try to cross the Aber Menai. Then we can deal separately with those left in Caer Seint."

"Not a bad plan," said Regenos. "But I see two problems. If they leave enough men in Caer Seint to hold the fort—and I think they will—they will be safe inside, with all our grain to feed them, while we starve outside their walls. Then their ships can bring in more soldiers, and take *us* in the rear."

"About the ships we can do nothing," said Maiorix. "Yet I think they will not sail our shores in winter. As to your other objection, O King, that applies also to Camulos' plan."

"True it is," said the King. "Who else has other ideas?" A general discussion followed, some supporting one plan and some another. At last Maiorix overrode the others and spoke.

"Here is what I say," he said forcefully. "Let us combine the two plans. First, our people must have food, however we can get it. Make an offer to the Red Crests to buy back the grain, even pay for it if you have to. Then, when we have it, and they are feeling pleased with our docility, strike first for Môn as I suggested, and crush their relieving force at the straits. Those left in Caer Seint will be without our grain to feed them, and if the Gods be kind, it will be too late in the year for their ships to sail. Thus we will hold Môn before spring, and still be alive to enjoy it. And if Caer Seint falls, we may get back the gold we gave for the grain as well, and no one will laugh at us for having spent it!"

"That is a good plan," said Regenos. "I like it. Has anyone else a better?"

"Yes," said Sennos, speaking for the first time, "and no. I have an addition to Maiorix's plan. After we buy back the grain, I will go to Môn with some of our forces. One of the local men whom the Red Crests trust can take them news that the Druids have returned, and are intending a human sacrifice. I will show myself as bait at some appropriate place, and when they come to take me—as come they will!—we can fall upon their troop and kill them, and then go on to take their weakened base before they can prepare to resist us. Then all the rest can follow as Maiorix has said."

"That is a bold addition," said Maiorix before the King could speak, "and, I think, a good one. But should you risk yourself so, Honored One? How if they strike you down before we can stop them?"

"I care not for that," said Sennos quietly, "if it helps to win back Môn." He turned to Regenos. "Let it be, O King, as I have said." Regenos looked back at him, unspeaking, for a long moment, while all the room held silent.

"Yes," he said at last, nodding. "It shall be as you ask, Sennos. Are we all agreed?" A chorus of shouts rocked the hall; no one dissented. "In that case," said Regenos, "I will send men tomorrow to bargain with the Red Crests. Long before midwinter we will strike our first blows, and may the Gods give us victory!"

All of them shouted their approval. Only Togi, watching from the back of the hall, was silent. He remembered his moment of *awen* from the day before, and he wondered who would pose as Sennos' sacrifice.

On the following morning, when the assembled chieftains went their separate ways, Togi rode with Bratronos and three other young warriors from his village. He was grateful to Cingetos for the loan of his gray pony; otherwise he would have been walking the weary miles on his own. "I think," said the Bard with a smile when they parted, "that you will be coming back soon when the war-bands gather, and will need him; if not, graze him for me until I come again."

Togi was both glad and sorry to see the last of Resta, at least for a while. There had been no leave-taking, for she had been absent on some errand that morning when he came back from the dawn ritual to make a hasty breakfast and gather his gear before going to find his pony. He had never learned her age; sometimes she had seemed much older than he was, and at other times, younger. Perhaps, if there was peace next summer... He put the thought aside. There was unlikely to be peace, and even if there was, he would have duties enough to keep him at home.

Home seemed just as he had left it. It would soon be time to drive the swine up from the oak woods, and the autumn slaughter would follow; there would be fresh pig-meat for the Samhain feast when it came, and fat blood sausages afterwards. And if the King's plans worked, there would be barley loaves to go with the meat; they might not starve this winter after all.

As well as the preparations for Samhain, however, the young men of the village were also preparing for war. Togi took the war-spear which Cunomoros had given him after his manhood ritual last summer from the dark corner of the hut where she lived, along with his and Tritos' hunting spears, and spent part of one evening sitting by the hearth, oiling and polishing her sleek gray blade and flawless ash-wood shaft. She was a new-forged spear, virgin and unblooded, for Cunomoros, not having been a warrior, had no weapon of his own to pass on to his son. Togi remembered the pride in the old man's face when he had produced her that night, and the thrill he himself had felt on first holding her—for of course Cunomoros had put magic and enchantments on her to strengthen her blows. Well, she was likely to get her first blood-anointing before long, he and she together. He hoped they would both stand the test well. He took her out the next day and practiced managing her on the gray pony's back. His people did not usually fight on horseback, as he had heard that some of the Red Crests did, but he did not want to look clumsy while riding to war.

This would not be his only spear, of course. All throughout the valleys, in the days between the war council and the summons, the village smiths were busy, forging new spearheads and fitting old ones to new shafts. Each warrior would need three or four light throw-spears, at least—more would be better—with which to thin the ranks of the enemy before they came to grips. Even after the war-bands rode out, the smiths would still be working, for no one believed that this would be a short war.

The summons came soon enough. The Red Crests, said the messenger, had agreed to sell back—at extortionate prices—some of the grain they had taken, and the King was calling in men from the eastern valleys to be ready to spring the trap. Togi was surprised to find himself named in the muster, but there was no reason given. Perhaps, he thought, it was at the Bard's request.

"I wonder?" said Cunomoros, when they talked it over that evening. "Would he not have mentioned it to you before you left him, if he had some special need of you?"

"Mmm," said Togi, looking up from the new leather thong he was threading through the loops of one of his worn rawhide shoes, the old one having shown signs of fraying. "He might. Or it might be something which has come to him since then. Who else could want me—?" He stopped suddenly, remembering his thoughts in the feast-hall after the plan had been agreed.

"You know something," said Cunomoros, nodding. "What have you not told me?"

Togi looked around the hut. His brother Tritos was listening silently but intently while whittling on a bit of wood which he was carving into a new spoon; his mother was working away at her loom by firelight; his little sister was already asleep beside her. "It is only a thought I had," he said slowly. "Sennos wants to set a trap on Môn for some of the Red Crests, by sending someone to tell them that the Druids have returned, and offering himself as bait. He thought that might draw them out of their camp to where they could be more easily killed."

"He may be right," said Cunomoros. "But what has that to do with you?"

"I am not sure," said Togi honestly. "Only, I had a—a moment of *awen* when he spoke of it. It may be nothing."

"Mmm," said Cunomoros. He had been sharpening his belt knife, stropping it back and forth on a whetstone. Now he looked down at it and carefully tried the blade on the back of his thumbnail. "From what you have said—and have not said—I can only give you this advice: do not trust Sennos. Do not trust him at all. There is nothing he will not do in pursuit of his ends."

"I know," said Togi softly.

Cunomoros nodded again. "I will make offerings," he said. And that was the end of the discussion for that night.

Valos was envious. He had been out in the pastures with the sheep on the day Ivo was killed, and so had missed that fight. "Not that my being there would have helped," he said, "but I would have liked to have thrown at least one stone at our enemies."

"You could have had my place," said Togi, "and welcome. But I wish you were going with us now."

Valos sighed. "So do I wish it," he said. "I envy you the loan of the Bard's pony as well." He grinned. "He is a fine little beast. But I doubt I could ride him so well as you do."

"Mmm," said Togi. They were grooming the gray pony, shaggy now with his winter coat, as they spoke. "I have had more practice, that is all."

"Two summers' worth," agreed Valos, "which I spent walking on the hills with the sheep. Ah well, if what I hear is true, we may all have a chance to meet the Red Crests before this is over—and I hope, throwing more than stones!"

"That," said Togi, bending to brush mud from the pony's legs, "is a true word. The Gods send that we triumph... You will aid Cunomoros with the sacrifices while I am gone?"

"Every day," said Valos soberly. "And my prayers will be with you."

"That," said Togi, and smiled, "I knew." And they went on grooming the gray pony.

The morning of his riding out dawned clear and cold, with the last sliver of the old moon hanging pale and thin in the bright sky. As always, Togi had been up before dawn to make the sunrise offering on the hill. As he watched the first rays of light touch the top of Penwyn, he wondered if he would ever see this sight again, ever stand thus with his father before the Gods. It was a solemn thought, but one which he did not share aloud. There was no need: he could see the same question in Cunomoros' eyes when their glances met. Unspoken, it linked them both, and sang in their joined voices as they lifted their songs of praise.

He would be the youngest of their war-band; the other young men of his year would remain at home to do the winter work and defend the people at need. Fifteen of them were going, all mounted, all lightly armed. Lugotorix was one of them, and the sight of him reminded Togi of Ivo. Dying was all too easy, and all too quick. Living could be a harder thing to arrange. One thing in the summons had seemed strange: they had all been told to bring their hunting bows. They had wondered at it, for the bow was not a weapon of warfare among the Britons: but they had obeyed.

The fortress hill was overflowing again with men when they arrived at Dinas Brân. The first familiar face that Togi saw as he rode into the courtyard was Cingetos'. "Hah!" said the Bard, seeing him. "Good, you are back! Sennos wants to speak with you as soon as may be."

"Was it he who summoned me, then, and not you?" asked Togi, swinging down from the gray pony's back.

"It was." Cingetos' expression was grim. "He has a role for you to play on Môn."

"I had guessed it," said Togi. "Where is he? I will see him as soon as I have stabled Llwyd."

"In his quarters," said Cingetos. "Have you been there before?"

"No," said Togi, "but I will find him."

A small dry-stone cell, thick-walled and thatch-roofed, at the western end of a storehouse near the low boundary wall of the compound: that was Sennos' home. The darkly weathered wooden door was closed against the late autumn twilight, but when Togi tapped on it, Sennos' voice called to him to come in. Inside, beyond the hanging leather curtain which helped to keep out the cold, he stopped, blinking in what seemed a blaze of light. Three candles burned in wall niches, and in the center of the room a fire leapt in an iron brazier. Beside it stood Sennos, feeding what seemed to be bundles of sticks into the flames. More were piled beside him: rectangular billets of wood, notched and carved with symbols, and larger flat objects gleaming with oil or wax which Togi belatedly recognized as writing tablets. Sennos was burning his books.

"Good," the old Druid said, looking up briefly. "You are here. We ride for Môn in two days, or possibly three: as soon as the messenger comes back from Caer Seint. The less time we must camp there, the better."

"Is it for Môn that you wanted me?" asked Togi, still looking around. Aside from the tablets, there was little enough to see in the room: a low bed-place with blankets; two wooden storage chests for clothes or other things, one of them standing open and empty; a small table against the wall half-covered with a litter of oddments; a row of clay jars on a shelf. Sennos' cloak and white hall-robe lay on the bed; he was wearing his traveling clothes of plain dark wool. He glanced up again at Togi and nodded.

"Yes," he said. "I want your help in baiting the trap for the Red Crests. It will be better if there are two of us there, at least. Will you come?"

"Of course," said Togi, "if I am needed." The words were out before he thought, but really there was nothing else that he could say.

"Good," said Sennos again, turning back to his task. Another bundle of waxed tablets went into the hungry flames, sending up more smoke to join that already making its slow way out through the thatch. "I will see you in the morning, then, as usual." He was half smiling, but it was a smile without mirth. "I have little more to do here, in any case. After we take Môn, I will not be coming back."

"And if we fail?" asked Togi.

Sennos' smile widened. "In that case," he said, "I will—still not be coming back."

First Blood

They crossed to Môn six days later—a crossing the like of which Togi hoped never to repeat. A bitter northeast wind which cut like a knife was driving hissing white-crested waves into the funnel of the Aber Menai, threatening to swamp the tossing fishing boats in their path, and the accompanying veils of drenching rain all but hid the distant shore toward which they strove. Clinging to the side of the boat with one hand and bailing with the other, in between retching his heart out, Togi felt every moment that he was about to die, and could not be sorry. It was with astonished relief that he heard the boat's flat bottom grate at last on the gravely shore, and gladly tumbled out into the foaming hip-deep water to help the boatman run her up the beach.

At least, he thought, the rain would hide them from the Red Crests. Their little army gathered itself together on the beach, and staggered up the dunes, laden with gear and weapons, to be met at the top by reinforcements: two old men and a girl, leading a bony old plow-horse. This last, they explained, was for Sennos' benefit: it was unfitting that the Honored One should walk. Solemnly Sennos thanked them and mounted his unlikely steed, and guided by the old men, set off into the gusty twilight, followed by Togi and their small band of rain-drenched warriors.

"Where are we going?" Togi asked the girl, who had dropped back to walk beside him. She turned a pale face toward him and pushed wet strands of dark hair back into the shelter of her hood.

"Rhiwlas," she said, "over the hills toward Traeth Coch. That is our village, on the west slope of Mynydd Llwydiarth. You will be safe there tonight; the Red Crests who live beside the Menai do not often come there, and anyway we will have watchers out."

"That is good," said Togi. "Is it far?"

"None too far," said the girl. "We will be there before moonset." Casting an eye up at the hurrying gray clouds, Togi wondered how she would tell. The moon, by his reckoning, was approaching her first waxing quarter, which would mark the first day of Cutios, the End-of-Autumn month, and would not set until almost midnight; it could be a long walk.

They squelched along through the twilight, following a faint path which wound its way around rocks and bogs and thorny clumps of gorse. Now and then Togi caught a glimpse of a distant hump on the skyline, a darker gray against the gray sky. "Is that your mountain?" he asked his companion. It seemed but a hill to him.

"Yes," she said. "It rises gradually on this side; the west side is steeper. The—the Priests used to have a holy place on its summit, or so my grandmother says, but the Red Crests burned it down. Maybe the Honored One will bring back the old ways."

"Maybe," said Togi. "I think that is his intent."

The night grew darker; they stumbled on through the gloom, following the dim shape of Sennos and the squelch of the plow-horse's plodding hooves. The booming of the wind covered other noises, but at least the rain had stopped. Looking up again, Togi saw that the clouds were breaking, and suddenly the hazy shape of the westering moon appeared through their tangled rags, seeming to hurtle through the heavens while the clouds stood still around her.

At the same time Sennos' horse stopped, and Togi heard a voice ahead of them raised in cautious challenge, followed by muffled thumps and grunts from behind him, as the sleepy marchers stumbled into one another. Then the horse began to move again, and Togi realized that the path had started down. On his right the mountain loomed out of the darkness, taller than he had imagined, and below him somewhere he heard the sound of rushing water. Soon he smelled a hint of peat smoke on the wind, and knew by that, and a distant blink of firelight, that they were approaching their destination—a loose huddle of dark buildings ranged around a courtyard.

They halted at last in front of the low thatched shape of a feast-hall, and Sennos slid off of his bony old mount with an audible sigh of relief, then straightened himself to his full impressive height. The fickle moonlight gleamed on his tangle of white hair, and dimly illuminated the small crowd of people who had gathered to welcome him. Old bent women and men, a few youngsters of Togi's age, and a scattering of small children: that was all. The missing generation had died in blood and fire with the destruction of their land. The scarred survivors gathered now, in hope or fear, around Sennos. Togi heard the forbidden words whispered, passed back and forth like a token through the crowd: *the Druids have returned.*

A woman came out from the hall, a tall old woman, thin and slow-moving. She carried carefully in her two bony hands a carved wooden cup, and brought it to Sennos. "Drink, O Honored One," she said, "and be welcome in our poor home. Long have our people served your kind, and glad we are to see you in your proper place once more."

Sennos laid his hands over hers for a moment, then took the cup and drank. "I thank you, old mother," he said, "for your welcome. Glad I am to walk this land again, and long may I dwell here."

"Come in, then, all of you," said the old woman, looking beyond him to Togi and the rest. "What we have is yours: use us as you will. If even one Red Crest soldier finds his death at your hands, we will have been well repaid." And turning, she led the way into the low-roofed hall.

Inside there was a bright peat-fed fire in the long central hearth, and food enough—cauldrons of steaming fish stew, and pitchers of a strange heather-scented ale. Sennos was seated at a trestle table near the far end of the hall, together with the tall old woman and the two old men who had served as their guides. The rest of the party, Togi included, found seats on the benches along the walls, where they were served by the women and girls.

Gathered thus in the firelight, their still-damp clothes steaming in the welcome warmth, they seemed a small enough army with which to start a war—perhaps two score of sturdy young men from the hills and valleys along the north coast, with a couple of experienced warriors from the King's *teulu* to lead them; Togi himself; and Sennos—facing a disciplined group of Red Crest soldiers like those who had killed Ivomagnos. Their chief weapon, Togi thought, would be surprise—if they could keep it. One loose tongue could cost them all their lives.

Looking up from his now-empty bowl, he found the girl who had helped to guide them there at his elbow. "The

Honored One asks you to join him," she said, her blue eyes sparkling with excitement. "He is making plans with the Elders now. In two days, maybe, we will spring our trap, and our land will once more be our own."

Putting down his bowl, Togi joined the group at the trestle table. Segovax and Licnos, the two older warriors, followed him. Once they had all found seats on stools or benches, Sennos looked around his council. "We will see the ground tomorrow," he said, "but from what our hosts tell me, the old *nemeton* on Mynydd Llwydiarth should serve our purpose well. There is good cover close enough for the ambush, and a fire lit there can be seen on a clear morning from the mainland. That will be the signal for our second party to cross the Menai and attack the Red Crests' base."

"How many of the enemy can we expect?" asked Segovax, a tall rawboned man in his prime whose scarred face spoke of old battles.

"I am told there are thirty or so of them at their base, as we thought," said Sennos, "and most of them horsemen."

"Perhaps a dozen will come, then," said Segovax, nodding. "They will leave at least half in reserve. That will be good. How soon can we expect them?"

"Probably the morning after tomorrow," said Sennos. "Tasgetos"—he indicated the elder on his left—"says he can send them word as soon as we are ready."

"They will come at once," rumbled Tasgetos, the taller of the old men. "We have fed them rumors already, and they will be expecting something."

"The first morning of Cutios will be good," said Sennos. "It is a day appropriate for sacrifices."

"We must make sure we are well armed and prepared," said Licnos. "I have seen the Red Crest horsemen in battle. Each of them carries javelins in addition to their long spear and sword, and their aim is good. They also wear helmets and good armor. We must kill them as quickly as we can, or they will ride over us and destroy us."

"That," said Sennos with a thin smile, "is why you have brought your bows."

The first-quarter moon had long set, and the last of the autumn stars were dimming in the sky as they went up the long hill. In the gray predawn light the land below them lay still and silent, blurred here and there with silver patches of fog, but except for a few feathery wisps of cloud near the zenith, dawn-pale against the darker blue, the sky above them was clear. They could not have asked for a better day, thought Togi, for the sacrifice: truly the Gods must favor this endeavor. He and the people from the village walked beside Sennos' mount, while the young men toiled along behind them, burdened with their weapons and gear. Togi's own spears and shield weighed heavy on his shoulders, and he carried his bow ready strung in his left hand: it was good to be prepared.

Just below the hill crest, they passed through a belt of young trees, second growth from the roots of the ancient oaks which had once encircled the hill. Some of the young men of the war-band stopped there, fanning out to take cover among the brown rustling leaves, and settling themselves to their ambush, their earth-colored cloaks blending with the dark earth beneath them, but Sennos and the rest of his party went on. Beyond the trees the clear hillside opened out again with a long view northward toward the sea, and the hill crest itself was crowned with a wide circle of low gray recumbent stones. In their center stood a tall pile of wood, brought up from the area around the village by the young men the day before. As yet unlit, it awaited its destiny—as did they all.

Within the circle Sennos reined his weary mount to a halt and slid stiffly down from its back, and a young boy from the village led the ancient horse away toward the trees. The old Druid was wearing white this morning, the same long white woolen robe he had worn in the King's hall. He had bloused it up above his belt to shorten it for riding; now he stood for a moment shaking it carefully down again, adjusting the folds until they hung just so, falling to his sandaled feet. The long sacrificer's knife with its bronze handle hung in its polished sheath at his left side, ready for use. His silver torque gleamed softly around his neck, half covered by his beard, and his white hair hung loose on his shoulders. He looked up at the sky, and something which might have been a smile stirred the dry skin at the corners of his mouth for a moment; then it was gone.

Six of them stood in the center of the circle that morning: Sennos, the three Elders from the village, Togi, and the girl—Tagia was her name—who had greeted them by the shore two days before. Today her dark hair hung long and loose on her shoulders, flowing in a dusky wave half way to her slender waist. Like Sennos, she also wore white, a sheep-colored robe which here and there showed the moth's tooth, made for a larger woman and carefully saved for this day. Her face was pale and solemn, and her blue eyes wide and dark, for she was to play the role of one of the sacrifices in their carefully staged play. Around them in a loose circle inside the ring of stones stood the rest of their small army, bows strung and ready, their spears standing point-first in the turf, and their round shields at their feet.

Slowly the late autumn sky brightened in the southeast. A little predawn wind fluttered Togi's cloak and blew strands of his dark hair across his face. Pushing them aside, he peered down the slope, wondering when the Red Crests would come. If they meant to interrupt the ceremony, they should be already on their way, but the belt of young trees hid the lower slopes of the hill from his sight. He tried to listen, but his own heartbeat sounded loud in his ears, drowning any sound which distant hooves might make on the rain-soft ground. Looking up, he saw the feathery clouds flushing pink with early light. Beside him Sennos said, "Light the fire."

Togi knelt and struck sparks onto his prepared tinder. His hand shook a little as he transferred the small flame to the waiting twigs; he was shivering with cold and excitement. When the fire had caught he pressed his palms to the ground for a moment, praying for the support of the Mother on whose breast he knelt. Then he stood up, looking southeast toward the distant peaks of Eryri, over which the sun would rise.

Beside him the fire lifted a crackling column of heat and smoke into the waiting sky. A grain of answering brightness appeared suddenly on the shoulder of Yr Wyddfa, blinked and brightened and swelled, and Togi joined his voice to Sennos' in the prayer to the rising Sun. Their voices rose together, mixed and blending. Clear and growing, in the following moment of silence, they heard the sound of hoof beats and the distant whinnying of horses as the Red Crest cavalry climbed the hill.

What happened next happened very quickly. As the Red Crests burst from the trees, a hail of thrown spears took them from behind. Some threw up their arms and fell from their saddles; others turned and charged back into the trees, their own spears leveled to strike their attackers; but the leader of the troop and three others spurred straight on toward the group standing within the ring of stones. They were confronted with a swarm of arrows, as the young men there turned, drew, and let fly. Horses screamed in pain as they were struck, men yelled. Togi's first arrow took the leading Red Crest in the eye and toppled him from the saddle. "Aim for their faces!" he shouted as he nocked his second arrow and drew, and Licnos' deep voice echoed his: "Aim for their faces!"

Arrows bounced off of helmets and armor, but men around Togi were also falling, as the surviving Red Crests threw their spears. He saw one coming toward him, and ducked sideways just in time; the sharp iron point tore through the left side of his tunic, drawing a hot line of pain across his ribs, and buried itself in the ground behind him. Ignoring the shaft, which was still tangled in the torn cloth, he drew and loosed again, but his arrow glanced off the soldier's cheek plate, missing his eye by a finger's breadth. Togi dropped his bow and tore his tunic loose from the spear shaft, then grabbed his shield and spear as the two surviving Red Crests—another had fallen with an arrow in his throat—drew their long cavalry swords and plowed into the crowd, striking to right and left and blocking spear thrusts with their long red oval shields.

One of them swung at Togi in passing, and he blocked the blow just in time, then dropped his damaged shield—the sword had cut it half in two—and turning, ran after the horseman and rammed his spear with both hands into the pony's guts. The beast screamed and fell, pinning its rider, and Togi turned his attention to the one Red Crest still mobile. He was dimly aware of shouts and screams from the battle in the woods, and of Sennos' voice raised in a high, triumphant chant behind him, but he had no attention to spare for them. Only the soldier mattered.

His own weapons were gone, and the Red Crest was wheeling his horse and turning toward him, but he could still act. With a savage grin, Togi stooped and grubbed a fist-sized rock from the ground, and threw it with all his might at the approaching soldier's head. It hit the man squarely between the eyes, and he yelled and dropped his sword, clapping his hands to his blood-streaming face and swaying in his saddle. Immediately other hands grabbed him from either side and pulled him from his pony. Spears rose and fell, and the soldier ceased to move.

Scooping up the dead man's dropped sword, Segovax yelled, "Follow me!" and led a charge toward the fighting in the woods, but Togi turned back, empty-handed, to look for another weapon. The gut-speared pony was still thrashing and screaming, smashing its trapped rider's leg deeper into the earth with every roll, but the other three ponies stood with hanging heads, two of them bleeding from arrow wounds. There were dead and wounded men of his own people around him, some of them being tended by villagers; Tagia knelt beside old Tasgetos, his head in her lap, and the skirts of her white dress soaked with his blood. Only Sennos stood unmoving beside their still-burning fire, his unsheathed knife gleaming in the early sunlight, and a look of savage satisfaction on his face.

Even as Togi found his bow and bent to pick it up, he realized that the sounds of battle in the woods below were ceasing. Laying the bow aside, he drew his belt knife and went to the wounded pony's head, but Sennos forestalled him. "This is my work," said the old Druid, holding out his long blade, and bending to seize the pony's halter.

"As you wish, Honored One," said Togi. He was becoming aware now of the pain from his gashed ribs, and the warm flow of blood down his left side under the rags of his torn tunic. "What shall we do with the other Red Crest?" For the trapped soldier, although disarmed, was still groaningly alive.

"That, too, is my work," said Sennos, and smiled. "We came here to make a human sacrifice, did we not? And the Gods have provided their own beast."

"Yes," said Togi, looking around their small battlefield again. "Yes, they have—but at what cost?"

"This is only the beginning," said Sennos, and with one deft movement cut the pony's throat.

Not one of the Red Crests escaped. The tribesmen carried their own dead and wounded—of whom there were far too many—down the hill for healing or burial, but the Red Crests they stripped of their weapons and gear, and left them on the hill for the carrion crows who were already gathering. The dead pony was butchered, and the meat brought down as well; there would be something better than fish stew in the cauldrons that night. Of the two-score young men who had climbed the hill that morning, only half came down again on their own feet; but the Red Crests' captured ponies carried several more.

Sennos had exchanged his plow horse for one of the captured mounts and led the procession. He had sent three wounded Red Crests to the Gods, and had seemed to grow larger and stronger with each sacrifice. It was a just and reverent thing to do in thanks for their victory, thought Togi; moreover, they had no need for hostages, who would have required precious food and attention. And the Red Crests would have done the same by them, had things been different.

After his initial elation at having survived the fight, he was feeling an inevitable letdown. The price they had paid for this small victory was high; what would the cost of the war be? And yet they had no alternative; they must all of them triumph or die. If only they could unite with the other tribes of Britain, and drive the Red Crests from their shores... But he remembered his foster-father's words. *The only force which could have united all the tribes at once,* had said Cunomoros, *was the Druids. And the Red Crests knew it, and for that reason they destroyed us...* Maybe, thought Togi, it is not too late: there are still a few of us left! But he was not sure that he believed it himself.

However, he was young, and once his wounds had been salved and bound, and his belly filled with ale and stewed horse meat, he forgot for a while his forebodings. He was alive, and twelve Red Crests were not: at the end of the day, that was what mattered the most. Instead he put the herb-craft and healing he had learned from Cunomoros to good use, helping Tagia and the other women to tend the wounded. To take life, and to give it: both were a part of the Druid's craft, as he was beginning to understand, and both were important to the balance of the world.

Segovax and Licnos had not stayed for the feasting; instead, once everyone had reached the village, they had set out with all of their warriors who could still fight for Castellum, the Red Crest's fort on the Menai. This, as a boy runner had come to tell them, was already under attack by a second group who had crossed the straits that morning on seeing the fire's smoke rise. Togi saw the results the following day, when he and Sennos, riding captured ponies, went to join the rest. The small earth-walled fort and the huddle of native bothies outside it were alike smoking ruins, but this time there were survivors: three wounded Red Crests, one of them an officer, awaited Sennos' decision.

"I would have put them to the sword," said Licnos dismissively, "but I thought you should see them first, Honored One."

"That was well done," said Sennos, frowning down at the prisoners. Two of them lay with closed eyes and tied wrists, their bloodstained cloaks beneath them, on the floor of the one unburnt timber structure remaining in the little fort. The third man, his roughly bandaged right arm thrust limply into the torn breast of his red tunic, sat with his back to the wall watching them. His ankles were tied together, but otherwise he was unrestrained. They had stripped his armor and insignia from him, but something in his bearing still spoke of authority. Looking at him, Togi saw a dark, square-set young man, perhaps ten years older than himself, whose face looked vaguely familiar under the blood and dirt which caked its left side. His black eyes were hard and bright, and his mouth was set in an uncompromising line. He had no illusions, thought Togi, regarding his likely fate.

"Take the first two out and dispose of them in whatever way pleases you," said Sennos. "They are too damaged to make a worthy sacrifice. The third one"—his pale eyes weighed up the officer thoughtfully—"we will keep in reserve. Find a slave chain somewhere, if you can, and shackle him to a post. That will take care of him for now." And he turned away, but Togi lingered for a moment. He had seen understanding move in the Red Crest's eyes when Sennos spoke, and he was curious.

"You speak our language," he said to the man.

"A little." The officer shrugged. "I have been in this island a while."

"You may not be here much longer," said Togi, a trifle maliciously. The spear gash along his ribs was aching.

"I know," said the officer.

Two men came in at that point and picked up one of the unconscious Red Crests by his legs and shoulders. The man groaned, but they paid him no heed, carrying him out like a dead thing and leaving a trail of dark drops of blood behind them in the dust. The officer's eyes followed them, but he said nothing. After a little while they came back for the second soldier, who opened his eyes and struggled weakly when they touched him. One of the tribesmen kicked him in the head, and he went limp. The other tribesman grinned, and they carried him out. Togi looked back at the officer, who still sat stonily watching. "Maybe," he said, "they will come back soon for you."

"Do you think I care?" said the officer. "You are savages, all of you."

"That," said Togi, "may be a matter of opinion." Something in the officer's voice, with its heavily accented British, was familiar. "You are the man," he said suddenly, "who came with the tax carts. You were in our village two moons ago, when Ivo was killed."

"What? Where?" asked the officer, surprised.

"On the mainland," said Togi. "You gave the order to kill the man who threw stones."

"Oh," said the officer. "Yes, I think I remember some such incident. What about it? It was my job."

"When Sennos cuts your throat, as an offering to the Gods," said Togi slowly, "I will help him. That will be my—*job*—on that day, O killer of men."

The two tribesmen who had taken away the wounded soldiers came back then, carrying an iron slave collar and chain. The officer sat unresisting while they fitted the hinged loop around his neck and locked it, and cut the thongs on his ankles. "Come on, you," said one of them, jerking the chain, and pulled him to his feet, but he hung back for a moment, his eyes still on Togi.

"When that day comes," he said, "I will remember you, savage." And he spat at Togi's feet. The tribesmen jerked the chain again, and he followed them out.

Togi smiled, and went to look for Sennos.

Caer Seint

Caer Seint was under siege. Fires burned in the native settlement along the river, but the first assault had failed to capture the fort. "At least we got the grain first," said Cingetos to Togi when the party from Môn arrived at the King's camp. "The problems came afterwards."

"What happened?" asked Togi, looking around. The smell of burning overlay the fainter stench of death in the cold air, but could not totally hide it.

"We made the payment, and they brought out the grain carts," said Cingetos. "Our men were supposed to attack once the drivers got them out of range of the fort. But there was some sort of argument, and steel was drawn on both sides… At any rate, we will have food this winter. But whether we can starve *them* out is another question."

The two of them gazed silently at the high turf-and-timber walls of the fort below them. It was situated on a slight rise not far from the confluence of the river Seint and the Aber Menai, with a good view all around.

"They built it fifteen years ago," said Camulos, coming to join them. "After they took Ynys Môn. I remember watching them, that first summer, while I herded my cousins' sheep, over there on the mountain." He gestured with an inclination of his dark head toward the hills across the river. "They dug the first turf for the walls from the boundary ditch, then brought in more from the slope on this side after they cleared it. I have never seen anything built so fast—the walls seemed to go up as if by magic! But that is the Red Crests—whatever they do, they do swiftly."

"How many of them are there?" asked Togi, still looking at the fort.

"At least a hundred, I think, before the fighting started," said Camulos, "and some of them horse soldiers. It might be more. How many did you kill on Ynys Môn?"

"A dozen with our ambush," said Togi, "and another score at their base by the Menai. And you?"

"Hard to say," said Camulos briefly. "We have not been able to clear our own men's bodies from the ditch, never mind count theirs. There was too much moonlight last night."

"Mmm," said Togi. "Perhaps the weather will change."

"Perhaps," said Cingetos. "A dark night would be our best friend."

"It would, truly," said Camulos.

"I will make offerings," said Togi.

There was an argument going on in the King's camp that evening between those who wanted to launch another attack at once and those in favor of waiting for more favorable conditions. "Did they have time to send out a messenger?" said Maiorix, shaking his gray locks. "That is the question."

"Na, I am not knowing," said Carnos. "I did not see the first blows struck."

"I did," said Camulos. Everyone looked at him.

"Well?" asked Regenos, who had been listening quietly from his big camp chair. "We are waiting. Tell us more. You were closer than most, except for Orgetos, and he was in the thick of the fighting. Did you see any break away?"

"Not on that side of the fort," said Camulos slowly. "Those who tried were struck down, and I think there were only two of them; most retreated to the gates under covering fire from the walls. But we were not on the seaward side to begin with, and they have another gate there. Who knows if a messenger got out that way?"

"Unless he took to the sea, we would have seen him," said Carnos reasonably. "They have cleared the ground so thoroughly around their walls that there is no cover for a mounted man, and hardly any for one on foot."

"In a boat?" asked Maiorix. "There were a few small ones in the river anchorage. Or one man might have swum the river without us seeing him."

"To find himself afoot in a hostile country? With winter coming?" asked Carnos. "That would be a desperate action indeed."

"And are they not desperate?" asked Camulos. "We outnumber them many times to one. And soon the sea lanes will be closing for the winter."

"Who knows what stores they have?" asked Regenos. "Camulos? Have you seen inside their fort?"

"Na, not I," said Camulos. "But some of my cousins may have. I will ask them."

"I do not think we will starve them out," said Orgetos, who had kept silent until then, nursing a wounded arm. "They will have got their winter stores in already, and not even greed would have made their commander risk finding his own table bare before spring. I say if we want this fort we will have to fight for it, and the sooner the better. The winter will not be kinder to us, here in our camp, than it will be to them in their snug barracks." And he shivered in a gust of cold wind which rattled the King's tent.

"Perhaps," said Regenos slowly, "it is an omen we need." And he turned to Sennos, who sat a little withdrawn from the group. "What omen can you give us, Honored One?"

"Na, I cannot draw wisdom from the sky, all in an eye-blink," said Sennos. "Let me make a proper sacrifice first, and then I will see what omen the Gods offer us."

"Fair enough," said the King, nodding. "When can you make your sacrifice, and what beast will you need?"

"At dawn I can make the offering," said Sennos. "As to the sacrifice… What prisoners have we taken?"

"Only the one you brought with you from Môn," said Orgetos. "We have taken none here."

"He will do well enough," said Sennos, nodding. "At dawn, then, we will see what the Gods decree."

Togi, listening from the fringes of the group with Cingetos, felt a twinge of discomfort. It was all very well to assist while Sennos cut the throat of a wounded enemy—a stranger. But this was a man he had spoken with—if not in friendship, at least as man to man. He tried to argue down his doubt: it was only right, in times of such great danger, for the tribes to offer this greatest of sacrifices to the Gods. His own blood-father, after all, had submitted himself to such an end. But Lovernos had chosen his fate: that was the crucial difference. Togi was quite certain that this Red Crest would not choose to die as a sacrifice to his enemies' Gods.

But how to avoid it? And who was he, anyway, to set his will against Sennos', and that of all his people? He knew from his lessons with Cunomoros that this sort of thing had often been done in the past. Indeed, Cunomoros himself had killed men for the Gods: he had said so. But who they had been, other than Lovernos, he had not said.

The meeting broke up with the arrival of a cauldron of stewed deer-meat for the King and his advisors. Togi took his portion gladly when his turn came, after the more important men had been fed, but even as he found a sheltered spot to sit and eat it, his mind was still niggling at his problem. What sort of event could prevent the planned sacrifice without bringing ill luck in its train? He knew that he himself could not intervene by somehow freeing the prisoner: he would be lucky in that case not to find himself taking the planned victim's place. Sennos, too, would find a special satisfaction in that act. And this time humor would not save him, nor would throwing stones. Or—would it?

Without realizing it, he had decided that he must act. He smiled a little at that idea: how surprised the Red Crest would be to find sympathy in one he had called *savage*. Well—not sympathy exactly. It was simply that his *awen* told him that this sacrifice, at this time, was wrong. And yet, was he being truthful with himself? Was he not merely reluctant to face up to his priestly duty? There had been a first time for feeling the wind of prophecy speak through his mouth, and seeing his words come true. There must also be a first time for shedding human blood other than his own. He knew that serving the Gods was not easy: he had always known it in his mind; now the knowledge sank deeper. Perhaps he should simply put his feelings aside and do his *job*.

He stood up to add his empty stew bowl to a pile being collected, and something in the movement shifted the position of his father's ring slightly, where it lay against the skin of his chest, under his tunic and cloak. *I wonder,* he thought, *what my blood-father would do? What counsel would he give me now?* Putting down his bowl with the others, he turned away from the King's tent. Neither Sennos nor Cingetos would miss him for a while, and he needed to walk and to think.

On impulse he turned uphill, away from the fort. The late autumn night had already fallen, but the waxing moon gave him plenty of light once he was away from the campfires. Three days into Cutios, she was, and another four from her fullness—no help there for night attacks against the fort. The sky was clear and dark, powdered with stars which sparkled like points of frost; only in the far west a faint haziness suggested approaching clouds. There was little wind, and sounds carried clearly in the chill silence. Behind him the noises of the camp faded as he walked.

The woolen or leather tents of the leaders and the crude brush shelters of the warriors formed a fire-lit crescent which stretched from river bank to Menai beach, cutting off the fort in its triangle of land. Beyond them, he could see torches burning at the corners of the fort and on its wooden gate tower; the helmets of the sentries occasionally caught sparks of the red light as they moved, walking their beats on the walls. No chance, he thought, of catching them unprepared tonight. In the native settlement by the river, where some of Camulos' cousins had sold heather beer and striped woolen rugs to the troopers until a couple of days ago, one or two fires still smoldered, but most of them had gone out by now. Otherwise land and water alike lay quiet and peaceful in the white moonlight.

Under his cloak Togi pushed his hand into his tunic and brought out the ring. In the moonlight he could just make out the worn design of the God with the wheel on its face. Closing his hand on it, he tried to feel again the contact he had sensed through it before with his blood-father, but that voice was silent. He would have to make his own decision this time. Nevertheless, he raised the silver thing to his lips before shoving it back into its place. It was a connection to his past, and a promise for his future—yes, and a reminder of his present burden. He sighed, and began to gather dry heather twigs for a fire. When he had built it, and made his sacrifice of blood and hair, he remained on his knees, opening his mind to whatever God might offer him advice. And at last it came, in a whisper of wind, a breath of salt air from the shore, carrying the taint of burning and the scent of the sea.

If the weather changed, and changed decisively enough before morning, an omen might not be deemed necessary: the Gods would have spoken already. But Togi was not sure Sennos would be satisfied with this. It might take more than a cloudy morning to deter the old Druid from his plan. Perhaps rain... He remembered his vision quests back in the spring. *Manannan, God of the Waters, God of the Sea,* he prayed, *come to me now, aid my endeavor. Give me the strength and wisdom to summon the storm...*

And the great voice answered in his mind. *You have called upon me, Fox Cub, and I have come. Ask of me now what you will.*

I ask your aid against my enemies, Lord, said Togi. *The rising of the winds, the roaring of the waves, the pounding of the rain. I ask you to send us a storm.*

What will you give me for this? asked the huge voice. *For nothing comes without a price.*

What sacrifice would please you, Lord? asked Togi. *I will give you what I can.*

Give me, then, this time, what you feel you can afford, said the great voice, and Togi felt that the God smiled. *Another time I may ask a higher price for my aid.*

Let it be so, Lord, said Togi. And the sea surge in his mind died away in laughter...

With an effort Togi came back to himself. He was still kneeling by the cold remains of his little fire, but the angle of his moon-cast shadow had moved two hands' breadths to the east. Slowly and stiffly he stood up and looked around. Nothing else had changed, but the hazy band of clouds still hid the western stars, and he thought that it was growing.

As he walked back to the camp, the sea wind began to rise.

Sunrise came cold, wet, and windy, behind a thick blanket of clouds. The King and his war leaders had risen betimes to join Sennos and Togi at the place appointed for the sacrifice, a spot just inside the sickle curve of the encircling camp, in clear view of the fort. The Red Crests had noted the unusual activity, of course, and now their men lined the walls, taking an occasional arrow shot at the tribesmen, but the later had discovered already the range of the Red Crest catapults and other projectiles, and had been careful to leave a good margin of safety when setting up their camp. Even with a following wind, the arrows could not reach them, and the Red Crests soon stopped trying in order to conserve their bolts.

Togi had lit the fire, a larger one than usual, and now was adding more fuel. The damp wood hissed and steamed as it was fed to the flames. Sennos was preparing to make the initial offering—a black yearling ram lamb from Camulos' flocks, currently being held by its donor. A wide brass bowl waited to catch its blood when its throat was cut, but the beast was restless, bleating and shying away from the crackling fire. Sennos frowned, looking back and forth, at the lamb, at the fire, at the sky. The rain, thought Togi, was getting heavier, and the clouds thicker, so that from moment to moment the morning grew darker, not lighter. Inside the dripping hood of his leather rain cloak, the King's face was also darkening with a frown: the whole ceremony was shaping up to be an ill omen indeed, not at all what he needed at this point in the war.

"Bring forth the prisoner," said Sennos to some of the *teulu*. "I want him ready now." The men looked to Orgetos, who nodded.

"Bring him," he said, and they went on their errand. Sennos turned back to Togi.

"Take the bowl," he said, drawing his sacrificer's knife from its sheath. "The time to begin is now."

The ram lamb was not convinced. It bucked and struggled against Camulos' grip, almost escaping, and when Sennos grabbed its right ear to hold it steady, it jerked away, so that the knife thrust which should have cut its throat cleanly only grazed its neck. At this it gave another leap, knocking over Togi, who was trying, crouching, to hold the bowl under its throat. In falling he in turn jarred Camulos, who also lost his balance. With a twist and a kick, the lamb tore itself free and set off into the open space ahead of it. It had covered half the distance toward the fort when a Red Crest arrow struck it. It fell, struggled for a moment to rise, and then lay still. A cheer went up from the walls, and the watching Britons stood silent.

Only Sennos turned back toward the little clump of men making their way through the crowd, the Red Crest officer in their midst. "This one," Togi heard him mutter, "will not get away."

Considered as an offering to the Gods, the Red Crest was not an impressive sight. Although he had somehow contrived to wash the dried blood from his face, his red woolen tunic was dirty and torn, and the three days' growth of black beard stubble on his square chin gave his gaunt face a disreputable look. He still carried his bandaged right arm thrust into the breast of his tunic, but his captors had taken off the slave chain, so that only the grip of the burly warriors on either side of him restrained him. He had been walking readily enough between them, but at the sight of Sennos, the bloody knife still clenched in his right fist, he stopped, and his mouth set into a hard line. Then, at their renewed urging, he walked on, into the clear space beside the fire. When he saw Togi, picking himself up from the mud, his eyes narrowed. "So, savage," he said softly, "you are here."

As if called by his words, the rain, which had been coming in spatters and snatches on the gusty wind, suddenly began to fall in a torrent, blotting out the landscape. The fort disappeared behind a gray curtain, and the more distant wings of the British camp as well. Half-extinguished, the fire began to smoke furiously, but Togi could spare it no attention. His eyes were fixed on Sennos' face, but his mind was listening for the voice of the God. He felt a sense of power growing around him, and a shiver went down his spine, not born of the cold or the rain.

The King was saying something, but at first his voice was drowned out by the noise of the rain, and he tried again. "...stop the sacrifice," Togi heard. "...again later...ill omen!"

Sennos paid him no heed. His white hair hanging in a soaked mass upon his shoulders, his face and clothes running with water, he was positioning the officer's captors where he wanted them. A wave of acrid smoke from the dying fire engulfed him and he coughed, but his hand with the knife was steady, and his gaze was fixed on his victim. The Red Crest stared back at him with wide dark eyes, and his lips moved silently as if in prayer.

Togi saw a flicker of light from the corner of his eye, and lurched forward as if to hold the offering bowl. His foot in its worn rawhide shoe slipped in the mud, and he careened into Sennos, knocking the old man off his balance. The two of them landed with a splash on the rain-soaked ground, and the sacrificer's knife went spinning to land point-down in the turf. And over them the heavens echoed again and again with thunder, as the God spoke. Releasing their prisoner, the men who had held him hastened to help Sennos, who was struggling to push Togi off of him and rise, and their former captive, after one frozen instant of surprise, took to his heels toward the fort, vanishing into the rain before anyone could think to catch him. And that was the end of the sacrifices for that day.

It had been, thought Togi, on his hands and knees in the mud beside Sennos, and doing his best to hide his own inward mirth, *the thing unexpected* indeed. The wonderful thing was that he had not planned any of it—it had simply happened at the will of the God. But he knew that he would have to watch his own back in the future when Sennos was around. Even if the old Druid believed this had been an accident—and how could he not?—Sennos would still never forgive him.

Ten days later, with the fort still holding out, two Red Crest ships sailed into the Menai from the north. The tribesmen watched as they anchored in the river near the remains of the docks, and some of the more energetic young men wanted to attack them. "No," said Regenos at a hastily assembled war council, "we have lost too many of our warriors already in our last three attacks. Let the Red Crests go if they will. We will burn their walls behind them, and bury our dead, and make our borders secure for when they come again." And over a rising clamor he continued, "No, O my people. I would love as much as any of you to slaughter them all, to feed their bodies to the crows, to burn their fort around them and bury them in its ruins! But I repeat, let them go if they will. I would not lose one more man of our forces, not one more drop of your blood, to harry their retreat. All those left to us we will need to defend our land next summer—or the summer after!—when the Red Crests return. For they *will* return, with their numbers undiminished, as they always have returned before. All the days of my manhood I have fought them, since first I could carry a spear. O leaders of my people, are not my words true?"

"They are!" said Orgetos strongly, and others echoed, "True! True!" Regenos nodded.

"Go then, some of you," he said, "and keep watch. If they bring reinforcements—if they begin to unload supplies—I will unsay my words, and we will fall on them together! But do not hinder the departure of those already here. For now, I only wish them gone."

Some of the young warriors, eager for blood, took him at his word, and went to watch the Red Crests. But Regenos had spoken truly. Before the day was over, black clouds of smoke were rising from the fort, and at the sounding of a horn, the men left in it marched out. They went in an orderly array, ten after ten of them, their big red-and-gold shields carried at the ready, and the pale sunlight glinting from their polished steel-clad shoulders and bright helmets. Togi, watching from a distance, saw the wide waving horse-hair crests on the officer's helmets, and the two wolf-skin-clad men in the lead, carrying, one of them, a pole with shining silver disks on it, and the other, a square red and gold banner with the charging boar which was repeated on the shields, and strange letters above it. *LEG XX*, he read, and frowned. They all marched defiantly, with a clash and a clatter of arms, but with a wary eye on the watchers.

The foot soldiers were followed by five more men on horseback, with oval shields and mail shirts like those of the men Togi had fought on Môn. Lances ready, they formed a rear guard for their fellows, but there was no need. Regenos' will held, and his men held their hands, although they pressed closer and closer as the Red Crests reached the river and began to wade out to their ships.

At last, when all but a handful were on board, the horsemen dismounted and stripped the gear from their mounts. Then with a whack on the rump, they sent their horses racing along the shore, and scrambled for the ships as the tribesmen closed in. A thrown spear caught one between the shoulders, and he stumbled, but his fellows dragged him aboard; then a hail of missiles from the ships drove the tribesmen back. The anchors came up, the big square main sails was raised, and with a flourish of oars the ships, heavily laden, headed for the mouth of the river and the open sea beyond, accompanied by a yelling of insults and clattering of arms from the watching warriors.

"They will be back," said Cingetos from behind Togi. "Like the swallows in summer, or the locusts, they will be back."

"I know," said Togi with a sigh. "But for now they are gone, and we can get in a spring crop on Môn before they return. Sennos leaves for there tomorrow."

"And you?" asked Cingetos, smiling. "Are you going with him, to refound the Druid order there?"

"Na," said Togi, and grinned. "For now, at least, I am going home, where I belong."

"So, I think, are we all," said Cingetos, "at least for the winter. Spring may bring with it another tale."

"I know," said Togi again. And this time he did not smile.

The fort lay in ruins. The Red Crests had burned most of their stores and filled the wells with rubble and dead bodies, but a little grain had been missed. The rest of the timber buildings and gate towers that had not already burned were put to the torch. The tribesmen buried their own dead with due ceremony, but the Red Crest bodies they left for the crows which were circling thickly overhead. Even some of the turf ramparts they breached and threw down into the ditch; any returning Red Crests would find little here that they could use.

Looking back from the hill shoulder for a last view, Togi thought that it could have been much worse. Môn was theirs again, and the Red Crests gone; but many a place would be empty at the Samhain feast this year. Of the fifteen men who had ridden out with him, three would not be coming back. That was a heavy loss for a small community, and many would have lost more. Yet they would have food this winter after all, and next year—if the Gods were kind!—no Red Crests to steal their crops.

It seemed a small victory for so much blood and pain, but Togi was coming to realize that much of life was made up of such small gains. It was a bitter truth at his age, but no less true for that.

Dark Waters

After the violent autumn, winter passed quietly. The people celebrated Samhain with feasting and good cheer, remembering their dead, then spent the cold evenings in indoor crafts and storytelling. For Togi, and for Valos too, whenever he had the time, there was also more study; as Cunomoros often said, learning was a lifetime task for a Druid. This winter he had thought of something new for both of them: the use of letters. Although the Druids taught most of their knowledge by rote, the better to train the memory, many of them could read and write as well, as Togi had seen in Sennos' room at Dinas Brân.

The subject had arisen when he was telling Cunomoros about the Red Crests' defeat, and described the flag they had carried while marching out. "That is another skill which you should have," Cunomoros had said, after looking at Togi's clumsy drawing of "LEG XX" in the dirt floor of their hut. So at his direction, Tritos carved them wooden tablets, much like the ones which Sennos had burned, and filled the shallow depressions on one side of each tablet with melted beeswax; and for the rest of that winter, using the angular characters of the Red Crests, Togi and Valos learned to write.

They also found that the tablets could have other uses, such as the drawing of crude maps. One evening, under Togi's fascinated eyes, Cunomoros recreated for them the shape of Môn, and pointed out the holy places he had once known there; then, smoothing the wax first with his thumbnail, he went on to sketch more generally the shape of Ériu's Land. "Here," he said, pointing to the north end of the blob he had drawn, "is the great Sanctuary where I studied, and here the rugged country—many are its lakes and mountains!—from which Lovernos came. And this"—he indicated a shallow curve on the east coast—"is the landfall for the River Boyne, great mother of waters, which flows past the mounds built by the Old Ones, in the days when the Gods still walked among us."

"Father," said Togi, who had been following a thought of his own, "can you show me how to reach the place where my blood-father died? I should like to visit it someday."

Cunomoros looked up in surprise. "Well," he said after a moment, "I can try... In truth, every step of that journey is engraved upon my heart, but whether I can draw it clearly and accurately enough... We shall see."

He smoothed the golden-brown wax again, and began to draw. "Here is our valley... here our stream, which joins a greater river... here the gap in the hills over which you must climb, and the foothills beyond... here the wide marshy plain—Red Crest land now, and dangerous... Cross it, so, bearing first for these hills in its center, and then on toward the higher ones you will see in the distance, aiming always two hands north of the sunrise point. When you reach the high hills, turn north along their base until you find a broad north-flowing stream. Follow it until it bends west and another stream joins it. Then look toward the winter sunset, and you will find the place you seek."

"Was that, then, the way which you went?" asked Togi.

"Not entirely," said Cunomoros. "We spent some time in the high hills, at a sacred refuge there, before Lovernos led us to the place which the Gods had chosen for his end. But by this route I think you will find it... When will you go?"

"In the middle of the Bright Month, after my next birthday," said Togi. He had not planned it so; the thought spoke itself, without his will; but he knew at once that it was fitting and right. Cunomoros nodded, as at a thing expected.

"Yes," he said. "I will try, before then, to prepare you for your journey, my son."

"Cannot you go with me, Father?" asked Togi. Cunomoros shook his head.

"I am too old," he said simply. "But take a friend with you to aid you." And he looked at Valos. Togi looked at the brown lad, too, and smiled.

"Will you come with me on this mad adventure, brother?" he said.

Valos grinned. "I was only waiting," he said, "to be asked. And now I cannot wait until we go!"

"Cunomoros says it is called the Black Lake," said Togi, "not only because the waters are so dark, although they are that, but because it is itself a Gateway to darkness." Valos nodded, and pushed back the hood of his cloak. It was a mild spring morning, gray and soft, and the drizzle which had been heavier earlier was now letting up.

"He has told me a little about Gateways," he said. "But nothing compared to what you have learned. Will you know, then, when we reach the—the place?"

"I think so," said Togi.

They were riding, rather than walking—Valos on the gray pony which Cingetos had left with Togi over the winter, and Togi himself on a little brown mare who had formerly belonged to a Red Crest soldier. She was his share of the spoils from his first fight on Mynydd Llwydiarth, and he was proud of her as he had been proud of few things before. He had taken her in preference to a mail shirt or a cavalry sword, and had not been sure at the time why he had made that choice, but now he was glad he had done so. She was not only fast, but also an easy ride, even without her Red Crest saddle and bridle, which had gone to another man. The only thing about her which concerned Togi was the Red Crest brand on her right hip, which might attract attention where they were going. On balance, however, he thought that they would be safe enough, since they intended to avoid all contact with the Red Crests—so far as was possible. And there had not really been another choice; they could not afford to be gone too long at this season, when there was so much work to be done on the land and with the herds.

Brushing a few stands of his dark hair back out of his face, Togi returned to the previous topic. "I think I will know the place when we reach it: Cunomoros told me many details, and my *awen* should also tell me if it is right. I am more concerned right now about the Red Crests. How much do you remember about them? You were, what, nine? when you left them?"

"Almost ten," said Valos. "I was born around Samhain—I cannot tell the day, their calendar is different. I remember a great deal, as much as any boy growing up among the *canabae*—the rag-tag of camp-followers outside the fortress walls—would know. The man who owned my mother—Marcus was his name—traveled from place to place with the *tax* detachments, and took her with him when he changed postings. We were on our way from the Twentieth's main base at Isca Augusta—that same LEGIO XX whose flag you saw at Caer Seint—to the new fortress which the Second is building on the north shore, when we were attacked, I never knew by whom. My mother grabbed me and ran, and dragged me into the bushes, where we lay still and hid—hid until the next day, when everyone was gone. Then we started walking toward the sunset. That trip is a blur to me, I could not lead you back on our track. All I know is that at last we came to your valley, and people made us welcome there, and we stayed... Yes, I remember a great deal about the Red Crests. What would you like to know?"

"All that you can tell me," said Togi seriously. "We have a long ride ahead of us, and nothing much else to fill the time, other than to keep watch for Red Crests, and hold to our direction. Pick something which seems good to you, and begin."

Valos smiled reluctantly. "That will keep me talking for some time. Well, then..."

He talked, and Togi asked questions, and time slipped by. At midday they stopped for a while to rest the ponies and stretch their legs, then went on. Now and again they passed farming villages, where men were breaking the soil with ox-drawn wooden plows, or sowing grain in fields already prepared; now and again they encountered shepherds or cowmen, or young men on the hunting trail, and stopped to exchange a few friendly words. These were still the lands of the Ordovices, held by tribes akin to their own, and safe. They slept that night in the hall of a chieftain, made welcome as honored guests for the tales Togi could tell of the war—although as strangers and fellow-tribesmen they would have been welcome anyway.

The next day they rode on, fording the big river which formed the boundary between the hunting runs of the Ordovices and those of the Deceangli, their ponies sending up splashes of clear water which sparkled like jewels in the early morning sunlight. The country was lower here and more thickly wooded; they rode more slowly, following a narrow game trail to the gap in the hills of which Cunomoros had told them. As they climbed, the pale misty green of the valley trees gave way to the bronze-gold of new oak leaves and the just-swelling buds of the alders, and then at last to the dark heather and sodden last-year's bracken on the ridge tops, where the sheep would soon be grazing. Today that land stood empty, except for the moving shadows cast by the hunting hawks overhead, and the flash of red which was a distant fox, trotting through the heather on some business of his own. The game trail dropped again, and they threaded a belt of thickly wooded broken hills, heading always, so far as they could, in the direction of the sunrise.

That night they spent in a small steading at the foot of those hills, and the next day set out across a different sort of country entirely, a land flatter even than that which Togi had seen on Ynys Môn, and without the enclosing presence of the sea. This was the land of the Cornovii, their last-night's hosts had told them—a powerful tribe who had already come to terms with the Red Crests. That might be a new danger, thought Togi, for although Cunomoros had taught him that hospitality was the common right and expectation of any traveling man, yet it was also well to be wary among strangers. "Not all men," his father had said sadly, "are to be trusted; and those who have submitted to the Red Crests may seek to buy favor with them by betraying their enemies. Tell the people whom you meet that you are on a quest, that you go to make offerings to your father's spirit at the place of his death, that you go on pilgrimage to fulfill a vow—all of these have some truth in them, have they not? But whatever you do, remember not to mention the Druids. To do so could put you in very great danger indeed."

Two days, at least, to cross the marshes, Cunomoros had said; but in fact it took them four. The first day they reached the central line of hills, and slept that night in a chieftain's hall within the banks of the ancient hill-fort which crowned the southernmost member of that chain. They were made welcome as always without question, but when Togi named himself as a pupil of King Regenos' Bard, traveling in response to the urgings of his *awen*, their hosts quickly became

more curious. He answered some of their questions about the
fall of Caer Seint, and found that, subjugated or not, they were
no friends to the Red Crests.

"They trample down those who oppose them," said one
of the older warriors, "and our King thought it wiser to make
submission while he could deal from a position of strength, but
we will never be their slaves, and they know it." He grinned,
showing missing front teeth. "Where does your *awen* lead you,
O Seeker? If one may ask?"

"One may," said Togi, smiling in return. His belly was
agreeably full of roast cow meat and good beer, but he had not
drunk enough to lose all caution. "And if I knew the answer, I
would tell you. I only know it takes me toward the sunrise, and
the distant hills I saw this evening from your walls. Can you tell
me how best to reach them? For this land is strange to me."

"Na, that is more easily said than done," said the man.
"But come with me tomorrow morning, and I will do my best
to set you on your way. For now, though—a student of a King's
Bard must know some songs and tales, must he not?"

"True words," said Togi, still smiling. "And if you can
find me a lyre, I will do my poor best to sing one." He had not
spent two summers with Cingetos without learning a fair
number of songs, and his trained memory sang them back to
him now. When the lyre arrived he tuned it, fumbling only a
little with the carved bone pegs. What to sing? A good
question… He smiled to himself. Yes, that was the song. Taking
the singer's stance, he struck a ripple of notes, and began.

"In dark waters lies the answer—
in dark waters deep and still
where the Gods have placed my treasure
in the pool beneath the hill.

Long ago in times forgotten
when the First Men walked this land,
they left there a thing of magic
for those who could understand.

No man's hand will ever reach it,
grasp or seize or pull it up,
yet it lies there for the taking
sweet as mead within a cup.

Gold and silver cannot buy it,
nor sword win it in a fight—
inspiration, precious *awen*,
gives it to me as my right.

Priest nor king cannot command it,
and the waters keep it still—
say its name, and you may find it
in the pool beneath the hill."

"A Bard's song indeed," said the Lord of the hall when the mild applause had died. "Yet it would please me better, Singer, to hear a tale of battle."

"That is easily done, Lord," said Togi. And after a moment's pause for thought, he sang an older song he had learned from Cingetos, a song of praise for the hero Caratacos, who, ten years before the fall of Môn, had fought beside the Silures and Ordovices against the invading Red Crests, and had been betrayed to his enemies by Cartimandua, the Queen of the Brigantes, and died far away from his people and his land. This song pleased the hall much better, and the Lord gifted Togi with a twisted silver bracelet. After that the drink went round again, and there was no more singing that night. Yet the first song he had sung echoed still in Togi's mind as he lay down to sleep. Was the answer indeed *poetry*? He did not know...

From the top of the northern hill next morning, the view to the east was clear. As he had promised, the gap-toothed warrior—Cagos was his name—led them there, and stayed to point out their best route. "There are two choices before you," he said, scratching his red-bearded chin, "and neither is good. You may strike to the north past our chain of hills, where the land is better for traveling, but also where the Red Crests swarm thick as bees on summer gorse. Or you can strike to the east, avoiding the bogs as best you may—beware any too-green ground! That will keep you clear of most of the Red Crests, but you risk losing your way in the forested hills which lie between you and the heights. I would suggest," he said, grinning, and casting an eye at Togi's pony, "that you chance the forests. The wild pigs and wolves are not friendly, but they will be less of a danger to one who rides a hip-marked Red Crest mare."

"There is much in what you say," agreed Togi, nodding, "and I am for the forests. Valos, what do you say?"

"I also," said Valos. "I do not fear the Charging Boar of the Legions more than that of the forests, but at least the latter are better eating. Let us go east."

And east they went. Mud and bogs and swarms of biting insects gave way gradually to brush and brambles and densely wooded low hills. They followed winding game trails when they could find them, and more than once lost their way under cloudy skies when the rain set in again. Twice they had to circle Red Crest working parties, where gangs of men in muddy tunics labored to move earth and sod along the line of a new-planned road. That first evening they made a miserable camp amidst sodden bracken and bilberry beside a pool where the frogs sang all night and the mosquitoes whined and bit them, and the next evening they lay beneath dripping alders whose lacey branches bore pale young leaves and this year's tiny green cones. But at last the ground began to rise, and they knew that they were finally approaching the hills. That third night they stayed at a poor farming village, and the next day the people there put them on a trail which led northeast to the river they were seeking. And that night they camped beside its banks at the foot of the high hills themselves, and knew that they were close to their goal.

Despite his weariness, Togi could not sleep. Instead he lay awake, watching the pale disk of the full moon climb slowly to the zenith amid her attendant stars. Tomorrow he would see the place where his blood-father had died, and where perhaps Lovernos' spirit still dwelled. Why had he really come on this quest, and what did he expect to gain by it? They had talked about it, he and Valos, earlier that evening, before the brown lad had wrapped himself in his cloak and fallen asleep. Valos

had been hesitant to ask questions. "You told me once," he had
said haltingly, "a little about *when* your blood-father died, but
not how or why. That we go to find the place of his death is
fitting, but—is there more that I should know?"

Togi added a few sticks of wood to their fire and stirred
it, so that the little red and gold flames leapt up brightly. "*Sa*,"
he said after a bit, "I had not thought... I had forgot that you
did not know. My blood-father died by his own will as a
sacrifice to the Gods, and was put into the earth at the sacred
pool we seek—at the Black Lake."

Valos nodded. "The place which you told me is a
Gateway. Yes, that I can see. But why—*why* did he die? I mean,
why did he make the sacrifice? Was he called?"

Togi was silent for a while, watching the fire. It had
seemed such a natural thing to him, that his father had made the
sacrifice; he had known it for as long as he could remember.
Now that he was asked directly, he had to think.

"I—do not know," he said at last. "Only that he made
it. Perhaps that is what I have come here to learn."

Now, as he lay awake in the moonlight, turning the
worn silver ring on its thong between his fingers, he could find
no better answer. Idly he noticed how much his hands had
grown in the years that he had carried it: probably it would fit
on his middle finger now. But he made no move to put it on,
no move to wear it: he did not yet have the right.

Perhaps he never would.

Morning came gray and misty. They ate a little of the
dried deer-meat they had brought with them—the supply was
running low—saddled the ponies, and set off northward along
the stream, following its western bank. It led them north and
then west, through thickets of alder and willow and then onto
flatter and marshier ground. In late morning Togi saw on the
opposite bank the incoming stream he had been told to watch
for, and drew rein. He had hardly needed that sight; he had
been aware for some time that he was approaching a place of
magic. It was similar to the feeling he had had on Môn when he
and Sennos had visited the Hill in the Black Grove—the Gate

of Initiation—similar, but not the same. He slid down from the mare's back, and said, "We are close."

"How do you know?" asked Valos, and then, "Na, I see the stream, but—never mind. By your *awen*." Togi smiled.

"Yes," he said simply, and then, pointing southwest, "This way."

They walked slowly in the direction of the winter sunset, leading their ponies, and circling sunwise around the boggy ground. When they came to a drier spot where the trees thickened, Togi said, "Here—we camp here."

Taking the ponies' bridles, Valos asked, "For how long?"

"Until tomorrow," said Togi, looking around. He knew he was close, close… Valos nodded, and began to unload their gear.

"I will set up camp," he said, "and then walk back to the river—there should be fish."

"That would be good," said Togi absently, taking his hooded cloak from the mare's back and putting it on. "I need to—to look around."

"Surely," said Valos, unbuckling the gray pony's bridle. "Go ahead."

Togi stood for a while at the edge of the trees, looking out over the marsh. The morning's clouds had thickened and hung low and threatening; he thought that it might rain before night. An ill omen? Perhaps, perhaps not. Time would tell.

How do you search for a ghost, he thought, *or a memory?* The place where Lovernos had died was somewhere close by, he was sure of it, but he could not find the focus of the power which he felt. Yet moment by moment it was growing stronger, almost as if it were reaching out to him in its turn. *Father,* he thought, *is it you that I feel? Your spirit, waiting, holding this land—for…why? Why did the Gods bring you here, requiring such an offering? And…will they require it of me, some day, in my turn?*

Silence. Under the lowering clouds, even the air lay still. The dark water, the stiff green reeds, the tattered white remains of last summer's cotton grass still clinging abjectly to its thin brown stalks—all waited, unmoving, under that heavy gray pall.

Waiting as I am waiting, Togi thought, *for a sign… for a word… for a breath of wind… for the breath of the Gods… for Inspiration!*

A drop of rain dimpled the water, leaving an expanding ring. Another joined it, and another. One or two struck Togi's dark hair, and he reached back absently to pull the hood of his cloak over his head. From its shelter he continued to gaze out at the water—*in dark waters lies the answer,* said the song in his mind, *in the pool beneath the hill…* That was where the answer lay, and there he would have to seek it—if he could.

Making himself a cushion of bog grass and reeds on the driest spot that he could find, he sat down on the folded skirts of his cloak. He was reminded for a moment of the nest of grass and blankets in which he had sat, four Samhain nights ago, awaiting a ghost, and he smiled briefly. This time, however, it was he who was the Seeker, he who was the traveler into another realm, searching for—what? The thing unexpected…? Closing his eyes, stilling his breathing, he felt the world around him begin to shift, as the Gateway opened. The Black Lake… the Gate into Darkness… black as the water, cold as death, and deep as the earth herself. Slowly, deliberately, with an effort of pure will, Togi loosed his grip on his own world, and passed through that Gate.

Behind him the light faded, until he stood in utter darkness. Yet he was not without sight: through closed eyes he saw the cavern around him, huge, echoing, empty—and not empty. At one moment it seemed full of treasures—red-gold breastplates and arm-rings, bejeweled scepters, fine-wrought weapons of silver and bronze and steel. In the next heartbeat there was nothing there but rugged piles of stones, rough and jumbled, the bones of the hollow earth. *Everything,* he thought, *and nothing: but none of it is mine. I seek a different treasure. Father, are you here?*

The vision faded, and he was in darkness again. Time passed while he waited, time unmeasured, marked only by the beating of his heart, and the dripping and gurgling of water all around him. And at last, as had happened so often before, he felt a presence; but this one was neither God nor spirit. *Who comes?* asked a voice in his mind: the voice of a man.

I come, said Togi. *I, Togidubnos, the Son of the Fox. Who asks?*

The one you seek, said the voice. *Why have you come here, my son?*

I come in search of knowledge, said Togi. He thought the presence smiled.

Then follow me, said the voice, *and learn.* And Togi followed... Through darkness and light, through water and stone, through earth and air and fire, through silence and sound, he followed. It was a very long way, and it was not far at all; it took him a lifetime, and only a moment; in the course of that journey his very being was agonizingly destroyed and recreated, and he felt no hurt at all. And at last he found himself standing in a fire-lit, stone-walled chamber, in something very like his own body and his own clothes, and facing a dark-bearded, white-robed man whose features were at one and the same time strange to him, and utterly familiar. He could indeed—though he did not know it—have almost been looking at himself as he might appear in ten or twelve years' time, if he lived so long. Togi only recognized the essence of the being facing him, which he had touched once or twice before in meditation and in dreams. "Father?" he said, and the man smiled.

"Let us sit," he said, gesturing to two wooden benches on either side of the small chamber, and took his own seat on one. After a moment, Togi followed his example. It was good to feel smooth polished wood beneath his buttocks, and cool solid stone under his feet; good after that unmeasured and unmeasurable journey to feel—almost—real again. The man across the chamber watched him in calm understanding. "Will you drink?" he said, and turning to a low table beside him, lifted a cup—a greeting cup of age-darkened, intricately-carved wood—and held it out to Togi. Their hands touched on the cup as it passed between them, and Togi felt warm human flesh. But this man—no, he would not think it. He lifted the cup to his lips, and tasted clear heather mead. Over the rim their eyes met, and again the stranger smiled.

"It is safe to drink," he said. "By my name and by my soul and by my *awen*, no harm will come to you here." This time Togi smiled in return.

"I believe it," he said, and drained the cup. Under the honey taste of the mead, sweet and bitter together, he felt it fill him with a cool fire. *This,* he thought, *is the wisdom I did not find in the salmon.* The thought exhilarated him; he felt suddenly as if he could work marvels; but the calm caution he had learned from Cunomoros asserted itself, and he remembered his reason for seeking out this man. "Honored One," he said, falling back on the formal address, "may I ask questions?"

"Surely," said the man. His voice was low and pleasantly husky. "Ask what you will; but some questions I may not be able to answer."

Togi thought for a moment. "You have not," he said carefully, "told me your name, although I have greeted you and spoken mine. Is it permitted to ask it?"

"It is permitted," said the man, "but there is no answer. I have no name now: I gave it away with my life."

Togi thought again. "In that life," he said, "were you he who begot me?" Again the stranger smiled in his dark beard.

"In that life," he said, "I was. Is this what you came to learn?"

Togi shook his head. "Not entirely, Honored One," he said. "I am here: someone begot me, and of him I have heard only good. But after he did so, I am told that he went away to this place—to the place where I was today—and gave his life to the Gods. Is this not so?"

"It is." The stranger nodded.

"Then, Honored One," said Togi, "is it permitted to ask the reason for that sacrifice?" The stranger was silent for a time, and his deep-set eyes seemed to be looking into a distance.

"It is permitted," he said at last. "I gave my life away that I might become a Guardian—a Guardian of our land, and of our people, and of all that we hold to be true and right and holy. I was not the first to die so, nor shall I be the last, although my death was more formal than most. Those of us who have given ourselves to the Gods, live knowing that we may someday be called upon to die for them. When that day comes, if that day comes, we all make the sacrifice required of us. Some make it gladly, and some reluctantly, but the end is the same."

"How will I know," asked Togi, "if that sacrifice is required of me?"

"You will know," said the stranger. "It is bred in you." He pointed at Togi's breast. "You have a ring which came to you from me, yet you do not wear it. Why not?"

"I have not yet the right," said Togi. "I am not yet a full Priest."

"On the day when you put on my ring," said Lovernos—and Togi knew now, beyond all doubt, that it was he who spoke—"your question will have been answered. On that day your fate will be fixed, and I will know that my sacrifice to the Shining Ones was accepted. But part of your answer, my son, you know already."

"What is that?" asked Togi.

"It is the consenting," said Lovernos, smiling like the sunrise, "which matters. It is the consenting which sets your spirit free." Turning to the table again, he picked up a dark wooden bowl which sat there, full of small russet apples, and held it out to Togi. "You have drunk my mead," he said, "and taken no harm. Will you eat now with me?"

Togi took the bowl, and looked at the apples. They were round and firm, deep red flecked with gold where the sun had caught them, and pale yellow-green where the leaves had sheltered them. He could smell their sweet autumn scent on the cool air. He looked up again at Lovernos. "You died in apple time."

Lovernos nodded. "I did." A trace of his smile still showed in his dark eyes, but his mouth in the frame of his beard was stern now. Togi looked again at the apples, trying to work out what exactly he was being offered. The feeling of exhilaration which the mead at first had given him had passed, and his head felt thick with weariness. There was magic, he knew, associated with this fruit, but... After a moment he looked up again and smiled.

"You said, O Honored One, that no harm would come to me here, and I believe you. I do not know the meaning of this gift, but I accept it." And choosing an apple, neither the largest nor the smallest, he bit into it, his eyes still holding Lovernos'. The fruit was perfect, crisp and juicy, sweet with a hint of tartness. He ate all of it but the core, and set that down on the bench beside him, next to the empty cup and the apple bowl. Lovernos nodded again.

"Yes," he said, "you consented to trust, and your trust is not betrayed. If you can trust in me, whom you do not know, how much more can you not trust in the Shining Ones, who hold us all in their hands? Rest now; you must go back soon, but you will go with my aid and my blessing. I am content, my son, with the bargain that I have made."

It was a long way; it was a short way; it was very hard, and very easy. When Togi opened his eyes again beside the Black Lake, he felt that he had been gone for an age and more; yet the gray daylight had not changed, and his hooded cloak was only a little wet on the shoulders. His body, too, when he stood up and stretched, was not very stiff; he could not have been gone from it for long. Slowly, thinking on what he had learned, he made his way back to their chosen campsite.

Valos was squatting by a fire, cooking fish spitted on green willow twigs, but he looked up at the sound of Togi's approach. "Is all well?" he asked.

"Very well," said Togi, squatting on his heels beside his friend. "Tomorrow we can start back."

"That will be good," said Valos, smiling. "I have had enough for now of sleeping in damp woods and avoiding Red Crests. It is time that I went back to my sheep."

Retribution

Cingetos had been right about the Red Crests. "Like the swallows in summer, or the locusts," he had said at Caer Seint, "they will be back." And back they came in the month of Cantlos, not long before Beltane, when all the world was bright and green and hopeful, and brought destruction with them.

The first that Togi heard of it was from Cingetos himself. He had been out all that day in the up-valley pastures, helping Valos with two late-calving cows, and came home at dusk, tired, wet, and very dirty, to find the Bard enjoying a cup of ale beside their fire with Cunomoros. "Ha!" he said, stripping off his belt and his filthy tunic, and stooping to pick up a clean one from the small pile of gear beside his bed-place. "My *awen* told me this morning that we would be seeing you again before long! What is the news?"

Cingetos laughed. "If you were expecting me, O far-seeing Priest, why were you not here to greet me?" Togi grinned.

"I might have been wrong," he said, handing the wet tunic to his mother, "and Valos said that the red heifers were for calving today. Only wait until I go to the stream to wash off this muck—then I will want all your news!"

"Haste back, then," said Cingetos, still chuckling, "or your father and I will have drunk all the ale, and the news may be harder to swallow dry."

"I know," said Togi, and went out again into the misty twilight, leaving the Bard staring after him.

He had known for a long time that this was coming, but had hoped that it would not be so soon. He had had plans for the summer, plans which might now never come to fruition. There was Seda, for instance, the girl he had come to know last year in the hill camp; Beltane night was coming, and he had sometimes hoped that she might spend it with him. And before Beltane, and much more important, was the Manhood Ritual: he would be helping Cunomoros this year, bringing the boys forward to him in the darkness when they were called, as Valos and other make-shift assistants had done in the years before. From now on that role would have been his, and his alone; it was an important part of his priestly training, for the time when he would someday take his father's place. But if it was to be war again already... He set the thought aside, as he was learning to do. Things would happen as the Gods and his fate decreed. He could only do his best to fulfill his allotted role.

When he returned, clean and dressed, but with his long hair still hanging loose and wet upon his shoulders, Cingetos and Cunomoros were still nursing their cups beside the hearth. His small sister was asleep in her bed-place, and his brother Tritos was somewhere else with his friends, but his mother had saved him his bowl of stew by the fire. He took it from her gladly with a word of thanks, for his belly was very empty, and holding it, squatted beside the other two. "What news, then, of the Red Crests?" he asked, beginning to eat. "For nothing else could bring you here, Cingetos, in this season."

"Softly, my son, softly," said Cunomoros in gentle rebuke. "Let our guest tell his tale in his own way."

"Na, na," said Cingetos, "I understand his haste. It is not war, Togi—or at least, not yet. Only we have heard rumors that the Red Crests are gathering a cavalry force—a large cavalry force—at their new fortress of Deva, and Regenos feels it would be well to be prepared."

"Valos and I were over that way, not so long ago," said Togi slowly, "in the lands of the Cornovii, and what we saw was mainly Red Crests building roads. But we did not go closer to Deva than we could help."

Cingetos nodded understandingly. "Nor would I, but some have done so. I do not come to summon anyone, not yet, but merely to spread the news, so that our people may be ready when the time comes. I do not think, myself, that they will strike soon, for they may wish to pillage, and there is little enough to be had from us at this season. Also there are whispers that Frontinus their leader may be leaving Britain soon, and he would not be wishing to leave in the midst of a war."

"All of these things, my friend, are uncertain," said Cunomoros. "But tell us more of what you were saying about Môn."

"Ah," said Cingetos, toying with his half-empty cup, "that is a better story." He drank a bit, and Cunomoros lifted the pitcher to refill it. "Na, save a little for later; I have had enough for now. Môn has been in part resettled, Togi, and those returning there have already planted their crops with what seed we could spare them. If only the Red Crests hold their hands until harvest... But it is not likely. We have seen their ships off the coast, but so far they have not attempted to land. Sennos orders all on the island now, and sends us word. He is settled at Rhiwlas, and offers to the Gods daily of what the people bring him, although"—and here Cingetos grinned—"he has taken no more Red Crest prisoners." Togi smiled.

"It was not my fault," he said, "that the last one got away."

Cingetos laughed. "I was there," he said, "and saw it. But that is by the way." He drained his cup, and stood up. "I am for bed now, in the hall. I ride on tomorrow to the east. Shall I take the gray pony with me?"

"Yes, for I have the mare now," said Togi, also rising. "It is good to see you again, Cingetos, though you do not bring good news."

"Wait," said Cingetos, "until I come again, to say that." And he went out. But Togi lay long awake that night before he slept.

The manhood hut was stuffy and warm, and its air thick with smoke. Bending forward, Togi dropped another pinch of dried mugwort on the hidden fire, then picked up the skin drum again. Its heartbeat rhythm, sometimes tapped with one or two fingers, sometimes with the whole hand, would measure out the minutes and hours to come for the ten boys lying blindfold in the dark. Togi knew what they were feeling; his blood beat with their blood, his mind moved with their minds. Behind the hanging curtain with him, Cunomoros was ready. All was as it should be for the beginning of the rite.

It had not started that way. Only the day before, a messenger had come from the King: the Red Crests were moving, along the north shore and through the southern passes in a pincer movement which would close on Caer Seint.

Bratronos and two or three of the older warriors had been summoned to a hasty council; they had left that morning, and only old Crotos had remained to set the fourteen-year-olds on their path. The boys—they seemed like children now to Togi, only a year older—had been restless and distracted, madly eager to be ready for the fighting they knew so little about, and it had taken a long time to get them settled. Even now he could hear one or two moving uneasily on their beds of skins. They would have strange dreams tonight.

Cunomoros' touch on his arm broke into his thoughts. "It is time," the old man said, barely above a whisper. "Bring the first one forward when I call." Togi stilled the vibrating drumhead with his palm, and slung the instrument's strap over his shoulder. Silently he felt his way around the curtain as Cunomoros unshuttered his lantern. Behind him the old man's voice, echoing strangely, called out the first boy's name, and Togi went to guide him as he arose. Then he returned to his drumming, and the hours passed like a dream. Ten times for the cup, ten times for the telling of their visions, and then it was the moment for the knife, and the test of blood. Valos had not stayed for this part of the ritual the year before, but for Togi it was different, as Cunomoros had explained.

"When you take my place," the old man had said, smiling, "you must know every detail of the rite: the way to hold the knife, the depth and placing of the cuts, and how to judge the proper heat of the iron. These things you will practice many times, at first on a dead animal, and then on your own living flesh, before you do them on the arms of the young men. But this year you need only watch, and aid me in small ways, as by making ready the firepot and the other tools." And he showed Togi the scars on his own thigh from the days when he had been a neophyte on Môn. "It is not appropriate to do in ritual," he had said then, "anything you are not prepared to suffer, if need be, in yourself. That is the thing Sennos would never understand, and one of the reasons he was not chosen as Archdruid on Môn."

"Yet that, I suppose, is what he thinks himself now," said Togi. Cunomoros sighed.

"Thinking a thing," he said, "does not make it so. Sharpen the knife now, my son, that all may be as it should be on the appointed day." Togi had thought about those last words for a long time. He did not think they only referred to steel.

He watched now as each boy in turn stood and held out his arm for the knife and the brand. Not one cried out, although some of their faces showed their pain. In battle it would be much worse; last winter he had seen too many men die, some of them screaming in agony. Before this summer was over, he thought, he would see more. One of them might well be himself.

He considered that thought as the bowl of blood went around, and shrugged. Sooner or later, every man living must die. He was not a boy now; he knew it for truth. These about-to-be men would learn the same in their time. That was the real lesson behind the manhood ritual: when the time comes to die, let it be for the sake of the tribe, for that is the blood bond, the oldest bond of all.

Three days later the King called them to war.

Togi crouched unmoving in a clump of brush on the steep hillside, looking down the narrow Glaslyn Pass. In the distance he could see the Red Crests, the sun glinting off their polished helmets as they moved, splashing slowly across the river in order to reach its wider west bank. As the scouts had reported, they were all horsemen. That would make the Ordovices' ambush more difficult in some ways, but it could not be helped. At least the narrow pass would slow the Red Crests' advance and make it harder for them to escape once they were in the trap.

His thoughts drifted back to the previous afternoon and the King's last council. Regenos would be leading this attack himself, having sent Orgetos and half his *teulu* north to help deal with the Red Crests there. "If we can defeat this force in time," the King had said, overriding objections, "we can hasten north to reinforce him—always supposing he still needs our help. No, I do not like splitting our army, either, but the Red Crests have given us no choice. We must deal with both parts of their attack at once, and hope that this group will indeed take the shorter road through the Glaslyn Pass, as I think they will, rather than skirting the mountains to cross the Lleyn ridge at Bwlch Derwen. The tides are high just now in the Aber Glaslyn, which should help them to make up their minds; also"—and here he had grinned like a hungry wolf—"I have taken pains to make sure that they know how close this route will take them to Dinas Brân, and how great is the richness of my court there—from which I will no doubt be away in the north, meeting their other attack! I have never yet seen a Red Crest army that did not like a bit of pillaging, if the chance arose!"

It seemed, thought Togi, peering through the thin screen of branches in front of him, that the King had been right. At any rate, the Red Crests had finished their crossing of the river, and the first of them were now entering the pass. They were coming slowly, well bunched up; that should help. He would not have much longer to wait.

His left leg was cramping, and he shifted his position slightly, being careful to make no movement which could be seen from below. They had all been in position since before dawn, and he had greeted the sunrise silently from this high perch. Turning his head slightly, he glanced along the mountainside, but even knowing that they were there, he could not see any of his fellows. They had all disappeared into the rocks as thoroughly as the morning mist which had half-hidden the river earlier.

The first of the Red Crests were passing below him now; he could hear the occasional jingle of harness, and the soft smother of hoof beats on the rough road, but the bulge of the hillside, and the bulk of the carefully loosened boulder in front of him, hid them from his view. He would have to wait for the signal from one of the watchers on the opposite cliff. It would not do to start the attack too soon.

Time passed; a chaffinch lit briefly in the branches of his bush and trilled a few notes, then flew on about its business. When would the horn sound? Surely the invaders must all be in the pass by now. Too late could be as bad as too soon. If they once got past the narrows... Even as he thought it, a hunting horn called from the mountain across from him, its bright summons echoing in the canyon below. Setting his back more firmly against the hillside, Togi braced his feet against the gray rock in front of him and pushed with all his strength. Slowly, reluctantly, it moved, and then with sudden speed, bounding down the hillside to join the cascade started by the other young men, and crashing into the mounted force below. Injured men and horses screamed, and a Red Crest trumpet brayed orders. Almost immediately these sounds were mixed with battle shouts and the clash of arms from north and south, as the men who had waited there, concealed in the trees, attacked the disorganized Red Crests from both ends. Grabbing his bow, Togi stood up and began to shoot, grinning savagely as he did so, and added his arrows to the rain of rocks and other projectiles still descending on the enemy below.

The battle was brief and bloody, and was over almost before it began. With half their men and horses already down, bottled in front and rear by yelling warriors, and unable to reach their tormentors above, the Red Crest troopers fought bravely, and bravely died. A few broke through to the south, to be hunted through the mountains by their pursuers, but the Glaslyn River ran red that day with their blood, and only a handful escaped to return to their half-built fortress at Deva. The Ordovices took no prisoners alive that day; but that night the King feasted his force in triumph at Dinas Brân, and there was horsemeat for all who wanted it.

In the north things went much the same in a different canyon. The two prongs of the Red Crest advance, both taken in ambush, were crushed into bloody rags, and most of the Ordovices came safely home again. But neither the King and his councilors, nor Togi and his friends, believed that the war was over: this was only a lull.

In that lull, however, there was time enough to heal the wounded, and to tend the herds and crops; time enough, too, for love. Togi had got his Beltane night with Seda, and for him, at least, liking had been added to lust. He might yet come to marry, he thought; after all, a Priest must pass along his craft to his sons as both his different fathers had passed theirs to him. But it was early days yet for such plans; the world was wide, and he knew in his heart that he had far to go in it. Ériu's Land still beckoned in his dreams.

He tried to tell Seda about this, lying out in the sun-bleached grass above the hill camp, late on one warm evening in Dumos. They had been kissing and touching, with little sighs and murmurings, and had paused to take breath and let their blood cool. Looking up at the high pale sky, just brushed with feathers of cloud, Togi was reminded of that morning last winter on Môn where their war had begun. "Someday," he said softly, "if the fighting ever ends, I am for traveling. There is so much yet that I still need to learn."

"Where would you go?" asked Seda. "They say that the Red Crests are everywhere in Britain. Cannot your father teach you all you need to know here?"

Togi shook his head. "Na, he tells me that there are crafts beyond his teaching. If I would learn them, I must go to the Sanctuaries—to the last of the Druid Sanctuaries—in Ériu's Land, across the Western Sea."

"That is a far journey," said Seda, turning to look more closely at his face. "How long would it take, that teaching?"

Togi frowned. "How can I know? It might take years. But at the end, of course, I would come back to you." He reached out to stroke her breast, but she stayed his hand.

"A women could grow lonely, with such long waiting," she said. "It might be that I had chosen another man."

"Mmm," said Togi. Rolling onto his side, he leaned forward and kissed her lips, lightly at first, and then more urgently. When he drew back, her blue eyes were smiling into his. "I am going nowhere soon," he said, smiling back at her. "Let us enjoy the time that we now have. Who knows what the autumn will bring?"

Reaching out in her turn, Seda touched his beardless cheek, then laughed when he turned his head to nip at her fingers. "Yes," she said, suddenly serious. "Who knows. Let us enjoy the time that is now."

Togi smiled, and leaned to kiss her again. As he moved, he felt his father's ring shift position on its thong inside his tunic, but for once he ignored its message. For today, he would enjoy the time that he still had; tomorrow would take care of itself soon enough.

Lughnasa came, and the harvest. It was bountiful this year, and the people began to hope. Then, toward the end of Anagan, when they thought themselves safe for the winter, the bad news came: the Red Crest armies were once again on the march.

"They are coming by the north shore again," said Cingetos, "and this time they are ravaging as they come. Rumor says that they have a new governor, and he is hot to prove his strength."

"Can his strength repel boulders?" Togi asked. Cingetos shook his head.

"I doubt it," he said. "But I also doubt they will make the same mistake again. They are a frighteningly practical people, the Red Crests."

Cunomoros sighed, and added a few pieces of wood to the hearth fire, which flickered now and then in the drafts from the autumn storm outside. Rain was drumming on the thatch, and Cingetos shivered, drawing closer to the flames. He had got soaked through on his ride that day, and still did not feel warm. "Let me make you a draught, old friend," said Cunomoros, seeing it. "Togi, fetch the brown bottle: you know the one I mean."

"Perhaps it would be better," said Cingetos reluctantly, for he had tasted Cunomoros' draughts before. "I have no time to lie ill; I must carry the message to three more valleys tomorrow." And he sneezed.

"Perhaps," said Togi, returning to the fire with the brown bottle, "you should rest here for a day, while I run your errands for you. I could easily take the message; you have only to tell me the way. It is not right, anyway, that you should do such work, you who are a Bard well-trained and famous." Cunomoros eyes' twinkled, but he said nothing, only taking the bottle and beginning to prepare the draught. Cingetos smiled weakly.

"Mine is not the only nimble tongue here," he said. "I ride on the King's errands because the chieftains all know me, and will take his orders through me, that they might through others decline. But if I feel no better in the morning—well, we will see. First, Cunomoros, I will prove the strength of your draught."

"Tell me now, when you have drunk it," said Togi, smiling at Cingetos' grimace of distaste. "Then, if you are unwell—despite my father's magic!—I will be off at dawn, and you need not wake."

"Perhaps," said Cingetos hoarsely, "I will do that. Only first, for the love you bear me, give me a cup of ale to take the taste away!" Laughing, Togi complied. "Now," Cingetos said when he had drunk it, "The first place that you must go…" The list was not long, and Togi carefully memorized it, reciting it back at the end to prove he had it correctly.

"And the message?" he said.

"The same to each," said Cingetos. His eyelids were drooping now, and he yawned. "To meet Regenos with all their warriors at the Conwy crossing, as soon as ever they can. Once the Red Crests cross that river—although the rain may delay them—I doubt that we can stop them short of Ynys Môn." He yawned again. "By the Gods, I am tired! Lend me your bed for tonight, Togi. I doubt my legs will carry me as far as the hall!"

"He will be in a fever before morning," said Cunomoros softly to Togi, once the Bard had lain down. "Do you prepare your gear now and be ready to ride at first light; I can make the dawn offering without you. Better for all of us that you make all speed with the news."

"I will make ready my weapons as well," said Togi, "for I think I shall need them when I return."

"Yes," said Cunomoros, nodding, "you will need to ride with the rest. I also shall have preparations to make, in case the Red Crests come this way. I fear that they mean, this time, to destroy us all."

Togi had a wet ride the next day, but he had expected it. He took the Bard's pony, so as to leave his own mare fresh for his return, and pushed the poor beast hard, slowing only where he must on the steep mountain trails, and splashing through the half-hidden fords where brown bog-water from the hills roared

-203-

in foam-flecked torrents around the black teeth of the rocks. One after another the mountain chieftains listen to his news, nodded gravely or angrily, and began their preparations. Hospitality was offered him in every village, but he turned away all but a few hasty bites of food, eaten on horseback as he rode on.

The autumn darkness was closing around him as he reached his last goal, and slid gladly from the back of his tired mount. "Rub him down well and feed him," he said to the boy who took his reins. "He has earned his rest today." And he made his way into the fire-lit feast hall.

Maiorix was the chieftain here, a grizzled elder whom Togi remembered from the previous autumn's war. It seemed that he remembered Togi, too, as his first words showed. "Ho, the Priest's lad who entertained us so at Caer Seint! Has old Sennos cast you off, then, that you ride about our mountains in the rain?"

"Na, lord," said Togi, laughing. "I serve another master today. Cingetos the King's Bard was to have brought you this message, but he lies ill in my valley, and I go about to do his work for him." Then, more soberly, "Alas, that the news is not better. The Red Crests have returned in great force under their new leader, and are ravaging the villages of the north shore as they move westward. The King sends out the call to all the men of the valleys, to meet him at the Conwy crossing so soon as ever you can; for let the Red Crests but cross that river, he says, and it will go hard with us to stop their advance, short of Ynys Môn."

"Ill news, indeed," said Maiorix, nodding, "but not unexpected. Well, we will be ready to ride out tomorrow, but for now, King's messenger, be free of my hall. Daughter, bring the guest cup, and find this young man good food and a place by our fire!" And turning away, he began to give rapid orders to the other folk who had crowded into the hall behind Togi.

The young woman who brought the guest cup had her father's thick mane of hair, but her curls were sun-gold rather than gray. "Be welcome in our hall, King's messenger," she said smiling, "and forgive my father's haste; it is only the urgency of your message which demands it."

"I would expect no less of him," said Togi, smiling back at her over the cup. "I have seen him speak in the King's councils, and know him for a man of decision and renown. For myself, I only need a little food, and a place to sleep—also the loan of another horse tomorrow, for mine is weary."

"All of that you shall have, and welcome," said the woman. "For has my father not made you free of his hall?"

"Indeed, and he has," said Togi, looking her over frankly. "My only sorrow is that I cannot linger here long enough to taste all its joys."

"Perhaps you might return in the future?" she suggested, her blue eyes twinkling.

"Perhaps," said Togi, "if the Gods be kind." But the words tasted hollow in his mouth, and he knew in his heart that he would never do so. The *awen* was not always a comfortable gift to have, he thought, as he followed the woman to a seat by the hearth. Sometimes the future was better left unknown.

The crossing of the Conwy lay at the top of its tidal range, where the river has been forded time out of mind. The village beside it—now deserted by its people, who had fled to the hills—was the place where Togi had first tasted salmon, in that long-ago summer when he first traveled with Cingetos. The river's waters had been clear green and placid then; today they were muddy brown, flecked with foam and debris which the rains had brought down from the mountains above, where the Bard still tossed in fever under Cunomoros' care.

Togi stood now amidst the ranks of assembled tribesmen, his right hand clenched hard on the polished shaft of his spear, and watched the enemy come. Back in the summer, he had thought the Red Crest cavalry forces large, but this army dwarfed them. A rolling tide of men, vast and unstoppable as the ocean, they seemed not so much to march as to flow across the land. Polished helmets and shining steel-clad shoulders gleamed brightly in the dappled morning light above their big red-and-gold rectangular shields, while here and there the transverse horse-hair crest of an officer, from which the Red Crests took their name, waved defiantly above the rest. In the front came a man carrying a tall pole topped with a gleaming golden eagle which glittered as he moved—the God of their army, perhaps, Togi thought. Troops of horsemen with green shields like those he had fought on Môn flanked the marching ranks, and in their midst rode a man with a high-crested helmet, and armor which cased his torso like a shining silver skin. The waiting tribesmen on the western bank began to drum their spear-shafts against their shields and shout, but the Red Crests advanced silently, remorseless as death.

Then, as they reached the ford, a horn sounded a bright string of notes. The marching ranks paused to adjust their positions, and then threw a volley of light spears across the river, driving the tribesmen back. The Red Crest soldiers began to follow them, wading steadily into the brown water without a break. Some of them fell, as the tribesmen began to throw their own spears in return, but more took their places; the numbers seemed endless.

As the first-comers reached the western bank, the yelling tribesmen surged forward to meet them, and blood began to flow. The tribal leaders tried to keep their men in order, but the younger warriors were eager to prove their valor in combat and could not be restrained. To the shouting of battle cries were added the thuds and crashes of blows and the screams of the injured. Slowly, foot by foot, as more and more of them came ashore, the Red Crests pushed their opponents back from the ford.

The front ranks of the tribesmen were forced back in close fighting, or fell to be trampled groaning underfoot. The air grew heavy with the stench of blood and urine and feces, and the ground slippery underfoot with these and other things, and treacherous with fallen men and weapons. Togi found himself jammed in the middle of the pack, crushed against two burly warriors in front of him and unable to move. The second rank of Red Crests had begun to throw their javelins again, the barbed weapons soaring over their own men and falling in the thick of their opponents. Togi struggled to raise his shield in order to protect himself from this iron rain, but he could not; there was no room. He was going to die helplessly where he stood. Fear and anger surged within him as he struggled; this was not the destiny for which he was born. *O Lugh of the Light,* he prayed silently, *protect your servant, that I may survive this battle to do your will!*

Then there were fresh screams from either side of him, and he saw that the Red Crest cavalry had come into action, swimming their horses across the river to attack the tribesmen's flanks. Behind him there was suddenly room to move, as the rearmost warriors turned and fell back toward the hills at their chiefs' urging: the ford was lost, and those who could must escape to fight another day. After a moment's wavering, Togi joined them, breaking into a run as the rout became general.

Behind him he heard a thunder of hooves: the cavalry was coming. On this rough ground he could not outrun a horse, but perhaps… Ahead of him was a low cluster of gorse bushes. Dropping his spear and shield, Togi dove headlong into it and rolled, ignoring the clutching thorns. The spear point that would have pierced his back in another moment passed harmlessly overhead, and the horsemen streamed by on either side of the obstacle, ignoring him. Gasping, he lay as still as he could in his refuge, listening to the screams from the battlefield. He knew that a warrior should stand his ground and die bravely for his people, but he felt he could help his people more if he was alive. There would be plenty more chances to die bravely after this day.

Presently he heard the cavalry returning at a trot, the soldiers calling out to each other as they rode. Togi could catch a few of their words thanks to Valos' coaching. He wondered if his friend—if any of his friends—had survived the battle, but there was nothing he could do for them. If the Red Crests camped nearby it might be difficult to get away, even after dark, but there was nothing he could do about that either. In the meantime, he was hungry and thirsty, and some of the gorse branches were digging painfully into his ribs and belly, but he went on lying still. At least he was alive, where all too many were dead.

The day passed slowly; he could hear Red Crests shouting from time to time, and thought they might be making camp somewhere to the north of the battlefield, no doubt to tend their wounded and bury their dead. He could hear screams and moans from that battlefield as well, and listening, he wept at his own helplessness. But not until night had fallen and the young moon had set did he leave his refuge.

His first care was to recover his spear and shield from where he had dropped them. The shield he could replace if need be, but the spear was his manhood gift from Cunomoros, and not willingly would he abandon her. Crawling slowly through the bilberry bushes and tussocky grass in the dark, and pausing now and then to listen for Red Crest sentries, it took him a long time to find her, but at last he felt her familiar shape under his left hand. After that the shield was easy. Slinging it cautiously across his shoulders, he paused for a moment, considering. The cries of the dying still wrung his heart, and his silent tears flowed unnoticed as he listened, but he knew there was only one thing he could do for them, and the Red Crests would be watching for any movement by the ford. Instead, kneeling in the shelter of another gorse bush, he prayed to his Gods to ease their departure, and to lead their spirits safely to the Land of Rest. Then he roughly wiped his tears and began his slow journey up the valley to the west. Now and then as he crawled he could see the blink of fires in the Red Crest camp, but only when he thought himself safe from their sentries did he get to his feet.

The sky overhead was clearing, and the stars gave him enough light to see by. They showed him, amidst the rocks and bushes, here and there a tumbled body. Bending, he touched, now an out-flung hand, now a bloody shoulder, but the flesh was cold. Then he found one who moved and groaned, and spoke in a thread of a voice he recognized. It was Vindex.

They had become friends of a sort in the summer camp the year before, joking and drinking together sometimes in the hall afterwards along with Valos and big fair-haired Pasutagos. The little dark youth had no laughter left in him now, only pain; the wonder, thought Togi, passing careful hands along his body in the dim light, was that he was still alive. "Vindex," he whispered, "O my brother! I hoped that you had escaped."

"Na, na," said Vindex, shaking his head feebly. "Spear...took me...from behind. Too late now...do you...have water?"

"Na," said Togi, "but...only wait." After the rains the ground was still sodden; he would not have far to seek. Leaving his shield and spear, he groped his way down the slope until he found a tiny trickle, and soaked part of his cloak in it. Retracing his steps, he squeezed the water drop by drop into his friend's parched mouth.

Vindex sighed, and muttered something, and Togi bent closer to hear. "Cold... Togi... how long?"

"Na," said Togi, "I am not leaving. I will stay with you as long as you need me." He thought privately that it would not be very long. He chafed his friend's cold hands, feeling for the thread of a pulse as Cunomoros had taught him to do. Vindex's eyes were open, gleaming in the starlight, but their gaze seemed unfocused. "Togi," he mumbled once, and Togi said, "I am here." Some unmeasured time later, he realized that he was alone.

Fumbling at Vindex's waist, he took his friend's belt knife, which might be of use to one of his younger brothers. He closed the staring eyes, and wiped his hands on the rough grass beside the body; then, taking up his own weapons, he resumed his journey.

None of the other bodies he saw that night was still alive.

The Ordovices struck again and again as the Red Crest army made its slow way over the Ddeufaen Pass and south along the coast to Caer Seint, but only in running fights from ambush. Togi played little part in these battles; his healer's skill, declared the King's doctor Lucotios, who had seen him bandaging the wounded, was worth more to the tribes than his single battle-borne spear. So Togi stewed poultices and ground herbs while his friends fought and bled, and did his best to heal those of them who came back; and every morning, wherever he found himself, he made the dawn offering to the Gods. It was often not much of an offering—a barley bannock, a handful of nuts, or a cup of heather beer—but it was what he had, or could get. The days of great public sacrifices were over, and the Gods, it seemed, had turned their faces away from their people. But he could not turn from the craft which was bred in his bones.

From their new base at Caer Seint—built higher up the slope than the old one, which still lay in weed-covered ruins—the Red Crests began to send out forays into the lower valleys. By now it was well into Ogron, and the moon which had been young at the Conwy fight had passed her fullness and begun to wane. The tribesmen began thinking of their homes, and winter; it was time to bring the herds down from their summer pastures, and to prepare for the autumn slaughter. Yet still they were here, shedding their own blood, while their wives and children labored unaided—if indeed they had not been cut down in their own fields, or driven into the hills by the Red Crests' ceaseless raids.

Togi was at the council when the decision was taken, standing beside Cingetos—for the Bard had come back at last, pale and shrunken and worn. Regenos sat with his chieftains, or what was left of them—too many had fallen in battle—and listened patiently to all that they had to say. There was gray in his beard which had not been there last winter, and new lines of sorrow etched in his broad brown face. His own eldest son, that new-made shining warrior, had died the day before on a Red Crest horseman's spear.

"Na," he said at last, "we can fight on and on, Ambiorix, but how many of us would be left to see the spring? I remember, though I was only a lad, the news from the Iceni lands, after Boudicca failed. The Red Crests will follow us into the mountains—they are doing so already—and wipe us out to the last man, if we do not sue for peace. We have made our gamble, and we have lost. Now we must try to get what terms we can."

"Once they have defeated us," warned Ambiorix, "they will turn their attentions to Môn."

"Then Môn," said Regenos, "must look to her own defenses. We are of her blood, but we are bled white; for now, we can do no more."

The terms were harsh. The tribute renders of the past were increased and made permanent. The tribes were to provide labor to work on the new fortress at Segontium, and on any other fortresses and roads the Red Crests should plan. All native trade was to pass through the Red Crest ports, and be subject to heavy taxes. And finally, there was to be a levy of one thousand young men, to serve as soldiers in the Red Crest armies abroad.

It was this last demand which almost ended the negotiations. The terms were being read aloud to Regenos and his councilors at a meeting with the Red Crests' leader—not merely the head of their army, but the new governor himself, Gnaeus Julius Agricola, who had personally led this campaign.

"What!" cried Regenos, astonished. "You cannot mean it! We are a poor people, and our losses have been heavy! Will you take our babes in arms, or our gray-beards, too? As well kill us all outright, and be done!"

A babble of talk broke out behind him, but the Red Crest governor held up one lean, brown hand, commanding silence, and silence he eventually got. "Let me explain. This levy is not a new thing; it has been enforced before on subject peoples—"

"It was enforced on the Iceni," said Maiorix, standing behind the King, "with the results you know, O governor of 'subject peoples'. Have a care that your demands do not bring a like response!"

"The care," said Agricola steadily, "must be on both sides. I was in Britain during that rebellion; I helped to put it down. I know what I am asking. My Emperor always needs soldiers, and the men of the tribes of Britain are some of the best. You shall have enough men left to till your fields and guard your flocks, even enough to supply the working parties I require, but not enough to launch another uprising against me and mine. Thus is the balance struck."

"And how will you chose your conscripts?" asked Regenos angrily, overriding the voices of his councilors. "I tell you that we have not so many young men left to spare."

"They would be chosen thusly," said Agricola. "It is known to me that among your tribes there is a warrior's mark, set upon the arm of every boy when he reaches manhood. All those within your lands who bear that mark, and yet have no gray in their beards, will be subject to conscription, and must present themselves to my officers at Segontium before the Winter Calends. Select those who come by your own methods; if the number be made up, all will be well, and I shall enquire no further. But if the number be short, any such young men which my officers find among you after that date will be hanged. Thus do I encourage compliance."

A babble of voices broke out again among the Ordovices, arguing and objecting, but Agricola and his men sat patiently silent. Togi, standing with Cingetos on the fringes of the crowd, found himself rubbing the scar on his left arm. Agricola spoke very fair British, and all the King's contingent had heard and understood his terms. *A frighteningly practical people*, Cingetos had called them, and he was right. If the levy was enforced—and it would be—those remaining would have no time to plan another uprising: all their efforts would be needed to survive. As for himself... But here his thoughts went no farther. First he must go home, and see his family again. After that it would be time to decide. And so far, Môn herself was still free...

A slight movement among the Red Crest officers caught his eye, and looking, Togi saw one of them staring back at him. It took a moment for the memory to come into focus, for the Red Crest, clean and shaven and properly dressed, looked very different from the battered captive Togi had first seen last autumn on Ynys Môn. Today his armor shone with much polishing, and the transverse red crest on his elaborate helmet waved proudly in the light morning breeze. Togi supposed that he had changed as much himself in the last year, for he had grown and filled out, and now wore the first proud smudges of a dark mustache on his upper lip. The officer went on staring for some moments, then smiled slightly, and gave a tiny nod of recognition. No question but that they would know each other, if they ever met again.

The cacophony of voices had died down, and Regenos was speaking. "We have no choice now," he was saying heavily, "but to accept your terms—all of your terms, O governor of Britain. Yet it is a shame on us which can never be washed out. But though we fought you to the last man, and took thousands of your men down with us, it would not benefit our children, who would starve just the same. Let that memory stay with you when you dine in your palace this winter, while we in the mountains subsist on grass and weeds." Then, standing, he turned his back on Agricola and faced his councilors. "O my people," he said, "I would have died gladly, rather than bring you to this day. If any wish my blood for it, let him but ask, and I will kneel and bare my throat to his knife. Yet I hope rather to live, and do all that I can to help us survive the misery which lies ahead, that our name and our line shall not wholly perish from the earth."

There was a little silence. Then Maiorix, who had become in some sense the leader of the King's *teulu* since Orgetos died five days ago, stepped forward. "For my part," he said, "I will have you still for my King, O Regenos, and I will stand for you against any who would contest that word. In making the decision to fight, and to make peace, you only spoke for all of us. Therefore the blame should not rest on you alone, but on us all. Does anyone here disagree?"

There were mutterings, but no one spoke up. Turning back to Agricola, Regenos said simply, "Governor of Britain, we all accept your terms."

Agricola nodded briefly in understanding. "Then let you carry them out. This meeting is ended." And standing, he turned and led his officers away.

"I cannot go," said Togi, his voice breaking.

"You must," said Cunomoros firmly. "You have no choice. You cannot stay."

"But who will help you if I leave?" Togi was almost in tears. They had been discussing the matter for some time, alone in the autumn garden behind their hut.

"Your brother Tritos will help me," said Cunomoros. "He is nearly a man."

"He is bound to his master," said Togi, before remembering that the wood-turner was one of those men who had not come back from the war.

There had been far too many of them. Of his age-mates alone, four had not come back; of the boys who he had helped to make men at Beltane, seven were missing. The older warriors had done better, but the number of widows in their village was not small. All over the highlands, the tale was the same, except where Red Crest incursions had made it worse. As to the coastal villages, better not to ask; most were no better than blackened ruins, with their erstwhile inhabitants left to feed the crows. And now the Red Crest's levy would take most of the able-bodied men who were left, leaving only the old and the feeble, the halt and the lame, to guard the herds and till the fields in their places. Those, and the women and children... "The Gods must hate us," said Togi bitterly, "so to destroy us."

"Think carefully before you speak," said Cunomoros. "Who are you to judge them? We are not the first people to have suffered so. Where are the Iceni now? Where are the tribes of Gaul? Were all of their Gods indifferent to their prayers? You have seen Môn in her devastation, Togi. Have I then forsaken the Gods whom I served there?"

"Na," said Togi after a pause, "you have not. And nor did my father Lovernos. He was firm to the end... I think that I must be made of weaker stuff than you. I cannot forget...the things that I have seen."

" 'Blood and death wait always in the way of the warrior,' " said Cunomoros, quoting the ritual. "In the manhood hut you once accepted this fate."

"I did. I did." Togi took a deep breath. "I will go to Môn, then. The Red Crests have not overrun her yet."

"Do you think that they will not?" asked Cunomoros quietly.

Togi shook his head. "Na, I know that they will. They did so before, when she was better defended. But it is—a first step upon my road."

"To Ériu's Land," said Cunomoros, nodding.

"To Ériu's Land," agreed Togi at last, and sighed.

So recently it had been his dream, to make that journey and study in his blood-father's land. Now that the journey lay before him, not only possible but required, he saw much more clearly all that he would be leaving behind. He sat on a rock near the top of offering hill next morning, after Cunomoros had made the morning prayers with him and gone down, and looked at the valley spread out before his feet. There was his father's house, and the bean plot they had hoed so often together; there the feast hall, where they had drunk with the other men; there the houses of his friends and cousins; there the storehouses, and the courtyard where they had fought the Red Crests, and where Ivo had died; there the winter barns for the ewes and the milch-cows; there the apple orchard, and the training ground where he and his friends had learned to fight; there the stream where they had sometimes swum in summer; there the sties for the wintered-over swine; there... But there were too many memories. Every rock and tree, every pebble and blade of grass, seemed to call out to him, reminding him of pleasures and pains gone by. Reminding him, too, of the friends with whom he had shared them... Valos had come back, but with a wounded shoulder which still gave him pain; big fair Pasutagos had lost his beauty for good. Bogos and Ambios lay somewhere near the Conwy crossing, their long-ago quarrels forgotten, and Vindex... His mind shied away for a moment; but no, he would not forget little Vindex, with his dark narrow face, and his bright laughter. Angrily Togi wiped away the tears which were blurring his vision, and stood up. It was time he went down; there was always work to do, and more so now than ever, with so many missing hands.

It was a few days later when the news came of the fall of Môn. It came, not by messenger this time, but at third hand, drifting up the valleys like smoke on the autumn wind, passed on from village to village by chance meetings of hunter or herdsman or traveler returning home. The Red Crests, it was said, had wasted no time once they had got the Ordovices' submission. Not pausing to build boats, Agricola had thrown his Batavian troops—trained to swim German rivers in full armor—across the Menai one morning, and taken the island's defenders by surprise. Farmsteads burnt, warriors cut down in battle, women and children slaughtered or taken away as slaves, Môn—or so the rumors told it—was more desolate now than it had been a year ago

"There is no haste now," said Cunomoros to Togi that evening. "You have more than two months before the Calends. Wait a little while, if you still mean to visit Môn, until the Red Crests have had time to settle in, or to return to winter quarters. Just now they will be stirring about like a kicked wasp nest, searching for anyone to sting. The seas will be no worse in Cutios, or even Giamon, and you will have had one more Samhain feast at home."

He did not say, *we may never see you again,* but Togi understood. So he stayed, putting off his preparations from day to day, and helping his kindred prepare for winter. The sheep and cattle were brought down from the hill-pastures, and the pigs up from the oak-woods where they had fattened on mast; the last berries were gathered from the wood-shore, and the hazels from along the stream; and the apples were safe in their store. The mornings were frosty now, and Penwyn wore sometimes a snowy cap after storms. And Togi's mother worked late and early at her loom, weaving the cloth to make him one last suit of clothes.

"It may be long and long," she said to him one evening when Tritos and the little daughter were already abed, "before I dress you again, my son, and I would not send you into the world in rags. Do not trouble to build up the fire; I shall not work much longer tonight."

"There speaks a liar," said Cunomoros fondly. "Do not believe her, Togi; if I did not stop her, she would still be weaving at cock-crow." And to his wife, "Less haste, belovéd; there will be time enough to finish it before he goes."

"Na, I know," said Togi's mother, smiling. "Yet still I wish to be beforehand with my work. Who knows what tomorrow may bring? Twice in my life now have I heard of the fall of Môn, that ageless refuge. The thing unexpected comes without warning to us all."

"True that is," said Cunomoros, and Togi nodded silently in agreement. "Sixteen years ago, it was, that I rode back up this valley to bring you a gift, and received a greater one in return. Lay aside your shuttle, Vera my wife, and give me that gift again." And reaching down his hand to hers, he tugged her to her feet. "Smoor the fire, my son," he said to Togi. "It is time we all went to bed."

Samhain night came clear and cold; but in the fire-bright hall, the feasting was muted. Too many places stood empty; too many horns and platters were set out for the dead. Togi was remembering Samhain nights before, especially the one when he had waited alone on Penwyn for the ghosts. Sacrifice, and the thing unexpected: the two thoughts twined together in his mind like plaited ribbons, like tendrils of bindweed climbing up a stalk. He looked at the dish of autumn apples on the table beside him, and remembered the one he had eaten with his blood-father in the spring. Trust, decision, consent: more tendrils joined the plait in his mind. He was bewildered, bemused by the pattern: if only he could understand its end...

"Still brooding, Togi?" asked Valos' voice beside him, as the brown lad laid a friendly hand on his shoulder. "Come and help me light the fire outside; we will be dancing soon." Like all the young men, Valos had made his decision about the levy. "The Red Crests bred and reared me," he had said the day before, shrugging. "If they will have me, I will go, to make up the numbers; but I doubt that they will take me. A man must be sound in wind and limb to serve under the Eagles; this limp of mine will likely excuse me from that. In which case, I will come home to aid your father, and to tend my sheep and cows: none of these will mind if my pace is sometimes slow."

"I hope you are right about the Red Crests not taking you," Togi said now, following his friend outside. "I could go to Ériu's Land with a lighter heart, if I knew that you were here to take my place with Cunomoros."

"I could never do that," said Valos seriously, and then grinned. "But I know what you mean, and I will give him all the help that I can. Now, if we were talking of your place with Seda—!"

"To that," said Togi, glancing back at the hall briefly, "you are also welcome. Things have been at an end with us, since I came back from the war."

"But surely she understands why you must leave?" said Valos, thrusting the torch he had carried from the hall into the bonfire's heart. "It is not as if you had any choice in the matter."

Togi shrugged. "She does, and she does not. I have talked as much as I can, but it makes no difference. I do not understand her at all."

"Understanding," said Valos wisely, "is not easy, with women." Togi laughed shortly.

"Good luck to you with her, then," he said. "I am through."

Crossing to Môn was not easy. Most of the fishing villages had been burnt, and their people scattered, but at last Togi found a boatman who agreed to take him across. Sitting in the stern of the little craft as the man sculled, he thought back to his leave-taking five days before.

His mother had wept, of course, and hugged him tight. "Goodbye, little cub," she had whispered. "Gods bless you. Take care."

Cunomoros had said little, but had given him his blessing; the old man's love for him had shone out of his eyes. "Walk always in the way of the Gods, my son," he had said at last, "and trust in their power. The pattern is not finished; your journey has only begun."

Tritos had been solemn-eyed and tongue-tied, but had pressed a small carved box into his hand. "It is not much," he had said gruffly, "but the best I could do, so far—I will do better in the future! And I will take care of all of them, until you come again."

The little sister had cried, seeing her mother crying, until he had picked her up and kissed her; then she had smiled. At last Togi had shouldered his pack—there was not too much in it, for he must go on foot, having lost his little brown mare in the war—and turned to go. That was when Pasutagos had hurried up, panting, with Valos not far behind.

"We feared you would be away without us," had said Valos, smiling. "We will come with you for the first hour, to set you on your road." That had lightened Togi's heart a little. They had talked of trivial things, and laughed, as though nothing was happening. "Well," had said Valos on parting, "take care, and keep clear of the women. If you ever come back, I will likely be here still."

"And I," had said Pasutagos with a grimace, "will likely be at the other end of the Empire, if I still live! Ah well, our fates make the pattern; we only do as they will. The Sun and Moon on your pathway, Togi; maybe we will yet meet again."

"Maybe," had said Togi, and smiled; but for once his *awen* was silent.

After that, there had only been walking: five days of walking, through sun and mist and rain; staying at night wherever he could find food and shelter; and always, always, keeping out of the Red Crests' way. That had been a bad time, with too many hours for thinking, and too much to think about. Now, with the shores of Môn drawing closer, it might be time for action again; and for that at least Togi was glad.

He had chosen to cross as far as he well could from Segontium; the Red Crests took too much interest in people on their doorstep, and might besides mistake him for volunteer labor. He was aiming for Rhiwlas, where last winter's war had begun; if anyone was left there after the Red Crests' depredations, it would be the best place to get word of Sennos, supposing the old Druid still lived. Togi felt there were still things to be settled between the two of them, still things to be said, and he did not know when he might come this way again. He was also, he admitted to himself, curious to see Tagia again. Something about her had stuck in his memory, and he was not so disinterested in all women as he had pretended to Valos. All in all, Rhiwlas seemed the best place to go.

"Almost there," said the boatman, looking over his shoulder, and Togi came back to the present. "Mind the rocks, and be ready to step out when I say—I do not want to ground her."

"My thanks," Togi said, shouldering his pack, and picking up his spear, which he had brought with him against all reason. Through the clear green water slapping against the sides of the boat, he could see the black rocks the boatman had mentioned, lying like teeth ready to rip the fragile craft to shreds. In a storm they would also do as much to a man, rolled against them by the pounding waves.

"Now!" said the boatman, and Togi stepped overboard, landing in the waist-deep water with a splash. It was cold, winter-cold, and he gasped, but kept his balance. The boatman, with a wave, backed his oars, then turned his craft and headed out to sea, while Togi made his slow way to the distant sand. He was, for the third time in his life, on Ynys Môn. Would it, he wondered, be the last?

The long walk to Rhiwlas in the morning sunshine warmed him, and he saw no signs of Red Crests. Now and then he passed plowed fields, but the farmsteads to which they belonged were empty and hearth-cold. No people, no herds, no dogs or playing children: only cloud shadows moved on the silent hills. A fear, half-admitted, began to grow in him: had he come to a dead place? He began to walk faster, in haste to reach his first goal.

Rhiwlas was still alive, if barely. The thin blue thread of peat smoke rising through the trees below as he skirted Mynydd Llwydiarth was the sweetest sight Togi had seen in days. He hurried on down the hill, hope rising in him, only for it to fall again as he came closer. The Red Crests had been here, too.

The village had not been large, but now there was little left of it. Most of the buildings had been reduced to ruins or piles of ashes; only the back portion of the hall was still standing, the peat smoke rising through its tattered thatch testifying to the persistence of life. A skinny brown dog lying in the dust before the entrance rose and barked at Togi's approach, and a woman's voice hushed it from within. A young voice, Togi thought, and perhaps familiar. "Hello, the hall," he called as he approached, and the dog barked louder. "It is a friend who comes." And in answer to his call, a woman came to the door.

At first he did not know her. Her long cascade of dark hair was pulled back roughly in a bun, and her oval face was thinner, and disfigured with healing scars. Not until she spoke did he recognize her as Tagia, who had walked beside him that night on the way from the shore. She spoke first to the dog again, to quieten it, and stooped to grasp its collar, then looked Togi up and down. "So," she said at last, "he was right for a change. You have come back."

"As you see," said Togi, approaching with a careful eye on the dog, which was growling steadily. "Am I not welcome here now?"

"To what little we have, yes," said Tagia, but there was no smile in her eyes. She stooped again and patted the dog, who ceased to growl. "He is a good watchdog," she said with a twisted smile. "Yes, come in, Togi. He will be wanting to see you."

She turned and went back into the ruined hall, and Togi followed her slowly, pausing to let the dog sniff him as he passed. Apparently satisfied, it lay down again with a grunt, but its yellow eyes were watchful. *You may be welcome*, they seemed to say, *but take care how you go*.

The back part of the hall had been clumsily partitioned off with woven branches, chinked with mud, to form a sort of room under the surviving thatch. Tagia stood waiting for him at the entrance to this area, holding back the leather door curtain. "Go in," she said briefly, "and I will follow. Yes, he will be glad to see you: I think he has only been waiting for that."

The room inside was dim and smoky and not large, but a peat fire burned in the central hearth and gave some light. Here at last there were people: a gray-haired woman kneeling beside the fire to stir a cooking pot; two small children sleeping together in a corner; an old man whom Togi recognized as one of the elders he had met the year before. Near the back of the room, partly screened from the firelight with hurdles, was a low bed-place, and in it lay Sennos—or what was left of him. His bone-thin hands lay folded on the blanket which covered him, and his eyes were closed; but as Togi walked toward him they opened, and seemed to burn in his gaunt face. "So," he said hoarsely, "you have come back, Fox Cub—and not before time."

"As you see," said Togi evenly, squatting on his heels beside the bed-place. "What would you have of me, Honored One?"

At the formal title, the corners of Sennos' mouth moved slightly in what might have been a smile. "Na," he said, "it is what *you* would have from me. I see you still do not wear your father's ring."

Togi glanced down at his ringless hands. "Not yet," he said, "but I hope to, one day."

"How if I make you Priest, then?" said Sennos. "I have the power—I am Archdruid now."

"Mmm," said Togi, thinking. "By what right?"

"By right of survival," said Sennos harshly. "I am the last Druid on Ynys Môn. No one here is senior to me now."

"Mmm," said Togi again. "I must think on this first. This is—unexpected." Sennos laughed shortly.

"Ah," he said, "you thought that I hated you, because you are your father's son. And in some ways, you are right. But I have a duty also to my order, which I must fulfill. Think if you must, Fox Cub, but do not think too long. My time in this body is short, and I am impatient to be away."

"What would this priesting involve?" asked Togi slowly. Sennos frowned.

"In the old days, the ceremonies were long and formal. I remember well my own. There were tests, and ordeals… But there is no way we can match that now. However… Do you remember the Hill in the Black Grove?"

"Of course," said Togi. Sennos' mouth twitched again at the corners.

"Yes," he said, "you wanted it, even then. Well, here is your chance. Go to the Black Grove—now, today, with no preparation. Enter the Hill if you are able, and stay as long as you must. Then come back, if you can, bringing with you what you found within. Then we shall see… Will you do it?"

Staring into the old Druid's pale eyes, Togi thought hard. Was this a gift of power, or a trap to destroy him? *Do not trust Sennos,* said Cunomoros' voice in his memory. *Do not trust him at all. There is nothing he will not do in pursuit of his ends…* But he remembered the Black Grove, and the power he had felt there;

and he needed that power now, more than he ever had before…

"Yes," said Togi, "I will."

"I knew that you would," said Sennos softly, and very slowly smiled. "After all, you *are* your father's son."

Some miles south of Rhiwlas that evening, Togi sat on a rocky ridge in the winter darkness and waited for moonrise. Thinking back, he smiled a little at his last conversation with Tagia. "Wait until tomorrow, at least," she had said quietly. "It is a long walk, and evening will soon be here."

"That was not in the bargain," had said Togi, swallowing the last mouthful of fish stew from the bowl she had given him. "Besides, I will be safer traveling by night. There will be moonlight later, and the Red Crests will all be asleep."

"Mind you do not walk into a bog, then," had said Tagia. "There are plenty of those, and they will *not* be asleep." Togi had grinned.

"You will have to come after me, then, and pull me out—or send your fine watchdog."

"I might," had said Tagia, looking at him thoughtfully. "I might even do that."

Now he was sorry that he had not taken her invitation to stay. Thus far his southward walk had been easy; he had followed the northeast-southwest trending ridge of which Mynydd Llwydiarth was the crest. But now he must strike eastward across the low hills and valleys which lay between him and the Menai, aiming for a destination which he could not see and which he had only visited once before. By day it would have been difficult enough; by night… He shrugged, and pulled his cloak closer around his shoulders against the chill wind. He would have to trust to his *awen* to lead him to his goal.

The moon was sinking into the west, and dawn was in the eastern sky, before he found it. He had blundered in and out of more than one bog that night, and was cold, wet, and exhausted—not the best condition, he thought wryly, for beginning an Otherworld quest. But the hill lay just as he had remembered it in its shallow valley, surrounded by its ring of half-burnt and fallen trees. He remembered that it had felt cold and dark to him even at midsummer; now in chill twilight, clad in frost-touched weeds and bracken, it loomed like some monstrous fortress of Winter himself. Circling sunwise around it, he came to the entrance, a gaping black mouth into the earth, half-hidden by tangles of bindweed and the dead stalks of rosebay willow-herb, still holding tattered remnants of their silky white seeds. No one had gone into that entrance in a very long time, certainly not within the last year. Whatever Sennos had sent him for, it was not something which the old man had recently placed there himself.

Togi hid his pack and his spear under a gorse bush, and walked slowly toward the entrance to the mound, feeling his way. He could sense the darkness inside the mound itself, and the presence of something waiting. This was more than an entrance, it was a Gate—a Gate between the worlds. If he could pass through it, he would find himself in another world—in the Otherworld— in the feast-hall, perhaps, of the Shining Gods themselves... As before, he touched the invisible barrier, and stopped, but this time he was prepared. Closing his eyes for a moment, he focused his mind and will on his task. Then slowly, step by step, he went on, as if leaning into a churning wave of water or a winter gale of wind. Three paces, four, five... His outstretched hands touched the hanging curtain of bindweed, and he ducked beneath it, and at once the pressure was gone. Straightening up cautiously, he sighed and opened his eyes.

They saw, by the faint moonlight which followed him in, a stone-walled and stone-roofed passageway, made by men little taller than himself. His mind, however, saw darkness—limitless darkness, spreading out like an endless plain in all directions. In that huge darkness, under a starless sky, his spirit moved like an ant on the boss of a great war-shield, tiny and insignificant and afraid. For a moment he reeled at the double vision, and felt himself falling; then, with an effort, he caught his balance and stood firm. Slowly, step by step, he went forward, along the dimly-lit passage and through the endless dark.

The light around him grew slowly fainter, but never quite faded; it seemed now to come from the stones themselves. The air was cold, and grew steadily colder, until he felt his very breath must freeze in his throat. He walked with the tips of his fingers brushing the walls which were and were not there, and his mind alert for danger. He knew that it waited patiently somewhere ahead.

At last, when he seemed to have been walking for hours, his hands lost touch with the walls, and he knew he was in the center of the mound. The icy silence here was absolute; not the sound of his steps nor his breath, nor the very beating of his heart, came to his straining ears. *This*, said the darkness, *is the place where all things stop, the place where all things end. Why, man, have you come to disturb our sleep?*

I come in search of a token, said Togi, *to prove my right to the name and status of Priest.*

What will you give us for it? asked the darkness. *For nothing, as you know, comes without its price.*

How shall I know, until my need is upon me? answered Togi. *When that hour comes, I will pay the price that is due.*

Come forward, then, and take what you will, if you can find it, said the darkness. *Then try, man, to find your way home again.*

Utter silence. Togi stood still and considered. He did not, in truth, know what he had come for, and he was not really sure that he could find his way back again. His legs ached, and his feet were weary with walking; he felt he could lie down and sleep, but he knew that this would not be wise. To search, in the dark, for an unknown and invisible something... No, that was not the way to go about this task. *What*, he asked himself, *did Sennos expect me to find? And perhaps more importantly, what do I want?* That, he thought, was the key to the question. Suddenly he smiled. The thing unexpected...

Not a ring, for he had one; not a jewel of any kind. Possibly a weapon; but what kind of weapon, then? A magical one, of course! And what he needed most, just now, was light...

The knowledge came as if he had always known it. He held out his hands before him, palm down and side by side, fingers curled as if they grasped a stick. With his mind he could see it—a slender rod of hazel, a little thicker than his thumb, smooth and peeled and white—and softly glowing in the darkness. He moved his hands slowly apart, seeing it lengthen, until it was almost as long as his forearm, then nodded to himself. There would be more work to do on it later—symbols to carve, letters to engrave—but for now, it would serve his purpose, and light his way home.

Holding it up in the darkness, he put the full force of his will into it, and suddenly its light sprang out, illuminating the vast room and the tall white stone which stood in its center. Carved patterns flowed across the stone's face like water; it seemed to dance in the glow from Togi's wand. The Light which lives hidden in darkness, the center of the mystery, life eternal and endlessly reborn, all-enduring as the Gods: that was the message of the stone. Togi stood gazing at it for a long time, drinking in its beauty. Once he started forward to touch it, then stopped, shaking his head. He had things still to do in the world outside, roads to walk, magic to make. He turned and found the door by which he had entered, and started back along the passageway which would take him to that world. Behind, in the darkness, he felt the stone still watching. It might have a long wait until the next Seeker would come.

The air outside was cool and fresh, and the sun was just rising. Thrusting the plain wooden rod he still carried through his belt, Togi greeted it, raising his hands and his voice in the dawn prayer. Then, suddenly so weary that he could hardly stand, he stumbled to the shelter of the gorse bushes where he had left his gear, and lay down. He would need to rest before walking any farther that day.

He came to Rhiwlas again at moonrise, having slept half the day, and thought at first that no one there was still awake, not even the watchdog. Then he heard a soft *woof,* and saw, in the shadows beside the ruined doorway, the pale shape of a human face. "I thought," said Tagia softly, "that it was you, but you are too late."

"How is that?" asked Togi, moving quietly toward her.

"Sennos is dead," said Tagia. "He died at dawn today."

"Mmm," said Togi, and sighed. "So I need not have hurried back."

"So it seems," said Tagia. She stepped into the moonlight and held out her hand. "He left you this."

Togi looked at the silver thing in her palm, but did not touch it. "His Priest's ring."

"Yes. He asked me, at the end, to give it to you."

"And his blessing?" asked Togi.

Tagia smiled. "That," she said, "was not mentioned." Togi chuckled.

"Sennos to the last. Did he leave anything else?"

"His sacrificer's knife. Do you want it?" Togi wrinkled his nose.

"I think not," he said. "Bury it with him."

"And the ring?"

"I am not sure—I suppose so. I will have to think." Togi sighed. "By all the Gods, I am weary. May I beg food and lodgings here, for tonight at least, before I go on?"

"It is waiting within," said Tagia. "And, in the morning…"

"What, in the morning?" asked Togi. He felt he could sleep for a week.

"There is a ship in the bay which will soon be going to Ériu's Land," said Tagia. "I bade them wait for a day or two, and then take you along, if you wish it." Togi laughed.

"Thank you, *cariad*," he said. "I could kiss you!"

"That," said Tagia dryly, "will not be necessary. But do you come in now, and enjoy my *offered* hospitality. That will be enough for tonight."

The Old Enemy

Togi sat on the Hill of Emain Macha in the late summer twilight and pondered the workings of fate. Three and a half years had passed since he had left Britain—three and a half busy, exciting, fruitful, and occasionally dangerous years. The ship which Tagia had held for him had taken him to Limni, an island off the east coast of Ériu's Land where a small trading station had long been established. From there a fisherman had agreed to take him to the mainland, to the *dun* of the local king at Droim Meánach. At first the king was minded to make him captive, for landless exiles had no status in Ériu's Land, and slaves were always valuable, but Togi's unexpected knowledge of his language, and his claim to be of the Druid kind, had given him pause, and a wandering poet's offer to escort the stranger across the hills to Temair solved the problem. There Togi had found men who remembered the fall of Ynys Môn, and accepted his story. Thus, by stages, he proceeded to the Druid Sanctuary near Emain Macha, where, with occasional excursions to the various sacred festivals, he had been studying under his current master for the last three years.

The first few months had been spent in improving his command of the Irish language, and reviewing his basic studies with his new teacher. Many of the concepts they discussed were familiar to Togi, but some were different, and excitingly so. The grounding Cunomoros had given him had been solid, so far as it went, but there were arts practiced by the Irish Druids which were beyond his knowledge—especially in the field of magic. Things Togi had felt instinctively but had not known how to apply were now made clear to him, and he practiced the necessary disciplines with a will. His greatest interest lay in those magical techniques useful in warfare, such as the summoning of mist to conceal an army, and the protective barrier known as the "Druid Fence". In these he showed promise beyond his years, but his teacher Fedelmid was troubled by the degree of his application. "Do not be in such haste to learn everything at once, child," he had said one day to Togi. "Knowledge without wisdom may be dangerous, and wisdom comes only with time and experience. You will have long years in which to perfect your art; do not rush so headlong into it. Where is your need for such haste?"

"Mmm," had said Togi uncertainly. "I am sorry to have offended, Honored One. I wish only to excel in—in all the arts you have shown me. I—I shall try to curb my haste."

"That would be well," had said Fedelmid, looking at him narrowly. "Let me hear now the other lessons you have prepared for today." Togi could not bring himself to admit the real reason for his impatience: his search for a way to drive the Red Crests from his homeland, and to keep her safe. Only in such a way, armed with such power, could he ever go home again; only thus keep faith with his blood-father, and with all of those he loved.

But time passed, while still he studied, and gradually he realized that it might take decades for him to reach his goal. He still dreamed sometimes of his home and family, but less and less often. Slowly, almost without noticing it, he had begun to build a new life here, among his new friends and mentors, a life where he was valued, and could hone his growing skills. And now that too seemed to be under threat, for his old enemies, the Red Crests, had reared their heads again. Even to Ériu's Land their threat extended; it seemed there was no limit to their greed for land and gold.

The rumor from which these thoughts had sprung had been brought by another Druidical student, returning that day from a visit to Temair, the seat of the King of Mide, south of the Boyne. It was nothing much in itself: only that while he was there, he had seen a small party of Red Crests—*Rómhánach*, the Irish called them—at the King's court. This was not entirely unprecedented, he said; there had been *Rómhánach* there before—usually traders. But something about this group had been different. Most of them had been, in the student's judgment, warriors; and that was a thing worth the mentioning, at least as idle gossip over meat.

Listening, Togi had scratched his chin in thought, where his young dark beard was sprouting. "What was it," he asked his friend, "which gave you that idea? Their dress, or their weapons, or something else about them?"

Aed, a lanky yellow-haired lad a couple of years younger than Togi, had frowned thoughtfully. "Na, I am thinking it was none of those, or at least, not those alone. Their dress was not much stranger than that of any outlander, and most men carry weapons who can, even the Men of Art. But they moved somehow as men who were used to fighting, and they kept always their eyes upon their chief. A youngish man, he was; dark, as they all were, but with a look of being used to command."

"How many were they?" asked Togi. "And where did they come ashore?"

"Half a dozen, I saw," said Aed, "but there might have been more. As to where they landed—na, the knowledge is not on me. From Limni, like enough. What difference does it make? They were only a few foreigners."

Togi had returned an indifferent answer, and presently walked out, as he often did, to be alone and think. His steps had taken him, not for the first time, to the Hill of Emain Macha. It was the closest unencumbered high spot, and except on festival days, it was quiet. He missed more than ever, at such times, the dark mountain peaks of his homeland, and the bright silence of their Gods. Those parts of Ériu's Land which he had so far seen were green and lush and kindly, but her hills were not the hills of his childhood, not the hills of his heart.

What should he do about this news? The thought of Red Crest soldiers peacefully at Temair—perhaps on a scouting mission?—worried him. So had they first come to Britain, to make contacts and evaluate the land's defense. Once let them get a bridgehead here, however, and he knew what would follow: invasion, destruction, enslavement—and the final suppression of the Druids. *That* he must prevent at all costs, for Ériu's Land was their last Sanctuary. He did not think that his superiors, however wise, truly understood their peril.

First, however, he must gather more information to prove or disprove his fears, and that meant a trip to Temair. The idea pleased him, and he suddenly smiled; after so long a time spent in rooted study, a little action would be a welcome change. Standing up and brushing off his short tunic, he started down the Hill, making his plans as he went, and still smiling.

He went first to his teacher's hut in one of a group of round wattle-walled thatched bothies, knowing that Fedelmid would be there at this hour. The Druid looked up at Togi's tap on the door-post, and his rather somber face lightened. "Enter, my child," he said. "What is your need of me? For I think that you come with some question in mind."

"It is an easy one, I think, Honored One," said Togi. "I ask your permission to journey to Temair's court. I have heard rumors of strangers there which intrigue me, and I would seek them out, and perhaps question them."

"Not hard the granting of that request," said Fedelmid, nodding. "Take what you will from the stables. Do you travel with a friend?"

"I had thought," said Togi, "of asking Ruad to accompany me, for she comes of that country and knows its customs well."

"A good thought," agreed Fedelmid, his dark eyes smiling at the name. "If she wishes it, she has my permission to go with you." Turning to his worktable, he took a slip of wood and carved three rapid strokes across it with a small knife. "There is my symbol; show it to any who enquires. When may I expect to see you again?"

"Before the middle of Dumen, I should think," said Togi, and Fedelmid nodded again.

"That will be well," he said. "Travel safely, and safely return."

The morning was bright and cool, and the chariot ponies were fresh; sitting in the two-wheeled cart, Togi had his hands full at first. He was keenly aware of the critical scrutiny of the red-headed young woman sitting beside him. "You would have done better," said Ruad dispassionately after a while, "to have let me handle them at first, as I suggested, but you are not doing badly—for a Briton. None but we Irish truly understand how to drive."

Togi grinned. It was an ongoing game between them, begun at their first meeting three years ago; now it had become habit, with neither of them keeping score. "That is as may be—not that I am agreeing!—but half of Britain is not covered with level bog. We have true mountains there—have you heard of them?—and prefer to ride our horses, not play about with little wheeled carts on the flat."

"That, of course, is your misfortune," said Ruad sympathetically, nodding. "But talk to me of mountains when you have seen those of the northwest. The Croaghgorm are truly a land of eagles, taller by far than your little British hills."

"I have not seen them yet," said Togi, still grinning, "but neither, of course, have you ever seen Eryri. Let us talk instead of Mide, and the Bend of the Boyne."

Ruad's green eyes sparkled, and she pushed back her long red hair from her strong-boned face. "The most beautiful and blessed land in the whole of Ireland. We have the greenest fields and the best cattle, the sweetest butter and the most intoxicating mead, the swiftest horses and the purest water. We have the sacred Boyne, greatest of rivers, which circles the mounds of the very Gods themselves. Truly there is no better place in all of Ireland, which as all men know—even the boastful Britons!—is the best of all the islands of the earth."

Togi laughed aloud. "Truly the Irish outstrip us poor Britons in everything, not forgetting the noble art of the boast! Now, to be serious for a moment, I have only once been at Temair, and that was in winter, three years and more in the past. What would we be likely to find there at this season? Would the King be still in residence, do you think?"

Ruad threw back her head and laughed. "Well, to be serious, if I must... Yes, Eochaid Finn should be there. He is growing old, and does not travel so much these days. You saw him, did you not, when you first came here?"

Togi nodded. "I did—a tall man, with yellow hair turning gray. I remember he had a fine hall, and many retainers, more than the king of my people at home."

"Yes, he is a king over many sub-kings—an *Ollam Ríg*, as we call it, a Chief of Kings. All of them furnish him with retainers, and with the food-renders to support them. He has, besides, his officers—his Druid and his Judge and his Chief Poet, his charioteer and his physician and his smith, along with many others."

"A great number, as you say," agreed Togi. "I was bewildered by it all at the time. If it had not have been for Dáire Dubh, the King's Druid, who questioned and believed me, I think I should have been quite lost."

"He is a wise man, and a generous one," said Ruad. "He spoke for me, when I wished to study to become *bán-draoi*. That is not usual, even among our people; but it is not forbidden, and my father agreed, so—here I am today!"

"On your way south again, with me, to see the *Rómhánach*," said Togi grinning. "*Hai mai!* It is good to be on the road again, with the sun and wind on my face, and—something of interest—ahead. I have been too long at my studies, and need to see more of life!"

"That," said Ruad drily, "you should find in abundance, in Eochaid's hall."

Two days later, entering that high-roofed building, Togi had to agree. From its carved and painted doorposts, to its blue and crimson roof-trees, to the intricately woven hangings which covered its walls, Eochaid's hall glowed with life and color. Its many supporting pillars seemed a young forest, and its throng of richly dressed men and women, great hounds and laughing children, seemed to fill all the space between their trunks. Shouting and singing, music and laughter, shook its walls; and its very air was heavy with the scents of roasting meat and strong ale, and blue with smoke from the hearth-fires that burned day and night in its heart. Compared to it, the fine hall of Regenos in Eryri seemed no more than a shepherd's hut, tenanted by a few wandering men.

Shouldering his way through the press with Ruad beside him, Togi looked around for Red Crests, and at first saw none. Despite the leaping fires and the smoking torches, the great room was dimly lit compared to the brilliant sunlight outside; some sections, moreover, were partitioned off with man-high wicker-work panels between the pillars, providing some privacy for those who sat within, but hiding them from his view. While he was still peering about, Ruad said at his shoulder, "There is Niall Chief Poet; let us ask him. He always knows everyone and everything, it is part of his craft."

Looking where she pointed, Togi saw a short, broad man with deep-set blue eyes and a sad face above his bushy gray beard. His many-colored cloak with its wide woven borders made Togi blink, and advertised his rank, while his jewels, from his great enameled gold brooch to his many rings and bracelets, would have served to pay the ransom of at least three minor kings. When Ruad went up to him and greeted him familiarly, he smiled. "A long time it is since I have last seen you, little cousin's-daughter, and you have grown tall. How does it suit you now, this life among the Druids?"

"It suits me finely, Niall Song-Smith," said Ruad. "And I have brought a friend today to greet you. He studies with me at Emain, and comes from across the sea."

"Ah, the lad from Môn," said Niall, looking at Togi. "I have heard tell of you; you came here—let me see—three winters ago, in late Giamon, not long after the *Rómhánach* finally subdued that island."

"I told you he always knows everyone," said Ruad to Togi, laughing. "Yes, Niall, you are right. His name is Togidubnos son of Lovernos, and he has come to seek knowledge from you."

"Lovernos," said Niall musingly, still looking at Togi. "Of that name I have heard—a little—as well. You are not unlike your father, so far as I remember him. He was younger than you are now when I last saw him, of course, but the resemblance is there... What knowledge does the son of the Fox seek of Niall *Ollam File*? I think I can guess, but better you should ask it of me yourself."

"A thousand thanks for your greeting, Niall *Ollam File*," said Togi formally. "The knowledge that I seek is not great, but Ruad assures me you will have it. Merely, I have heard rumors of *Rómhánach* here in Temair's halls, and come to prove the truth of that rumor. Tell me, if it pleases you: is this so?"

Niall smiled. "Courteous that speech, and well spoken. Yes, there have been a few of the *Rómhánach* here for a while, and I believe they have not left. I have not seen them today, but the evening is young; they may yet appear. What is your interest in them, Son of the Fox?"

"I am curious, *Ollam File*, as to what they do here," said Togi seriously. "It might be that they pose some danger to this great land."

"They merely talk, and give small gifts to kings and nobles," said Niall lightly. "They are only a handful; how could they possibly be a threat?"

"That I think you know as well as I do, *Ollam File*," said Togi. "Better, perhaps, for your knowledge is greater than mine. Yet a small leak in time may empty a wine skin, and a gap in the wall serve to let the whole flock out. So the *Rómhánach* came, I was told, first to Britain; now they rule her. I have fought their armies; I know of what I speak."

"That," said Niall still lightly, "may be true of Britain. Yet before they could rule us, they must first conquer our land. Do you think they could do so with little effort? I doubt it. I have been *Ollam File* since before you were born, and I too have bathed my spear-point in blood. We are a quarrelsome race, we people of Iérne, not easy to lead or to drive, and fighting is what we live for. The *Rómhánach* might find that they had a wolf by the ears."

"Your knowledge of your land is as a river to my raindrop, *Ollam File*," said Togi. "Yet the *Rómhánach* might do great damage, even though at last they failed. Better it would be to keep them from these shores, if it were at all possible."

"Better for them, at least," said Niall with a chuckle. "Yet I thank you, Son of the Fox, for your concern. Look, there they are, coming in the doorway now; yet I do not feel that I am in danger today!"

Togi turned to follow the Poet's gaze. Through a momentary gap in the crowd, he saw a little clump of five or six men by the entrance to the hall. Unlike the soldiers with whom he was familiar, these wore no armor, being dressed only in loose woolen tunics of white or faded red, bloused above their belts to bring them above the knee, and heavy red cloaks clasped on the right shoulder. This attire, and their short-cropped dark hair, unusual among the Irish, marked them out as strangers, but Togi had to admit that they did not look very threatening. He saw them for only a moment before the crowd closed between them, but thought that they might be making for the center of the hall. "Na," he said, turning back to Niall, "I agree that they do not look very dangerous. I remember now that there are no serpents in Iérne."

Surprisingly, Niall gave a crack of laughter. "Well spoken, lad," he said. "I will carry your words in my mind. So, now that you have found them, will you beard these—serpents—in their den?"

"Yes," said Togi, "I think I will speak to them, if I can. To acquire knowledge before action is always commendable, or so I was taught."

Niall nodded. "When you have seen them, come back and tell me your conclusions. We will drink a cup of wine together then, we three, and talk."

"You spoke him fair," said Ruad as they made their slow way through the crowd, "and he likes you. He would not else invite you to drink with him. This is good: he has much power to help or to hinder, has Niall Song-Smith. I have known him since I was only a little girl."

"He seems to know a great deal," said Togi, "more than I would have expected."

"He moves among kings," said Ruad, "and has all their ears. Once convince him of a thing, and soon all will believe it. But he does not at once speak all that is in his mind."

"Mmm," said Togi. "That I do believe. Hush, now—here they are."

The five Red Crests stood in a loose clump near the central hearth fire, most of them gazing idly around. One, however, who might from his stance have been their leader, was speaking to a well-dressed older warrior, whose multicolored clothing and gilt torc suggested nobility. "A minor king," whispered Ruad at Togi's shoulder, "from the Ulaid lands, I think, though I might be wrong." The discussion continued for some time with apparent earnestness, and something changed hands; then the warrior turned away to rejoin a group of his friends. The Red Crest leader glanced idly around him, perhaps to see if anyone had been watching; then his eyes met Togi's, and he paused with a frown.

Togi smiled and stepped forward. "Greetings, Red Crest," he said in British. "I see you have not met your end in battle yet."

"So—so," said the soldier. "I thought you looked familiar, savage. Have you found more Druids here to serve?"

"I have," said Togi evenly. "In truth, I am well on my way to being one. But tell me now, what brings you to these shores?"

"A whim," said the Red Crest, "to see how other tribes of savages live." His eyes went past Togi to Ruad, who was watching this interplay with interest, and widened in appreciation. "But I see you have found yourself a woman here?"

"Not mine," said Togi, and to Ruad in Irish, "This is a Red Crest I met more than once in Britain. Shall I tell him your name?"

"Why not?" said Ruad lightly, and to the Red Crest, still in Irish: "I am Ruad ingen Domnall mac Eochu mac Aed of the Loegaire. How are you called?"

"Centurion Quintus Fulvius Rufus," said the Red Crest, and in the same language: "I am sorry I speak little of your tongue."

"So—so," said Togi, smiling more broadly. "A man of many talents. Et Togidubnos filius Lovernos nomine meus est. Now that we are all acquainted, who are your friends?"

The centurion laughed and introduced them. They were all a few years older than he was, steady-looking square-built men with lean brown faces who obviously spoke no Irish, but gazed at Ruad with an appraising warmth in their eyes which brought the color flooding into her cheeks.

"And are they also curious about foreign lands?" asked Togi at the end, speaking again in British. "I would not have thought it so easy to visit here, for men in your profession."

"As to that, said Fulvius Rufus smoothly, "they are thinking of going into trade when they finish their army service, and came with me to see what Hibernia offers. Clearly it is a rich island, and I would say their prospects are good."

"That supposes, of course," said Togi thoughtfully, "that the natives are friendly." Fulvius Rufus smiled.

"I think they will become so, once they know us," he said.

"Has that been your experience in other lands?" asked Togi.

"In—some other lands, certainly," said Fulvius Rufus. "But friendships need time to ripen."

"Yes, that was what I was thinking," said Togi, and smiling turned away.

"I somehow do not think," said Ruad as they made their way back through the crowd, "that you two are friends."

"And you would be right," said Togi, smiling at her. "I will tell you the tale of it someday, but not just now. Let us find a space and eat before we see the *Ollam File* again, lest I find myself cup-bitten in his presence. Besides, I want to think on what we have just heard."

They found a place at one of the trestle tables which ringed the hall, and servants brought them plates of bread and steaming bowls of stewed pig-meat in rich broth. Both hungry from their day's drive, they ate in silence for a while. "Tell me now about the Centurion," suggested Ruad when Togi's bowl was empty. He smiled, and between bites of bread he complied.

"I saw him last near Segontium four years ago," he finished, "when King Regenos sued for peace. He was with the Red Crest governor Agricola then, one of his retinue. I think he is here scouting out the land for Agricola's next advance."

"So his jesting with you seemed to indicate," agreed Ruad. "My *imbas* says that your fates are intertwined."

"That may be so," said Togi, frowning, and rolling a last bit of bread between his fingers. "Well, it shall be as the Gods decree. Are you finished? I think it is time we went to talk with Niall *Ollam File* again."

"And drink with him?" asked Ruad slyly, teasing.

"How not?" said Togi, and met her eyes, and smiled.

Niall greeted them with raised eyebrows and a questioning smile. "So, I see that you have returned safely from your meeting with the threatening *Rómhánach*. Did you have civil converse with them, then?"

"We did," said Togi, taking a seat at the table opposite the Poet. "Moreover, the leader of their group is known to me from past meetings. I saw him last in the retinue of Agricola, their governor and war-leader, when he took the surrender of my King."

"Ah," said Niall, "I have heard of this Agricola. He is said to be in Alba this summer, making war on the Segoves and Novantes. From their country, of course, it is not far across the narrow waters which lie between Alba and the Ulaid lands. I begin to think that you may have some reason for your suspicions, Togidubnos."

"I agree, Niall Song-Smith," said Ruad, who had seated herself beside Togi. "We had some bantering talk with Fulvius Rufus, their leader. It is clear they are all soldiers, and the others under his command."

"Do you know the man Fulvius Rufus was talking with before we joined him?" Togi asked her.

"Na," she said, "but I am sure that Niall would know him. He looked to me to be of the Ulaid: a client king, perhaps, for he wore a five-colored cloak and a good gilt torc."

"What was he like?" asked Niall, interested. "There are several here today who might fit that description."

"A warrior in his prime, and well-seasoned," said Ruad. "Dark-haired but graying, with a scared face and a wide mouth. His left eyebrow is a little twisted from some old injury."

"Lugaid mac Eogan of Béal Feirste," said Niall softly, nodding. "The very man in the very place for a landing. I begin, cousin's-daughter, to be convinced."

"It looked also," said Togi, "as if Fulvius Rufus gave him some gift or payment at the end of their discussion. A token, perhaps, to seal their bargain."

"That would be likely," said Niall. "Lugaid has had ever a hunger for gold. Moreover, he is used to it; his river is a port for traders, and he demands his cut."

"He might get more in this trade than he bargained for," said Togi. "Who is his over-king?"

"Oengus mac Fergal," said Niall. "He is not here, but one or two of his family are. Let you be patient for a day or two, my children, while I make inquiries; if this plan really is afoot, I should like to know it."

"We will wait gladly, Niall cousin's-uncle," said Ruad. "But if what we suspect is true, what then can we do?"

"That," said Niall a trifle grimly, "is another question entirely. Quite possibly, not very much, but knowledge is strength. At least if they come, some few of us may be prepared."

The Price Demanded

"Honored One," said Togi at the end of a day's lesson, "One more question, if I may." Five days had passed since his return from Temair with much to think about. Niall had confirmed his guess as to Lugaid's identity, and also discovered that the Red Crests had been visiting other kings' courts in Ériu's northeast. They had also been speaking to supporters of Tuathal Teachtmhar, an exiled claimant to the Kingship of Temair, now rumored to be gathering men in Alba with the intention to return. All of these things, said the Poet, made a pattern which he did not like; he would speak to others of Oengus' client kings when chance offered, but could do little else at the moment. Togi had returned somewhat gloomily to Emain Macha, and had since been thinking hard.

"Yes?" said Fedelmid. "What is that question, my child? You have asked already a many of them today."

"It concerns," said Togi slowly, "that defense of armies called the Druid Fence. You have told me a little about it, and I have practiced diligently the disciplines involved. Do you think I might be ready to attempt it soon?"

Fedelmid frowned. "Na, that is a serious magic we are discussing. Even I would not use it lightly, and I am forty years ahead of you in my art. Only the greatest of Druids could so protect an army, and one or two of them have died in the attempt. Put it out of your mind, child, and work instead on the arts I am teaching you. I have taken you to task before for this unseemly haste."

"I ask your pardon, Honored One," said Togi. "And of course you are right. But my curiosity pricks me still. Why is this magic so dangerous to him who works it? I had thought, at the worst, it would only fail in its intent."

"There speaks your inexperience," said Fedelmid sternly. "The higher magics are worked through the Druid's own life force. Yes, he draws for the power he wields on the Gods and spirits—and there, too, the working may have its price!—but it is his own mind and will and spirit which shape and focus that power. If his skill and strength are not great

-241-

enough for the task, the balance may slip and destroy him. Then, even if he lives, he may never be the same."

"Surely, though, it would depend on the scale of the working," persisted Togi. "To protect a great army would require more magic than for a small band."

"That is possible," admitted Fedelmid reluctantly. "But for now I urge you to put the subject out of your mind. Believe me, child, when I say that you are not ready for such magic. In twenty years, perhaps, you might attempt it, but not today!"

"Thank you, Honored One, for your answer," said Togi. "I will do my best to put it out of my mind."

For a little while, he even tried to do so. But as the summer wore on and more rumors came from the northeast, he found his thoughts drifting back to the Druid Fence—to that, and to other forms of magic which could be used in war. He did not ask Fedelmid about them again, but once or twice tried questioning other of the masters at Emain on related topics, and from the fragments of knowledge so obtained, he began tentatively to put together a plan.

He had been chosen to attend the festival of Lughnasa at Tailtiu this year: a high honor, recognizing his degree of application and progress in his studies. He traveled south again, this time without Ruad, and with half his mind still fretting about what the Red Crests might be planning for the north. The festival itself fell late this year due to the intercalary month Quimon which had started the five-year cycle, the last of this thirty-year age. Because of that, the harvest itself was almost finished: a good one for a change. Togi wondered, looking at the golden stubble in the fields he passed, if it had also been a good year in Britain. For the sake of his own people, he hoped so. A little news had trickled across the sea to him these last few years, but the most of it was ill hearing: with so many of their young men missing, dead or taken for the Red Crest army, the Ordovices were struggling even to survive. Togi put the thought away, as he had learned to do; there was nothing now he could do to help them. Perhaps, someday... But someday might never come.

At Tailtiu he was pleased to see Niall *Ollam File* again. "I have news for you," the Poet had said in greeting him, "but it will have to wait until the first ceremonies are over, and we have time to be alone. It would not be well to spread this tale abroad."

"News from the north?" asked Togi.

Niall nodded. "The same."

Togi thought about it for the rest of the day, in between the sacrifices and other observances. That evening during the open-air feasting he sought the Poet out. "I am eager," he said after their initial greetings, "for the news you promised me. Where can we go?"

"In the open field is as good as any," said Niall quietly, and then louder: "Come, I will show you the view that I meant."

They climbed to the top of one of the mounds where sacrifices had been offered earlier. The fire there was still burning, but no one else was about. For such a low hill, Togi thought, the view was surprising; far in the south, he could see the summits of the Wicklow Mountains, from which, he had heard, it was possible to see Yr Wyddfa on a clear day; then sunwise around the horizon, Sliabh na Caillighe, Sliabh Guaire, and Sliabh Breagha, all of them a day's travel or more away. In the middle distance to the east was the low green ridge of Temair; closer to them in the south, the looping course of the Blackwater River could be seen glinting through its screening trees. "It is a fair country," he said softly, half to himself. "I should like to see it all someday."

"Perhaps you will," said Niall. "I have been at my travels for thirty years—a full age!—and have not yet seen it all; but my traveling days are not finished. And one place I think my travels will take me soon is Béal Feirste. Should you like to come with me, when the festival is done? I think your superiors will give you leave, if I ask."

"I should like it above all things," said Togi, feeling a familiar thrill of excitement. "Do we go, then, to prove the source of your news?"

"We do," said Niall, smiling thinly through his bushy gray beard. "I should like to test the hospitality of Lugaid mac Eogan, and also that of Oengus his over-king. As a Chief Poet,

I am allowed a retinue of four and twenty, but on this occasion I think a few less will suffice."

"And is Lugaid's hospitality like to prove generous?" asked Togi, smiling.

"That," said Niall, "is the thing which we go to test. I have heard that he has been acquiring large numbers of cattle and swine, and great store of other provisions. I cannot imagine—well, I can, but not in public!—what he will do with the half of it, or where he found the silver to pay for it all. He might indeed be preparing to feed an army…"

"Or an invasion?" said Togi. "Yes, I see your point. In that case, I think we may not be welcome."

"Perhaps not," said Niall lightly. "But no one dares to turn a Chief Poet away, for fear of the songs which might come of it. It will be entertaining to see our host's face when I arrive!"

Lugaid's face, when he found a crowd of visitors at the gates of his *ráth* half a month later, was indeed a brief study in consternation; but he pulled himself together and bade them loudly to come in. His guest-house was not large enough to hold them all; they spilled over into his feast-hall and stables, and the *Ollam* and two of his favorite pupils took over their host's own bedroom. No man, as Niall had rightly said, dared turn a Chief Poet away, or indeed deny him any request he might make. There was nothing for Lugaid to do except to feign happiness, and to hope that his inopportune guests would not remain for long.

"I could have laughed aloud," said Togi late that evening, as he and Niall and Ruad were settling down on Lugaid's goose-feather bed, "at his face, when he saw us on his doorstep. Never did I see a man look so chagrinned."

"I liked best," said Ruad, "how his eyes grew larger and larger, and his face redder and redder, as more and more of Niall's retinue came through his gate."

Niall chuckled. "Ah, that is not the first time in my life I have had such a pleasure, but certainly this occasion has a savor all its own. Now, my children, be serious for a moment. Did you see any sign of an extra store of arms here?"

"Na," said Ruad, stretching luxuriously at Niall's right, "and I searched all about, while you two were swilling ale in the hall. No one suspects a wandering woman, although I met one or two lads who were friendlier than I liked. I soon," said Ruad reminiscently, "set them to rights."

"Ah, well I know the lash of your tongue," said Togi, teasing. "Have I not the scars on my heart to prove it?"

"Enough, enough, children," said Niall, laughing. "Now, I heard nothing"—here he lowered his voice—"at Oengus' court that would lead me to believe he is part of this conspiracy, if conspiracy it is. I begin to think our host's part is only to provide a welcome for the invaders when they come. I have, however, talked with some lords of this district who would not be happy with such an occurrence, and I think they will send war-bands quickly enough when the *Rómhánach* arrive. Our part, if we are still here, will be to delay them if possible; but I am not sure how such a thing could be achieved."

"It would depend," said Togi slowly, "on how many come. Agricola's armies are very large, but I do not think he would risk many thousands on such a venture, leaving the Segoves and Novantes newly conquered at his back. But some hundreds, at least, I think we must expect to see: and we are five and twenty."

"Well stated, our problem," said Niall tartly. "And your solution?"

"Magic," said Togi, "might succeed, where force of arms would fail. I have a plan…"

"Well," said Ruad after a moment, "let us hear it."

"It will depend," said Togi, "on many things, not least the tides and the weather. But… You have heard of the Druid Fence?"

"More than that," said Niall tersely, "I have seen it. And do you think that *you* can work that spell?"

"I am not sure," said Togi honestly, "but I mean to try."

"You realize, of course," said Niall, "what that magic might do to you, if you fail?"

"If I fail," said Togi, "I think it will not matter. If I fail, the Red Crests will have won, and we will all be dead."

"What a cheerful thought," said Ruad, yawning, "to take with me into my slumbers! Good night, Togi—pleasant dreams to you, as well!"

If Lugaid had hoped to be soon rid of his unwanted guests, he was disappointed. Days passed, while the Poet and his retinue settled in more snugly. Seafood from the bay, bilberries and wild honey from the hills, beef and mutton and pork from the best of the herds—all these and more they demanded as a matter of right. It was noticeable also that Niall's students—with one striking exception, all lean and fit young men, many of whom seemed more at home with weapons than with words—had excellent appetites, not to mention a bottomless thirst for the best of wine and ale.

Then a wet spell set in, with almost daily mists and showers, not weather to tempt even the most eager traveler onto the muddy roads. Lugaid's face grew longer and longer as he watched his provisions diminish, and his eyes, Togi thought, had acquired a hunted look—as a man's must when he has promised to the *Rómhánach* things that he might now be unable to provide. Togi could have laughed more than once to see Niall tease him, suggesting an imminent departure at one moment, only to contradict it the next, but the thought of what might happen before long extinguished his mirth. The autumn equinox had passed, and the month of Ogron was beginning. If Agricola meant to cross the narrow seas before winter, he must strike soon.

Unable any longer to bear the tumult in the hall, he had taken to walking. The *ráth* was set on the north bank of a river which flowed into the ocean at the western end of a deep narrow bay, forming a fine protected harbor. Behind it, the encircling hills rose steeply, and Togi headed by instinct for their heights. Ruad accompanied him sometimes on these rambles, but not often; she was not fond of hill-walking, and preferred the joys of the hall. "I can understand," she told him once, "your need for silence; I have such a need myself at times. But surely you could get it without scaling a mountain? There is plenty of quiet along the shores of the sea."

"Na, I suppose that for each, it is what we were bred to," said Togi. "I never saw the sea, or any wide water, until I was twelve years old; I am a man of the mountains in my heart. But these, of course," he added, teasing, "are only little hills."

Ruad laughed. "Ah well, have it your way, Man of the Mountains. I will see you when you return from—your little hills!"

So it came about that on a cloudy day in early Ogron, Togi, seated alone on Black Mountain, saw the first of the Red Crest ships approach the bay. He did not notice her at first, for he had been thinking deeply, running over once again in his mind the steps which create the Druid Fence. Only when he came to the end of the list and looked outward again did he see her, making her slow way into the bay under oars against the gentle west wind. Behind her came one, two, half a dozen others. Togi watched them for a moment, judging their speed, and let out his breath in a sigh. The time for waiting was over; and the thing long expected was here. Now it was time for his plan to begin in response.

Standing up, he started back down the mountain, not running, but covering the ground in the hill-man's rapid gait which should get him to the *ráth* well before the first Red Crests arrived. The moon was almost full; the high tide would not come until well after sunset; and there would be plenty of moonlight to speed their messengers tonight. If the Red Crests did not come ashore until morning, they might find warriors assembled to greet them—warriors, and perhaps something more. At that thought, Togi smiled and quickened his pace.

One by one, half of Niall's young men slipped quietly from the feast-hall, took horse, and rode away from the *ráth*. He had only needed to say to them, "The time has come;" all the rest had been arranged. Those who remained made sure of their weapons, then began to clamor for food and drink; between this noise, and the shouts of the over-driven servants, it was some while before Lugaid realized that half his guests were gone. He did not, thought Togi, watching him closely, seem delighted at the change, but there was really nothing that he could do. The swift autumn twilight had already fallen, and the

Red Crests ships were safely anchored well out in the bay, beyond his reach until morning. Even if he sent a boat to them with a message, they were unlikely to begin their landing on unknown ground in the dark. A little time, therefore, had been won to prepare the Irish defense.

"We are fortunate," said the Poet to Togi under cover of the hall noise, "that they have picked this time of month for their arrival. Our messengers will have easy riding; also, the tidal range here may be greater than they know. Grounded ships will be hard to refloat if they must retreat, and hard to defend against fire arrows. Manannan may gain a rich harvest from this field."

Togi smiled. "I also will find the moonlight useful. Ruad, come out with me now, and help me lay the fire. I do not think Lugaid will notice our leaving, and if he does—why, we will keep good watch."

"As shall I, and distract him, if need be," said Niall a trifle grimly. Go, then, children: I will wait on your return."

They slipped from the *ráth* quietly, hand in hand, and if anyone saw them—why, who would think it strange that a young man and woman should go out together into such a moonlit night? The sky had cleared with sunset, and the gibbous moon hung rich and golden above the low hills which formed the south side of the bay. She threw a path of golden light across the water, dimming the reflections of the lanterns on the sterns of the anchored Red Crest ships. By her light Togi led Ruad to the place where he had stacked his supplies in preparation for this ritual.

"I have gathered wood from oak and alder, hazel and holly and ash," he said quietly. "These need to be laid in the right order with strengthening charms, and two sets of prayers are better than one." Ruad nodded.

"Male and female also have their virtue," she said. "Let us kneel to our work, and begin. Have you also offerings?"

"I have," said Togi. "Enough, I think, for the work at hand. Take you the east side, and I the west, and between us we will make our magic."

They worked for a while in silence except for their muttered invocations, one and then the other of them adding sticks and twigs to the rising cone. The moonlight softly silvered their intent faces, and gleamed now and then in their eyes. At length Togi said, "That is enough for now," and sat back on his heels with a sigh, critically regarding their creation. Silently Ruad watched him with a faint smile. After a few minutes he looked up and met her gaze, and just for an instant sat entirely motionless, as thoughts which he had no time to pursue streamed through his mind. Then with a sigh he stood up, and stretched down his hand to help her rise, although she did not need it; she came to her feet as lightly as a springing fawn. For a moment they stood hand-clasped, looking into each other's faces, while a current of energy seemed to run through their joined arms; then, with an effort, Togi stepped back, dropping her hand. "That will be all for now," he said quietly. "I think I will lie down here and sleep for a bit, so as to be rested; I must begin my magics long before the dawn. Let you go back to the hall now, and tell Niall that all is ready."

"Niall can wait for a while," said Ruad as quietly. "I would rather stand watch here while you sleep." Then, when Togi did not answer at once, she added, "If an enemy should come upon you, helpless, it might be the worse for all our plans."

"Stay, then, if you wish," said Togi after a moment, and lying down, wrapped his cloak around him and closed his eyes. Ruad found a stone at some little distance from him and sat down upon it, so that the bushes around them hid her from any casual passer-by. She neither moved or spoke, but Togi was aware of her, and it was a long time before he could compose his mind for sleep.

The moon was low in the west when he awoke. He lay silently for a while with open eyes, looking up at the stars and listening to the sounds of the night, then sat up. Seeing his movement from the corner of her eye, Ruad turned her head. "All is still," she said, just above a whisper. "Unless you need me, I will go back to the *ráth* now."

"Go, then," said Togi; and then, "Na, wait one moment." Standing up, he pulled his blood-father's ring from the neck of his tunic, and slipped the worn leather thong over his head. "Keep this safe for me," he said, holding it out to her, "until—until I need it again."

She took it slowly, looking first from his face to the dangling moonlit silver and back again; then nodded and slipped the thong over her own head, settling it beneath her red hair, so that the still-warm metal nestled between her young breasts. "I will keep it," she said softly, "until—until you ask for it—which will *not* be long!" And turning, she started back toward the *ráth*. Togi watched her out of sight, then gave himself a little shake, and turned to his own work.

That work was magic. He began slowly, scrutinizing again the pile of wood which the two of them had built, and adding here and there another stick or twig of one kind or another. He walked around and around it, considering it from all angles, yet never forgetting the night around him, and the creatures which moved in that night. The sky which had been clear when he lay down to sleep had acquired a faint haziness, and tendrils of rising mist now blurred the lights of the anchored ships. Seeing them, Togi smiled: things were moving as he wished. Soon he would begin to mold them more closely to his will.

Stripping off his cloak and belt and tunic, he made his way slowly down to the sea, and there left his sandals. The water lay far out across an expanse of pale sand and mud, dappled here and there with smooth rocks hairy with dark weed, but he walked steadily on until he reached it. The tide had turned, and was advancing now toward him, making little runs as each foam-edged wave lapped farther up the wide beach. Togi walked into it, shivering as the icy water crept slowly up his legs to his belly, and then to his chest. When he was shoulder deep he stopped and ducked his head under, then stood still while the water trickled down his face and dripped from his short beard and long dark hair. Beyond the cold, beyond the wave-chop and the currents, he could sense the surging power of the Sea God. *O Manannan*, he prayed silently, *God of the Dark Waters, I have called to you before and you have answered. Now I call again, I, Togidubnos, asking that you will lend your power to me, to aid my working tonight.*

There was a long pause, while Togi tried not to shiver. He could feel the Sea God coming closer with each rising wave. *O little Foxling,* said Manannan suddenly in his mind, *what do you offer me, in return for my strength?*

Ask what you will of me, Lord, said Togi. *I will pay the price demanded, for my need is upon me now, as never it was before!*

He felt the Sea God smile. *This, then, is the price I ask for my service,* said the huge voice in his mind. *Ten years away from the home which bore and bred you: ten years of exile, to wander Ériu's Land, and to serve my will whenever I may call. Will you pay the price demanded this time, little cub, or will you decline?*

I will pay the price, Lord, said Togi steadily, but he felt a deep sense of loss. *Only give me the strength to turn back this threat which comes from the sea!*

The bargain is struck, said Manannan, *and what you ask, I will give you. Be ready, Fox Cub, to use it now aright!*

And with that he was gone. Slowly, shuddering with cold, Togi turned and walked back up the beach. He felt sorrow at the forfeit he must now pay, but also a great joy that his first request had been granted. Behind him as he walked, the sea mist rose and thickened, wrapping the anchored ships with its silver veil. But he still needed more power before he could work all of his will.

Back by his unlit fire, Togi dressed again swiftly, then stood for a while in thought. To work his spell he also needed the power of the Earth, from which all life comes and to which it all returns. That meant appealing, not to a God, but to a local Goddess: Ériu herself, from which the land took its name. He had learned much of her in his last three years of study, but only lately, with this need in his mind, had he approached her in trance. Now he must do so again, and try to make his bargain, for without her aid there was no way that he could succeed.

Taking a sack of mixed grains which he had prepared and brought with him, he began to pour it out onto the ground, making elaborate patterns around the unlit fire. Oats and barley, emmer wheat and rye, he poured out in offering, speaking in his mind to the Goddess as he did so: *O Ériu, Earth Mother, I return to you now some small part of the fruits which you have given us; your riches I pour out in offering upon your land. Hear my prayers now, O*

Ériu, and accept now my offerings; draw near me, O Goddess, and heed my small request. To his grain-patterns he added mead, the bees' blessing, and pure water gathered from seven holy springs. *O Ériu, all good things from your plenty you give us; I give them in return, in order to ask for your aid.* Then he knelt, and bowing himself forward, first kissed the ground, then pressed his forehead and his palms against it. He remained that way for a long time. Slowly the night noises, the sound of his own blood and breath, even the sense of his body, all faded, and he was aware only of the greater body on which he knelt. Earth and root and plant, stone and deep-flowing water, all of these he touched and understood. Beyond them, within them, lay her spirit. *O Ériu, here am I, Togidubnos, a stranger in your land, but nevertheless your child. Hear me now and grant the thing I ask, now in the time of my sore need.*

In his mind at last a great voice spoke, blood-warm and generous. *O outling child,* it said, *why do you come here, and by what right do you ask now boons of me? Are there not others who could fulfill your request, who before have known your worship? I am of this land, not that from which you come.*

O Ériu, said Togi, *I am here, on your island, and here it is, for its defense, that I need the power of Earth.*

What do you offer me then in return? asked Ériu. *For nothing in magic comes without a cost.*

I offer the price which I paid to Manannan, said Togi. *Ten years of exile, serving you here in your land.*

There was a long silence, and he feared he might be rejected. At last the great voice said, *Yes, this time I will accept your offer. Be ready then, child, to use the power you ask.*

O Ériu, Earth Mother, said Togi, *I will strive to use it well and wisely, and well to you will I fulfill my word.* And with that, the Presence was gone.

Slowly Togi came back to his own body, and thrust himself up stiffly to his knees, and then to his feet. He had committed himself to ten more years of exile, but he had now the second of the powers he needed. For the third he must wait until sunrise, but that would not be long. Already the mist-shrouded moon had set, and the foggy east was growing faintly gray. Seating himself on the stone where Ruad had sat earlier, Togi wrapped his cloak more tightly around his shoulders, and composed himself to wait. In this, he thought, he had had much practice: in some ways, he had been waiting for this day all his life.

Through the thickening mist he could faintly see the shape of Black Mountain and its brothers, and he kept his eyes on Dubhais, the highest point of the chain. When the first sunlight touched that lofty head, he was ready. Kneeling, he struck sparks to light his fire and blew on them gently; then stood to watch the small climbing flames. Twig after twig caught fire, and their smoke ascended to the heavens, mingling with the salt-bitter silver mist. Facing the east, Togi called on Lugh of the Light. *O Sun God, O Fire God, Light of the World and Wielder of Lightning, I have served you with prayers and offerings since I could stand. Here I am, Togidubnos, asking your aid now. Great Lugh, hear my voice, grant my prayer!*

The brightness swelled in the east while still he waited; then, with the rising sun, the Bright One spoke. *Here am I, Lugh; you have sought me. Tell me now, Fox Cub, of your need.*

I seek your strength and power, Lord, against my enemies, who would extinguish, should they triumph, the fires of your morning praise.

Tell me, then, said the bright voice, *for my aid, what do you offer? What gift will you give me, in return for my gift?*

Ten years of my life, Lord, in exile from my homeland, to wander Ériu's island, and serve you whenever you call. This is the price I paid to Ériu and to Manannan; I have nothing else to give you, except my life.

The gift is good, said Lugh. *Take now what you ask of me, and be ready, Fox Cub, to use it aright!* And in a moment, in sun-dazzle, he was gone, while Togi's fire still burned between him and the sun.

He was ready now; he waited only for the signal to begin. Through his mind there passed a snatch of memory: Cunomoros' voice, speaking of Lovernos' death. *For himself,* the old man had said, *he kept nothing at all... His very life he gave in the end, as a sacrifice to the Gods...*

From the anchored ships Togi heard the bright sound of a trumpet. Drawing the sharp knife which he wore on his belt from its wooden scabbard, Lovernos' son smiled.

The Druid Fence

Almost without pause, the trumpet's voice was answered from behind him by the brazen clamor of a *carnyx*, its Celtic brother. Niall's war-bands had arrived, then, and were in position. On the water, the galleys had their oars out, and were beginning to move, the staccato cracks of the horators' hammers, setting the time for the rowers, blending in a blurred stutter of sound. The leading ship, flying some sort of bright banner—was it Agricola's? The mist made it hard to tell—headed for the docks at the river's mouth, while the others formed a line abreast and advanced across the now-flooded shallows toward the curving shore.

Togi laid the shining blade of his knife across his left palm, and closing his fingers on it, drew it across his flesh. The bright blood sprang out, reddening the blade and dripping to the ground. Reaching back, he gathered the mass of his long dark hair left-handed, and hacked it off roughly with the knife at the nape of his neck, then dropped the bloody offering into the fire.

"To the Gods who bred me, to the Gods who fed me, to the Gods who led me, I offer myself today," he chanted, repeating the boyish verse of his first dedication. The offering crisped to nothing in the flames, and again he smiled. Laying down his knife, he picked up the rod he had made by magic in the Hill of Bryn Celli Ddu, and ran his left hand along it, wetting it too with his blood.

> "Powers of the Sea, be mine,
> to raise the mists which hide and blind!
> Powers of the Earth, now rise
> to show as phantoms in their eyes!
> Powers of the Sky, let fall
> the lightning, and destroy them all!"

he chanted, and from south to north sketched sunwise with his rod a line a little inland from the beach. Along that line the sea-mist began to rise, drifting upward like smoke from a ground fire and thickening as it rose. In that smoke moved shapes insubstantial and dimly seen, shapes of men and shapes of monsters, creatures born of darkness in the very long ago when Gods still walked with men upon the earth. Behind him the *carnyx* spoke again, as the war-bands advanced under cover of the Druid Fence to await their foes.

Togi stood with spread arms, the focus and conduit of the magic which burned and flowed through him like cold fire. His eyes were wide and unfocused, his mouth a little open in a sort of ecstasy. This was the power for which he had longed and worked and suffered all his life, the power which he had first tried to shape into a weapon when he was ten years old, now unimaginably magnified and strengthened by the aid of his Gods. Dimly he knew in some corner of his mind that he could not sustain this flow for long—no human brain or body could—but he thought that he could last long enough—long enough to throw the Red Crests back from Ériu's shores, and to keep the Druid Sanctuaries free from their destroying influence for a few more years. That was all one man, in one lifetime, could hope to do, and if he did not live beyond this day, the price he paid would still have been worth while, and he would have kept faith with his father—with both his fathers. No one could do more.

The galley which might be Agricola's was approaching the dock now, and Togi lost slight of it behind the earthen bank of the *ráth*. Dimly through the Fence he could see that the others were anchoring in the shallows; the beat of the horators' hammers ceased, and they laid in their oars. Immediately soldiers began disembarking, splashing into the chest-deep water and forming up there before heading for the shore. With that part of his mind not engaged in magic, Togi tried to count them, but they were too many, and he could not spare the concentration. The barrier which he had created would be facing its first test soon.

From the direction of the *ráth* he heard shouting. Ruad and Niall would still be there, with enough spears, he hoped, to keep them safe. Would the Red Crests attempt to take them prisoner? Niall had not thought so, but he could be wrong. Togi did not know; he could only follow his course. The Red Crest soldiers were beginning to come ashore.

They came splashing their way through the shallows, tall solidly-built men holding their line as they came, their big green and gold shields—they were auxiliaries, not regular legionaries—at the ready, and their mail-clad shoulders and heavy helmets gleaming balefully in the foggy light. He could see their spear-points bobbing above the shield-line as they marched, and remembered the rain of those missiles at the Conwy ford. This time he was not trapped in a press of warriors; this time he would not be fleeing for his life. Taking a deep breath, he sent even more energy into the Fence.

As they reached the land, the advance of the Red Crests slowed. Before them was a bank of slowly moving mist, full of dark shadows and strange flashes of light. What they made of it was hard to tell, but on what seemed to be an order they all threw their javelins, which rained harmlessly down on bushes, trees and sand. Nothing came back from the mist, and slowly the green-and-gold line began its advance again. Hobnailed boots trampled sand and salt grass; storm-battered gorse gave way before their shields. Their ranks passed by on either side of Togi, not noticing that they did so, and the mist took them into its heart, and darkened their eyes.

There, at last, they met resistance: sharp spears emerging from the darkness to pierce their shields and their mail. Men stumbled and fell, and were trodden down by their fellows; the front ranks paused, and again threw their javelins, but to no avail. Somewhere in the distance they heard horn calls, eerie and unnatural; sweat poured down their faces, as their eyes darted left and right.

At their optios' commands they resumed their advance, through gorse and thorn and brambles, and found themselves treading a bog where no bog should be. Spears struck at them randomly out of the mist; the very air thickened; they gasped for breath in blinding heat, or shivered in cold. Swarming clouds of insects, and slow moving *things* underfoot, troubled them next; and always, always, the spears. There were gaps in their ranks now, and their lines were no longer even. From being eager to fight, they had become more eager to flee. But the Eagles' iron discipline drove them onward, toward enemies invisible but all too real. If only they could find someone to fight and to kill!

Sweat poured down Togi's face too now, and his outstretched arms were trembling. Every surge of the enemy he felt in his body and bones. He had never imagined such pressure, such weight, such exertion, as the whole Red Crest army thrust itself against the Fence. He heard screams, shouts, horn calls, but had no attention to spare for them. His whole mind and will were directed toward maintaining his magic. If it faltered or failed, he knew that he would be finished, but he did not know for how much longer he could continue to hold.

Gnaeus Julius Agricola stood on the walls of Lugaid's *ráth* with his adjutants beside him, and looked out into murky darkness which should have been afternoon sunlight. He had seen strange things before in his Imperial service, but this Hibernian sorcery was beyond his experience. "Are you sure," he said to one of them—Centurion Quintus Fulvius Rufus, recently detached from the Twentieth Valera Victrix—"that you are seeing what I see?"

"Yes, Governor," said Centurion Fulvius Rufus steadily, "I think I am. Some of their Druid magic, it would seem."

"Hmm," said Agricola, tapping his teeth with a fingernail. "If it continues, the landing may have to be abandoned. This will not look good in a dispatch—it will not look good at all. The new Emperor will not be pleased."

"I agree, Governor," said Fulvius Rufus, thinking of some of the rumors he had heard about Domitian. "But perhaps I have an idea."

"Act on it, then," said Agricola tersely. "We have lost touch with most of the forward units of the cohort, and five of our seven ships are aground until the turn of the tide. If you cannot get a capitulation, I will settle for a truce, to get our men off safely and refloat the *liburnae*. I might spare the men, but I cannot afford to lose this much of my navy; I am going to need them next year against the Epidii."

"Yes, sir," said Fulvius Rufus, saluting. "I will see what I can—arrange."

"Do so," said Agricola, and turned his dark face back to the darkness outside the *ráth*.

Togi was only aware of a gradual lessening of pressure. *The Red Crests,* he thought muzzily, *the Red Crests are falling back.* He did not know for how long he had been maintaining the Fence; he no longer knew anything but fire and ice and pain, and a great emptiness inside him, as if all his flesh and bones were crumbling away from within. There was a roaring in his ears, a blindness in his eyes; he no longer seemed anchored to the earth. But for as long as strength remained to him, he would continue to uphold the Fence. He no longer remembered that he could stop.

The Red Crest units were indeed falling back. They had found and killed a few natives, but at a hugely disproportionate cost, and they were confused, weary, and increasingly afraid. Good plain fighting, with plenty of blood and death—preferably the other fellow's—was one thing, but this sort of murky magic was not at all to their taste. Some of them remembered the stories of the Priests in the forests of their German homeland, and began to mutter charms against witchcraft under their breath. The trumpets sounding retreat had never been so welcome, and the Governor's adjutant, appearing in their ranks, did not have to urge most of them twice.

Fulvius Rufus, rounding up stragglers, heard unexpected laughter, and found two of the troopers beside the crumpled body of a young man which lay near a burnt-out fire. One of them had just wiped a knife blade on the young man's tunic, and was stripping the belt off the body to get the scabbard which went with it, while the other cast disconsolately around through what seemed piles of trash. "Did you kill him?" asked Fulvius Rufus, seeing a pale but oddly familiar upturned face. The young man's left hand and arm were bloody, but otherwise he had no obvious wounds.

"Na, he dead already," said the knife-acquiring trooper. "Nothing else here; come on, Alaric, time we go."

"Just a moment," said Fulvius Rufus, on one knee beside Togi. "I think he is still alive. Bring him along; the Governor may have a use for him."

"You had to stop," grumbled the second trooper to his mate, slinging Togi's limp body over his broad shoulder. "Well, if the Governor wants him, I guess we take him there." And leaving the clearing, they tramped on toward the sea, with the Governor's adjutant following rather thoughtfully behind.

A bucketful of sea water struck Togi in the face, and slowly he regained consciousness. He was lying on his back on a hard surface, and he was cold and wet and unutterably weary. Above him a pale sky—was it morning or evening?—moved slowly back and forth as if he were dizzy. But he was not dizzy, only weak and confused, as if he had been ill for a long time. Around him were creaking and groaning sounds, the slap and splash of water, and a regular pounding noise which made his head ache. The moving sky worried him, and he closed his eyes again, only to get another bucketful of water in his face, and a hard boot in his ribs. He tried to fend it off, but his arms were too heavy, and when he lifted one wrist, he heard the rattle of chains. A loud voice was shouting; he understood one word in ten, but enough to know something of where he was. How or when it had happened, he could not remember; but the Red Crests had taken him prisoner, which meant he was going to hang.

Another voice spoke nearby, and the shouting ceased abruptly. This voice sounded vaguely familiar, and when he opened his eyes again, it was to see a Red Crest face he should know. He frowned; his head felt thick; "I...know you?" he mumbled.

"Yes," said Fulvius Rufus in British. "Yes, I think that you do." And to the optios beside him in Latin, "He is awake now—bring him, and follow me."

Togi was pulled to his feet by rough hands, and half-dragged, half-carried along a strange wooden floor. The world was still heaving rhythmically about him; but holding up his head with an effort, he realized that this was because he was on a ship—a Red Crest ship, which was making her slow way eastward against the tide. Somewhere behind her the sun had already set in crimson clouds, and she followed a silver track cast toward her across the waves by the low moon. On her either side, her many oars, pulled by men or magic somewhere beneath his feet, churned the sea like wings, and above him her square-set linen sail billowed gently in the following breeze. The shores of the bay she was leaving were already indistinct and distant in the twilight; before long she would escape from them, to cross the narrow seas toward Britain. And once in Britain, in the Red Crests' hands… But Togi's thoughts stopped there, as his escorts had stopped, before a lean, dark man in an elaborate breast-plate and armor, whom he had last seen four years ago at Caer Seint.

"So this," said Gnaeus Julius Agricola in Latin to the Centurion standing beside him, "is your Druid. He looks rather young for the role, does he not?"

"I believe, Sir," said Fulvius Rufus, "that he is still a student."

"Hmm," said Agricola, looking Togi over, "if that was a student's work today, I should not like to meet his masters." And to Togi in British, "What is your name?"

"Togidubnos son of Lovernos," said Togi, trying to stand erect in the hands of his captors. His command over his body was coming back, and also his memory; he remembered, if not too clearly, all that he had done that day. "As your warrior says, I study the Druid path."

Agricola's eyes opened wider. "And understand Latin, it seems. Now where would a Druid in Hibernia have learned our tongue?"

"In the same place, I think, where the Governor learned his British," said Togi levelly. "You speak to me in my language; you know from which land I come."

"You are arrogant, my young friend," said Agricola. "Did you alone really cause all of the magic I saw today? I find that hard to believe."

"The Governor may believe what he wishes," said Togi.

Agricola frowned. "I believe," he said, "that Druid or not, you stand here in chains before me. Shall I drop you overboard now, and turn my ships back? Will you stop me?"

"How many men, I wonder, did the Governor lose today in battle?" said Togi. "I do not think you would be leaving only for fear of my magic, if you still had all the warriors you landed with this morning."

"That," said Agricola ruefully, "has some truth in it." And to Fulvius Rufus in Latin: "What do you think? Are there more like him in this benighted country? If so, I understand why the Druids must at all costs be suppressed!"

"Well, sir," said Fulvius Rufus, "I am not sure. On the one hand, the Druids on Mona did not seem to have any of these sorts of tricks up their sleeves, so it may be that it is only an Hibernian—ah—thing. On the other hand, he is clearly one of the Ordovices—look at the tribal mark on his left arm."

"One of the Ordovices," said Agricola thoughtfully, "who did not appear for the levy four years ago. Yes. That, of course, is another point. He had better go back to that country, to serve as an example to his fellows. They are still restless there, from what I hear."

"Restless," said Fulvius Rufus meditatively, thinking of the reports he had seen. "Restless. Yes, that is one way to describe it."

"The highland tribes are always reluctant to own when they are beaten," said Agricola, and sighed. "That is the problem with the Britons; they do not know when to quit. And this"—looking back at Togi, who was frowning hard as he tried to follow the discussion—"if I mistake not, is another example. You had better take charge of him, Centurion. I think I will go to my cabin now; call me when we are approaching land."

"Yes, sir," said Fulvius Rufus, and to the optios, "Take him back to where he was and stay with him until I come. I have some things to do first, but I will not be long."

Togi was escorted back along the heaving deck, past groups of weary soldiers, some of them wounded, sitting patiently here and there with their mud-spattered kit, and occasional gray-tunicked sailors who regarded them all with scorn, to the place near the ship's stern where he had awakened earlier. The optios pushed him roughly down onto the deck, as if he had been an animal, and telling him bluntly to stay there, took a seat on either side of him. Struggling up to a sitting position, Togi drew up his knees against his chest and leaned back against the wooden side of the ship, wrapping his arms around himself for warmth, for he was still wet and cold. He had not understood much of the latter discussion between the two Red Crest officers, but what he had understood had not boded well for him. But there was not much he could do about it, with two large men watching him, one on either side of him, and chains on his wrists, unless… What, he wondered with a faint smile, was the Thing Unexpected which might still save him tonight?

For a little while he amused himself with thoughts of daring or magic. He would creep into the Governor's cabin after moonset, and take him prisoner at knife-point. He would raise by magic a storm which would engulf and sink the ship. He would somehow release all the rowers below—he knew that they were slaves—from their benches, and lead them in a rebellion. He would hide—somewhere—in the ship, and escape to swim ashore before they reached land…

He sighed a little, and shifted position, shivering. His belly was empty—he had not eaten since the previous evening—and his mouth was parched with thirst, but his mind was clear now. None of these plans, he thought, diverting though they might be, had the least chance of success. He could not take the Governor prisoner, or release the slaves, or hide, while he sat here a guarded prisoner; and as far as working magic went at the moment, he was more likely to sprout wings and fly. Sinking the ship, besides, would not aid him to escape, unless by making an enormous offering of the whole of it to Manannan, he somehow won the God's favor…

Manannan. There was an idea. He owed the God one debt already, and he rather thought that Manannan might like to collect it. Togi began to smile, and was still smiling, some while later, when Fulvius Rufus came back.

"Well, you look cheerful," said the Red Crest, gazing down in surprise at his prisoner. Togi blinked.

"Na," he said, "I was only thinking…"

"Yes?" said Fulvius Rufus after a moment. "Thinking what?"

Togi's smile widened. "On the fate that my *awen* tells me is coming to you soon."

Fulvius Rufus chuckled. "It is a prophet that you are, then, as well as a magician?"

"Of course," said Togi. "It is part of my training as a Druid." Narrowing his eyes, he peered up at Fulvius Rufus. "I see a fate on you…"

"Yes?" said the Centurion, intrigued despite himself. "A fate?"

"On you and all your army," said Togi, glancing at the soldiers on either side of him, who flinched slightly. "These, too, will be caught up in it. A great change…"

"What change is that?" asked Fulvius Rufus. Togi sighed.

"Na, I have lost the thread of it," he said sadly. "I am too weary, and my mouth is too dry for much talking. Forget what I said."

Fulvius Rufus was amused, but said to one of the optios in Latin, "Go and get him a cup of wine—officer's grade, not sour vinegar."

"Yes, sir," said the optio, and went off shaking his head. In a little while he came back and gave the cup to Togi.

"Ah!" said Togi, and sniffed it, then looked up at the Centurion speculatively. "You must want to hear this prophecy badly." Fulvius Rufus grinned.

"It will help to pass the time," he said. "And I am curious." Togi smiled, and sipped the wine, feeling it spread a gentle warmth through his body. It was of good quality, sweet and harsh together, like that he had first drunk at Dinas Brân, the night he had stayed with Lucotios and his daughter Resta. A fair maid she had been; he hoped no ill had come to her… But this was no time to sit dreaming of girls.

Finishing the wine, he set the cup carefully down on the deck beside him, and looked up again at Fulvius Rufus. "My thanks to you," he said. "That was good wine."

"Are you ready, then, to prophesy?" asked Fulvius Rufus, still looking amused. "Or do you need more?"

"This will do," said Togi. "But for a true prophecy, I shall need two other things, one of which you may not be disposed to give me."

"Yes?" said Fulvius Rufus, taking a grip on a stanchion as the ship heaved more strongly in the growing swell. She must be reaching the mouth of the bay now; he thought; it would soon be time to bring this entertainment to an end.

"These chains." Togi held up his manacled wrists. "The iron impedes the *awen,* grounding my inspiration and holding me down. Surely this is known to your holy men, that to prophesy a true Priest cannot carry metal at all?"

Fulvius Rufus frowned, remembering a long bloody knife in a madman's hand. Something wrong there, he thought; but he might as well humor the boy. "Take off his chains," he said to the optios.

"But, sir!" one of them protested. "That is against orders, sir." Fulvius Rufus frowned.

"I am giving you now," he said coldly, "a different order. There is nowhere he can run to; take off his chains."

The optios exchanged glances; better to humor the Centurion. One of them produced a key, and reluctantly undid the locks. The chains slid clattering to the deck, and Togi sat rubbing his bruised wrists for a moment; then, holding to the side of the ship, he pulled himself to his feet. The deck heaved again, and he staggered, then caught hold of the railing. This was good, he thought; it would make his next request more believable.

"Well?" said Fulvius Rufus. "Are you ready?"

"Almost," said Togi. He stood swaying on the deck, a gaunt, pale-faced figure with wild rough-cropped hair and wilder dark eyes, and suddenly seemed older and larger than he had been moments before. "I shall need a piece of wood—some tree-stuff to aid my Druid magic," he said. "It does not matter what kind."

"Wood?" said Fulvius Rufus, puzzled. "But the whole ship is wood, man! What do you mean?"

"A staff," said Togi impatiently, "a rod, a stick, a beam, something to channel the *awen.* Hurry, man, or the moment will pass, for we are leaving the land, and my spell may not hold on the open sea!"

"Get him a piece of wood," said Fulvius Rufus to one of the optios. "There must be some broken oar-shafts on the rowers' deck, one of them will do."

"Sir!" said the optio, now convinced the Centurion was as mad as his prisoner, and staggered away down the heaving deck. Presently he came back bearing a seven foot long piece of oaken oar-shaft, as thick as a strong man's wrist and smoothed with much wear. Togi took it lovingly in both hands and held it vertically, one end against the deck and the other reaching above his head.

"Now," he said with authority, "I am ready to prophesy. And you, Quintus Flavius Rufus, should stand ready to hear what I say."

"Yes?" said the Centurion, impressed despite himself. The optios on either side of the prisoner stepped cautiously back, giving him uneasy looks, and a few sailors passing within earshot paused to listen as well.

"Far north in the island of Britain your general will travel," said Togi, feeling the true *awen* stirring in him as he spoke, "and you will go with him, suffering many wounds. Four years he will war there, and great fame he will garner, but the best of his conquests will soon fade away like the mist. But you, Fulvius Rufus, you will live out your days in Britain, and leave your seed to hold the land that you win."

"Yes? And how long shall I live there?" asked Fulvius Rufus with an uncertain grin. Togi's eyes were gleaming in the moonlight, and his voice had become deeper and stronger, as if some other voice spoke through his mouth. Despite himself, the Red Crest shivered; this was much more than he had bargained for.

"An age and more shall you be in Britain," said Togi, "and you shall not die until you look on my face again. But as for Ériu's Land..." He paused, looking puzzled.

"I did not ask about Hibernia," said Fulvius Rufus.

"I answer your thought, foreign soldier, as well as your words," said Togi, and there was a horn-call note of triumph in his voice. "Your people shall never rule in this island."

"We shall, you know," said Fulvius Rufus. "We will be back."

"Oh, yes," said Togi, still with that strange intonation. "Some will come back, and leave their bones in this land, but not in a thousand years will they come to rule her." He paused, and when he spoke again it was in something more like his normal voice. "You may come back, Fulvius Rufus, but you will never rule here, and your forays will be forgotten like cloud-shadows on the hills. But we—we Druids—we shall be remembered, though we pass into legend, and all our works into dust. And we will come back."

"When?" asked Fulvius Rufus, shaken and confused. "When will you come back?"

"We will come back," said Togi, smiling, "when the world is reborn." And grasping his oar-shaft more tightly, he turned, clambered swiftly with its aid onto the rail, and leapt out from there into the waiting sea.

He had forgotten the oars. Fortunately he was close enough to the stern of the ship to avoid them, but their turbulence still roiled the water into which he plunged feet-first. The impact tore the oar-shaft from his grip, hard though he held it, and down, down he went, into the night-black sea. Its chill took his breath away, so that he struggled not to breathe in water, kicking and clawing desperately back toward the light. There was pain in his chest like a sword-blade, and the sight of his eyes was darkening. *Manannan!* he called frantically. *Great Sea-God, help me now!*

Giant hands seemed to lift him, and at last he reached the surface, choking, coughing, and frantically sucking in air. As his sight cleared, he saw his oar-shaft close at hand, and swam toward it, getting an arm across it at last. This helped keep him afloat, and he clung to it, gasping, while his pounding heart gradually slowed to its normal rate. *O Manannan,* he thought, *once again I thank you! Preserve me now, take me safely to land!*

In his mind, he heard the huge laughter of the Sea-God. *Little cub, little cub, you ask much of me today! How if I leave you now to swim alone?*

Why, then, said Togi, *if I drown, Lord, I fear it will be very hard for me to pay my debt to you.*

The Sea-God laughed again. *A bargainer after my own heart! Content you, Fox Cub, you will not drown tonight!* And with that, he was gone.

Togi sighed. He was cold and very tired, and from his low position in the water he could see no signs of land. For a while he did not move, for the rest of the Red Crest fleet was passing, ghostly shadows in the moonlight except for their lanterns fore and aft, and he did not wish to attract their attention. One passed him so close that he thought he could feel the spray from the oars, and hear the rhythmic grunting of the men who pulled them above the relentless beat of the horator's hammer. Then they were gone, and he was alone with the sea and the moon. She and the stars gave him his direction; the waves were pushing him southwest, and the tide should still be flowing into the bay. His belt was gone, and he had no way to lash himself to the oar-shaft; if he fell asleep he would lose his grip on it and drown. Slowly he began to swim, holding onto the hard wood and kicking. He had never given up at anything before in his life, and he was not about to start now.

Sometime before midnight, as the moon was starting her decline, he came ashore at last on the south side of the bay, and loosening his cramped fingers from the oar-shaft with an effort, crawled up the rocky shore and collapsed on a patch of dry sea grass. That was where Ruad and Niall, still doggedly searching, found him the next morning. They thought at first that he was dead, he lay so still; but when Ruad turned him over, he yawned and opened his eyes. "I have come back," he said hoarsely to her.

"I knew that you would," she said, helping him to sit up, and Togi smiled.

"I was not sure, for a while," he said. "But...the Gods were kind, and I still have things to do."

"In Ériu's Land?" asked Ruad, and Togi nodded.

"Yes," he said, "in Ériu's Land. I have not seen the half of it yet."

"There will be time for that," said Niall, and Togi smiled again, thinking of his promises.

"Yes," he said, "there will be time. There will certainly be time."

End and Beginning

Togi sat again on the Hill of Emain Macha in the early summer twilight, and watched two figures coming toward him across the fields below. It was a few days after Beltane, and all the world around him seemed flowering and green; from the woods below he heard small birds singing fiercely, and above him the bats darted swiftly back and forth through the mild air. He had loved watching them as a child; almost he had thought he understood their language. Now he was too old to hear their shrill voices, but the memory remained. He remembered, too, what Cunomoros had said about them: *That is their protection; no one knows where they will be next. Remember that, if you are ever pursued, and do the thing unexpected.* It had been good advice, some of the best his foster father had ever given him; it had saved his life more than once, and would probably do so again, for he knew that his travels were not over.

Thinking of his family, he smiled. He had heard news of them not long before, from the physician Lucotios, who had left Britain again to travel abroad. King Regenos was dead, and things at Dinas Brân were changing; also, his daughter Resta had married Cingetos the Bard, who had recently left the court. Lucotios had decided to return to Gaul, but had come first to Ériu's Land, as he said, to obtain and to deliver news.

"The winter cold has been in my bones of late," he had said, "and I remembered the years I spent in Gallia Naborensis, before my daughter was born. That is a better place to wear out one's old age, in that land of sunshine, and a physician can make his living anywhere. Resta has her own life now, and does not need me."

"Cingetos is fortunate," had said Togi with a laugh. "A very fair young woman, your daughter is!"

"So I think," had said Lucotios, smiling. "And Cingetos agrees. He sent me with news for you, if I could find you; and once I arrived in Ériu's Land, it was not hard. Your family, he said to tell you, are well; your brother Tritos has recently married; also your friend Valos, who has taken on most of your father's work."

"That is good hearing," had said Togi. "Valos must have succeeded, then, in avoiding the Red Crest levy."

"So it would seem," had said Lucotios. "But the tribes have suffered, none the less, with so many of their young men missing or dead. They have had some incomers from the Decangli and Cornovii lately, even some from the Demetae and the Silures in the south, and by and large they are welcome—there is always work for another pair of hands. The Red Crests, however, having defeated us, have become less demanding under their governor Agricola, and usually leave the people enough grain to live on, if the winters are not too hard."

"I wish," had said Togi, "that you were going back to Britain, and could take my family some news of me. I cannot go back; I have made—commitments—here; and besides, if the Red Crests were to find me there, I would hang."

"As to that," had said Lucotios, "there is a little trade now into Segontium. I expect, if you were to inquire at Droim Meánach or Limni, that you could find means to send a message. I am going back that way myself before long, and could start one on its way."

Togi had thanked him, and taken his advice. In the end he had sent a waxed tablet, with a small package attached to it containing Sennos' ring. Maybe it would arrive safely, and maybe it would not; but he wanted it off his hands, and Cunomoros was the man to deal with it: he was, after all, probably the last survivor now of the Druids of Ynys Môn, and therefore it was his by right.

Thinking of that ring reminded him of his own changed status. Three days before Beltane, while he had been finishing his morning mediations, he had been summoned to the presence of the Archdruid of Emain Macha himself. The young student who brought the summons had not known the reason, and Togi had gone in some puzzlement, assuming he was to have a small part to play in the festival. So, indeed, it had proved, but not as he had expected. He had reached the Archdruid's room to find several of the other Masters there, apparently concluding a discussion.

Togi had stopped at the door, waiting respectfully until the Archdruid looked up and noticed him. "Ah, come in, lad," the old man had said. "We have been speaking of you. Fedelmid was just telling me something of your adventures with the *Rómhánach* last autumn, of which I had only heard a little before."

"Yes, Honored One?" said Togi, entering as he had been bidden. "It was—no great matter."

"'No great matter'," said the Archdruid thoughtfully, as if savoring the words. Beneath his jutting white eyebrows, his dark eyes looked amused. "He says that you created the Druid Fence singlehanded, and maintained it for some part of the day, helping to defeat an invading army. And this was 'no great matter'? I am glad to know it."

"Mmm," said Togi. "My apologies, Honored One. That was not quite what I meant."

"So I would think," said the Archdruid. Except for his eyes, his face was stern, but his mouth twitched a little at the corners in the frame of his white beard. "Grabán Bric, how many times have you made the Druid Fence?"

"Three times, Honored One," said a lean, sinewy, gray-haired Master from Connacht. "Three times for the battle-hosting of my King."

"And did you find the undertaking 'no great matter'?" asked the Archdruid.

"Na, I did not," said Grabán. "I count it no easy magic at all."

"I would agree," said the Archdruid. "Fedelmid, how many times have you made it?"

"Five times," said Fedelmid harshly, "and I think it cut a year from my lifespan every time."

"Ah!" said the Archdruid. "Yes, it might well do so. And what would you think of a student who did it alone?"

"I think that he was an arrogant fool," said Fedelmid, "and so I have told him." Almost the Archdruid laughed.

"Congal?" he said to a little wizened Master. "Would you agree with that judgment?"

Congal chuckled. "I would. But I think also I might ask him why he did it, before deciding whether he should be sent away in disgrace."

"Well?" said the Archdruid sternly to Togi. "What defense can you give me for this unauthorized action against your teacher's express words? For it is not a light thing here, so to go against a Master. The penalties, as you should know, can be severe."

"I have no defense, Honored One," said Togi slowly, "except that I believed it was necessary at all costs to prevent the *Rómhánach* from establishing a base in this land. Gaul they conquered long ago, and destroyed the Sanctuaries there; much of Britain they have also overrun. You know as well as I do, I think, what they did on Ynys Môn; to be a Druid in Britain now is not allowed. My father gave his life to defeat them, and I would do the same. Indeed, when I set the Fence against them that day, I did not expect to survive; I am here today only because our Gods were merciful. Yet I know also that I have defied my Master, and gone against his words. Put what penalty on me you will; I shall not complain."

"Fedelmid?" said the Archdruid. "What do you advise?"

"Na," said Fedelmid, "I cannot say. He did wrong, but for right reasons. I would forgive him, but it is not only for me to decide."

"Grabán?" said the Archdruid. The lean man shook his head, but he was smiling.

"I would not forgive him," he said, "but you know what punishment I advise."

"Congal?" said the Archdruid, and again the corners of his mouth were twitching, as if determined to show amusement despite his will.

"I am with Grabán," Congal said. "It is a fitting punishment, after all."

"I think, then," said the Archdruid, "that we are all agreed." He turned to Togi. "The penalty, Togidubnos, that we put on you for your defiance of your Master, is to leave the Sanctuary of Emain Macha, and walk the land of Iérne for a year and a day. Thus is your transgression punished. But before you go"—and now the Archdruid was openly grinning—"I think a change is due to your status. Will you be ready to be made Priest in the Beltane rites?"

It had struck him like a blow in the belly, and it was a moment before Togi could gather breath to reply. "Yes, Honored One," he had said when he could speak, "I think I will be ready."

"Then you had better go away now," had said the Archdruid, still grinning, "and prepare."

"Yes, Honored One!" said Togi, and bowing, left.

The next three days had passed in a blur, of which he remembered only snatches clearly. First had come his own self-questioning and doubt; he did not think he was ready for this honor. After long thought, he brought his uncertainty to Fedelmid. The gray-haired Master had listened patiently as he poured it all out. "Yes," he said at the end, "so it comes to all of us. If you were not uncertain, I would advise the Archdruid to delay. It is time, though, that you went back into the world for a while, to learn from its people and events day by day, and for that you will need *nemed* status—for only the Men of Art have privilege equally in all our lands. Do not worry too much, child," he had added when Togi still looked uncertain. "You have the core of the thing in you, and you will grow into the role. After all, you were bred to it, were you not? I think that in some ways you have been already a Priest for many years."

So Togi had bowed to his wisdom, and went on with the preparations. Ruad was delighted with the news, but downcast when she heard he was leaving. "But," she had said, "I may never see you again!"

"I will be back in a year," Togi had said, grinning. "You will hardly have time to miss me." Ruad sighed.

"Then we had better spend as much time as we can together," she had said, "before you go." And they had indeed spent some snatched hours together, and those hours had been sweet.

His priesting had come toward the end of the Beltane rituals. He had not been the only candidate, but he had been the youngest, and for all of them it had been a great and shining day. "I remember your father," the Archdruid had said after Togi had recited his vows. "He was my student for a while before he went to Ynys Môn. I think you will never be unworthy of him. What name will you take now, Lovernos' son?"

Togi had thought long about that, for it was normal for a new Priest to take a new name, but there was really only one answer. "I will be called *Mac Criomthann*," he said, "the Son of the Fox." For of course that was what his new name meant in Irish; he and others had called him so before. The Archdruid had smiled.

"Yes," the old man had said, "that is fitting… By Lugh of the Light, and Ériu our Mother, and Manannan the Lord of the Sea, I bless you today. May you always walk with wisdom in your father's path, Mac Criomthann, Lovernos' son, and may Sun, Moon and Stars, earth, water and air, aid you on your way."

He would remember, he thought, until he died, the moment when he had finally put on his blood-father's ring. The touch of it on his hand had seemed strange at first, and then natural; and the link that it gave him with Lovernos had grown stronger still. He had never tried it on since his mother had first given it to him; it had been far too large then, but now it fitted as if made for him. Perhaps, he thought whimsically, it had been; or perhaps it was he himself who had been made to fit the ring. He only knew that he would wear it for the rest of his life.

The two people he had been watching breasted the last rise, and stopped before him. "I knew," said Ruad, "that I would find you up here, O Man of the Mountains. Did I not say so, Niall?"

"You did, cousin's daughter," said the Poet. "And you were right." And they sat down, one on either side of Togi, on the grass.

"Now that you have found me," said Togi, "what shall you do with me?" And he reached over and took Ruad's hand.

"Niall has a proposition to lay before you," she said, interlacing her fingers with his.

"What is that?" asked Togi, smiling, and turning to the Poet. "If I can offer you any aid, I would be glad to do so."

"It is not aid, exactly, that I am wanting," said Niall, watching the two of them with amusement. "But I understand that you will be leaving Emain Macha soon."

"That, alas," said Togi, "is true. I have already overstayed my time."

"In that case," said Niall, "I wonder if you might care to journey with me for a while? I am on my way to the northwest, and I should be glad of your company on the road."

"I should be honored," said Togi, "to travel with you. I have long had a desire to see that country, from which, I think, my blood-father came."

"That thought was in my mind also," said Niall, and smiled. "I leave in three days' time. They will not turn you out of doors here in the meantime, will they?"

"If they do," said Ruad, "he will have company." And to Togi, "Shall we go down now?"

"Yes," said Togi, standing up, "let us go." And still hand in hand with Ruad, and with Niall walking beside them, he started back down the Hill.

Though he went bound in service to the Gods, he thought as he walked, and might never go home to Britain, he had many good years before him, and Ériu's Land was wide. He was free to wander, and to learn, and—here he squeezed Ruad's hand, and felt the answering pressure of her slender fingers—to love. Looking up again at the bats, still tracing their unexpected courses across the twilight sky, Mac Criomthann smiled.

Afterword

In a book concerning British and Irish Druids, it is as well to be forthcoming about one's sources. These are, unfortunately, scanty indeed, and I have nothing new to bring to the table. We have a handful of mentions of Druids in Gaul and Britain by classical writers, who undoubtedly had their own agendas for what they wrote; and we have archaeological evidence for various prehistoric European religious practices, some of which seems to fit the classical writers' descriptions; but nowhere do we have an artifact stamped "Made by Druids". For a summary of the evidence from different points of view, I recommend: Green's *Caesar's Druids,* for a pro-Druid viewpoint which discusses much of the more recent archaeological evidence; the first chapter of Hutton's *Blood and Mistletoe,* for a skeptical view of the historical material; and Freeman's *The Philosopher and the Druids,* for a pre-Caesar viewpoint which takes in quite a lot of other interesting territory along the way. There are, of course, many more books about the Druids, and I have read quite a few of them, but they all of necessity rework the same ground.

After considerable reading and thinking in the process of constructing this story, my own conclusions on the subject are as follows: we know very little about Britain in this period (other than what Tacitus has to say); we know even less about British Druids (i.e., they may have existed, and if so were probably on Anglesey at some point in the 1st century AD, but we have no idea what they were doing there); and we know rather less still about Ireland and Irish Druids (if any). Ireland was where it is today; there was some sort of (probably complex) "Celtic" society there, speaking (probably) a Goidelic language; there were probably religious / magical specialists of some kind (who may or may not have called themselves Druids) in that society at the time in question; there is a possibility (supported to some extent by archaeological discoveries of Roman material) that Agricola may have sent some sort of military expedition to Ireland, most probably in late 81 AD, with outcome unknown; if he did send such an expedition, they most probably crossed from the vicinity of Galloway (Scotland), as he was operating in that area at the time with the required manpower and naval support; Agricola (according to Tacitus) had in his entourage at that time an exiled Irish noble of some sort who could have served as a focal point for such an expedition. What any Druids (if they existed and were interested) might have had to do with this is entirely conjecture. It's a good thing I'm writing fiction and not history, or this would have been a very short book!

I usually include in my books a list of the chief people and places involved, with notes as to which ones are historical (or mythological) and which invented. In this case, however, there is so little historical material that it is easier to simply list those which are *not* fictional. The three Roman governors mentioned—Gaius Suetonius Paulinus, Sextus Julius Frontinus, and Gnaeus Julius Agricola—are historical persons; so, of course, is Boudicca. Tuathal Teachtmhar, mentioned toward the end of the story, is a legendary Irish king who may have had some historical existence. The man whose preserved body was found in Lindow Moss in 1984—the prototype for Lovernos—certainly existed, but his exact date and his story are still a matter for scholarly debate. All other persons mentioned in this book are fictional, which is, of course, not the same as unreal.

On the other hand, the only wholly invented place name in the book is that of Castellum, the Roman base on the Anglesey side of the Aber Menai, which has no documentable existence. My only other conscious tampering with history concerns Segontium (later known in Welsh as Caer Seint). Excavations to date indicate that the Roman fort there slightly postdates most of my story, probably having been constructed after Agricola's conquest of the Ordovices. I have therefore located Togi's Segontium under the Anglo-Norman castle of Caernarvon, the building of which would have doubtless obliterated any traces of an earlier ruin. Regenos' fort in Snowdonia is based on the post-Roman (and possibly Arthurian) site at Dinas Emrys, slightly relocated and enlarged. Togi's home valley is also invented, but corresponds most closely geographically to Cwm Penmachno in north Wales; I have, however, rearranged the local topography to suit my own purposes. The Hill in the Dark Grove—Bryn Celli Du—is real, as is Mynydd Llwydiarth, although the latter lacks the stone circle with which I have endowed it; but any use of either place by the Druids is speculative at best.

Regarding other story elements, the initial conquest of Ynys Môn by Suetonius in 60 or 61 AD is historically documented, as is Agricola's reconquest of the island after defeating the Ordovices in 77 or 78 AD. It is not known what his settlement with that tribe entailed, but Tacitus says that "he cut to pieces almost the entire fighting force of the nation." The demand for young men to serve in the army, which amounted to a sort of slow genocide, was practiced by the Romans in a number of locations, and may have been one of the contributing factors to Boudicca's revolt. It is also true that the Druids had been suppressed throughout the Roman Empire under Claudius in 54 AD. The calendar system used in this story is based on an interpretation of the Coligny calendar developed by John Bonsing, and available online.

Finally, one of the most apparently fantastical elements in my tale—the Druid Fence—has an actual basis in history, if a slender one. The entry in the *Chronicle of Ireland* for 561 AD includes the following item: "The battle of Cúl Dreimne in which Diarmait son of Cerball was defeated... Fráechán son of Tenusán was the one who made the druidical fence for Diarmait son of Cerball. Tuatán... was the one who cast the druidical fence over them. Maglaine leapt over it and he alone was killed." (Charles-Edwards 104).

The Druid's Son developed as a sort of spin-off or prequel to material in my *Storyteller* series, which is set in Britain and Ireland in the 6th century AD. As to whether it forms the beginning of its own series... As the Storyteller frequently says: *That, O my children, is a story for another day!*

—G. R. Grove, October 1, 2012.

Selected References

Primary sources:

Caesar, Julius. *Seven commentaries on the Gallic war.* Oxford New York: Oxford University Press, 2008.

Charles-Edwards, T. M., trans. and editor. *The chronicle of Ireland.* Liverpool: Liverpool University Press, 2006.

Koch, John, trans. and editor. *The Celtic heroic age : literary sources for ancient Celtic Europe & early Ireland & Wales.* Aberystwyth Oakville, CT: Celtic Studies Publications. Distributed by David Brown Book Co, 2003.

Tacitus, Cornelius. *The Agricola and the Germania.* Harmondsworth, Middlesex New York, N.Y: Penguin Books, 1970.

Secondary sources:

Bhreathnach, Edel. *The kingship and landscape of Temair.* Dublin: Four Courts for the Discovery Programme, 2005.

Bonsing, John (2007). *The Celtic Calendar.* Online at http://caeraustralis.com.au/celtcalmain.htm. (8/26/2012.)

Bowen, Keith. *Bugail Eryri : pedwar tymor ar ffermydd mynydd yng ngogledd Cymru.* Llandysul: Gwasg Gomer, 1997.

Breatnach, Liam. *Uraicecht na Ríar : the poetic grades in early Irish law.* Dublin: Dublin Institute for Advanced Studies, 1987.

Brunaux, Jean Louis. *The Celtic Gauls : Gods, rites, and sanctuaries.* London: Seaby, 1988.

Burkert, Walter. *Homo necans : the anthropology of ancient Greek sacrificial ritual and myth.* Berkeley: University of California Press, 1983.

Campbell, Duncan. *Mons Graupius AD 83 : Rome's battle at the edge of the world.* Oxford: Osprey, 2010.

Casey, P. *Excavations at Segontium (Caernarfon) Roman fort, 1975-1979.* London: Council for British Archaeology, 1993.

Cool, H. E. M. *Eating and drinking in Roman Britain.* Cambridge: Cambridge University Press, 2006.

D'Amato, Raffaele. *Imperial Roman naval forces, 31 BC-AD 500.* Oxford New York: Osprey Publishing, 2009.

Dixon, Karen. *The Roman cavalry : from the first to the third century AD.* London New York: Routledge, 1997.

Evans, David Ellis. *Gaulish personal names : a study of some Continental Celtic formations.* Oxford: Oxford University Press, 1967.

Fields, Nic. *Boudicca's rebellion AD 60-61 : the Britons rise up against Rome.* Oxford, UK Long Island City, NY: Osprey Publishing, 2011.

---. *Roman auxiliary cavalryman : AD 14-193.* Oxford: Osprey, 2006.

Fowler, P. *Farming in the first millennium AD : British agriculture between Julius Caesar and William the Conqueror.* Cambridge New York: Cambridge University Press, 2002.

Freeman, Philip. *The philosopher and the Druids : a journey among the ancient Celts.* New York: Simon & Schuster, 2008.

Goldsworthy, Adrian. *The complete Roman army.* London: Thames & Hudson, 2011.

Green, Miranda Aldhouse. *Caesar's Druids : story of an ancient priesthood.* New Haven Conn: Yale University Press, 2010.

---. *Dying for the Gods : human sacrifice in Iron Age & Roman Europe.* Stroud, Gloucestershire Charleston, SC: Tempus Pub, 2002.

Hutton, Ronald. *Blood and mistletoe : the history of the Druids in Britain.* New Haven, Conn. London: Yale University Press, 2011.

Hyland, Ann. *Training the Roman cavalry : from Arrian's Ars tactica.* Phoenix Mill Dover, NH: Alan Sutton, 1993.

Jones, Barri. *An atlas of Roman Britain.* Oxford: Oxbow, 2002.

Joy, Jody. *Lindow Man.* London: British Museum Press, 2009.

Kelly, Fergus. *A guide to early Irish law.* Dublin: Dublin Institute for Advanced Studies, 1988.

---. *Early Irish farming : a study based mainly on the law-texts of the 7th and 8th centuries AD.* Dublin: School of Celtic Studies, Dublin Institute for Advanced Studies, 1997.

Koch, John. *An atlas for Celtic studies : archaeology and names in ancient Europe and early medieval Ireland, Britain, and Brittany.* Oxford Oakville, CT: Oxbow Books, 2007.

Lynch, Frances. *A guide to ancient and historic Wales : Gwynedd.* London: H.M.S.O, 1995.

MacLeod, Sharon. *Celtic myth and religion : a study of traditional belief, with newly translated prayers, poems and songs.* Jefferson, N.C: McFarland, 2012.

MacNeill, Máire. *The festival of Lughnasa : a study of the survival of the Celtic festival of the beginning of harvest.* Dublin: Comhairle Bhealoideas Eireann, University College, 1982.

Matyszak, Philip. *Legionary : the Roman soldier's (unofficial) manual.* London New York: Thames & Hudson, 2009.

Ó Cróinín, Dáibhí. *A new history of Ireland.* Oxford New York: Oxford University Press, 2008.

O hOgáin, Dáithí. *The sacred isle : belief and religion in pre-Christian Ireland.* Woodbridge, Suffolk, UK Rochester, NY; Cork, Ireland: Boydell Press Collins Press, 1999.

Peterson, Daniel. *The Roman legions recreated in colour photographs.* London: Windrow & Greene, 1992.

Raftery, Barry. *Pagan Celtic Ireland : the enigma of the Irish Iron Age.* New York: Thames and Hudson, 1998.

Rees, Alwyn. *Celtic heritage: ancient tradition in Ireland and Wales.* London: Thames and Hudson, 1973.

Ross, Anne. *The life and death of a Druid prince : the story of Lindow Man, an archaeological sensation.* New York: Simon & Schuster, 1991.